The WOMAN before WALLIS

The

WOMAN

before

WALLIS

BRYN
TURNBULL

A NOVEL OF WINDSORS, VANDERBILTS
AND ROYAL SCANDAL

mira

ISBN-13: 978-0-7783-6102-2
ISBN-13: 978-0-7783-8819-7 (Library HC edition)

The Woman Before Wallis

Recycling programs
for this product may
not exist in your area.

This edition published by arrangement with Harlequin Books S.A.

For questions and comments about the quality of this book, please contact us at
CustomerService@Harlequin.com.

Mira
22 Adelaide St. West, 40th Floor
Toronto, Ontario M5H 4E3, Canada
BookClubbish.com

Printed in U.S.A.

To Hayley

The
WOMAN
before
WALLIS

ONE

THELMA CONSIDERED MANHATTAN HER HOME, though she hadn't lived there for over ten years. To her, it was a city of firsts: she had smoked her first cigarette there, a Lucky Strike stolen from a nun's desk drawer at the convent and passed around the dormitory after bedtime. She and her twin sister, Gloria, had rented their first apartment on Fifth Avenue: an attic brownstone, which, at sixteen years old, they were far too young to live in unchaperoned but did so anyways, stuffing the living room with flowers and leaving the icebox empty. Her first encounter with the society pages had been at New York Harbor: she was eight at the time, mobbed by reporters at the behest of their diplomat father in an attempt to turn the tone of a negative press scrum. The next day's papers would run pictures not of Harry Morgan on his recall to Washington but of his twin daughters, Thelma and Gloria, walking down the gangplank in matching pinafores.

First marriage, thought Thelma, gripping the sable collar of her coat more tightly around her neck. *First divorce.* She stayed on deck long enough to watch the ship slip past the redbrick build-ings of Southampton before seeking refuge from the chill air.

Though Thelma felt uneasy at the prospect of being away from David for nearly six weeks, she knew that she had little choice: Gloria's trial had become a media sensation, chewing up columns on front pages across America and Europe. The cus-tody battle, dubbed the "Trial of the Century" by reporters who squeezed onto the courthouse steps each day, was a nightmare for her sister, forced to defend not only her right to raise her own daughter but also to preserve her own good name. Thelma still rankled at the letter Gloria had sent her: *For Reggie's sister to believe what's being said about me is bad enough, but to know that the rumors came from our own mother is too much to bear...*

Thelma knew that the stories would continue long after the trial concluded—it was inevitable, given that it revolved around a Vanderbilt daughter with a Vanderbilt fortune.

She had received the letter five days ago and booked passage on the earliest steamer bound for New York. If it had been ei-ther of her other siblings—Consuelo or Harry Junior—in this situation, Thelma would have offered what help she could, but as her twin, Gloria held Thelma's allegiance the strongest. It was how it had always been: one supporting the other.

There was only one consideration weighing on Thelma's mind which made it difficult for her to focus on what she would find in America.

"Shall I come, too?" David had asked days ago at Fort Belve-dere. Dismal weather had driven Thelma, David and their guests indoors, an afternoon of weeding David's gardens mercifully re-placed by card games and needlepoint round the drawing room fire. David laid his embroidery hoop to one side, the half-finished rose pointing sightlessly at the ceiling.

Across the room, Wallis Simpson, perusing the contents of the bar cart, turned.

"Don't be silly," she said. From a club chair in the corner,

Wallis's husband, Ernest, folded down the corner of a newspaper. There was a momentary silence as Wallis's long fingers trailed delicately along the crystal tops of several heavy decanters before she selected one.

"You can't possibly think it's a good idea for him to get caught up in this mess," she said, glancing at Thelma as she poured a neat scotch. "You've seen the papers. Can you imagine the sort of froth they'd work themselves into if the Prince of Wales stuck his oar in? I don't mean to offend you, Thelma," she said, "but it's just not seemly for him to get involved, don't you agree?"

David's brows knitted together as Wallis handed him the whiskey. "I feel so terrible about it all," he said. "Gloria's a decent sort. She doesn't deserve all this…surely there's something I can do?" He looked up at Thelma, his spaniel eyes imploring.

Wallis sat down. "You can let Thelma go to support her sister," she said. "Gloria needs her family, sir, not the distraction of a royal sideshow."

"Wally's quite right, sir," said Ernest, resting his newspaper on his lap. "You'd be hindering more than you'd help. Couldn't fix me up one of those as well, could you, darling?"

David exhaled, but didn't look convinced. "Perhaps," he said, as Wallis returned to the cart. "I wouldn't want to add any more controversy to this ghastly business, but I hate the thought of you going on your own."

Thelma sat beside him, smiling at the thought of what David's advisors would say if he so much as commented on the Vanderbilt trial, let alone sailed to America.

"They have a point," she said, taking his hand in hers. "I don't think there's much for you to do. But thank you for wanting to help."

He smiled, worry carved into the lines of his face. "Of course," he said, and kissed Thelma on the cheek. He picked up his needlepoint, lifting the embroidery hoop to inspect the stitching more closely. "Just don't stay away from me too long. I don't think I could stand it."

Perching herself on the armrest of Ernest's chair, Wallis caught Thelma's eye. She smiled, red lips curling in a wide, reassuring grin.

Thelma had been involved with Edward, Prince of Wales—David to those who loved him—for nearly four years now, but she'd never quite shaken the sense of insecurity that came with being part of his life. David's charm, his naivete and, critically, his wandering eye, made him easily distracted; and while Thelma had few qualms about him seeing other women while he traveled abroad on official tours, she couldn't help feeling that this time—these six weeks apart—might prove problematic. Though David had been sorry enough saying goodbye to her at the Fort, there had been something imperceptibly different in his kiss: it had felt a few degrees colder, somehow. The change had been subtle, but enough to make Thelma question whether she ought to shorten her trip. Taking a seat at an empty table in the tearoom, Thelma recalled the luncheon she'd had with Wallis yesterday in London, unsure if the meal had quieted or amplified her worries.

They had met at the Ritz Hotel. She couldn't count the number of times she'd come here on David's arm, to dance in the ballroom or dine in a private suite with one of his brothers. Yesterday, it had been just her and Wallis at a quiet table in the back of the Winter Garden. Given the chilly mist that had settled over London, the restaurant was near to full, diners in cream-colored chairs seeking refuge from the fog. The room was dominated by a baroque fountain, its gilt glamour reflected in the gold scrollwork that ran along the walls and the ceiling.

"You seem distracted today, Thelma—is it nerves? I always go a little queer before traveling. The effort of it all," said Wallis, handing the menu back to the attending waiter. In her typical fashion, Wallis was the best-dressed woman in the room:

she wore a butter-yellow afternoon dress expertly tailored to her slim figure, its high neckline accentuated by an amber and gold brooch nestled in the hollow of her throat. Her hair was pinned into immaculate curls, which, along with her burgundy lips, drew attention away from her square jaw. Seated next to a marble column, Wallis looked at home, her own modest charm magnified by the striking beauty of the room around her.

Thelma pulled a cigarette case and lighter from her handbag. "I don't know," she said. "I hate to leave David. He can get so *melancholy...*"

Wallis lifted her teacup, dismissing Thelma's concerns with a sweep of her hand. "He's a man—they don't stay blue for long. We'll allow him one afternoon to moon over you before finding some suitable distraction."

"That's my concern," said Thelma. "I don't mind distractions so long as they don't become permanent. I'll be gone such a long time—what if someone turns his head?"

Wallis looked at Thelma, frowning. "I can't pretend it's not a possibility," she said. "He will be awfully lonely without you."

Thelma positioned the lighter so the flame caught the end of her cigarette, her heart sinking. "Well," she said, feigning a confidence she didn't truly feel, "nothing to be done for it now, I suppose. I'll have to rely on you to look after him for me while I'm gone."

There was a moment in which Thelma worried she had said the wrong thing—but then Wallis smiled. "Of course," she said, setting her cup back in its saucer. She reached a hand across the table and patted Thelma's arm. "You can count on me. Now, before I forget, would you mind picking up a few odds and ends for me while you're in New York? Some things are so difficult to find here..."

Much as she adored Wallis, Thelma knew she was a cruel choice of chaperone: her brash demeanor was off-putting to many of their friends, so much so that David would likely have no fun at all while Thelma was away. She smiled as she thought of them, David and his guard dog, before chiding herself. That was unkind: if Wallis kept Thelma topmost in his mind, Thelma would have plenty of reasons to thank her. She didn't truly believe David would follow through on his dreams of marriage, but she did, at the back of her mind, wonder.

Thelma looked around the tearoom, filling properly now that they were out of the harbor. She never dreamed of being made queen if he did propose—consort, perhaps, maybe a duchess of some kind—though, as she was already a viscountess through her marriage to Duke, perhaps she was being greedy. Still, she could only imagine what her mother would say. "Marry money," she'd told Thelma and Gloria from the time they were young. "Marry money and you'll never want for a thing in your lives."

It was advice that Thelma struggled with. She had rejected it, espoused it—embraced it, even, though the notion sat heavily on her at times. It was this idea, or some form of it, which had led to her marriage to Junior; to Duke and her title as Lady Furness; and finally, to her relationship with David. Thelma leaned back in her seat, feeling the thrum of the ship as it passed through the English Channel.

It was the foundation on which, for better or worse, Thelma Morgan had built her life.

TWO

July 1925
Hôtel Ritz, Paris

THELMA SURVEYED THE DRESSES HER MAID HAD laid out and dismissed them all with a wave of her hand. She'd arrived in Paris only hours earlier, and while she shared Gloria's happiness at being reunited, she was exhausted from nearly two weeks' travel, looking forward more to her bed than to making small talk with Reggie and Gloria's assembled guests. For one thing, Elise hadn't had the time to unpack all of Thelma's luggage, including the only dress she owned that would look suitable next to Gloria's spectacular new wardrobe. For another, Thelma wasn't quite ready to put a brave face on being Gloria Vanderbilt's poor relation just yet.

She looked down at her bare hand, missing the heavy sapphire that she'd worn for nearly three years. When she first met him, Junior Converse had seemed like a worthy match: impulsive, adoring and wealthy, he was a decade older than her, with breathless dreams and a silver screen smile. His family had money in railroads, he told her—Thelma had never seen him work, but he always had enough to throw the best parties with the best people, constantly turning up at Thelma's apartment with champagne and jewelry, cigarettes and flowers.

They'd eloped when Thelma was seventeen and ran out of Junior's inheritance less than a year later. He developed a knack for speculating and gambling, and for coming home late at night—if at all. At eighteen, Thelma miscarried—a grueling, bloody ordeal that had left her barren. In the clinical light of the hospital room she'd finally seen Junior for what he really was: a boy pretending to be a man. A person so caught up in his own groundless dreams that he was incapable of seeing the harm he caused to others. When she'd gotten out of the hospital, Thelma had gone home, taken Junior's gambling money from behind the loose brick in the chimney and left her sapphire ring on the dining table. She spent the next year in California, fighting for a divorce while attempting to make a name for herself as an actress, trading on her notoriety as a society-page divorcée to win bit parts in second-rate productions.

Thelma rested an absent hand on her flat stomach, shying away from memories that were best left undisturbed. Perhaps fate had been kinder in letting the child slip away.

Turning her attention back to Elise, Thelma dismissed the second set of dresses. The blue Lanvin she'd bought two years ago; the Florrie Westwood with the gathered waistline.

"Haven't I got something in gold?" she said, dropping onto the daybed. The maid dove back into the wardrobe, hangers clicking as she sorted through the evening gowns. Thelma refastened the tie of her dressing robe, its cuffs showing signs of wear: Gloria would have to take her shopping soon.

As if she'd overheard Thelma's concerns, Gloria entered the bedroom, followed by a maid carrying an armload of evening gowns. "I thought you might want to look through a few of mine," she said, directing the maid to Thelma's wardrobe.

In a strange twist of fate, Gloria's relationship with Reginald Vanderbilt had begun just as Thelma's marriage to Junior was ending. He and Junior knew each other casually, occasionally sharing boxes at the Belmont where Reggie ran a string of horses. At a dinner party Thelma and Junior hosted before the miscarriage, Thelma had arranged for Reggie and Gloria to sit together—she'd felt a bittersweet triumph when they were the last couple on the dance floor, turning in slow conversation as the other guests drifted out into the wintry night. If their meeting was the only good thing Thelma could salvage from the wreckage of her marriage to Junior, she would take it.

Elise took the dresses, throwing Thelma a look of relief as she laid them out on the bed. Gloria parsed through them, pulling out one, then another, to hold up against Thelma's chest. Marriage suited her: Gloria had always been more prone to illness than Thelma and was slender to the point of skinniness. Thelma had been sorry to miss the wedding—sorrier still to miss the birth of her niece, Little Gloria. The delivery, Mamma had told her, had been a disaster: Gloria had needed a caesarian operation, and a subsequent bout of diphtheria had laid her up in hospital for the first six weeks of Little Gloria's life.

Now, though, she looked healthy. She had put on some weight, the curves of her figure mirroring Thelma's own.

"I hope you don't mind," said Gloria. She handed Thelma a backless black evening gown, and Thelma slid behind the dressing curtain. "I got so excited that you were finally coming, I couldn't resist throwing a little party. It's all very good having Reggie and the baby, but it's not the same without you here."

Thelma slipped out of her robe. She knew what Gloria meant: though they both had other girlfriends, it simply wasn't the same as having each other. During her year in California, Thelma constantly found herself turning to address her absent sister. When Gloria had greeted her at the train station, Thelma felt something click into place: a half made whole again.

"How are you? How is living with Reggie?"

From the other side of the curtain, Thelma heard Gloria sigh.

"It's wonderful. Isn't that awful? I don't mean to gloat, but I've never been happier. And it's not just the money, either. We have so much fun together, just the three of us."

Thelma came out from behind the dressing curtain, adjusting the neckline of the sleek outfit, biting back a sullen retort: Reggie and Gloria were never alone—not with the baby, nor with each other. Their suite of rooms at the Hôtel Ritz were full to bursting: Gloria and Reggie had brought their staff from New York, and the baby now traveled with a retinue of her own, including Thelma's mother. By every measure, Gloria's marriage to Reggie had been a success: when she signed the marriage document, she became part of one of the wealthiest families in America. Looking down at the spectacular dress Gloria had thrown her way like a hand-me-down, Thelma could see that her sister had quickly become accustomed to her husband's lavish way of life.

Gloria pursed her lips. "Not that one—you look sallow." She pulled a cream-colored Vionnet from the pile. "Try this one, then we can go visit the baby."

Thelma tried on the second dress. She didn't begrudge Gloria her good fortune, but she couldn't help being envious. Thelma's time in California had been an ordeal of lawyers and penny-pinching; she'd not bothered to think about her future, beyond obtaining the divorce she so desperately sought. Now with that battle behind her, Thelma couldn't avoid the reality of her financial situation much longer.

She came out once again. Gloria nodded her approval, and Thelma went back to change into her dressing gown, adjusting the turn at the cuff to hide a spot that had begun to fray.

They left the maids to retrieve jewelry and walked down the hall to the nursery. Gloria knocked but before they could enter Little Gloria's nurse stepped out, pulling the door shut behind her.

"The baby is sleeping," Nurse Kieslich pronounced. With her pigeon-puffed chest and broad shoulders, she looked more like a linebacker than a nanny: she stood straight-backed, her hand curled around the doorknob.

"Mamma hired her," Gloria had told Thelma earlier that day, "and she does seem devoted to the baby but she's so *stern* all the time. The way she looks at me, I don't think she likes me one bit."

Seeing Nurse Kieslich standing guard at the nursery door, Thelma suspected that Gloria was right. Kieslich stared down her nose at Gloria, with an expression that bordered on insolence.

"You would do well to remember she is my child," said Gloria, lifting her chin, "and I'll decide when it's appropriate to see her."

Kieslich raised her eyebrows but released her hold on the door.

The room was lamp-lit and comforting, a cloud-white cradle in one corner. Gloria pulled aside the bassinet's muslin curtains and reached in.

"Who's Mamma's good girl, then?" she said, lifting the child into her arms.

Little Gloria yawned, rubbing her eyes with a puffy fist. She was more toddler than infant now, her chubby legs dangling down Gloria's front as she nestled her face in the crook of her mother's neck.

Gloria kissed the crown of her head. "Would you like to hold her?"

Thelma lifted the child into her arms. "She's so much bigger," she said. A year ago, Thelma had made a rare visit to New York to visit the newborn. At the time, Gloria had been laid up in the hospital with diphtheria; Mamma had been caring for the baby in her absence, moving a cot into the nursery so she could sleep beside the crib. Thelma had yearned to hold her niece, but Mamma wouldn't let her: What germs might Thelma have brought, coming from Gloria's hospital bed? By the time Gloria had recovered, Mamma had hired Nurse Kieslich, and had moved her belongings permanently into one of Gloria and Reggie's guest bedrooms.

Mamma had a close hold on Little Gloria, but this evening she was out. Thelma took full advantage of her absence, holding Little Gloria close and inhaling her sweet scent, imagining, for the briefest of moments, that she was holding a child of her own.

A deep voice behind her broke the silence of the nursery. "She likes you."

Reggie Vanderbilt was standing at the nursery door. He came forward, resting a hand on Gloria's shoulder as he kissed Thelma on the cheek.

Though he wasn't a tall man, Reggie dwarfed Thelma and Gloria both, his square frame giving the impression that he took up more space than he truly did. "Perhaps we'll be welcoming a cousin for Little Gloria to play with before long."

Thelma looked down as Little Gloria grasped her finger with an unsteady hand. "Perhaps," she said.

As a brother-in-law, Thelma couldn't ask for more than Reggie Vanderbilt. Gregarious, fun-loving and good-natured, Reggie was generous to a fault, always insisting on more: more food, more wine, more laughter. He lived in excess, racing cars and horses, hosting parties for hundreds—and though Thelma disapproved of his gambling habit, he adored Gloria, and that was enough.

"Of course she likes you," said Kieslich as she set the folded blanket back in the crib. "She's a baby—she likes anyone who holds her."

"Yes, thank you, Nurse," muttered Reggie, exchanging a look with Gloria. She stifled a smile and took Little Gloria to settle her back in her crib.

"Troll," said Reggie, once they were out of earshot. "If I wasn't so afraid of what your mother would say, Gloria, I would sack her. You ladies get dressed, we're expected downstairs in an hour."

The private dining room at the Ritz was bright, electric lights in chandeliers sparkling over the soft glow of candles. A dining table laden with flowers stood at one end of the room, and a three-piece band sat on a raised dais at the other, rehearsing a jerking, rhythmic piece as Gloria flitted past, setting handwritten place cards on the table. She and Thelma had come down early, instructing the maître d' to squeeze in another setting.

"I know it's last minute, but Beth telephoned—a friend of hers is in town, Lord Furness, have you heard of him?" said Gloria, bending over the table with a fountain pen in hand to write a new place card. She looked up as a waiter arrived with a wicker-seated chair. "Reggie has. Apparently, he's got more money than God. No—move that one," she said, motioning to the waiter. Gloria picked up Lord Furness's place card and switched it with the one next to Thelma's seat. "Who knows?" she said. "Reggie and I met at your dinner party—one good turn..."

Thelma picked up the place card, watching the ink dry as she played with its edges. "I don't know," she said. "My divorce was finalized only a few weeks ago... How would it look?"

Gloria snatched back the card and set it down. "It's dinner," she said. "That's all. You've been estranged from Junior for over a year. It's time you started thinking about your future."

Thelma frowned but let the card stay where it was. Gloria was right—she generally was, where Thelma was concerned. Still, she felt unsettled about the prospect of meeting someone new. She had fallen for Junior in the space of an evening—and spent the next three years atoning for it.

"It's dinner," Gloria repeated, and pushed a glass of champagne into Thelma's hands. "Not the rest of your life. We ought to go. Do I need to touch up my hair?" They walked out of the dining room. "I'm not so sure about that maid of mine, she doesn't use nearly as many pins as Joan used to. *French...*"

They went into the Petit Bar, which, along with the private dining room, Reggie had rented for Thelma's party. She couldn't help but marvel at the deference with which people acquiesced to Reggie's demands—but then, that was the power of a Vanderbilt. She thought back to the juvenile conversations she used to have with Gloria, the dreams they shared before falling asleep in matching cots. It had all worked out for Gloria: a fairy-tale romance with a man who adored her. How very different Thelma's own life had become.

Thelma felt a pang of longing as Reggie pulled Gloria close and kissed her tenderly, releasing her as the first few guests began to trickle through the bar's painted-glass doors.

Though part of her still felt that the night would be better spent resting, Thelma put on a good face for Gloria. She picked up her glass of champagne and joined her twin at the door, smiling at the familiar faces, allowing Gloria to make introductions to the new ones.

Thelma brightened as a man escorting a woman in an unseasonable fur stole walked into the room. She turned to Gloria. "You didn't tell me Harry was coming!"

Gloria laughed. "I wanted it to be a surprise," she said, as Thelma pulled him into a hug.

Thelma hadn't seen her brother since before her marriage. Back then, Harry had been readjusting to civilian life—and to a body permanently impacted by war. He had been gassed at Argonne, which had left him with a permanent tremor. Thelma looked him over, watching him blink back the tears that perpetually welled in the corners of his eyes. He'd regained some measure of control, it seemed, but he hadn't lost that look of panic that had followed him since that day.

She pulled back. "You look like Papa," she said.

Harry laughed. "A little less up here—" He rested a shaking hand on his thinning hair, then patted his waistline, "—and a little more around here. May I present my wife, Edith?"

She grasped Edith by the hands. Petite and blonde, with a sparrowlike tilt to her chin, Edith was someone Thelma had only heard about in Gloria's letters. "I'm so pleased to finally meet you," she said.

Thelma drew Harry and Edith into a corner of the bar and

they began to chat, Harry tactfully avoiding any mention of Thelma's divorce.

Fifteen minutes later, they were interrupted by the ring of a spoon against crystal. Thelma looked over at Reggie, standing at the bar with his glass high in the air.

"Gloria and I are so pleased you could join our little party," he said, beaming at the crowd, "and I'm especially pleased to welcome my sister-in-law, Thelma, back to Europe. *Bienvenue*," he said. He raised his glass in a toast and Thelma lifted hers in response.

He drained his glass, then set it on the bar. "And now," he said, "we eat!" He held out his arm to Gloria and she took it; together, they walked through to the dining salon. With a nod to Thelma, Harry and Edith followed suit, guests pairing off to walk down the marbled hall. She looked round the emptying room, worried, for a moment, that she would have to walk through alone—then a man stepped forward and held out his arm.

She hadn't noticed him among Gloria's guests: he was older than her by a fair bit, of average height, with average features. His hair—strawberry blond—was parted down the middle and waxed back from his temples, his blue eyes morning pale. His only truly distinguishing feature was his suit: he wore an exquisitely tailored dress coat that cut close to his slim figure. A high collar and white bow tie; black-and-white wing tip shoes. *British*, Thelma thought, admiring the cut.

He smiled. "I spoke to Mrs. Vanderbilt on my way in and she tells me I have the pleasure of dining with you this evening. May I take you through?"

Thelma smiled back. "Certainly, Lord Furness," she said, resting her hand on his arm.

"*Marmaduke*," said Lord Furness, as waiters cleared plates. Despite his stiff jacket and collar, Lord Furness had visibly relaxed during his dinner: he leaned back in his chair, one leg crossed over the other, hands raised to the back of his neck. "I ask you—*Marmaduke*. Though," he frowned, his northern accent strengthening, "I daresay it's the reason I've been successful. Give a boy a bleeding poem for a name and he'll have to amount to something to stop him getting his lights knocked out in the schoolyard."

"*Duke* is a dashing alternative, though, wouldn't you say?" said Thelma. She had enjoyed Lord Furness's company at dinner more than she'd anticipated: conversation flowed easily between them, so much so that they had forgotten the other diners around them.

Lord Furness nodded. "Sounds better—stronger," he said. "My friends call me Duke."

Thelma smiled, picturing Lord Furness as a redheaded youth, rangy and ambitious, shaping his identity with quiet conviction. "Did that happen often? Getting your lights knocked out in the schoolyard?"

Furness chuckled. "More than a gentleman would like to admit. And you? Any childhood ghosts?"

Thelma shrugged. "A few playground crushes—perhaps the odd encounter with a bully or two. But we never stayed long enough in one school to develop any real rivalries. With Papa's work in the diplomatic service, we were always moving from one place or another."

Furness set down his glass. "How did you find that? Moving from place to place?"

"How did you find growing up in Yorkshire? You get used to what you know," she replied.

"I suppose so," he said. "And what are you used to, a girl like you?"

Thelma smirked, casting an eye around the room. "I'd like to say I'm used to this," she said, taking in the crystal chandeliers; the waiters, silent and attentive; the free-flowing wine and daringly fashionable guest list, "but I'm afraid my husband and

I were used to a slightly different standard of entertaining. Former husband," she clarified.

"I'm sorry," said Furness. "I didn't realize—did he pass recently?"

"He didn't. Divorce." She waited for his reaction. *Oh*, she recalled an American friend telling her once, her nose wrinkling with distaste, *they don't have divorce over there; they have affairs.*

Furness cleared his throat. "Any man would be mad to give you up," he said. "I was lucky in my marriage to Daisy, God rest her soul. Not everyone is, I suppose."

Thelma reddened, and the room grew quiet. At the head of the table, Reggie rang a dessert spoon against his glass.

"My friends, thank you once again for joining us this fine evening," he said, getting to his feet. "My lovely wife tells me I am to lead us all to the dance floor with her equally lovely sister. Thelma?"

Thelma rose, the men standing in unison as Reggie claimed her hand. The band began to play the same jilting tune they had been rehearsing when Gloria set the place cards, and Thelma and Reggie began to dance. From the corner of her eye, Thelma saw Gloria pull Harry onto his feet, and within minutes they were surrounded by other couples.

"You've certainly done a number on Furness," said Reggie quietly. "Beth Leary might be upset with you."

"Really?" said Thelma. She looked over Reggie's shoulder as Lord Furness began to dance with Beth. The sight irritated her—but then Furness turned, sweeping Beth around, and met Thelma's eye.

Thelma looked away, pleased. "She's welcome to him, but it might be a wasted effort," she said.

Reggie's wheezy laugh quickly turned to a cough. "You and I know that," he said, "but I'm not sure Beth does. I'll warn you, though, you'll have stiff competition for that one, Miss Leary aside."

"Whatever for?"

"I thought Gloria told you—Duke Furness's wealth makes me look cheap. Though at the rate we're spending it…"

Thelma waved off Reggie's self-deprecation. "Well, Gloria mentioned it…"

"Shipping," said Reggie. "Had a near-flotilla at the turn of the century—sold them all off during the war. When prices dropped after the Armistice, he bought everything back for a fraction of what he paid. There were complaints, of course—improprieties—but still, money talks. Thirty million, I've heard. Pounds."

Lord Furness and Beth circled once more and he looked over Beth's shoulder, his pale eyes crinkling as he smiled.

"…Wife died, had to be—oh, five, six years ago? He's been alone ever since, though not for lack of trying. Half the women in St. James would give their left arms for a shot at him."

The song ended and Reggie slowed, tucking his hand into his waistcoat as a red flush of exertion rose in his cheeks. His thick neck bit at the edge of his straight collar; Thelma knew there would be a line there, red and raw, when he removed his collar points at the end of the night.

"I'll be straight with you, Thelma. Gloria knows you've been unhappy—well, no wonder, given that shark you married. She frets about you. It would mean so much to her if you made an effort to rebuild yourself. If you've caught Furness's eye…" Reggie pulled a cigarette case from his pocket, his gaze steady, "Well. Worth a shot, don't you think?"

They left the dance floor, drifting slowly, almost accidentally, toward Lord Furness and Beth.

"Good evening," said Reggie. "Ah, a slower number, much more my speed. Beth, would you do me the honor?" He held out his hand and Beth dithered for a moment before accepting, a slight slump to her shoulders as Reggie pulled her away.

Thelma's stomach lurched as Lord Furness shifted closer. She had enjoyed their dinner-table conversation, but now, knowing the hope that Gloria and Reggie had placed on them was disconcerting. And the wealth… She'd known Furness had money, but what did it say about her that, since hearing the figures, he'd become so much more attractive?

"Dreadful music, this," said Lord Furness. "I know of a cracking group playing at a club across town… Reggie wouldn't mind, would he?"

Thelma looked across the room. Reggie was making a concerted effort to distract Beth, while Gloria, in defiance of the song's tempo, was dancing the Charleston with Hannibal de Mesa.

She frets about you.

At the end of the evening, Gloria would clasp hands with her husband and take an elevator to the top floor of the Ritz, kiss her beautiful daughter good-night and spend the early hours in Reggie's arms. Tomorrow, she would take Thelma shopping for dresses made of fabric that would slip through her fingers like water, the Vanderbilt name all the capital she needed to live a life of comfort.

Thelma let her hand drift across the bar-top, as close to Furness's as she dared. "I shouldn't think so," she said. "Give me a minute."

Furness beamed. "I'll get my coat," he said, and Thelma dashed to the dance floor.

Gloria knew what Thelma had come to say. "Furness?" she said, barely missing a step.

"Can I take your cape?" asked Thelma.

Gloria laughed. "Tell him if you lose it, he'll have to buy me another." Hannibal lifted his arm and Gloria whirled under it, the beaded fringe of her dress whipping as she moved.

Thelma met Furness in the hotel lobby, his coat slung over his arm. "Ready," she said, drawing close. He put his hand on the small of her back. "Where to, Lord Furness?"

"Please," he said, "call me Duke."

THREE

LITTLE GLORIA LET OUT A SQUEAL OF JOY AS Thelma and Gloria entered the nursery.

"Up!" she commanded, holding out her pudgy arms. Gloria lifted her out, offering her cheek to the toddler before setting her down on the carpet. Thelma lowered herself to the ground as well, arranging the hem of her dress while Little Gloria pushed herself up on unsteady legs and lurched toward the toy chest.

Across the room, Nurse Kieslich watched Little Gloria's tottering procession.

"Am I to assume that you are pushing back Little Gloria's luncheon? It's to arrive in twenty minutes, and if you insist on disrupting her schedule—"

"It's disrupting, is it, for me to spend time with my daughter?" Gloria shut the wicker lid of the toy chest and sighed. "Very well, then, it's disruptive. Little Gloria will have her luncheon in forty minutes. Thank you, Kieslich, that will be all."

She turned her attention back to Little Gloria. "Well?" she said, dangling a toy rabbit in front of her daughter. "How was it?"

Thelma smiled, pulling a set of building blocks from the toy chest. "He's very nice," she said. Duke had seemed determined to fit the whole of Paris into a single night, taking Thelma from club to club until her feet ached in protest. They'd ended the night at the flower market, strolling hand in hand as they watched merchants open sidewalk stalls, lifting armloads of sunflowers, peonies, freesias, iris and lavender from the wooden flatbeds of small trucks in the dim half morning, lining tulip-filled tin pots on cobbled street corners. Later that morning, she'd awoken to the biggest bouquet of roses she'd ever seen, six dozen at least, set in a display that looked more suited to the hotel lobby than her bedroom.

Thelma smiled. "No," she corrected herself. "He's very *keen*."

"Do you think you'll see him again?"

"He certainly hopes so," said Thelma.

"That's not an answer," replied Gloria, grazing the rabbit's ears against Little Gloria's fingertips.

"I know," said Thelma, "I just—it's the money, Gloria, I don't know if I can—"

"Why ever not?" said Gloria.

Thelma hesitated, passing a block from hand to hand. "He's lovely…but is it terrible for me to say that the most attractive thing about him is his wealth? When I think of what Mamma—"

"Mamma would turn backflips if she knew—mind, she doesn't notice much these days beyond the baby. Isn't that right?" she said, addressing Little Gloria. "Your Naney loves you—and it's suffocating your daddy and me!" She pulled the child into her lap, who kicked at the air with slippered feet. "For all her faults she's right, you know," she continued. "Reggie and I—well, for all that he's a spendthrift, we've got his family to take care of us. You can't live on charity forever, Thelma—goodness knows Papa can't afford to help you, and Reggie and I are already supporting Mamma. If Furness is showing interest in you, don't you think you ought to give him a chance?"

"It seems disingenuous," said Thelma. "And after Junior..."

"Furness is Junior's opposite in every way," said Gloria. "Your husband was one of the most reckless men I've ever met, and from what I've heard Furness is an even keel. He's a good prospect, Thelma. He's already made money—he already has children. You won't have any surprises, and that might be a good thing. Comfortable."

Thelma smiled, thinking of the roses. "We got on awfully well last night," she admitted.

"See? There you are. Like can become love," said Gloria. "You'll see him again? Good. He's invited us to dinner tonight."

"So soon?"

"He spoke to Reggie this morning. A man like him—he's not going to waste time," said Gloria. She got to her feet, but as she straightened she swayed alarmingly, blood draining from her face.

"Gloria?"

She gripped the side of the crib, squeezing her eyes shut. Thelma stood to steady her; pressing a hand against Gloria's forehead to check for fever.

"It's all right," said Gloria, but Thelma led her to a rocking chair, as Little Gloria shifted across the carpet in search of more building blocks.

"It's getting worse," said Gloria. She leaned forward, her head between her knees. "Since the delivery." She opened her eyes as color slowly flooded back to her cheeks. "The doctor says it's heart attacks. From the diphtheria. Not much to be done for it, I'm afraid."

"Deep breaths," said Thelma. Gloria inhaled through her nose, letting the breath out with a hiss. "We've got time."

Behind her, Thelma could hear Little Gloria scuffling about on the carpet. She let out a whimpering sound, wavering on the edge of tears—well, she'd have to wait, thought Thelma, focusing her attention back on Gloria as the door swung open.

Mamma walked in with Nurse Kieslich, carrying a luncheon tray. "Why is Little Gloria alone?" she said.

"Gloria had one of her attacks."

"There we are, *caro*—upsy daisy," said Mamma, lifting Little Gloria from the floor. She quietened, snuggling against Mamma's chest. "Well, seeing as you're poorly, you might as well go and have a lie-down. Kieslich has Little Gloria's meal. It shouldn't sit."

"We had asked for more time with her," said Thelma. "Another twenty minutes."

"Nurse Kieslich explained the situation to me and I quite agreed with her. Children need schedules," said Mamma. "You know when her playtime is." And with that Gloria and Thelma were dismissed.

"Better?" asked Thelma. She had brought Gloria into the sitting room and settled her onto a daybed with a blanket over her legs.

Gloria nodded. "Truly, though, it's getting worse," she said, her face knotted with tension. "And when I think of Reggie's troubles…"

Thelma exhaled. She'd had her suspicions about Reggie's health: his red face; the broken veins. "What do the doctors say?"

Gloria played with the hem of the blanket, knotting loose threads together. "We came back from Vichy two weeks ago— the doctors in Newport recommended he take the cure," she said. "He wouldn't stay. Said it didn't take."

Thelma watched Gloria worry the blanket, her brow furrowed. "The doctor called me while he was in treatment," she said. "He said I had a right to know if Reggie wouldn't tell me himself. He's got—cirrhosis of the liver, I think it was called. Too much rich food, too much drinking. Not enough exercise…"

Thelma's stomach dropped at the mention of cirrhosis. "Well, that can be fixed, can't it?" she said. "Rest and fresh air—"

Gloria laughed bitterly. "Have you met my husband?" she said. "I love him dearly, truly I do, but he would choose wine over air. The doctors say he's only got a few more years if—if he doesn't change his habits."

"So change them," said Thelma. She could feel a quiet sort of panic setting in—at Reggie's diagnosis, and at Gloria's quiet resignation. "It's his health, Gloria, you can't afford to take risks."

"That's why we extended our trip," said Gloria. "Reggie agreed—a change of scenery, a few months away from the Newport crowd, they're all as bad as he is. But you saw him last night, drinking and carrying on... He was coughing up blood the other day, Thelma. *Blood.*"

Thelma hesitated, "You're sure?"

"He tried to pass it off as a nosebleed, but he's a terrible liar. I don't think he can do it, Thelma. I don't think he's taking this seriously at all. And me with my heart..." Gloria began to cry; she looked too small against the cushions of the daybed, too young to have such worries. "What will happen to Little Gloria if—if—"

"Don't be ridiculous," said Thelma. She shifted from the armchair to the daybed, collecting Gloria into a hug. "Nothing's going to happen. It won't come to that."

"Won't it?" said Gloria. "Watch him at dinner, Thelma. Watch him, and you'll understand why I worry I'll be a widow by the time I turn twenty."

"A daughter in the nobility—well, it would make up for Consuelo's faults," said Mamma. She had called on Thelma and Gloria as the maids served afternoon tea, sinking into Reggie's armchair with a restless Little Gloria in her arms. The mere mention of Thelma and Gloria's elder sister was enough to cast a shadow on her face: two years earlier, Consuelo had divorced a French count to marry a diplomat's son.

"Mamma, I've met him once," said Thelma.

"And look at the impression you made on him," Mamma replied. "This is an opportunity—give him reasons to believe you
would make a good wife. Read a newspaper—you'll want him
to think you're worldly."

Thelma took a madeleine from the tea tray, balancing it on the
edge of her plate. "And would you like me to grow two inches
as well, so that he can kiss me more easily?" she said. Beside her,
Gloria hid her laugh behind a hasty cough.

"He's tall?" Mamma replied. "Wear your sister's highest
heels." Little Gloria squirmed free of her grasp and thumped
across the room; for once, Mamma let her go. "When you ran
off with that Converse fellow I thought you were ruined," she
said. "All I had worked for, wasted on that reprobate…" She
trailed off and watched Little Gloria kneel to open the back of
a splendid doll's house. "When you divorced him, I was sure
you'd never be accepted into society again. It's why your father
and I let you run off to California. Society has a looser sense of
propriety there."

Thelma's face grew hot, and she lowered her plate with the
uneaten madeleine to the table.

"Quite frankly, I'm astonished he's showing an interest even
after Reggie told him you were a divorcée," said Mamma. She
leaned back and settled her hands above the rise of her stomach. "And I'll tell you this—another opportunity won't come
along easily. Wealthy men don't look far for distractions. Think
carefully about the advantages Lord Furness would give you."

"Surely it's not quite as dire as all that," said Thelma, feigning bravado. She wished Gloria wasn't in the room; she wished
Kieslich wasn't listening. "I can take care of myself—"

"Can you?" Mamma had taken to drawing her eyebrows on
higher than they naturally sat; she would have looked ridiculous,
if she wasn't so unnervingly stern. "Your father and I have our
differences, Thelma, but I know how expensive your divorce

was for him. Do you expect to live on Gloria's good will? Or are you planning to train as a secretary?"

Thelma looked down. She'd tried, in California—she'd made pictures, posed in magazines, turned up at all the right parties—but Hollywood hadn't wanted her, not on her own terms. She could have stayed, she supposed, and found herself some elderly studio executive, following the path of a thousand young starlets into vanity projects that would never make it into theaters, filling the family coffers with cheaply set jewels from new-money admirers—and still Mamma would be there, telling her she'd failed.

"Well," said Thelma, not bothering to hide the bitterness from her tone as she looked up. "We know Gloria and Reggie can't support us both."

She could feel Gloria staring at her but held Mamma's gaze, waiting for the rebuke. Then Mamma sighed.

"No," she said. "They can't."

Thelma couldn't bring herself to respond.

"Think about Furness's wealth. And his title—what that might do for you. You would be able to move to Europe permanently, and leave the stain of your divorce behind you." She reached forward and took the madeleine from Thelma's plate. "Think about that—then tell me a little effort wouldn't be worth your time."

FOUR

THELMA SLID INTO THE BACK OF THE MOTORCAR, reaching up to ensure that her jeweled headpiece hadn't gotten dislodged by the movement. Beside her, Gloria reached over and batted Thelma's hand down.

"You'll ruin it," she said as the chauffeur pulled away from the curb. The expansive lights of Place Vendôme gave way to the narrower streets of Rue de la Paix, storefronts glittering as they passed. Ciro's wasn't far, but Thelma was glad they'd driven. It gave her a few moments to collect herself.

Thanks to Gloria's intervention, Thelma was wearing an intricately patterned dress with a zigzag hemline that brushed the backs of her knees. She'd borrowed Gloria's spectacular pearl necklace—a gift from Gloria's mother-in-law, so long that, even though Thelma wound it twice around her neck, it still fell below her waist.

The motorcar turned onto Rue Daunou, the sidewalks closing in further as they rolled down the cobbled street. They stopped outside the brightest building, light spilling out of square windows and splashing onto the sign out front. Even within the confines of the motorcar, Thelma could hear the pulsing beat of an orchestra.

The chauffeur parked at the curb, and as Gloria stepped out she waved: Reggie was standing on the street corner.

"Came out for a breath of fresh air," he said, taking a final puff from a blunt cigar. He had come to Ciro's from a poker game at a nearby club; Thelma wondered how he'd done, but his expression betrayed neither victory nor defeat. In the yellow glow of the restaurant's lights, Reggie looked sallow, his complexion the color of antiqued paper; but he grinned nonetheless, dropping his cigar stub onto the curb. "Furness is inside."

Gloria twisted her hands around the strap of her handbag. "The doctors told you not to smoke," she said, "Did you—"

"Quite all right—stuffy inside, that's all. I got a bit light-headed." Gloria looked unconvinced; Reggie laughed and kissed the crown of her head. "I'm right as rain, my dear. Now, we're being rude—Furness is in there alone." He settled Gloria's hand in the crook of his right arm and offered his left to Thelma.

The restaurant was alive with sound, a five-piece band leading dancers, packed elbow to elbow on the dance floor, in a waltz. Couples nearly bumped into each other as they sought to avoid the tables closest to the dance floor, where unlucky diners snatched their cocktails out of the way of fringed hems and the tips of tailcoats. Reggie was right: it was stuffy, sweat and cigarette smoke overpowering the smell of roast beef as waiters laden with dinner plates weaved past. Surveying the room, Thelma was grateful for Gloria's insistence on wearing a new dress: the women dripped with jewels and beading, feathered headpieces and filigreed bangles, cocktail rings with stones the size of thumbs.

Reggie led them into a smaller, quieter dining room with a long oak bar and Thelma's pulse quickened as she caught sight of Duke Furness at a corner table: she enjoyed the momentary,

all-too-familiar look of confusion on his face as he tried to de-
cipher which twin was which. She gave a short flutter of her
fingers and Duke smiled, rising to his feet.

She broke away from Reggie and Duke kissed her on the
cheek; she rested her hands on his arms, feeling the weave of
his tuxedo beneath her fingers. He wore a different, no less
extravagantly cut, suit from the one he'd worn the night before, abandoning swallowtails for a single-breasted dinner jacket
with peaked lapels. He looked handsome—dashing, even—in
his finery.

The same, however, could not be said for Reggie. Though
Gloria had told Thelma that Reggie had had several new suits
made before they left Newport two months ago, Reggie looked
overstuffed, his solid belly straining at his silk waistcoat. He
called for the waiter, who came with four glasses of champagne
on a tray.

"Delighted to see you again, Miss Morgan," said Duke, pulling out Thelma's chair. "How are the roses?"

Thelma lowered her voice and Duke leaned in to hear her.
"Truly, Lord Furness—they're too much. Far too much."

Duke beamed. "Nonsense." He tucked a hand in the pocket
of his waistcoat and reached for his drink. "A girl like you ought
to have flowers, and a fellow like me ought to give them."

Reggie motioned for the waiter, holding up his empty glass.

Perhaps she'd chosen not to see it before, but after her conversation with Gloria it was clear that Reggie drank two cocktails
for each one of Duke's. As dinner progressed, he was gregarious to a fault, calling the waiter over whenever their drinks
fell past the halfway mark, leaving a bottle of champagne reserved on ice. Despite the noise of the other diners, Reggie's
voice boomed over the rest, his barking laugh a constant punctuation to the music. When the waiter removed the remains
of their main courses from the table, Reggie knocked over his

water glass; Gloria rescued her napkin from the deluge, her face twisted in polite anguish.

Thelma touched Duke on the arm. "Tell me, how is London at this time of year?" she asked as Reggie dabbed water from his front. "I'd so love to go for the season. I've never been."

"Haven't you?" said Duke. "I'll not lie—this is a dull month for London. Everyone's off at their country homes—it's why I spend so much time in Paris. But Ascot's coming up—good fun, that. Reggie would enjoy it, eh, Vanderbilt?" said Duke, casting across the table. His voice faltered slightly as he saw Reggie and Gloria in the midst of a terse, whispered conversation.

Reggie dropped the soaked napkin on the table. "What's that, Furness? Ascot? Yes, well—could be a laugh. We could bring a string of ponies from Newport. Host a polo match with Nada and George, if I get my act together. Yes, why not?" He shifted in his chair to look at Duke head-on, planting his arm on the table as he leaned forward. "But that's not for a month— plenty of time to waste on the continent until then. Could go to Longchamp, watch the races there? Horsepower rather than horses, eh?"

Duke gave Thelma a sidelong glance. "I rather thought I'd stay through to June, if I found an excuse—hunting's rubbish this early in the year, and Dickie and Averill won't thank me hanging about London while they throw their parties. Longchamp sounds like a damned good time. Damned good."

"Excellent," said Reggie, shifting to his feet. "That calls for—a toast, I think—"

A fresh tray of drinks appeared as if by magic, and Reggie lifted his glass to shoulder height. Beside him, Gloria made an involuntary noise: a choked sort of cough.

"To friendships, old and new," he said. He drained his glass in one and wiped his mouth on a napkin, then lowered himself back into his seat and circled his hand in the air for another round.

"A bottle of White Rock, if you'd be so kind," Gloria murmured as the waiter picked up Reggie's empty glass.

Reggie glared at her when the waiter returned with the mineral water and covered his glass with a beefy hand. "Scotch," he said, meeting his wife's eyes with a level stare.

Thelma and Duke sat in silence. From the other room, the music swelled louder.

Beneath the table, Duke took Thelma's hand, stroking the back of her palm with his thumb.

"Tell me, Gloria, how do you find Paris compares to Newport?" he said.

Gloria turned away from Reggie and smiled at Duke, her voice unsteady as she launched into a comparison of American and European society.

Thelma turned her hand under Duke's so that they were facing palm to palm and squeezed.

FIVE

THE GARE DU NORD WAS WRAPPED IN A THICK fog of steam that mingled with the crisp air carried in by the trains as they rolled into the station. Though it was still mid-August, the day held the promise of autumn to come.

Reggie and Gloria's train stood at the farthest platform, belching exhaust in a periodic wheeze that made it look as though it was bound to depart earlier than scheduled on its own impulsive whim. The platform was packed with people: shouts echoed as families caught sight of each other for one final goodbye; porters, lugging heavy carts and trunks, shouldered their way toward the carriages, faces stern beneath trim caps.

After their night at Ciro's, Duke had sent Reggie, Gloria and Thelma tickets to a show in Montmartre; two weeks later, he invited them to a villa he'd rented in a seaside town. The foursome rang in Bastille Day at the Deauville Casino, Reggie losing thousands of francs at the baccarat table, Duke quietly making up the difference; in August, they went to the racetrack and bet on the horses that Reggie, with his years of authority in

the sport, had picked as the likely winners. As the summer progressed, Thelma was surprised—and pleased—to find that her
affection for Duke continued to grow: so much so that, when
Duke asked Thelma to come with her to his Scottish hunting
lodge at the end of the season, Thelma had accepted.

It could have been the perfect summer, but for Reggie's de-
clining health. Two weeks ago, Reggie had collapsed getting
out of the motorcar and Gloria, finally, had put her foot down.
She'd taken Reggie to Vichy for the cure, but Reggie, reluctant
to miss the opening day of the Newport Horse Show, had cut
his treatment short. Now, they were returning to New York
with a hired doctor in tow.

Duke saw them first, standing at the entrance to the first-class
coach. He put his arm around Thelma so as not to lose her and
charged forward, lifting his hat high in the air.

"We were worried you might not make it," said Reggie,
enveloping Thelma in a cloud of cigar smoke and brilliantine
as Gloria and Duke said their goodbyes. Thelma gripped him
tightly, hating how weak his arms felt around her. "Best of luck
in Scotland." He released her, inhaling the last of his cigar as he
stepped an extra few paces away from Gloria and Duke. "He'll
be a lucky man to have you. Lucky indeed."

Thelma warmed at his words. She arched an eyebrow, play-
acting for his benefit. "But who's to say I'll have him?" she replied, and Reggie chuckled.

She sobered. "Take care of yourself, Reggie."

Reggie's cheery expression dimmed. He threw his cigar stub
onto the train track and took Thelma's hand. "Promise me, my
dear," he said in a low voice, "that you'll look after them. When
the time comes."

The train let out a blast of steam. A conductor blew a piercing
note on a whistle, and Gloria threw herself into Thelma's arms.

"Tell me everything—absolutely everything. I can't wait to

hear about it," she breathed. She let go and Reggie helped her onto the train.

"Second and third compartments, darling," he said, and Gloria disappeared into the depths of the carriage. Reggie stepped up, but lingered at the carriage door.

He looked at Thelma. With Gloria gone, Reggie let fall the armor of relentless enthusiasm that had carried him through the day. He looked, quite simply, ill: the world no longer a game, but already a memory.

Thelma nodded, and the strain in Reggie's face lightened. He touched the brim of his hat, then turned to follow his wife.

Two weeks later, Thelma stepped off the train in Inverness at six in the morning, bundling herself in the thick of her overcoat as she searched the platform for Duke. She'd taken the overnight service from London, and while she hardly would have blamed Duke if he'd only sent a chauffeur to collect her from the station at this early hour, she was pleased to find him leaning against the ticket counter, dressed in his tweeds and looking every inch the country gentleman.

He bent to kiss her. "Made it, then," he said fondly as he led her toward a waiting car. "How was your trip?"

"I wish I could tell you I slept, but I'm afraid I barely shut my eyes. I hope you don't have some horrid Highland tradition where everyone wakes at seven to walk the glen—I may need a nap before I'm civil."

Duke opened the car door and Thelma climbed inside as her maid helped the footmen strap a hatbox onto the boot. "We aren't much for traditions up here," he replied. "If a warm nap and a hot bath is all you're good for today, that's fine with me."

The drive from Inverness took less than an hour, the car cutting through Highland mist as they passed rolling mountains covered in purple heather. Thelma curled into Duke's chest, smiling at the easy intimacy between them, and at Duke's evident pleasure in seeing her. She felt as though she was dreaming as the peaked roofline of Affric Lodge came into view: a compact gray-stone mansion with a fairy-tale turret, perched on a tree-lined outcrop overlooking a wide loch.

"Is that it?" she said, nudging Duke in the ribs. "That old mess?"

Duke laughed, snugging Thelma closer in a proprietorial sort of way. "It's not as grand as you might think," he said. "It's not got electricity, nor a telephone. How will you stand that, I wonder? Averill's always on about it. Says she loves the hunting but feels cut off from the world. A telegram's not enough for her, I suppose."

Thelma didn't respond; she fit her hand in Duke's, studying his ruby signet ring.

"What?"

"Suppose your children don't like me."

Duke snorted as the car trundled up the drive. "Why wouldn't they?"

Notwithstanding its size, Affric Lodge was airy, its immense picture windows coaxing in the morning light that had broken through the fog. After freshening up, Thelma came down to find Duke in the dining room, helping himself to an array of breakfast foods while being regaled by a redheaded youth telling an animated story.

Duke cleared his throat when Thelma entered, and the young man sprang to his feet.

"Pleased to meet you," he said, offering his hand in a warm imitation of Duke's manner.

Thelma smiled. "You must be Christopher. How do you do?"

He beamed. Christopher was a miniature of his father, Duke's handsome features set in a round, guileless face. "My friends call me Dickie," he said in a trimmed Eton accent, "and I hope you will, too. I'm sorry Averill isn't here to meet you, she's out stalking." He sat back down and helped himself to a mountain of scrambled eggs. "One of the gillies spotted a ten pointer just the other side of the loch yesterday afternoon."

"Afraid her old man would nab it if she didn't get after it first thing in the morning, eh?"

Thelma took a square of toast, letting the conversation between father and son wash over her. She was relieved to have been afforded a few more hours' grace before meeting Duke's eldest child. According to Duke, Averill—only four years Thelma's junior—hadn't inherited her mother's gentle charm: she was strong-willed and obstinate, and shared Duke's passion for hunting and riding.

"I may have made her slightly more in my image than I'd planned after Daisy died," Duke had told her, furrowing his brow but smiling nonetheless. "She was thirteen when it happened. Old enough to understand, but young enough not to know what to do about it all. She followed me around like a damned puppy for months afterward. I couldn't have her out on the moors with nothing to do so I gave her a shotgun, pointed to the birds and told her to have at. Rather a good way to cope, as it turned out, I think."

Averill returned from stalking in time for afternoon tea, which had been served on the lawn overlooking Loch Affric. Though she had saved her new trousers for tomorrow's sport, Thelma was wearing a jacket over her afternoon dress: the sun might have been sending ripples of light across the water but, as Elise reminded Thelma while she was dressing, it was still Scotland in late summer.

"Father!"

A young woman, wearing tweeds that rendered her nearly invisible against the forest backdrop, walked toward them from the side of the house, her strides growing longer as she approached the tea table. She took the final few steps at a run, launching into Duke's arms, her long auburn hair masking her features as she buried herself in his shoulder.

Thelma stood, but Averill gripped the back of Duke's jacket a moment longer before turning to Thelma.

Though not conventionally pretty, Averill Furness looked strong, her face lean and freckled from the day's hunting, ice-blue eyes beneath sharp, arching eyebrows. A shotgun on a thick leather strap rested between her shoulder blades; she unhitched it and handed it to a waiting footman.

"It's not loaded. Thelma, is it?" she said coolly.

Thelma shrank from Averill's steady gaze. It would have been helpful, she thought, if Averill had left the shotgun with the gillie.

"I'm pleased to meet you. Duke—Lord Furness—has told me so much about you," said Thelma.

"Likewise," said Averill. She glanced at Duke, then made a renewed effort at smiling. "Welcome to Scotland. No luck on the stag I'm afraid, Father," she said, settling into the chair Thelma had vacated. She reached for a scone. "Disappeared across the burn about ten miles out."

"You'll find him tomorrow," said Thelma as Duke pulled out his own chair for her. "A big creature like that can't be too difficult to find."

Averill didn't look up. "He's got ten thousand acres to hide in," she said, splitting the scone in half, "but perhaps he'll wear a little flag on his antlers."

"Steady on," said Duke, chuckling. He rested a hand on Thelma's arm. "Stalking can take days," he said. "Sometimes weeks, even if you're an old hand at it like Averill. We'll go after it tomorrow, what do you say? Three heads are better than one. Four, if Thelma feels like giving it a go."

"Oh, I don't think so," said Thelma. "I prefer eating animals to hunting them. You go—I'll be perfectly fine walking the loch."

"Not on your own, surely?" said Duke. "Averill can stay with you. Dickie and I—"

"Oh, don't be silly," said Thelma, as Averill looked up in alarm at the suggestion of staying behind. "Besides, I'm sure you have lots to talk about."

Averill let out a breath. "It's my stag," she muttered.

"Well—only if you're sure," said Duke.

Thelma looked at Averill, who was demolishing the scone with single-minded purpose. "I'm sure," she said.

Over dinner, Thelma was able to get a better measure of Duke's relationship with his children. He treated them as friends, skimming over the formalities Thelma expected from an upper-class family: he teased them constantly, quizzing Dickie about his most recent school term, interrogating Averill about the condition of their family estates, which she'd been overseeing during Duke's frequent absences to Paris.

"Have you given any further thought to a new horse for Burrough Court?" asked Averill as plates of venison pie swimming in gravy were delivered to the table.

Duke nodded, lifting the pie's crust with his fork. "I have. We'll have two new horses—I trust you to make the selections yourself."

"Two?" Averill took a sip of wine, her eyes flickering to Thelma. "Should I take it that you're looking for a gentler mount?"

"That was my thought, yes," he replied. "Thelma, do you ride?"

"I've only tried once," she said. "It was a disaster, I'm afraid."

"Really?" said Dickie. "Good gracious, you must tell us all about it."

Thelma set down her cutlery. "It was during my—well, my misguided career as a film actress," she said.

"The pictures!" said Dickie. "Did you live in Hollywood? Do you know Mary Pickford?"

"As a matter of fact, I do," said Thelma. "I lived in Hollywood…oh, over a year ago now. But this was before California. I was in New York, and Sammy Goldwyn introduced me to a friend of his who was directing a small film."

"Which one?" asked Averill, picking at a piece of fluff on her sleeve.

"It's called *A Society Scandal*. Gloria Swanson plays the lead," said Thelma, and Averill looked up. "I thought it would be a good start to my acting career, so I said I would do it. Only, my character had to ride a horse."

She leaned back in her chair, recalling those first few moments on set. "I had never even touched a horse, let alone ride one, but that seemed like such a small detail so I told the director I could ride sidesaddle. We were filming in Central Park, and when I got there, I was shown to this enormous beast. I got into the saddle and managed to—to sort of nudge it under the ribs." She gestured, recalling the horse's stubborn refusal to budge. "Finally, it started to move, but as we went under the bridge a group of children in roller skates clattered overhead. It spooked, of course, and bolted."

Averill smirked. "You had no idea what to do, did you?"

"Not a clue. All I could do was hold on to the reins and pray that it didn't throw me off. The production assistants were running after us, waving their arms and shouting. I only hoped the horse wouldn't trample some poor bystander."

"What did you do?" asked Duke.

"What *could* I do? I waited for it to slow. I was afraid it was going to take me halfway to New Jersey," said Thelma. "So there—my one and only adventure on a horse. But as I see it, I've only got room for improvement."

Dickie laughed, and reached for the decanter.

"The horse likely hadn't been properly exercised," said Averill. "That's often the case with new riders. The horse is skittish as it is, and if it's not given enough time to work out its nerves…"

She shrugged and shared a glance with Duke. "I'll give you a few lessons. See if we can't get you jumping hedgerows."

"Shall we tell them tonight, do you think?" Duke asked as he pulled the oars of a gray-hulled rowboat and sent the little vessel gliding across the loch. They had been at Affric Lodge nearly a month now and had settled into a domestic routine more stable than Thelma, living between cities and hotels, had experienced in years. She felt she might just fit into the fabric of Duke's family: under Averill's guidance, she had become a proficient rider, able to bring Dickie's slender roan up to a gentle canter; with Dickie, she learned how to fly-fish, standing in the river behind the house in a pair of Duke's old waders, attempting to make the small bundle of feathers at the end of her line fall delicately on top of the water.

She lounged in the bow of the skiff, watching Duke row. He'd rolled up his shirtsleeves to the elbow and had dispensed with his suspenders, letting them hang loosely against his legs as he strained against the oars. His skin had become nearly the same reddish gold as his hair and he was smiling, the lines on his face smoothed by the breeze coming across the water as the afternoon sun stretched long across the mountains behind him. She'd never seen him so contented.

"I think we ought to," said Thelma, "though I doubt it will come as a great surprise."

Duke's grin broadened as he pulled on the oars. "I can't imagine it will," he replied. "It's a yes, then?"

"To what? You've not properly asked," she said, with the hint of a smile in her voice.

Duke stopped rowing. He leaned toward her, resting his hands on the oar handles. "I hope you're not expecting me to go down on one knee. We might end up in the loch."

Thelma leaned forward, too. She'd worried about her feelings, once: Did they match the depth of his? But here, in his element, Duke had shown her the life he was prepared to give her—and a love she wholeheartedly returned. She placed a hand on his cheek and kissed him—a long, crushing kiss, question and answer bound together. She'd played this moment out a thousand times and seen a thousand different futures: theirs the whirl of a summer romance, the madness of a fling transformed into the long and storied courtship of a couple meant to be.

She'd played this moment out a thousand times, but had never felt as sure as now.

They broke apart and Thelma leaned back on the gunnels of the skiff.

"Just so you know," she said as Duke picked up the oars, "my answer is yes."

Later that evening, Thelma sat at her vanity as Elise set her hair for dinner. Would Averill and Dickie be surprised at the news? Having gotten to know them, Thelma realized that Duke's children always expected their father to remarry: Averill had said as much one evening as they brushed down the horses after a day on the moor, letting slip the fact that Duke hadn't brought any other women to Affric Lodge.

No, thought Thelma. They wouldn't be surprised.

She thought about writing to Gloria. Perhaps Duke would take her into town tomorrow to send a telegram.

Elise set a pair of amber combs in Thelma's hair, then stepped back, nodding with satisfaction.

"It looks wonderful, Elise, thank you. The brown gloves, I think," said Thelma, as someone knocked on the door.

Duke hadn't yet changed out of his rowing clothes. His shirt-sleeves were still pushed up, his suspenders still loose at his sides. He clutched a creased telegram between his hands.

Thelma knew its contents without being told. The air rushed out of her lungs as though she'd been struck in the chest, feeling Gloria's grief—her own grief—hit her.

"Reggie," she said.

★ ★ ★

The day after they received the telegram Thelma and Duke traveled into Inverness to place a transatlantic telephone call at the Royal Highland Hotel. "There was nothing they could do," said Mamma, her voice sharp over the wires. "Internal hemorrhages—horrifically violent death, so I'm told. Alice wouldn't let Gloria see the body. A kindness, I suppose…"

Thelma shied away from the image of Reggie, bloated and bloody against his bedsheets, his fate long since sealed by the vices he was too proud to give up—or too aware, perhaps, that doing so would make no difference. "I'll leave for London immediately," she said. "I'll buy a ticket to New York."

"You will not," said Mamma. "What on earth could you accomplish here?"

Thelma let her outrage stretch across the silence. "I could mourn my brother-in-law," she said.

"The funeral is in three days. You can't possibly make it in time. Stay with Duke—let him comfort you."

Thelma hung up the telephone, shaking at Mamma's callousness, hating the fact that she was right. She spent the day of the funeral alone in Duke's Arlington Street town house, surrounded by his austere collection of marble statues that looked more like graveyard monuments than works of art, dazed at the devastating change in Gloria's fortunes.

Soon after, Thelma received more shocking news from New York: Gloria was bankrupt. Although he had provided generously for Gloria in his will, Reggie's profligate spending—and his penchant for handing out IOUs—had left him so heavily in debt that, after probating the will, Gloria was declared virtually penniless. Aside from a $2.5 million trust fund for Little Gloria, every cent of Reggie's estate was earmarked for creditors; and, being only nineteen, Gloria was unable to serve as guardian over Little Gloria's sizeable inheritance.

"They've put a team of lawyers together as Surrogates to

safeguard the money until she comes of age," Gloria said, when Thelma telephoned. "I can collect the interest from her estate, but only if the money is used to provide for her well-being. For myself, I've got nothing. No money—no husband."

Thelma's cheeks burned when she thought of how unflinchingly she had accepted Reggie's charity. Now, Gloria was forced to sell their honeymoon farm, all of Reggie's magnificent purebred horses, even Little Gloria's old crib.

"He owed $14,000 to a butcher. A butcher, Thelma," Gloria continued, her voice numb. "How on earth does a man run a $14,000 debt to a butcher?"

Thelma gripped the telephone cord as Gloria explained that the lawyers would be holding an auction at Reggie's farm in Rhode Island.

"I'm coming," said Thelma. "You can't possibly go through that on your own."

SIX

October 9, 1934
RMS Empress of Britain

THE WOOD-PANELED TEAROOM HAD BEGUN TO fill with passengers seeking refuge from the chill wind that blew off the sea, but Thelma was already stationed at a small table beneath a lacquered oriental painting of willow trees. She studied the painting, admiring the play of brown and gold in the leaves—did it look different in the morning light?—but was interrupted by the thud of a newspaper hitting the table.

"I've been looking for you all over this damned boat," said Harry. He took the seat opposite Thelma's and called for a waiter. "Did you see yesterday's headline?"

Every newspaper in Europe, it seemed, was following the trial, basking in Gloria's misfortune. "Vanderbilt Widow Penniless Without Heiress Tot;" "Fight To The Bitter End For Vanderbilt Girl." There would be more articles waiting when they landed—Thelma was sure of it, given the scene she'd made when she boarded the *Empress* in Southampton.

She'd been mobbed by reporters at the dockyards, a swarm

of them shouting questions over one another as she and Harry walked up the gangplank.

"Lady Furness!" shouted one reporter, his voice cutting through the shipyard commotion, "Do you know your own mum will be testifying against Mrs. Vanderbilt?"

"I do," said Thelma, "and she's mad to do so. Absolutely mad."

The reporters scribbled, and one young man raised his pen. "What do you say to the maid's allegations about Nada Mountbatten? Will Her Ladyship come to Mrs. Vanderbilt's defense?"

Thelma gripped the railing to still her shaking hand. "All I have to say," she said, "is that my mother is mad to indulge this fantasy. Absolutely mad."

Thelma shook her head, thankful that she'd been able to escape into the sanctuary of the ship.

"Nada won't come," said Harry, his fingers trembling as he folded the newspaper. "She's sending a lawyer—wants to keep away from all this." He let out an involuntary noise and closed his eyes, waiting for the tremor to pass. "Friedel is, though. He's told reporters he'll be leaving on the *Bremen*."

"Good." Prince Friedel Hohenlohe, Gloria's former fiancé, had been heartbroken when Gloria rejected his proposal—but what choice did she have, when Mamma had accused him of wanting to do Little Gloria harm?

Thelma could have laughed at the accusations, if they weren't such a threat. According to Mamma, Gloria neglected her daughter to the point of cruelty—a claim that Gertrude Whitney, Reggie's sister, had accepted far too easily, far too quickly. Yes, Gloria entertained friends on a regular basis, but never at her daughter's expense. Yes, Gloria traveled frequently, but she made sure that Little Gloria wanted for nothing, regardless of whether they were in Paris or Biarritz, New York or London. Hadn't that been the point of Mamma joining her household in the first place?

And where had Gloria learned about motherly love? All

through their childhood, Thelma and her siblings had been dragged from country to country according to their mother's changeable whims: Consuelo had been stashed away with a family friend in the United States from the time she was thirteen, and Thelma and Gloria had barely seen Harry as children, closeted away in a Swiss boarding school.

Harry sipped his coffee, looking at Thelma over his shaking cup. "I wanted to talk to you about what you said to those reporters this morning."

"What about it?" said Thelma. "I'm right, aren't I? Mamma is mad, and that's all there is to it. The public ought to know."

Harry sighed. "Maybe so, but discrediting her on the front page won't help Gloria's case."

Thelma's irritation—with Harry, with Gloria, with Mamma—spilled over. "I'm *trying* to discredit her," she said. "She's mad as a cat. The media ought to know what sort of person is behind all the ridiculous accusations Gertrude's accepting as fact."

"And it will," said Harry. "But it's for the lawyers to bring it all out in court. They have a strategy, and we won't help by creating another arena for combat."

Thelma exhaled, biting back her next retort—hadn't Mamma's side already claimed that battlefield? "It just—it makes me so cross, Harry."

"I know." Harry signaled for the waiter, who came with a billfold. "Promise me you'll speak to Gloria's lawyer before you make any more statements to the press."

Harry signed the bill and stood; Thelma finished the last dregs of her tea and followed him through the first-class corridor in silence. When they reached Thelma's cabin, Harry cleared his throat.

"I need your word, that you won't make any more unauthorized statements, Thelma," he said. "You can't do that to Gloria."

Again, Thelma refrained from snapping. Lawyers wouldn't help Gloria's reputation—not when the judge had closed the courtroom to reporters for the rest of the trial. How could Harry not see that? Gloria had to be vindicated by her friends, her family— those able to defend her outside the courtroom, as well as those fighting within it. "It's ghoulish," she said. "I won't let Mamma spread such lies—"

"I can't stop you from speaking your mind, Thelma, but please consider your actions," Harry replied. "Calling Mamma names in the papers—can't you see how that looks?"

She pictured two fishmongers' wives, brawling in the streets. "You're right," she said. "Of course."

Harry nodded, the twitch in his cheek more pronounced than earlier. "You're a good sister," he said, with a sudden smile. "You and Gloria...always two of a kind, aren't you? The Magnificent Morgans." He sobered, stepping away as Thelma crossed into her berth. "You can't fight this battle for her. Remember that when we get to New York. As difficult as it may be."

Thelma shut the door to her stateroom. The Magnificent Morgans, she thought, recalling a newspaper article from their days as New York socialites. They had always been magnificent, her and Gloria—the world knew it, which was perhaps why it was so taken with Gloria's trial. She turned Harry's words over in her mind: *You can't fight this battle for her.*

It came from a good place, really, but Harry didn't under-stand. Thelma would always fight Gloria's battles. Just as Gloria had always fought hers.

SEVEN

April 1926
Newport, Rhode Island, USA

DUE TO COMPLICATIONS INVOLVED WITH THE estate, the auction at Reggie's Newport farm was delayed until spring, giving Thelma time to move her possessions from Paris to London. To provide a suitable mourning period, Thelma and Duke agreed to keep news of their engagement quiet until Thelma returned from America. They spent a quiet Christmas together in Scotland and Thelma set sail in mid-April, arriving in Rhode Island the week of the auction.

When Thelma arrived in Portsmouth, Gloria was there to greet her, looking too small on the platform, her mourning clothes hanging off her thin frame like a shroud. She wrapped Thelma in a silent hug before leading her to the motorcar that would take them to Newport.

"I have to let them all go," she said, watching the chauffeur walk around to the front seat. "Reggie had meant to give his staff a nice settlement, but I can't even afford to keep a housemaid on the—on the amount of money—" She fell silent as the automobile lurched forward.

"I had no idea it would be so sudden," she continued. She reached across Thelma's lap, seeking comfort; Thelma grasped her hand, wishing she could provide something more substantial than reassurance. "We had talked, of course, but we thought he had more time..."

"There's never any way to be prepared," she said.

"No," said Gloria. "But to leave me with *nothing*... I had no idea."

Thelma thought of Duke's healthy vigor; his many homes, scattered like leaves across Britain and Europe. Duke's wealth was concrete, tied up in dockyards and steel hulls, bricks and mortar. If anything were to happen to him, Thelma would be well cared for—but then, Gloria had thought the same thing.

"Little Gloria is provided for. At least there's that," she said.

Gloria nodded. "My lawyer tells me I can't be guardian of her property until I turn twenty-one. Her person, yes, but not her property." She rooted through her purse and pulled out a handkerchief emblazoned with Reggie's initials. "I can use the interest from the inheritance to maintain her standard of living—but what about mine? What on earth am I to do?"

They motored onto a narrow strip of land, the road barely the width of the car. On one side lay the Atlantic Ocean; on the other, a bay eroded into a marsh.

"Would Reggie's family support you?" asked Thelma.

Gloria folded the handkerchief. "They've been very good to me," she said. "Gertrude's husband paid for the funeral."

The automobile slowed as it entered a seaside town, clapboard colonial houses on tree-lined lots, white sailboats turning on mooring lines in the blue distance. Thelma opened the window and salt air breezed in. Newport would be an idyllic place under different circumstances.

The car crept closer to the sea, where the green spaces between houses grew wider. Down long driveways, Thelma could see the peaked roofs of massive homes. They were elegantly haphazard, palatial and incongruous: beaux arts mansions beside French châteaux, English manor homes next to Italian palazzos.

They turned down a drive flanked by a set of massive wrought-iron gates. Thelma couldn't help but marvel at the sheer size of the estate beyond: built by Reggie's parents, The Breakers was needlessly large, a statement rather than a summer home. Six footmen flanked the front entrance, standing to attention as the motorcar came to a stop under a heavy limestone portico.

"Good morning, Mrs. Vanderbilt," said one as he opened the door. Behind him, the others came noiselessly to life, unbuckling Thelma's luggage from the luggage rack.

"Thank you. Is Mrs. Vanderbilt home?" asked Gloria.

"She is, ma'am. Shall I lead you in?"

"No need."

Though Thelma was becoming used to Duke's old-world wealth, the Vanderbilt estate was an entirely different form of opulence. It was almost offensive in its display of family fortune, though Gloria barely blinked as she led Thelma through the front door. The great hall, with its gilt ceilings and immense marble columns, dwarfed Thelma, her footsteps echoing as they walked. She felt as though she'd stepped into the Renaissance, and had to remind herself that the mansion, with its quaint cottage name and sweeping crimson carpets, had been built only thirty years ago.

Gloria led Thelma into a wood-paneled library with a spectacular stone fireplace. Books sat in glass-fronted alcoves; damask-covered chairs and couches fought for prominence against a bright Persian carpet.

Preoccupied as she was with the room itself, Thelma nearly didn't see the white-haired woman in a high-backed chair by the fireplace. She didn't stand as Gloria grasped her hand, but looked at Thelma with a placid expression.

"It's lovely to meet you, my dear," she said, "though under such unfortunate circumstances."

"Mrs. Vanderbilt," said Thelma. "I'd like to offer my deepest condolences. Reggie was such a dear, dear friend."

Alice Vanderbilt smiled. She was a diminutive woman with papery skin and a stern face, her scrawny neck rising out of a sea of pearls. Like Gloria, she was dressed in black—though, according to Gloria, black was the only color Mrs. Vanderbilt wore, ever since her husband's death twenty-six years ago.

"So kind," she said. "My Reggie—our Reggie," she conceded, looking at Gloria, "spoke so fondly of you."

She gestured toward a tea tray on the coffee table. "I hoped you might join me for some refreshments, but I wonder—Gloria, would you be so kind as to go make sure Thelma's things are put in the green bedroom?"

"Of course," said Gloria and she turned, her footsteps heavy as she made her way back down the hall.

Mrs. Vanderbilt watched Gloria's retreating figure. "We truly appreciate you coming," she said.

"I would have come for the funeral if there had been time," said Thelma, settling into a chair. "How is Gloria?"

Mrs. Vanderbilt shook her head. "I worry she's not keeping up her strength. The shock of it all—and now this horrid business with Reggie's estate. She was such a bright young thing when they met, but now…"

"What's she going to do when the estate is settled?" asked Thelma. "Will she stay with you?"

Mrs. Vanderbilt smiled. She leaned in, her hands folded in her lap. "It's not terribly sensible, is it, having older and younger generations under one roof?" she said. "Gloria has to think about her future, and about the sort of environment in which she plans to raise my granddaughter. I'll not give unsolicited opinions, but perhaps she ought to consider being with those from whom she draws strength."

Thelma frowned, thinking of herself in London and Consuelo, stationed in Paris with her diplomat husband. "Perhaps she ought to return to Europe. For a time, at least."

Mrs. Vanderbilt nodded. "A change of scenery might be a fine thing for her."

The door to the library opened once more, as Gloria returned. "All sorted," she said.

Not for the first time that afternoon, Thelma noticed the deep blue shadows that had gathered under Gloria's eyes, like mourning veils.

They arrived at Sandy Point Farm the next morning, an hour before the auction.

"The lawyers tell me I'm only to take what I owned before the marriage," said Gloria, as they stepped out of the car, "which doesn't leave me with much. It all fits inside a single trunk."

Though there was a flurry of activity at the stables where the auction was to take place later that afternoon, the main house was empty, its doors thrown open in anticipation of bidders to come. Thelma walked arm in arm with Gloria through the echoing rooms. The contents had already been removed, but Thelma could see touches of Gloria's hopeful handiwork: new curtains, barely faded. Fresh paint in the sitting room.

Thelma left Gloria on a bay window downstairs and walked through the bedrooms alone. She had been to the farm before, shortly after Reggie and Gloria's wedding: she had sat in the back of the carriage as Reggie drove his Hackney horses to and from parties, and had laughed with the women, flirted with the men. Where were Reggie's friends now, she wondered— the party guests, the high society horsemen? They had disappeared: fearful, perhaps, that Reggie and Gloria's misfortunes might be contagious.

Thelma found Gloria in the drive, conversing with an elegant older woman in a magnificently embroidered jacket.

"Thelma," said Gloria, as the woman turned to greet her, "meet Gertrude Payne Whitney. Reggie's sister."

Thelma shook Gertrude's hand, looking for a hint of her brother-in-law in the woman's gray eyes. In looks, at least, she was Reggie's opposite: tall where he was short, willowy where he had bulk. Given her success as a sculptress and an art patron, Thelma had expected someone more gregarious, but Gertrude seemed solemn and reserved—though, Thelma acknowledged, the circumstances didn't exactly lend themselves to levity.

"I'm pleased to meet you," said Gertrude. "I hope you don't mind my intrusion, Gloria. I wanted one final look at the place."

"How difficult it must be for you," said Thelma.

Gertrude looked up, squinting, at the house. "Difficult for all of us. We were close, Reggie and I—I only wish he'd taken better care." She looked at Gloria, and despite her reserve Thelma could see the sympathy in her eyes. "For all our sakes."

Gloria attempted a smile. "Gertrude's been just wonderful. She's caring for Little Gloria while all this business with the estate gets sorted out."

"That's kind of you," Thelma offered, but Gertrude didn't seem disposed to accept her praise.

"It's nothing at all," she said. "I'm happy to have her—she's a lovely girl."

They stopped talking as three men in coveralls walked past, carrying a marble bust that had once stood in Gloria and Reggie's sitting room.

Thelma shivered, despite the heat of the day. "What a horrible business," she said, once the men were out of earshot.

Gertrude watched the men carry the bust into the stables and Thelma wondered whether it was one of her pieces. "I'm sorry this is the side of our family you have to see," she said. "My brother was many things, but his generosity got the better of him. I wish his estate could care for Gloria in the manner he'd intended."

Thelma was surprised by her frankness. "I'm sure it will," she said, more for Gloria's sake than out of any sense of conviction. "Once the financiers have a chance to look at the books, we'll see that today was for the best. I'm sure of it."

Gertrude reached into her handbag and pulled out a cigarette case. "None of this is for the best," she said, "but it's the best we can do. We all make our choices. It's a pity, Gloria, how Reggie's choices are impacting you."

Gloria smiled, looking close to tears as a flatbed truck pulled into the driveway.

Thelma took her by the arm, lending her what strength she could. "We really ought to be getting on. It was lovely to meet you, Mrs. Whitney."

"Of course," said Gertrude. She looked back to the house, dropping ash onto the pavement. "I'll stay a little longer, if that's all right with you."

The first automobiles were beginning to pull up as Thelma and Gloria drove away from Sandy Point, filled to bursting with people and wicker baskets. Looking at the threadbare incomers, Thelma knew they couldn't afford to buy anything at the auction—a napkin, perhaps, or a silver spoon, sold off one by one. No, they came to peer behind the curtain of high society, to run their hands over Gloria's memories.

Their Rolls Royce trundled up the drive, the only car to move against the current. Moonlike faces stared through the glass windows, fingers pointing as they recognized the Vanderbilt Widow.

That evening, Mrs. Vanderbilt made the tactful suggestion that Thelma and Gloria take their dinner on trays in Gloria's bedroom. "Things look better after an early night," she said. Given the informality, Gloria had changed into a dressing gown. To Thelma, the pale pink silk was a welcome change from Gloria's solemn attire.

"A comfortable household," Gloria said finally, pushing a piece of asparagus congealing in butter onto her fork. "That's all I'll be able to afford, if I'm lucky."

"It's something," said Thelma.

Gloria abandoned her plate and stared out the window. Two stories below, the Atlantic Ocean buffeted itself against the coast. "Did you see them today, Thelma? Those people—" She rubbed at her eyes with a slender finger. "You know, I haven't had a moment's peace since it all happened. The newspapers have been relentless."

Thelma had seen the headlines generated by Reggie's death, the clear glee with which the newspapermen were recounting the fall of a giant. "Reggie Died Broke!" Thelma had been given a newspaper in New York City before boarding the train to Portsmouth, black letters emblazoned across the front page: "Gloria Junior World's Most Expensive Tot—Mother Left Penniless."

"Have you given any thought to moving abroad?" asked Thelma. "At least until things quiet down." She recalled Mrs. Vanderbilt's words. "Perhaps a change of scenery…"

"I had been thinking, perhaps, France," Gloria replied slowly. "Reggie and I were so happy there…"

"You'd be closer to Consuelo and me," said Thelma. "You ought to be with family."

Gloria stared down at the waves breaking below. "If I stay here, I'll only ever be Reggie's widow," she said.

"Perhaps moving to Europe will give you a chance to regain yourself," Thelma replied.

Gloria smiled half-heartedly. "It would be a start."

They were interrupted by a knock at the door. Gloria's maid opened it and accepted a telegram that she passed to Thelma.

"Duke?" said Gloria.

Thelma nodded. Unbeknownst to Gloria, Duke had sent five

telegrams to The Breakers already; in deference to Gloria's feelings, Thelma had tried to hide them.

HOPE DAY WASN'T TOO DIFFICULT STOP WHEN DO YOU ANTICIPATE
RETURN STOP WITH GREAT AFFECTION DUKE.

Thelma folded the telegram and tucked it under her napkin. "Nothing that can't wait."

"He loves you," said Gloria.

Thelma paused. "Yes," she said quietly. "I believe he does."

Gloria's face crumpled delicately, a softening and a steeling all at once—then she looked up.

"I love you for coming to help me," she said, "but I'll love you more if you go back to Duke."

Thelma frowned. "Don't be silly."

Gloria reached across the table. "If this whole terrible experience has taught me anything, it's that life is short. Go back to Duke and enjoy every moment of it. For me, darling. Please."

EIGHT

AFTER HER SOMBER WEEKS IN NEWPORT, THELMA'S return to London was welcome—and busy, given preparations for her wedding. As it was a second marriage for Thelma and Duke both, they planned for a quiet ceremony—but that didn't mean the society pages hadn't caught wind of it.

"If anyone turns up with a camera I'll knock them into next week," said Duke, practically growling after a friend from Manhattan sent Thelma a newspaper clipping chronicling Duke's courtship in astonishing detail. "New Lady For Lord Furness?" it read, above a photograph of Thelma and Duke entering the Embassy Club.

After sorting out the particulars of the reception luncheon, Thelma traveled to Paris with Gloria and Consuelo to find a wedding dress.

"*Bois de rose, madame*," Jean Patou had told her, holding a subtle pink fabric against her face when she arrived for their appointment at the House of Patou. "Exquisite with your coloring." Consuelo and Gloria sat in the fitting room with teacups in hand while Thelma stood on a platform between them, holding her arms aloft as a seamstress draped crepe de chine across her shoulders.

"An improvement from my first dress, don't you think?" asked Thelma.

"Second marriages are an improvement in all respects," said Consuelo.

Thelma smiled as the seamstress pulled the fabric tight across her chest. She didn't feel the same wild triumph that she had felt when she'd married Junior, but rather, a contented sort of happiness.

"You have so much to look forward to," said Gloria. She'd moved to Paris only weeks ago, installing herself—and Little Gloria and Mamma—in a narrow town house near the Bois du Boulogne. "Those first honeymoon months are such a joy."

"Everyone congratulating you," added Consuelo. "Wanting to hear about the ceremony, the presents."

"And then you settle into routines," said Gloria. "I always enjoyed that, whenever Reggie stopped somewhere long enough to build them. We had such fun. Even when Mamma criticized us, we had fun."

Thelma swiveled, causing the seamstress to protest as several pins came loose. "How is Mamma?" she asked.

"She's a nightmare," said Gloria. "I'm surprised, really, that I didn't anticipate it." She paused, playing with a scrap of organdy fabric. "She seemed fine when Little Gloria was in America for the funeral, but she had a complete fit when I told her we were moving to Paris. She told me France is no place for a child."

Consuelo smirked. "She told me Little Gloria was nearly kidnapped on the train from Le Havre."

"I don't know where she gets these notions," Gloria said. "Mamma lost sight of her in the compartment. The conductor had to stop the train, she was so hysterical."

"What happened?" asked Thelma. From somewhere near her

midsection, the seamstress fixed the pins back into the fabric as Patou barked orders in rapid-fire French.

"Kieslich had taken her to watch the tracks from the caboose," Gloria sighed. "Mind you, Kieslich is no better. Do you know, she refused to allow Little Gloria to eat food prepared by the Ritz? She brought a hot plate up to the room and cooked all of Little Gloria's meals in the bathroom before I put a stop to it."

"Have you considered dismissing her?" said Thelma.

"Many times," said Gloria. "But Little Gloria loves her so... and with Reggie gone..."

"It might be heartless to deprive her of someone else," Consuelo finished, nodding. "I understand, but you're her mother. You have the final say in how she's raised."

"Do I?" said Gloria. "Between the lawyers, the financiers, Reggie's family, Mamma and Kieslich, I feel as if I'm raising my girl by committee."

"So long as they know you're the head of the operation," Consuelo replied. She turned to Thelma. "Darling, that color is divine on you. Truly."

The morning of Thelma's wedding dawned rainy and gray— an ill omen to anyone else, perhaps, but Thelma took it as a sign of her British life to come. The streets of Westminster were quiet as Duke's car pulled out from the service entrance to the Ritz Hotel: to avoid reporters, Duke had let slip that the wedding was on Tuesday afternoon, but quietly arranged for the registrar's office to open on Sunday for the ceremony. Glancing at the rainy entrance to the Ritz Hotel as they turned onto Piccadilly, Thelma could see that Duke's ploy had succeeded: only one reporter was stationed at the front door, his shoulders hunched against the weather. He would be disappointed once he found out that his soggy vigil had been in vain.

Seated next to her, Averill grinned as they took side streets to Hanover Square.

"All rather cloak-and-dagger, don't you think?" she said. "How are you feeling?"

Thelma flushed. "Nervous," she said, plucking a stray petal from her bouquet.

Averill pulled a dainty hip flask from her handbag. "I brought it for Father," she said. "You ought to have seen him at breakfast—he was just about green."

Thelma took the flask, savoring the warm heat of the brandy as the car pulled up in front of the registrar's office. Careful not to catch the hem of her coat on the motorcar—or to trail it in the puddles dotting the sidewalk—Thelma handed the flask back to Averill and stepped under cover of the chauffeur's umbrella.

Gloria and Consuelo were waiting at the front door. Not for the first time, Thelma wished that the wedding could have been held in a church; she glanced across the green of Hanover Square to the bell tower of St. George's, barely visible as it peeked over the rooftops. Even if she had been able to overcome Duke's aversion to a religious ceremony, it would have been impossible to hold the wedding there—*The Times* had been parking a reporter outside the church for a week now.

"You look lovely," said Gloria. Even accounting for her obvious partiality, Thelma agreed: Patou had designed a flawless gown, long-sleeved, with silk-covered buttons tracing down the line of her back. She wore a matching floor-length jacket with lynx-fur trim along the sleeves and hem and a silk turban that swept her features back in a manner she found exceedingly elegant.

Mamma, dressed in black, was inside. She wiped away a rare tear as Thelma came into the building with Averill. "You look so beautiful," she said. "And on such a happy occasion. Think, *mi belleza*—in an hour's time you'll be a peeress."

Gloria led the procession up an imposing wooden staircase with wrought-iron railings, pausing at the top to allow Averill to arrange Thelma's train. At the far end of the second-story corridor, framed by an oak-trimmed window, stood Duke, dressed as immaculately as ever and accompanied by Dickie, light glinting off their matching copper hair. He looked up at the sound of Thelma's approach, and any lingering nerves she may have had fled as she met his gaze.

It would have been awfully hard, Thelma later reflected, to be upset. Despite the clinical feel of the registrar's office and Mamma's tactless jabs, Thelma couldn't have been happier when she allowed Duke to take her hand and lead her into the small office where they became man and wife. It would have been very difficult, she thought, to see how anything else mattered.

Late that evening, Thelma lay in bed, Duke sleeping softly beside her. He had been so different from Junior, thought Thelma, feeling her hips ache slightly as she turned and drew her hand along the side of his torso. He hollowed, only slightly, at the waist; she paused at the soft deposit of flesh around his hips, goose pimples rising at her touch. Thelma had despised any hint of excess fat on Junior: it made him look womanly, hips rounding over belt loops, the fall of his trousers catching on idle excess. On Duke, the bulk seemed to fit—a heavier figure, perhaps, for a man with more substance.

He had been more generous than Junior as well, not demanding a performance from her but offering himself, wholeheartedly. His skill was evident; as was his happiness at being united, once more, with someone he loved.

Thelma, too, was happy, listening to the rise and fall of his breath, feeling his reassuring heat as he shifted beside her. Despite all her first husband's shortcomings Thelma had missed this: the simple pleasure of sleeping in the same bed with someone she loved.

Duke rolled in his sleep, reaching his arm out to pull Thelma close. She settled back down, letting the rhythm of his breath coax her eyes closed.

NINE

THREE WEEKS LATER, THELMA CAME DOWN TO breakfast to find Duke nestled behind the pages of a newspaper, a white envelope perched on Thelma's place setting.

"We've received an invitation," said Duke. "Thought you might want to be the one to open it."

Thelma opened the envelope and read aloud:

"'*Lord and Lady Londonderry request the presence of Viscount and Viscountess Furness to a ball...*' Oh, it is nice, to see it written out like that," said Thelma, admiring the look of her title printed on the card.

"Read the bottom," he said.

"'*Decorations*,'" she said. "What's that?"

"You need to bone up on your knowledge of high society, my dear. It means royalty will be there." Duke snapped the newspaper straight, looking pleased. "Not a terrible introduction to it all, is it?"

Duke offered his arm to Thelma as she walked up the stairs to Londonderry House. From within the stern exterior of the

Park Lane mansion, she could hear the sound of the ball: music echoed off the stone building, wrapping around Thelma as she walked through the front door.

Her free hand brushed across the white satin skirt of her dress, falling in thick folds from her waist to the floor. The top was form-fitted, with small mirrors sewn into the fabric that caught the light as she walked. She wore a thin, glittering tiara: a present from Duke. She'd never worn such finery in all her life. Even Gloria's wardrobe, purchased on Reggie's overextended credit, paled in comparison to the spectacular excess of her outfit. With no small amount of self-awareness, she knew that her outfit had cost more than the rent on the apartment she'd once shared with Junior.

Though Londonderry House had an ascetic facade, its entrance chamber was warm. It was dominated by a marble double staircase that hugged three walls, symmetrically framing a stained-glass skylight above. Thelma and Duke mounted the stairs, following the noise of the party and the steady current of guests to an immense ballroom.

While Thelma had been impressed by the nouveau riche opulence of Alice Vanderbilt's home in Newport, Londonderry House's grandeur stemmed not only from its gilt and marble, but from the sheer sense of permanence that it exuded. Calla lilies and white roses overflowed from five-foot vases set along the length of the ballroom, filling the air with perfume. Undercut by the smell of candles and alcohol, food and sweat, the effect was nearly overwhelming.

The room glittered with light cast by half a dozen chandeliers, crystal splashing off the gilded walls and mirrors. Hundreds of people were there, and Thelma clutched Duke's arm, worried that if she let go he would be swept away on the tide and not emerge again until next week.

Immense marble statues stood in recessed alcoves, and Thelma nudged Duke as they passed. "Could you just imagine knocking one over?" she whispered. Duke chuckled, leading her farther in.

Thelma had only vaguely understood the reference to decorations but she could see that it was mainly an instruction for the men: they wore military medals and jeweled badges against the clean backdrop of their tailcoats. Dozens wore sparkling crosses on red ribbons that glittered just below the knots of their bow ties, complemented by magnificent red or blue sashes that cut across the fronts of their waistcoats.

For all their decorations, though, the men were nothing compared to the women. It seemed that all the safe-deposit boxes in Mayfair had been emptied for the evening: everywhere Thelma looked, she saw tiaras, diamond bangles, set-piece necklaces and gleaming rings. Women wore the most remarkable ball gowns, delicate layers of organdy and crepe de chine that floated along the ground as they moved. Some had chosen avant-garde, drop-waisted dresses with layers of thin silk or weightless lace that skimmed across their hip bones—a style that Thelma, petite and curvy, could never hope to achieve with any appropriate level of elegance.

If a woman was without a tiara, she wore peacock feathers high in her hair. Strings of pearls reached well below waistlines; long trains and oriental shawls trailed on the marble floor.

Duke took two glasses of champagne from a footman in Georgian dress and handed one to Thelma.

"Well?" he said.

Thelma beamed. "It's remarkable."

Duke huffed, raising his glass to his lips. "It's a damned waste of money, but I'm not covering the bill so I'll enjoy it just the same."

"Can we dance?"

"I'm not much good at it," he said, "but for you, yes."

They moved through the crowd of revelers, Duke keeping a reassuring hand on Thelma's back as they nudged through the ballroom. They had only made it partway to the dance floor when Duke stopped to clap a man on the back.

He was handsome, with a premature shock of white hair and his left sleeve pinned to his shoulder. He was accompanied by a woman in a magnificent gray dress—one of the few who, like the men, wore a glittering medal pinned on a sash.

"Thelma, might I introduce you to two dear friends? G Trotter," he said, "and Lady Sarah Wilson. Lady Sarah is the first woman war correspondent in Britain—possibly in the world," he continued, as Lady Sarah, tall and graceful, her dark hair shot through with gray, waved away Duke's accolades. "G, Lady Sarah—my wife, Thelma."

"I had heard you'd become an honest man once more," said G, in a voice that sounded as though it had been matured in an oak barrel. "And given this lovely creature, I can see why."

"G is a very dear friend," said Duke.

"Too dear, on occasion," said G, smiling at Thelma. "The number of times I've reached the bottom of your husband's liquor cabinet—well, perhaps a story for less civilized company," he said. "It's a pleasure to meet the woman who's finally tamed our Duke. We had wondered what it would take for him to settle down, but I can see you were worth the wait." He reached for Thelma's hand and raised it to his lips; Thelma was instantly charmed.

She turned to Lady Sarah, who looked at her with a sharp, but not unkind, gaze. "I'm so pleased to meet you," she said.

Thelma smiled. "Duke speaks so highly of you," she said, and it was true; Duke had told her, several times, about Lady Sarah.

Her husband had been the aide-de-camp to Baden-Powell during the Boer War and she accompanied him to Mafeking, Duke had once told her. *When the* Morning Post's *correspondent got himself arrested by the Boers, Lady Sarah stepped in and covered the siege of Mafeking on her own. Was decorated by King Edward for her troubles, and well deserved, too.*

"Does he?" said Lady Sarah. "How kind of you to say. Has Duke introduced you around London yet?"

"No," said Thelma. "We've been traveling so much I've not had the chance to spend much time in the city."

Lady Sarah smiled. She looked as though she was studying Thelma for something—for the spark that had ignited Duke. "You must let me take you to tea."

"I'd like that."

"Well, can't hang about all evening, old boy," said Duke, clapping a hand once more on G's back. "Lunch at the club tomorrow?"

G nodded, and Duke kissed Lady Sarah's hand before leading Thelma to the dancers as the orchestra began to play a fox-trot.

Duke was stiff yet competent, rotating methodically with his hand on Thelma's back. He'd danced in the years since his first wife's death, of course—he'd danced with Thelma in France, the night they met—but perhaps not with feeling. Not with the same interest, nor a partner willing to match his pace. He adopted a more fluid gait as the song progressed, and Thelma enjoyed his slowly building confidence, as though he was remembering a half-forgotten talent. By the time the band shifted into a new number Duke had visibly relaxed.

"Keep going?"

"Of course."

Thelma tightened her fingers around Duke's, but the band fell quiet. Around them, the other dancers paused, murmuring—then the band launched into a thrilling rendition of "God Save the King."

As one, the room turned to face the ballroom's entrance. The crowd shifted and reformed as a threesome moved into the ballroom.

"Lord and Lady Londonderry, and the Prince of Wales, I imagine," murmured Duke.

"How can you tell it's him?" asked Thelma, rising onto the balls of her feet.

"His brother's darker."

The procession moved slowly, stopping to greet those around them; after an appropriate interval the orchestra struck up once more.

Duke looked at Thelma, eyes crinkling. "Would you like to meet him?"

"Oh, no," said Thelma. "I wouldn't know what to do."

"It's not difficult," he said, "and he's a rather decent fellow, all things considered. Curtsy, call him 'sir'—that's about the extent of it." He handed Thelma a glass of champagne and positioned her closer to the trio, not directly in Lady Londonderry's path but close enough.

Thelma watched the prince with interest. He was younger than she had expected; she knew he was in his thirties, but the prince looked almost boyish, his expression youthful yet weary at the same time. She was surprised at his height: she had imagined him tall, as she pictured all public figures, but he was just a shade taller than Thelma and exceedingly slim. Exceptionally handsome, too: impeccable and fine featured, his hand darting, almost compulsively, to his bow tie as he spoke.

Beside him, Lady Londonderry caught Duke's eye. She touched the prince gently on the arm and he followed her to greet Duke and Thelma.

"Sir, may I present Lord Furness and his new American bride?" said Lady Londonderry. "Lady Furness, His Royal Highness, the Prince of Wales."

The prince inclined his head. Duke bowed at the neck and Thelma, recalling long-disused lessons from finishing school, curtsied.

"Lady Furness. Welcome to England," said the prince.

Thelma rose. "Thank you, Your Highness," she said. His eyes—pale blue—were almost disconcertingly steady. She col-

ored: back in New York, she and Gloria had once had a magazine cutout of him on their wall.

The orchestra began to play the opening strands of "Blue
Danube," and the prince held out his hand.

"This is one of my favorites. May I?" he asked.

Thelma's legs trembled as the prince led her onto the dance
floor. She glanced back at Duke, who winked.

The Prince of Wales lifted his hand to Thelma's upper back
and stretched his other arm to one side, lifting his palm in invitation. Thelma took it, and he smiled.

"Are you ready?" he murmured.

Thelma smiled back. "Yes."

It was as though the prince had begun to breathe. He danced
naturally, confidently, with a conviction he didn't seem to have
when walking; he whirled Thelma around so quickly that,
had she been dancing with any other partner, she would have
thought him reckless. Couples around them moved aside, making room for them to sail across the ballroom.

Unbidden, memories flashed one by one into Thelma's mind:
Mamma, snapping a butter knife at her elbow as she and her
brother learned to waltz in the living room, telling her to hold
her frame; she and Gloria at fourteen years old, attempting a fox-
trot in time to a rusty-sounding gramophone recording they had
smuggled into their convent dormitory. A dashing young man at
Consuelo's first wedding, graciously allowing Thelma's blunders
at her first real dance, with her first real partner. She had danced
countless times since then, gaining a measure of proficiency and
pleasure in her movements but it had never felt so effortless as
this—as though she were floating across the dance floor.

Too soon, the music ended. The prince came to a standstill,
and lifted Thelma's hand. His lips were soft against the back of
her fingers; he held her gaze, his eyes twinkling as though at a
joke that only he had heard.

"Thank you, Lady Furness," he said. He straightened, and
escorted Thelma back to her husband.

TEN

October 10, 1934
RMS Empress of Britain

THELMA LEANED OVER THE RAILING ON THE upper deck of the ship, squinting in the cold sunlight as she watched passengers on a lower deck. Farther down, sailors moved in twos and threes, bracing lines on lifeboats and watching clouds build in the far-off horizon. A cold wind blew off the sea and Thelma pulled her shawl close, watching the water in the engine's wake churn in a furious, sparkling froth.

The *Empress* was due to dock in Montreal in one day's time. From there, she and Harry would travel by train to Grand Central Station—a passage arranged by David's private secretary. He would have returned to London from the Fort late last night, Thelma knew, stopping at York House before going out for dinner at the Ritz or Quaglino's, no doubt already planning his next escape from the city. She wondered who he would invite to the Fort next weekend: Piers Legh, presumably, and the Simpsons. Perhaps the Duke of York and Elizabeth. She hoped he would find someone more enthusiastic than Ernest to help with the gardening—or maybe Wallis, with her unique combination of charm and forcefulness, would convince David to stay indoors.

She found an empty lounge chair on the sunny side of the top deck, next to a smokestack that sheltered her from the worst of the wind. Bundled in her shawl, her face upturned to the sun, Thelma was warm enough to linger: she lit a cigarette and closed her eyes, listening to the low thrum of the ship's engine and the chorus of waves hitting the steel hull, the relentless murmur of the ocean, swelling and falling around the unshakeable boat. They had left the seagulls behind, but Thelma kept expecting to hear them nonetheless, and she let herself fall into a doze.

"Did you hear what the maid said? Three men in her bed *and* a woman. No wonder the family's horrified."

Thelma tensed. The voice was coming from the other side of the smokestack: it belonged to an American, her accent harsh to Thelma's ear after so many months in Britain.

"I'm told it's all true," someone replied. "Every word. My lady's maid, who happens to be on friendly terms with her cook, told me."

"I certainly hope not. That poor child. Raised by wolves... Alice Vanderbilt would be spinning in her grave."

"Gertrude may have taken on more than she bargained for," said the second voice. "Gloria seems inclined to fight tooth and nail. But if the allegations are true, what choice does she have?"

"If they aren't, Gertrude's taking a mighty risk. To hear Gloria tell it, Gertrude all but kidnapped the child. The nurse took her in broad daylight—said they were going to feed the ducks, but she took her to Gertrude's studio instead. Apparently, Little Gloria was hysterical—it took three doctors to calm her down."

"Surely that's not the behavior of a healthy young girl? No wonder Gertrude felt there was just cause... And if the allegations are true..."

"If they're not..."

"I heard her sister's on this ship." Thelma drew her shawl up around her chin. "Can you imagine? I'm told the grandmother is the cause of the whole mess. Says Gloria planned to murder her for the inheritance. That sounds awfully far-fetched to me, but after the Lindbergh tragedy..."

"Wouldn't wish it on anyone."

The voices paused. For a moment, Thelma worried they'd moved down the deck.

"You know," said the first voice, "the question, I think, isn't about whether the child is in physical danger but spiritual danger. I mean—" she lowered her voice further and Thelma pictured her leaning close to her companion, glancing about for eavesdroppers "—caught in bed with a woman?"

"Can you really trust someone with predilections like that to raise a child?"

"If the allegations are true..."

"If they are," said the low-voiced one, "and she loses, I would be on the first ship back to France. That sort of behavior may be tolerated in Europe but certainly not in good Christian society."

The voices drifted away, and Thelma stayed buried a moment longer before she sat up, seething. She lit another cigarette, looking up and down the deck to see if anyone else had overheard.

For the next few days, at least, Thelma would have to ignore what people said about the case. It was all hearsay and baseless opinion, given by those sanctimonious enough to think that their opinions really mattered. Beyond what sparse telegrams might be received by the ship's messengers, Thelma and Harry were traveling in the dark: whether new allegations had thrown the trial into further disarray, Thelma wouldn't know until they landed in Montreal.

Prince Friedel Hohenlohe was meant to be coming to New York, too: Nurse Kieslich had named him directly in her testimony, claiming that he had shared Gloria's bed in Biarritz and Paris. Well, that was to be expected—they were engaged at the time. As for the maid's allegations against Gloria and Nada... Thelma exhaled, smoke dissolving on the salt air. If she was being honest, Thelma wasn't surprised to hear that Gloria's servants had talked. Subtlety had never been Gloria's strong point.

ELEVEN

June 1929
Burrough Court
Leicestershire

THELMA LEANED OVER THE BASSINET AND DANGLED a ruby bracelet, catching the heavy sleeve of her house-robe with her free hand to keep it from brushing across the baby's face. Gurgling, the child reached up, his pudgy arms waving unsteadily as he reached for the jewels.

"Like his mother, he is—can't resist a bit of sparkle."

Thelma started, curling the bracelet back into her grasp. She hadn't expected Duke at their Leicestershire estate until Friday, as he was preoccupied with a takeover of a rival shipping business. Thelma wrapped her house-robe tighter, embarrassed to have been caught lounging in her pajamas midday.

Duke crossed the room and pulled Thelma in for a kiss. "We were able to come to an arrangement this morning," he said. "Thought I'd come to celebrate in person. How's the little man, then?" He leaned over the bassinet and ran a finger gently along the curve of the baby's cheek.

"I just woke from a nap," said Thelma. "If I had known you were coming, I would have gotten dressed."

Two years into her marriage to Duke, Thelma's life had taken an unexpected turn: she had become a mother. Having been told she was barren after her miscarriage, Thelma initially thought her symptoms were a fluke—an alarming stomach bug, recurring like clockwork every morning—but a doctor had confirmed the diagnosis on a trip to London.

Thelma worried about how Duke would react. Prior to the wedding, she'd told him about her condition, and he'd taken the news with typical sangfroid.

"It's no concern to me," Duke had said. "I've already got an heir—and I'm quite fond of your figure as it is." He'd smiled, then patted her on the hand. "A baby would get in the way." When, with some trepidation, Thelma told Duke of the pregnancy he'd changed his tune entirely. "Another Furness!" he'd shouted, lifting Thelma to whirl her round the bedroom. But as her pregnancy progressed, Thelma was aware that the terms of their relationship were shifting—inevitably, perhaps, and not for the better.

Though Duke was excited, Thelma was haunted by memories of her miscarriage. Nightmares of dying in bed, doctors sawing through her stomach to release a breech baby, wrenched her from sleep on a near-nightly basis. "Isn't it something, knowing you'll have a child soon?" Averill had said, cupping Thelma's swelling belly. But Thelma found it difficult to find joy in her condition—not when so much could go so disastrously wrong.

When she confided her fears in Duke he had laughed, not unkindly. "Daisy went through it twice, and she was such a slip of a thing," he said. "The doctors know what they're doing—they'll be there if anything goes wrong. Try not to let it worry you."

When her stomach lurched alarmingly at the end of her seventh month Duke had summoned a team of doctors to the house.

The premature labor lasted nearly twenty-four hours: a haze of injections and instructions, issued in faraway voices.

The next day—March 31—Thelma was presented with a wailing, squashed-looking newborn. Her boy, Duke told her. Their boy. But Thelma's recovery took longer than she anticipated, and her doctor prescribed two months of bed rest in the country, leaving Duke to shuttle back and forth from London when he could.

Alone at Burrough Court, Thelma tried to muster some enthusiasm for the new baby, feeling, somehow, detached from it all—that someone would realize she didn't know how to care for a child; that fate had made some mistake. Mamma had hardly been a role model for motherhood, keeping Thelma and Gloria close throughout their childhood because they looked pretty— a "matching set", she'd called them. How could Thelma raise a child with an example like that?

She studied the baby while he slept, memorizing his wisps of hair, his seashell ears, and while she knew, on the face of it, that she ought to love him, she couldn't quite bring herself to be happy.

"Have you chosen a name yet?" said Duke, wrapping his arms around her. "We can't call him 'Little Man' forever."

"I was thinking 'Anthony'," she said, looking at the baby's wrinkled feet. "'Tony.' Does it suit him?"

Duke fitted his chin in the hollow of Thelma's shoulder. The scent of his aftershave mingled with the nursery smell of baby powder and another something spicy that Thelma couldn't quite place.

"Anthony," he said. "Tony Furness. Does it sound a bit exotic to you?"

"I like it," said Thelma.

Duke kissed her on the cheek. "Then 'Tony' it is. I'll speak to the priest about arranging the baptism." He snugged his arms around Thelma once more, his fingers sliding across the painted peacocks on her robe toward the drawstring.

Thelma twisted out of his grasp. "Darling, please," she said fixing the drawstring's loose ends. "The doctors say I'm not ready yet." In fact, the doctors had told her she was ready to resume marital relations a week ago, but Thelma couldn't stand the thought of making love. She had turned Duke away from her bed when her body began distorting to make room for the baby. After catching sight of herself in a mirror at a dinner in London a few weeks later—her stomach straining the front of her dress, her back twisting into a sibilant curve to accommodate the extra weight—Thelma retreated from society altogether, using Burrough Court as a refuge and doctors' orders as an excuse; telling Duke that she would return to London when the brutal business of giving birth was over and done with.

But even after the baby arrived, her body continued to warp. Without the child stretching within her, her stomach became flabby, lined with accusatory veins of stretch marks; her breasts pendulous, throbbing with the weight of milk within them. Even her face had changed, her cheekbones retreating under a layer of fat and blemishes.

Duke had grumbled when Thelma first demanded separate beds. "You think I mind a few wobbly bits?" he said. "For God's sake, I've two children already! I've seen a pregnant woman before, damn it!" But Thelma had insisted, not least because of the way his eyes seemed to slide, sidelong, to other women when they entered a room.

Duke persisted, stroking the silk on Thelma's shoulders. "Well, we mustn't disagree with the doctors," he murmured, "but there are other things we could do, aren't there? Other ways to while away the afternoon...?"

Thelma shied away from the thought of herself, big as a whale, manipulating Duke on their bed. "Really, darling," she said, pulling away. "It's the middle of the afternoon."

Duke sighed and straightened his tie.

"I'm leaving for London after tea," he said, holding the nursery door open for Thelma as they walked out.

"So soon?" she said. "I hoped you might stay the night."

Duke looked down the hallway. "You know I want to more than anything, my dear, but it just isn't feasible. We came to an agreement, yes, but there are still particulars to iron out, and Withy is insisting..."

He trailed into silence and pulled a gold case from his breast pocket. He clicked it open and took out a cigarette, clamping it between his lips as he rummaged in his pocket once more for a lighter.

"You ought to come with me," he said. He pointed at Thelma, cigarette perched between his first and second fingers. "A night out. That's what you need."

"You want me to come with you? Like this?" asked Thelma, but before she could protest further Duke kissed her, heat from the smoke warm on his lips.

"This really is ridiculous, your fussing," he said. "You realize, do you not, that you look as beautiful as ever?"

Thelma rolled her eyes, and Duke squeezed her hand. "I mean it," he said gently. "Come to London. We can go to the Embassy Club. You can wear one of those lovely frocks of yours."

"And Tony?" said Thelma, though she could feel herself warming to the idea. It had been so long since she'd been out, and she missed Duke terribly. What's one more stone? she told herself. Elise would find her something loose-fitting to wear.

"Nanny will take care of him. It's what she's here for." Duke frowned. "It's not doing you any good, cooped up here. Isn't doing *me* any bleeding good either, truth be told. Come to London. We'll have fun, you and me."

TWELVE

THE EMBASSY CLUB WAS HOT AND LOUD, A FUGGY mist of smoke hovering over the crowded couples on the dance floor. Thelma tugged at the sleeve of her dress: the gold lamé strained hideously across her bust, and she could feel a seam digging, persistently, into her armpit. When she was slimmer it had fallen carelessly across her torso, bunching elegantly at a dropped waist; now, it pulled across the plump stomach that the baby had left her, curling in a defeated heap under her belly.

"You look beautiful," Duke murmured. They stood at the top of the red-carpeted staircase, looking down on tables of women clutching cigarettes, men leaning back in their chairs with rock-glasses balanced on their crossed legs. An orchestra played in a pit below a stage at the end of the room, the singer crooning "Carolina Moon."

"I'd look better if I'd had the chance to visit my seamstress. I wish we'd planned this properly."

"Spontaneity is a virtue," said Duke. "Think of Reggie and Gloria—off at a moment's notice, no regard for rules…"

"And look where they ended up," Thelma muttered, tugging at her dress as it began to creep back up her stomach. Duke was silent: she could tell he was shocked by her callousness but his disapproval stoked irritation, rather than shame. She took his arm and let him lead her to the bottom of the staircase to greet the maître d'.

"A pleasure to see you again, Lord Furness, a pleasure..."

"Good evening, Luigi. Here to see G, has he arrived yet?"

Thelma could feel a bead of sweat making its way down her inner thigh as the maître d' led them to G's table, thinking there was no possible way that the room had been so warm when she'd last visited. She searched for a waiter with a tray of drinks as they walked to a square booth framed by palm fronds where G, seated next to a dark-haired woman in green silk, raised his arm in welcome.

"Thelma! You lovely girl, when Duke told me you'd be joining us I didn't quite believe him. How's the baby?" he said.

"He's well, G, thank you," said Thelma, as Duke pulled out a chair for her. Thelma sat, feeling the dress strain against her bust. "Good evening," she said to the woman.

"Nancy," she said, holding a cigarette aloft with thin fingers. "Old friend of G's. I've heard of you, of course, but it's a wonder we haven't met formally before now."

"I've been rather busy," said Thelma.

Nancy laughed. "So I've been told. Babies do have a ghastly tendency to get in the way of things, don't they? Thank heaven for nannies—I doubt I would have made it past infancy if my mother had raised us on her own. She'd have given us all away like a litter of puppies."

"You have siblings?" asked Thelma, taking the cocktail that Duke had lifted off a waiter's tray.

"Sisters. I don't know how my mother would have managed." Nancy finished her cigarette and flicked the end into an ashtray.

"I shudder to think," said Thelma, glancing at Duke. Though

he was speaking to G, he kept looking over at a group of women standing near the dance floor with drinks in hand. They were all young and slender, shoulders and hips thrust forward in contrived slouches. A heavy-lidded blonde with overlarge lips met Duke's eyes; he smiled and held her gaze, playing with the stem of his glass.

Mamma's voice echoed in Thelma's head, a snippet from a long-ago conversation. *Wealthy men don't look far for distractions.*

She finished her cocktail and stood. "Dance with me?" she said to Duke.

He turned his attention to Thelma. "Certainly," he said. As they walked to the dance floor, the blonde leaned in to whisper something to her friends.

"Are you all right, my dear? You're trembling," said Duke, as the band played a horn-heavy waltz.

"Am I?" said Thelma. "Nerves, I suppose. It's been some time since we've danced."

Duke squeezed Thelma's hand. "Too long," he agreed.

From over Duke's shoulder Thelma watched the blonde girl search the dance floor for him. She met Thelma's eye and blinked, diverting her gaze. "It's a wonder you haven't forgotten about me—taken up with some pretty young thing."

"Don't be silly," he said. "I've missed you. We all have."

"Including her?" said Thelma, nodding to the blonde.

He looked at her sharply. "I'll pretend I didn't hear that," he said.

"Which part?" Thelma stepped back, her ears ringing. "Oh, Duke. I hope you aren't thinking she's interested in anything other than your bank account." She knew she was deliberately antagonizing him, but she felt a perverse recklessness—as though she could wound without leaving a mark.

Duke leaned in. "I hope you know, Thelma, that jealousy is a terribly overrated emotion."

"Overrated, darling, but occasionally warranted," she replied.

The song ended and the dance floor began to clear. A cabaret of ten female dancers in beaded dresses skipped onto a stage above the orchestra arm in arm.

"Look here," said Duke, "I don't know what you're playing at but I won't have it, you hear me? This—this bitterness, this moping—"

"Who's moping?" snapped Thelma. On the stage, the cabaret began to kick their legs along to a loud American ragtime.

"I don't understand you—truly I don't," said Duke. He ran a hand through his hair, and the scent of pomade bloomed around him. "You just had a baby, for Christ's sake—you ought to be happy! You seem to be under the assumption that motherhood has made you a troll. Well, it hasn't. You look the same as you ever did, but for that bloody scowl on your face."

Thelma felt a pang of guilt but pushed it aside. He had no idea—no *clue*, how it had been. The pregnancy. The birth. Shunted away to Burrough Court like an invalid, while Duke gallivanted about, charming insipid beauties...

"I can't pretend to know what's going on in that brain of yours, but I miss you," he said. "I miss how it used to be. Come to bed with me tonight."

He trailed his fingers across Thelma's cheekbones, tucking a stray lock of hair behind her ear. Thelma could feel her conviction breaking, her anger dissipating as his hand ran down her arm, her torso—then it brushed over the stubborn chunk of her hip.

Thelma stepped back. "G's waiting for us," she said.

Duke deposited Thelma next to Nancy without another word and began, with apparent effort, a conversation with G. Thelma stared at him, oddly calm, before Nancy reached across the table and prodded her forearm.

"Terrible costumes," she said. Thelma laughed half-heartedly, twisting in her chair to watch the dancers with feigned interest.

She wasn't entirely sure why she was being so difficult with Duke but his conduct tonight—his conduct ever since she had gotten pregnant—grated at her. His relentless attempts to pull her into bed. His assumption that he could flit back and forth from Burrough Court at his leisure, his work taking precedence over her, over the baby.

Above all, Thelma's anger stemmed from her growing suspicion that Duke was whiling away his time in London by choice, rather than necessity. His trips to Burrough Court had taken on the tone of a chore—as though seeing her was a duty he had to get through in the course of his week. *And can you blame him?* said a small, calm voice in the back of her head.

Thelma glanced at Duke, who was conversing with a club-girl who had just sold him a packet of Turkish cigarettes. He nodded his thanks and she turned, pocketing more than the cigarettes were worth.

Duke opened the carton and tapped out four cigarettes, handing them to G and Nancy before passing one to Thelma. She fitted it into her cigarette holder and allowed him to light it, his hand curled steadily around his lighter as she bent toward the flame. She sat back up and Duke flipped the lighter shut, glancing, almost involuntarily, at the blonde as he stowed it in his pocket.

Thelma felt something snap.

"We must be at the most popular place in London," she said. Onstage, the chorus girls had filed off the stage, making way for a lithe couple in Spanish costumes. Thelma gave an empty laugh. "It feels like I've been gone longer than a few months. Why, I don't know half the people in here."

"That's not true," said Duke. "Betty Lawson-Johnson is just on the other side of the dance floor. We'll go say hello."

Thelma turned to Nancy, smiling. "But still. So many new faces, don't you think? So many *pretty* faces." She leaned back in her chair. "G, who do you think is the prettiest girl here?"

G chuckled. "Steady on. That's a dangerous question."

Nancy grinned. "You can't say it's Thelma or me—that's cheating," she said. "But if you *don't* say it's Thelma or me, then you're beastly."

"Duke, who do you think is the prettiest girl here?" said Thelma, reaching for her glass of champagne.

Duke puffed at his cigarette, frowning.

"*I* think it's that girl over there. The blonde one, in the gray dress," she continued. She smirked and lowered her voice to a stage whisper. "Duke thinks she's pretty. He's been staring at her all evening."

Duke reddened, and Thelma laughed. "Oh, come now. It's just a bit of fun," she said. She finished her drink, enjoying the petty rush of power. She locked eyes with her husband: he looked away and drained his glass of champagne.

"You think she's pretty, don't you, G?" said Thelma.

"Who, her? Yes, very pretty." G waved for a waiter to bring another round.

"See, darling? G thinks she's pretty, too." She tapped her cigarette against the ashtray, knocking dust. "Go ask her to dance. See if she's pretty up close."

Duke flipped the carton open and pulled out another cigarette. "Don't be silly," he said.

"Spoilsport. Afraid she'll turn you down?" She considered Duke with mock-seriousness. "Perhaps you're too old for her. Ten pounds says that you can't get her to dance with you."

G raised his eyebrows; Nancy grinned. "A challenge! Go on then, Duke."

Duke set down his half-smoked cigarette, stubbing it with delicate precision. "You don't want to do this," he said, smiling for G's and Nancy's benefit.

"Ten pounds is a princely sum," said Thelma, her heart beating fast in her throat. Onstage, the Spanish dancers bowed and left as the orchestra returned to its regular repertoire. "Do it. For me."

Duke looked at Thelma for a long moment.

"For you, my dear—anything," he said.

He made his way toward the group of women and tapped the blonde on the shoulder; he said something that made her laugh, then held out his hand.

She took it and followed him to the dance floor.

The music began to play—a slow, tender tune—and the girl rested her hand on Duke's shoulder. Duke put his arm around her waist. He looked down at her—she was several inches shorter than Thelma—and smiled.

"What d'you know—ten pounds to Duke. Well done, him," said G.

Thelma's heart sank. "Well done, him."

THIRTEEN

THELMA'S RELATIONSHIP WITH DUKE DECLINED slowly, inevitably, after their evening at the Embassy Club, and while Thelma regretted her spiteful conduct, she couldn't quite bring herself to apologize. The next day, Duke drove Thelma to King's Cross, excusing himself from making the drive to Burrough Court himself because of business—and although he telephoned her diligently, every afternoon at four, he did not leave the city for two full weeks.

"I could come down to London for a few days," Thelma suggested during one of their telephone calls.

There was a momentary silence on Duke's end of the phone; Thelma worried that the line had cut out.

"No, darling. My commitments will keep me far too busy to give you the attention you deserve. Perhaps I'll come up next week," he said, his tone perfectly cordial.

Over dinner one evening in July, Duke announced that he was planning a holiday to Monte Carlo.

"Really? How exciting. Shall I bring a bathing costume? Will it be warm enough?" asked Thelma.

Duke looked up. "Actually, darling, I had thought to go on my own," he said. "You don't mind, do you? Only I'll be spending the whole time at the baccarat table. Won't be much for you to do, I'm afraid."

Duke remained in Monte Carlo for nearly a month, and though he continued to telephone every afternoon Thelma knew it was only for show. She'd heard rumors—whispers at dinner parties, sidelong glances during evenings out—that Duke was entering the casino every evening with the same woman on his arm. Apparently, his affair was common knowledge—so much so that one of Averill's friends, invited to the town house for lunch one afternoon, had given Thelma a sympathetic look over her cup of coffee.

"I think he's being perfectly ghastly," she said to Thelma when Averill stepped out of the room.

Thelma had been rattled by the realization that Duke's life— her life—had become sitting-room gossip.

"I'm sure I don't know what you mean," she replied, but she excused herself just the same. She went to Duke's study and sat at his desk—papers neatly organized in stacks and folders, pens scattered artfully across the leather blotter. She looked at the telephone, spooling the loose cord between her fingers, willing it to ring, then picked up the receiver and instructed the operator to connect her to Duke's hotel in Monte Carlo.

Thelma slipped her shoe from her foot and balanced it from the end of her toes, bouncing it up and down as the operator tried the connection. She swiveled the chair, cord wrapping around her, and looked up at the painting behind Duke's desk.

It was a Cubist piece, by an artist Thelma had heard of but didn't know well. She had often wondered how something so abstract could appeal to Duke's cut-and-dried approach to the world, but he would spend hours staring at it, rotating in his chair in idle moments to appreciate how the light transformed it throughout the day, time giving it the illusion of life and temperament: distant at dawn, warm at dusk.

It's a woman, Duke had told her once, sweeping a hand across Thelma's sightline to connote the curves of a body. *She looks so sad... Can't you see it?*

Thelma couldn't. Each time she grasped an understanding of the woman's form—a glimpse of breast, the curve of a shoulder—the rest of the pieces would fall apart, leaving her staring at a mass of browns and grays.

I don't, she had told him, *but I can appreciate it, I suppose. If it appeals to you.*

Of course, it appeals to me, Duke had replied. *She looks like you.*

There was a quiet click on the telephone as the operator came back on the line.

"I'm terribly sorry, Lady Furness." Underneath the tinny tone of the connection, the operator's tone was delicate, as though she, too, understood the implications of the exchange. "Lord Furness is not registered at the Hôtel de Paris."

"I see," said Thelma. "Thank you." She let the operator ring off and dropped her hand, receiver limply trapped between her fingers, into her lap. She fitted it back into its cradle, a chill seeping into her chest.

She could hear Averill and her friend laughing in the sitting room. The clock on Duke's desk ticked in time with her heartbeat, a noise that seemed to fill the empty space.

The telephone rang, breaking the illusion of silence. It sounded twice before someone picked it up elsewhere; moments later, the butler tapped on the study door.

"It's Lord Furness, my lady. Shall I—?"

"I'm not at home," said Thelma. She stared at the painting, striving to form its shapes into a coherent whole. "Williams, would you fetch my pocketbook?"

The butler retrieved Thelma's handbag and she sorted through its contents to find her checkbook. She leaned over the desk as she unscrewed the cap of Duke's fountain pen, nib pressing into the leather blotter as she wrote.

Thelma sat in Lady Sarah's drawing room, knitting her fingers together.

"He's having an affair—he's all but admitted it," she said. "It's unbearable, it really is. Everyone knowing, everyone judging..."

Lady Sarah sighed. "I'm so sorry, my dear." She called her butler over, and spoke to him in an undertone. "A cocktail, I think, for Lady Furness."

"What do I do?" asked Thelma as the butler poured two glasses of sherry. Thelma took hers absently, resting it on the arm of the chair.

"If I could only tell you how many times I had this same conversation with Daisy, God rest her soul." Lady Sarah took her cocktail and the butler retreated. "I've seen this story play out many times before. He's used to having things his own way—most men are. Really, Thelma, you mustn't take it so seriously."

"How?" she replied. She set down her glass. "How can I possibly allow—"

"Thelma," said Lady Sarah. "I've known Marmaduke for many years, and much as I adore him he can be a very selfish man. He will have his affairs—these women will come and go—but you're the one he married."

Thelma shook her head, picturing a lifetime of smiling, willful ignorance. "How can I spend the rest of my life with someone unfaithful?" she said.

Lady Sarah smiled. "My dear, half the people in Mayfair are conducting affairs this very afternoon." She paused. "You know, it's not seen as a stain, here, for couples to live separately. Many do."

Thelma pictured it: separate bedrooms, separate social outings. Strained silences, on those rare Sunday afternoons where they both found themselves in the same house; feeble attempts to play at happiness when Duke's career demanded it. Leaving each other, cordially, at the end of the evening with transparent excuses to cover the excitement of spending the night with someone new.

"I don't think I can do that," she said. "I'm considering speaking to a divorce lawyer."

Lady Sarah raised her eyebrows. "I know divorces are common in America, but they simply aren't done here," she said. "Think about what you would lose. How would a divorce affect your son?" Lady Sarah's tone was firm and unsentimental. "It would impact Duke's business. You certainly wouldn't be permitted in society, nor at court." She was so matter-of-fact, thought Thelma, discussing her failing marriage as one would the weather. "In America, it might be common practice to pick oneself up after a scandal, but such things follow, here. Mayfair has a terribly long memory."

"In America, it simply isn't *done* for married men to go on public holidays with their mistresses," said Thelma.

Lady Sarah smiled faintly. "Can't you see that you're married to a good man—and he is a good man, Thelma, despite his lapses. You have a child with him. You have a comfortable life. What good would a divorce do?" She placed her hand over Thelma's. "He loves you, my dear. I know it might be hard to see it now, but he does. Give him time, and you'll see. Marmaduke always comes home."

The day Duke was due to arrive home from Monte Carlo Thelma lingered at the house. She couldn't bear the thought of seeing him, yet dreaded the possibility that he might spend the night with his latest conquest. Her conversation with Lady Sarah had done nothing to calm her doubts; she'd spent the night tossing in bed, watching the clock creep closer to dawn. She wouldn't divorce Duke—Lady Sarah had convinced her of that much, at least—but Thelma didn't want her husband thinking she'd simply accepted his infidelity. She'd been there once before.

Duke turned up early in the afternoon, his arrival heralded by a flurry of activity from the town house servants. In the sitting room, Thelma put her book down to listen: his genial greeting to Williams in the entrance hall; the soft thump of his brief-case on the floor.

"Where's Thelma?" she heard him ask. She stood, waiting, as his footsteps grew louder.

Thelma wasn't sure what she had expected—that Duke's be-trayal might be visible: lipstick on his collar, a bead of sweat run-ning down his temple. But he looked entirely himself: slightly rumpled, perhaps, in his traveling clothes, but with the same smile, the same careworn lines tracing down the sides of his mouth.

"Hello, darling," he said, standing in the doorway. Thelma made no move to go to him, although her stomach lurched ter-ribly when his eyes met hers. "You look well."

She had worked hard, in Duke's absence, to regain her figure and she felt a fierce tinge of vindictive pride as he looked at her with unexpected fondness. "How was Monte Carlo?"

Duke folded his gloves one over the other and tucked them into the pocket of his overcoat. "Same as ever. You've been well?"

"Very," said Thelma. She half dreaded that he would try to kiss her; she half hoped he would.

"Well," he said, clearing his throat. "Lovely to see you. Wil-liams tells me Dickie and Averill are coming for dinner—good, good. Perhaps you and I might find a moment before to say hello properly, but for the moment I—"

"No, please," said Thelma. "Go make yourself comfortable."

"A few things I need to take care of…"

He turned on his heel and Thelma watched him go, disappointed. She sat back down and picked up her book. If that was the best he could manage after a month apart...

Duke stormed back into the sitting room, color high in his cheeks. He had a piece of paper in hand: the check Thelma had written, the day she telephoned Monte Carlo.

"What's this?"

Thelma turned the page. "Oh?" She laid the book down. "You know, it occurred to me that we hadn't settled up for our little bet at the Embassy Club—remember?"

Duke was rigid, his knuckles white against his tan.

Thelma smiled. "I think the verdict is fairly clear, don't you? You won, darling."

Duke sputtered. He tore the check once, then again. "What rot," he said, letting the pieces drift to the floor. "It was a joke, a bloody joke—"

"It was," said Thelma. "But the joke, it seems, was on me."

Duke stared at her.

"I think I'll go to Burrough Court tomorrow," she said. "Spend a few days with Tony."

FOURTEEN

THOUGH THELMA WORRIED THAT HER WEEKS AT Burrough Court would feel like a defeat, she found that the countryside gave her a rare sense of sanctuary, as opposed to the loneliness she'd felt before. Distance was a welcome distraction—and while she was not prepared to forgive Duke his infidelity, she began to consider how their marriage might look, under changed circumstances.

Thelma also found that Burrough Court gave her an opportunity to spend time with Tony. At four months old, he was no longer an indistinct newborn but an infant, his features drastically different from when she'd seen him last: his lips were thin, and perpetually upturned in a Duke-like smirk, his eyes alert and following as Thelma drew a finger across his sightline. She marveled at his laughter, his constantly changing expressions, his wild tuft of strawberry blond hair.

She had worried, those first few nights in the country, that the resentment she had felt toward Tony throughout her pregnancy would continue to grow: that he would become an unwitting reminder of her failure to hold Duke's attention. To her overwhelming relief, though, Thelma found the more time she spent with Tony the more she loved him: the dumpling-like feel of his stomach as he slept, the shrieking laugh he gave when Thelma touched his feet. Tony had nothing to do with it all. It had been her own insecurities, and Duke's, that had caused the rift. Thelma would have been confronted by Duke's infidelity one day or another. At least Tony could bring her some consolation.

It wasn't only Tony that brought Thelma joy—Averill, too, had become a real friend. She was up each morning in Wellington boots, ready to tromp through the fields and meet with the farmers who worked them. She dug the kitchen gardens and broke in the estate's horses. She even pressed Thelma into the service, assigning her chickens to tend: each morning, Thelma was sent out to the coop to collect fresh-laid eggs, admiring the white, blue and green shells. This year, Averill was particularly busy, as she planned to show the estate's livestock at the upcoming county fair.

"Father insists on throwing me a coming-out ball—can you believe it?" asked Averill one evening. She lifted her hand, inspecting the mud still caked under her fingernails from a day in the stables. "I can't imagine what he thinks I could possibly get out of it."

"It's customary," said Thelma. "And it would mean so much to him if you'd let him make a fuss. Who knows? You might meet someone you like."

"What I'd like is for him to take me hunting somewhere exotic," said Averill. "Africa—somewhere with real sport."

Thelma laughed. "There's plenty of sport in a London drawing room. Stand at the back and watch the young men try to pick off the weak ones in the herd," she said. "Anyone who gets caught unawares at the punch bowl..."

"Trouble is, you can't shoot those leopards when they get too close," sighed Averill. "And their heads don't look particularly fetching displayed on the study wall."

Thelma's time away from London gave her a chance, too, to see Gloria. Living in Paris with Little Gloria and Mamma, Gloria was more easily able to visit, but her trips were rare: on a regular basis, Gloria traveled to America to discuss Little Gloria's upbringing with the lawyers, which was a particularly contentious issue now that Gloria was engaged to be married.

Thelma was thrilled that, after everything Gloria had gone through, she'd found happiness once more. Tall, well-spoken and several years older than Gloria, Gottfried zu Hohenlohe-Langenburg—Friedel—was a German prince, with a family castle in Langenburg and the upright posture of a man born to privilege. The marriage announcement was made; Gloria chose a lilac wedding dress, and a dress in a matching shade for Little Gloria.

The only trouble, Gloria confided in Thelma, was Little Gloria herself.

"I've been back and forth from America so many times I feel like a tennis ball," Gloria complained. She had come to Burrough Court to introduce Little Gloria to Tony; on arriving, Little Gloria had peered over her cousin's cradle with quiet interest before asking to go outside to see the horses. At four and a half years old, Little Gloria had grown into a dark and inquisitive child, with her father's distinctive eyes and overlarge mouth.

They led Little Gloria out to the paddock, where Averill, in her riding boots and breeches, was putting a horse named Chestnut through his paces. Thelma waved, and a groomsman came to the paddock gate to let Little Gloria in, lifting her by the waist to see the pony eye to eye. Little Gloria held out a hand—confidently, without any childish trepidation—and patted the horse softly on the nose.

"She's Reggie's daughter, all right," said Thelma, as Little Gloria asked Averill whether she could sit on the horse's back. Averill nodded, and the groom lifted Little Gloria into the saddle.

Gloria agreed. "She is—and Mamma's, and Kieslich's. And Gilchrist's, and Gertrude's. First they told me I shouldn't raise her in Paris—now they're telling me Germany is no place for a child. What's the harm in Paris? She's learning French, she's learning manners—and the parties! I've never had any interest in moving back to New York, and I don't see why they think Little Gloria would be better off there." She smiled. "It's all irrelevant now that I'm engaged. We'll live in Germany—Gloria's so excited. I told her we'd be living in a fairy castle. Mamma is furious."

"Why?" asked Thelma. "I would have thought she would be thrilled to have you married to a prince."

"Not when it interferes with Little Gloria," Gloria replied. "She's livid—keeps going on about the importance of raising her American. Truly, it boggles the mind. You and I were brought up on the continent and we're fine."

"We were brought up on *several* continents," said Thelma.

"See? Living in one place would be much more stable," said Gloria. "I've told the Surrogates that I plan to raise Little Gloria in Germany with Friedel until she's old enough for boarding school in New York."

In the paddock, Averill had begun to lead the horse in slow circles, Little Gloria clutching the reins. Dust clouded up as the horse walked, catching the afternoon sunlight.

Gloria tapped a hand against the paddock railing. "Mrs. Vanderbilt approves of the marriage, so that really ought to be the end of it," she said. "If she thinks Germany is good enough for Little Gloria, it should be good enough for the Surrogates."

"Why don't you apply for primary custody?" asked Thelma. If Gloria, now twenty-two, gained primary custody of her daughter, she could keep Little Gloria in Europe indefinitely.

"I've considered it," said Gloria, "but my last visit got all tied up in bartering over the cost of our town house in Paris."

In the paddock, Averill slowed the horse to a halt. Gripping the pommel, she swung up onto the saddle behind Little Gloria, reaching past the child for the reins as she nudged the horse into a gentle canter. Little Gloria shrieked with delight, gripping the horse's mane between her fingers.

"It's strange," she said slowly. "Mamma can't stand Friedel—she sits across from him at the dining table and positively scowls." She waved to Little Gloria, who waved back, her arm pumping ecstatically as she bumped up and down in the saddle. "But Friedel can handle her. And he's so good with Little Gloria—he says she needs a father figure. He thinks Kieslich spoils her terribly."

"Does she?" asked Thelma.

Gloria laughed. "Of course. So does Mamma. She insists on calling her an heiress, but Little Gloria now understands what that means. The other day, she asked for a second helping of cake and told me she can have anything she wants because it's her money keeping a roof over our heads. Mamma's voice, coming out of a four-year old child...it was disconcerting."

Thelma waved away a cloud of midges. "What did you say?"

"I told her it wasn't proper to say such things, but I couldn't stay and argue. I was on my way to meet Friedel." She waved once more as Averill brought the horse up to a trot. "You ought to come to Germany this summer. Friedel's invited me to meet his parents at Schloss Langenburg."

"I'd love to," said Thelma, "but with Duke and Tony..."

Gloria turned to look at Thelma. "How is Duke?" she asked.

Thelma shrugged. "Lady Sarah tells me he's moved on from his latest conquest. Apparently, he was in Rome last week with someone new. A war widow."

"I would never have believed it," said Gloria. "When I think about the two of you in Paris..."

"I'm told it's his way," said Thelma. "Lady Sarah thinks I should get a separate flat in London."

"Well, I hope you aren't moldering out here on your own," said Gloria. "Perhaps you ought to consider what living separately could mean. Find someone fun in London. What's sauce for the goose, and all that."

"A lover?" said Thelma. "Wouldn't that make me as bad as him?"

"Better a lover than a martyr," said Gloria. "Don't allow Duke to have all the fun."

In the paddock, Averill had begun to walk the horse toward them, Little Gloria bouncing with the motion of the horse. Averill looked up, grinning.

FIFTEEN

THELMA RETURNED TO LONDON, AT DUKE'S request, to help him plan a dinner party.

"To keep up appearances, I suppose," Thelma said to a sleeping Tony when she came into the nursery to say goodbye, but she knew it was more than that. For Duke, it was an opportunity to dine with business associates and return social favors; for Thelma, with Gloria's words echoing in her ears, it was an opportunity to return to her life in London.

Duke seemed genuinely pleased when Thelma arrived from King's Cross, pulling her into an embrace that was so easy, so natural that it felt as though the past few months hadn't happened.

"How's Averill?" he said, taking her hand as he led her through to the study. "And Tony? You know, I was thinking of coming to watch Averill at that county fair. We could make a day of it. Have Cook prepare a lunch…"

"That sounds nice," said Thelma. In her absence, the orderly mess of Duke's study had descended into chaos: stacks of paper had multiplied, spilling over the desk and onto the floor.

He sat on the couch and patted the cushion beside him. The butler had laid out a small luncheon of cold chicken and new potatoes on the coffee table.

Thelma looked at Duke as he poured two glasses of mineral water, noting his new tiepin, the slightly different way he combed his hair. "It's good to see you," she said, truthfully.

"And you," said Duke. He smiled, and Thelma felt the corners of her mouth lift in response. "The country seems to be treating you well. Any luck with the horseback riding?"

Thelma laughed. "Averill tries her best," she said, "but even she admits I'm better suited to a coach-and-four than a saddle."

Duke put a hand on Thelma's knee—casually, as though it had strayed there by mistake. "Then I suppose I'll be buying a coach-and-four," he said. He rested his head against the back of the couch. "It's good to talk again," he said. "The telephone just isn't the same."

Lightly, Duke's hand began to move up and down her leg. His fingers brushed against lace overlay of her dress; her slip whispered, silk against stocking, under the weight of his hand as he inched it slowly past her garter.

She knew she ought to pull away. Duke didn't deserve this—but it had been months since she'd felt true affection, true desire.

Duke kissed her. "I've missed you," he murmured. He slipped his hand under her dress, her skin electric beneath the pads of his fingers. She shifted beneath him, kissing him as he pushed her skirt even higher.

Afterward, they settled down to the business of planning the dinner party.

"Cook's sorting the menu—I don't much care what we have, so long as it's food," said Duke. "What I need from you is help with the seating arrangements."

He handed Thelma a list of names—thirty or forty, split down the middle by sex so they could determine who to put where.

Thelma barely saw the guest list. It felt as though nothing had changed: Thelma could suddenly see everything she'd given up these past few months—and for what? Duke had been as enthusiastic as ever. He didn't care about the pregnancy, nor her appalling conduct at the Embassy Club. He cared about her happiness—and she, unbelievably, had pushed it away.

Impulsively, she leaned over and kissed Duke on the cheek. He chuckled as she leaned against him and began to read.

Her stomach dropped. A name at the bottom of the list, hastily scrawled in contrast to the neat penmanship of the other names, stood out on the paper. It had been added by Duke: a careless addition, it seemed, to even out the numbers.

All the buzz in Thelma's head—the excited chatter, the restless hope—fell silent.

"I figured we can put G anywhere, he's fairly easy to get on with—"

"Duke, darling," said Thelma. "This name at the bottom of the list…"

Duke looked over, patting Thelma on the knee. "Who? Oh—yes, I figured we can put her somewhere near the Pevensies, they're old friends."

Thelma froze. "You can't possibly think I'd allow her in the house."

"Why not?" said Duke. "She's a friend."

"She's more than a *friend*," said Thelma. She stood. Duke was unbearable once more, the lingering feel of his hands dirty, clammy—

Duke stood, too. "I won't have you sneering at her," he said.

"I don't believe you. I don't *believe* you," said Thelma. "You ask me to allow that woman into my home? After making *love* to me, Duke, you ask—"

"It's *my* house, and you'll accept her in it!" Duke slammed a fist on his desk, so forcefully that several sheets of paper slid off the tops of their piles and drifted to the floor.

He pointed at her. "You will accept her into this house," he said. "I won't hear another word against her, do you understand?"

Stunned into silence, Thelma nodded.

Duke smoothed his hair back. "Good," he said. He sat on the couch and reached for her hand. "Forgive me, darling, I—I lost my temper. Cowardly."

Thelma wrenched out of his grasp and left the room.

SIXTEEN

THELMA LEFT LONDON EARLY THE NEXT MORNING, and though Duke apologized again for losing his temper, he refused to relent.

"Clearly, we are at an impasse," he said, walking Thelma toward her idling car, "and I'm sorry for it. But there really is nothing more to discuss."

For days afterward, Thelma drifted through Burrough Court, sliding from grief to seething anger to self-pity—and a weakening hope that she might one day find happiness in a life estranged from her husband.

"How do you stand it?" Thelma asked Lady Sarah over the telephone.

There was a pause at the other end of the line. "You stop feeling sorry for yourself," she replied. "It's happened to many women before you—it will happen to many women after. Duke will come to his senses, but don't sit about in Leicestershire waiting for it to happen." Lady Sarah paused again. "And Thelma? For pity's sake don't cause a scene."

While Thelma brooded, Averill had Burrough Court in an uproar preparing for the Leicester Fair. As her first show since taking on management of the estate, Averill had a lot pinned on success. It would prove, she told Thelma, that she was more than a society girl with a hobby.

"Father only ever signed the bills," she said, "but this place—it's so much more. The farming, the shooting, the hunting—all those things don't appear out of thin air. I want to learn how to run it."

The evening before the Fair, Averill prowled the drawing room, fretting about the clouds that had settled heavily over the fields.

"Blasted rain," she said. "Gordon tells me it's going to start this evening—nothing for it, I suppose, although it will make transport a nightmare..."

Thelma, curled on the divan, barely registered a word. Duke had sent a telegram to Burrough Court that morning, wishing Averill luck in the Fair. Even after their last argument, Duke tended to include some polite message for Thelma in such missives, but this telegram ended abruptly, with nothing to indicate that he knew Thelma was there.

Averill trailed off. "You aren't listening, are you?"

Thelma looked up. "No. Of course, darling." She smiled at Averill—her relentless focus, so very much like her father. "I'm sorry. I've not been good company this evening."

Averill sobered, the manic light of last-minute planning leaving her eyes. She circled back and sat. "I'm sorry, too, you know," she said. "He can be so pigheaded at times."

Thelma smiled. "So can I."

"A Furness family trait, I'm afraid. It's no wonder you fit in so well," said Averill. "You know what? You ought to come to the Fair tomorrow. Help calm my nerves."

Thelma thought of Duke's telegram, sitting at the bottom of a wastepaper basket in the study. If he wasn't going to be there for Averill, at least she could be. "Yes, why not?"

★ ★ ★

The next morning Thelma set out for Leicester Fair, bundled against the relentless drizzle in the back seat of her motorcar.

Don't cause a scene, Lady Sarah had told her—and while Thelma felt she was sparing the world the sight of her misery, she clearly hadn't considered the effect that her moping was having on Averill.

Thelma watched the gray fields pass by, the car slowing as it entered a small village. She never truly felt like a stepmother—she was too close in age to Averill and Dickie to feel any real sense of responsibility—but it was unfair to air her unhappiness in front of Duke's children. Had Gloria been there, Thelma would have been able to rely on her, as a distraction and a source of strength. As it was, though, Thelma was letting her emotions get the better of her.

The car pulled around a corner and an immense warehouse covered in red-and-white bunting came into view.

"Just a few moments here, m'lady," said the driver. The car joined a stream of automobiles and carriages slowing to let out the passengers that streamed into the warehouse, collars turned up against the wind. Many were under the temporary refuge of black umbrellas, while others held sodden newspapers over their heads.

The driver stopped in front of a series of wooden duckboards laid across the wet grass and Thelma stepped out, buttoning her coat. The brim of her hat lifted slightly, the breeze hinting at more inclement weather to come, and she snugged it down, the boards beneath her feet sinking into the muddy earth as she walked inside.

The Fair was bustling with visitors: farmers and their proud wives, townsfolk in rough-spun tweeds, small children darting like minnows between their parents' legs. It was noisy, the assembled din of farmers, animals and visitors creating an incoherent buzz. From some unseen corner of the building she could hear a horn band, punctuated occasionally by the lowing of cows.

Thelma walked on. The building was as large as a football pitch, if not larger; tables and fencing created makeshift alley-ways down which, presumably, she would find livestock. Signs hung from the rafters: Pigs and Sheep, Rabbits, Poultry. Thelma kept to the main thoroughfare, admiring the domestic offer-ings that lay on tables festooned with bunting: home goods and handiwork, preserves and pottery.

A large show ring stood in the center of the building, its white railings freshly painted. It was flanked by low stands filled with spectators—an oddly large crowd for a farm show, thought Thelma, but then what did she know of farm shows? Within the ring, a line of sheep stood in the company of freshly scrubbed farmers. A handful of men in suits and top hats huddled opposite, occasionally stepping forward to inspect the sheep more closely.

"They'll be bringing in the cows next," said a heavyset woman in a worn apron, sitting at a gingham-covered table laden with pies and tarts. She folded her hands comfortably over her stom-ach and looked up at Thelma with a matronly smile. "Short-horns, then longhorns—then's the 'orses—not sure 'ow many classes that'll be—and after they'll be moving on to baking." She beamed. "Imagine—the Prince o' Wales, eating one of my pies!"

"The prince?" said Thelma, looking at the show ring with renewed interest.

"Sure enough, m'lady. Come for the Fair."

Thelma walked closer and people moved to make space for her next to the railing. She leaned forward—surely Averill would have mentioned whether the prince was going to be at the Fair?

In the ring, a white-whiskered man held up his hand, then pointed at one of the sheep. The crowd broke into applause and the farmer holding the sheep's lead stepped forward and bowed in front of the slender judge holding a blue ribbon: the Prince of Wales. The farmer rose as the prince, smiling, pinned the ribbon onto the sheep's collar. The crowd applauded, and the prince waved, sending them into cries of approval.

The white-whiskered judge announced a short break while the next set of livestock were brought in—"Shorthorns," Thelma heard someone mutter—and the crowd broke into casual chatter.

The prince looked round and Thelma, instinctively, waved.

He met her gaze—then to Thelma's astonishment, he broke away from his handlers and walked to the side of the ring.

"Lady Furness," he said. Thelma curtsied, pleased—surprised—that the prince had recalled her with such ease.

"Your Royal Highness," she said. The prince smiled, his eyes—that startling blue—fixed on her.

"I meant to congratulate you on the birth of your son. One hears these things in the clubs now and again."

"Thank you, sir," she replied. "We named him Anthony."

The prince held up his handful of ribbons, weighing them in a gloved hand. "Quite the to-do, these shows," he said. "My understanding of agriculture is rather limited but I must say, I think I've gotten rather good at the judging end of things."

"It must make quite the change from London, sir," said Thelma.

The prince reached for the knot of his tie and Thelma smiled, recalling the gesture from a long-ago ball.

"Indeed, it does," he said. "I find I'm so much more at home in the country—particularly country as lovely as this. Have you been in Leicestershire long?"

"Several weeks, sir. My husband has an estate in Melton Mow-bray."

"But you'll be returning to London soon?"

She thought of her last disastrous trip to Arlington Place. "I should think so, sir."

"I don't suppose you'd be game for having dinner one night this week—say, Thursday?"

Thelma nearly laughed out loud but caught herself at the last moment, turning the noise into a deferential cough. The prince looked at her expectantly. His eyes flicked, briefly, to the neckline of her dress.

Thursday. It was the night of Duke's dinner party. But an invitation to dine with the Prince of Wales wasn't come by lightly…

She thought once more of Duke, his happiness and anger rolling in unpredictable waves. His ludicrous expectation that Thelma would allow him to set a double standard for their marriage; his petulant silence when she didn't acquiesce. Thelma knew how the dinner party would unfold: she would sit, staring daggers at his mistress while the other guests whispered pity behind their hands.

"I would be honored, sir," she said.

The prince smiled. He patted the rail of the judging ring once, decisively. "Wonderful. Shall we say six o'clock? York House, St. James. I'll send a car." He looked back at the line of cows. "Well, best get back to it." He smiled more broadly, the corners of his eyes crinkling into crow's feet that, despite his youthful appearance, betrayed his age. "What a pleasure to see you, Lady Furness. I look forward to better making your acquaintance."

When Thelma left the Fair, the rain had finally given way to sun. It was late: a few final stragglers were wrangling their livestock into carts and buggies as Fair organizers pulled the bunting down from the rafters. Averill, exhausted, accepted Thelma's invitation of a ride back to Burrough Court, leaving the estate farmers to transport her prizewinning animals home. She fell asleep within minutes, her head pressed against the window as the car trundled over dips and rises in the road. In its last gasps, the sunset strived to make up for the gray day, throwing brilliant hues of orange and gold across the rolling hills; outside, midges circled in lazy clusters, clouds against the deepening sunlight.

She nudged Averill awake as they pulled into the drive. To Thelma's surprise, Duke strode down the front steps as the car rolled to a stop, opening Averill's car door. "Your first Fair—

your first set of ribbons, so Gordon tells me! Well done, my dear," he said, kissing Averill's dust-covered cheek. "I would have come for the day myself, but business…"

Thelma walked past, but he called her back.

"Not so fast, darling. Come around to the side." He tucked Averill's hand in the crook of his arm and Thelma followed in their wake, her jaw set.

A pony trap stood in the stable courtyard: it was a gleaming gray, its burgundy seats matching those in Duke's Lagonda.

"A little something to commemorate your first Fair," said Duke as Averill, forgetting her fatigue, climbed into the chassis. He gave Thelma a sidelong smile. "And for Thelma, given her riding abilities."

"It's beautiful, Father," said Averill, running her hands along the body.

"It's nothing," said Duke. "A reward for hard work."

Thelma walked around the carriage, quietly indignant. To her, Duke's generosity was an insult: an attempt to buy Averill's affections without bothering to witness her success firsthand.

She circled back. "You should have come," she said, as Averill kneeled to inspect the carriage's wheels. "She was something special."

"You'll have to tell me all about it over a drink," said Duke. He raised his voice. "I'd say you've earned it, Averill!"

The evening was cordial, if not warm. Before changing for dinner, Thelma found a valet setting Duke's bedclothes on the wingback chair in their bedroom—an indication, if Thelma needed one, that he intended to spend the night with her. Perhaps he would attempt a reconciliation; perhaps she would claw his eyes out. To her surprise, Thelma found that she didn't much care either way.

Thelma watched Duke at dinner, smiling and laughing as though all were right in the world. He was lighthearted and charming, even reaching across the table at one point to grasp Thelma's hand.

And everything's fine, thought Thelma. *Just like that?*

As the butler served cheese, Thelma spoke up. "Webb, would you ask Elise to pack me a suitcase for tomorrow? I'll be going into London. Let her know I'll need something suitable for dinner out."

Duke knocked a corner of cheese off a wedge with his knife. "Oh?" he said. "Who will you be dining with?"

"I thought Averill and I might take in Ascot—that is, if you weren't planning to use the tickets yourself."

"I suppose so. Who are you dining with?"

Thelma dabbed her lips with her napkin. "The Prince of Wales, dear," she said, setting the napkin back down with delicate care. "He's invited me to dinner on Thursday."

Averill perked up. "Really? Goodness, I wondered! Gordon said you were speaking to him," she said. "How exciting."

Thelma looked at Duke. He was smiling—a horrible, fixed expression that made him look as though he had just swallowed paint.

"Thursday," he said. "Did you forget our dinner party?"

Thelma avoided his eye, delighting in her triumph. "What could I say? He's the Prince of Wales."

Duke gaped for a moment, a series of expressions crossing his face in fleeting succession—anger, hurt, surprise, shock—and Thelma's sense of satisfaction grew.

"Well," he said. He patted his waistcoat. "That's a rare treat for you, Thelma. Do enjoy it."

Thelma picked up her knife. "You know, darling," she said, "I think I will enjoy it immensely."

When she retired for the evening, Thelma noticed that Duke's bedclothes were no longer on the wingback chair. In a fluid movement, she took off her jewelry and unhooked the back of her dress, letting it slide to the floor. Truth be told, she preferred having the bed to herself.

SEVENTEEN

ON THE EVENING OF HER DINNER WITH THE
Prince of Wales, Thelma sat at her vanity, toying with the emerald necklace that Duke had given her for their second anni-
versary. She held the necklace against her chest, admiring how
her dress—a scoop-necked Lanvin—would allow the jewelry
to take prominence. Was it too simple?

Thelma found the prospect of dining with the prince intimi-
dating. In accepting his invitation, Thelma was acknowledging
an inevitable truth: that, rather than fighting for her marriage,
she was giving in to Duke's infidelity—and opening the door for
her own. *Live your life,* Lady Sarah had told her. While Thelma
hardly expected to embark upon an illicit romance with the
Prince of Wales, she knew that gossip would spread: before long,
it would be known that Lady Furness was accepting invitations.
She clasped the necklace into place and left the bedroom.

Thelma paused at the top of the staircase, watching the servants prepare for Duke's dinner party below. In Thelma's ab-

sence, Averill had stepped in to perform as hostess. To Thelma's mind, it was a preferable outcome for all involved.

The entrance hall was gloomy, dim light spilling in from the half-moon window above the front door. Sconces made little difference: if anything, their orange glow cast a sallow pallor on peoples' faces. As Thelma walked downstairs, the front door opened and Williams, his head obscured by a bouquet of peach-colored peonies, walked in, swaying precariously under the blooms. Walking in from the sitting room, Duke stepped aside to give the butler room to pass.

"You're off, then?" he said, looking up at Thelma. He hadn't yet changed for dinner—guests weren't expected for another hour.

Thelma nodded, fixing her gloves in place as she walked down. "The prince is sending a motorcar. I'm looking forward to seeing York House, I'm told it's beautiful," she said.

"It's lovely. At least the bits I've seen," said Duke, holding the front door open for her. "He'll likely have you in the gallery, if there's a decent crowd. There's a cracking painting of Waterloo just opposite the doors."

"I'll look for it," Thelma replied. She stepped out and Duke followed, the sound of traffic filling the silence between them.

"You're all set for tonight?" she asked.

"What? Oh, yes—should be a laugh."

"You ought to go upstairs and change," said Thelma. She gestured to his suit. "Can't have you greeting our guests in that."

They shared a polite laugh as a black Daimler pulled up at the curb.

"That's me," she said. It was another mild evening; she idled on the doorstep, lingering heat from the afternoon sun warm on her shoulders.

Duke hesitated, then kissed her on the cheek.

"Have a lovely time."

The drive to St. James's Palace was short—truthfully, Thelma could have walked if she wanted. The car turned onto Bennet Street, then again onto St. James before doubling back onto Cleveland Row, slipping into a small alleyway between the red bricks of the palace and a powder-blue building next door. They paused at a set of wrought-iron gates, where the drive rolled down the window to exchange a few words with a guard before moving on.

They stopped in front of the heavy brick arches of St. James's Palace. A footman opened Thelma's door, nodding as she stepped out.

"Welcome to York House, Lady Furness," he said. "May I show you in?"

Thelma, expecting the din of guests to be audible from the front drawing room, was surprised at how silent it was in the palace. The gallery—its doors flung open—was empty, and her footsteps echoed as the footman led her up a grand staircase. As they walked along a second-story corridor, Thelma was relieved to hear the scratch of a gramophone.

She followed the footman into a large sitting room with white walls and gilt trim, windows framed by soft green curtains. It was surprisingly comfortable, decorated for daily use rather than pageantry: The marble fireplace was flanked by chintz sofas, a half-filled ashtray and a paperback on the walnut coffee table between them. An immense Empire desk stood at the opposite end of the room under an ornately detailed map of the world, and a portrait of Queen Mary presided above the fireplace mantel.

The Prince of Wales stood beneath the portrait of his mother, his hands clasped behind his back.

"Lady Furness. I'm delighted to see you."

"The pleasure is entirely mine, Your Highness," said Thelma, curtsying. He wore a midnight blue tuxedo over a white waistcoat, his hair slicked back in a blond coif. He touched the knot of his bow tie, tucking one hand in his pocket.

"I hope you don't mind the informality—I thought we might have a drink here and then go out on the town."

"That sounds ideal, sir," she said as he led her to the sofa.

"Martini? I'm rather partial to gin, but I'm sure we can manage something else if you prefer…"

"Gin's fine," said Thelma, glancing at the open door as she sat, waiting for the footman to return with another guest. Her heart quickened. Would they truly be dining alone?

He began to mix drinks at a nearby bar trolley. "Correct me if I'm wrong, Lady Furness, but I believe you're American?" he asked, peeling a twist of lemon and dropping it into a glass.

"Half-American, sir. My mother's from Chile," said Thelma. She looked up at the portrait of Queen Mary and straightened, perching on the end of her chair.

The prince poured gin and vermouth into a chrome shaker and swirled it, ice clattering against the metal. "Yes, that's it," he said. "I had the pleasure of meeting your sister in South America, oh… two years ago?" He circled back to Thelma, a martini in each hand.

"You know Consuelo?" said Thelma as she took her drink, the mention of her sister a welcome point of commonality.

"She had just married—let's see—a chap from the American foreign office," said the prince. He settled onto the sofa opposite Thelma. "Stationed in Oslo, if memory serves."

"It does indeed, sir," Thelma replied. "I must say, your recollection is remarkable."

The prince stretched an arm across the top of the sofa and crossed one leg over the other. "A party trick," he said. "Yet when I ought to remember something of real importance—" he held up his hand, his fingertips touching in a delicate knot "—*poof*. The politicians don't think much of it. They've all mastered the same trick, so we stand about at parties spouting facts until someone knocks our heads together."

"I suppose it's better than the alternative," she replied. "Freezing up. That happens to me far more frequently."

The prince lit a cigarette and fitted it into the corner of his mouth. "I don't believe it," he said. "You've lasted five minutes with me—that's more than most. You should have seen those poor souls at the Fair go rigid when I walked by."

"Did you enjoy your time in Leicestershire?"

He tapped his cigarette in a nearby ashtray. "Where are my manners—would you like one?" he asked. Thelma declined: between the martini and the shock of finding herself alone with the prince, she felt light-headed enough.

"You know, people always ask if I enjoy those sorts of things," he continued. "I enjoy meeting the people, but I can't stand the formal bits. Bowing, shaking hands—give me a few hours to talk to someone, a real Englishman." The gramophone shifted into white noise, the needle scratching gently on the vinyl. "I will say that I feel a certain affinity for Leicestershire. I used to join the Quorn regularly, you know, till Father put a stop to it." A dark look passed over his face and Thelma, worried she'd upset him, searched for something to say.

"Why did he—His Majesty—not want you hunting?"

"Well, it wasn't so much the hunting as the steeplechasing. The government felt it was too dangerous. Didn't want the future king breaking his neck going over a hedgerow. They'd have me packed in cotton if they could."

Thelma smiled. "You don't strike me as the type to accept that sort of treatment," she said as the prince got up to change the record. "You ought to come to Burrough Court for a fox hunt. We've a lovely estate, it wouldn't be any trouble."

The prince brightened; he put the needle down and sat next to Thelma as music filled the room. "Say, there's a thought. I'll see if we can arrange it."

Thelma was surprised at how easy it was to talk to the prince. He was so very unkingly, with his self-deprecation and easy charm: he had a clipped, almost strained voice that lacked the gravitas of his lofty position, and a casual warmth that made

Thelma feel as though he could be any young man she'd found in the lobby of the Ritz. He hardly looked the part, either—more a film star than a monarch. He was heartbreakingly slim and handsome, with a dreamy, winsome expression that gave her the impression that he'd stepped off a cellulose reel.

He got up to change the record again, Josephine Baker melting into Noel Coward. "One of my favorites," he said. "A dear friend got me this album for my birthday last year—good gracious, *actually* last year, almost to the day. Can you believe I'll be turning thirty-five on Tuesday?"

"I can't," said Thelma truthfully. Aside from the crow's feet, he could have been in his twenties.

The prince smirked. "And yet, I have to ask permission from my parents to go riding," he said.

"Well, when you're such an important figure..." said Thelma.

He waved her equivocation aside. "I'm no more important than anyone else," he said. "I've three brothers who could take over if I were to top it. It's no fun, this *princing* business, I'll tell you."

"But you must have some fun, surely?"

He set down his drink. "When my schedule permits it," he said. "On evenings like this." He fixed his eyes on Thelma, his hand inches from her shoulder. "I'm having rather a lot of fun with you tonight, Lady Furness."

"And the evening's far from over," she replied, surprised at her daring.

The prince eased back into the sofa cushions, looking pleased. "I was thinking we could dine at the Hotel Splendide—they've a cracking band."

Thelma set down her glass. "Lead the way."

After dinner, the prince dropped the car off at York House and insisted on walking Thelma home. "A little fresh air might do us both good," he said, offering her his arm as the chauffeur tailed them out of the compound.

"This has been a truly wonderful evening, Thelma—may I call you Thelma?" he asked, flicking aside the tail of his jacket to put his hand into his pocket.

"Of course, sir," she said. "I've had a lovely time. You danced every bit as gracefully as I recalled."

"Well," said the prince, "when one spends as much time at dances as I do, one's bound to remember his steps. I do enjoy it, though. Makes me feel part of the crowd."

Thelma recalled how the other couples had shifted to make space for them on the dance floor, watching the prince out of the corners of their eyes.

"That's a lovely thought," she said.

They turned onto Arlington Street. The prince looked at the Ritz, tilting his head toward the marquee lights. "My favorite. Perhaps we could go sometime?" he said, and Thelma warmed at the prospect of another evening out.

Arlington Place was dark. No doubt, all of Duke's party guests had long since gone home. How different a night she would have had if she'd stayed.

"Thank you again for a lovely evening," she said.

Folding over at the waist, the prince set his lips against the back of her hand.

"Please let me call on you again."

"I would be honored," Thelma replied. She curtsied, the formality of the movement awkward after their casual evening.

"I'll likely be busy until after my birthday," said the prince, "but expect to hear from me soon." He waved and began to walk down the street.

She walked up the stairs but paused before entering, resting a hand on the doorframe as she looked back.

The prince had already begun to make his way down Arlington Street, his hands tucked once more in his trouser pockets, the cut of his tuxedo jacket giving him the illusion of bulk he didn't truly have. His chauffeur walked several paces behind him, holding an umbrella in case of a late-evening downpour; his car followed, its headlights extinguished.

The prince reached Bennet Street, then changed course for the Ritz Hotel, disappearing through the side-door entrance.

Williams was waiting inside. He collected Thelma's shawl, folding it over his arm. The rest of the house had already gone to bed but the front hallway was still lit, dimmed sconces sending dark shadows across the marble floor.

"How was dinner?" Thelma asked.

"Very successful, my lady. Lady Averill was well received," said Williams.

"And Duke?" asked Thelma, removing her silk gloves.

"He's gone out, my lady," said Williams.

"Well," she replied, "I'm glad to hear he had a pleasant evening. Good night, Williams."

"Good night, my lady."

EIGHTEEN

THELMA DESCENDED THE NEXT MORNING AND found Duke in the breakfast room, his face hidden behind a newspaper. Emblazoned on the front page was a large photograph of the prince, looking off into the distance.

"Good morning," said Duke. He set down the paper and tapped the photograph. "His birthday is next week." He sounded amused. "I hope you don't forget."

"Good morning," said Thelma. Williams poured her a cup of tea and set down a bowl of fruit. "How was your night?"

"Very decent," said Duke. He lifted the newspaper once more and twitched it straight as he reached for an apple. "Betty Lawson-Johnston was asking about you. Very excited when she heard your news. How was dinner?"

"Lovely," said Thelma.

The newspaper twitched again, and Thelma heard the blind sound of Duke biting into the apple. "Who was there? Any of our lot?"

"It was a rather small guest list."

"Oh? How small?"

There was a long, tense silence. "Just me," she said.

Duke lowered the newspaper. "Oh. Will you be seeing him again?"

Thelma hesitated. "I believe so."

"I see." Duke took a piece of toast from the rack and scraped butter across it. "Well, I'm pleased for you. From what I hear he's a good sort."

Thelma looked up. "You're pleased?" she said.

"Of course. Look, my dear, I've been thinking, and I've decided that if I'm going to be stepping out on my own it's only fair that you do as well. Beats ghosting about Burrough Court." He finished his toast and reached for a napkin, knocking crumbs onto the tablecloth. "Besides—not a terrible thing, making friends with the Prince of Wales."

Thelma raised her eyebrow. Whatever she'd expected from Duke, it hadn't been this. "We met once for dinner. I hardly think that makes us friends," she said.

"No, but he'll see you again. The prince and I agree on one thing—you're too beautiful to ignore."

"You're not upset that he wants to see me again?"

"Not at all," he replied.

"And you aren't afraid he might fall in love with me?" she said, only half joking.

Duke smirked. "You don't know the Prince of Wales as well as I do. He's very much in love with Freda Dudley Ward. Touchingly devoted to her—circles back like a homing pigeon." He stood and circled the table. "So, you see, I know you're quite safe in his hands. Shall we invite him to the country?" He set a hand on Thelma's shoulder and kissed the top of her head. "Must dash, business to attend to. Dinner at Café de Paris? G will be there. I'm told they've changed the lineup in their cabaret."

Thelma set out from the town house later that morning to meet Lady Sarah for luncheon, the motorcar's wipers beating furiously against the rain.

She hadn't expected Duke's reaction to her dinner with the prince—nor the revelations he'd seen fit to share. Though she knew that Duke's flippancy was hiding more than a little hurt, she knew that there was some truth in what he'd said.

The prince never held on to women for long. His penchant for romantic conquests was common knowledge among Thelma's set. He paid particular attention to married women—that much was common knowledge as well. Perhaps he thought they would expect less from him.

All right, she told herself. If she was nothing more than a temporary interest to the prince, was that so bad? As Duke said, friendship with the Prince of Wales could only bring advantages. And Duke had given his blessing, more or less.

In terms of the drawbacks, Thelma could only see one true danger: that she might develop feelings for him. The prince was, undoubtedly, attractive. And he was the Prince of Wales—that was an overwhelming consideration, and one she couldn't ignore.

The motorcar pulled up in front of Selfridges and a doorman with a wide umbrella came out to open her door. She followed him toward the store's entrance, glancing with amusement at the window display.

It showed a pastoral picnic: an afternoon at Ascot, perhaps, or a day in the Lake District. Several mannequins, dressed in white, were arranged in the window, faceless men in top hats, blank women in lace gowns, holding parasols or toy animals. Some were standing; some sat on red-and-white checkerboard table-cloths. Standing on a small easel amid the picnic was a painted portrait of the Prince of Wales in an oval gilt frame.

The bottom third of the window was dominated by a hand-painted sign.

Selfridge & Co.
Congratulates His Royal Highness On His 35th Birthday.

Thelma scrutinized the portrait of the prince. It was a good likeness, though his hair was thicker than the portrait made it out to be. She touched the back of her hand, where his lips had lingered at the end of the night. His eyes, too, were a different shade of blue. The color the artist used was a touch too artificial.

Thelma walked inside.

She went past the displays of perfume and makeup, rows of red lipstick lined under glass countertops, powder puffs balanced against open jars of rouge. She looked over the latest offerings as she passed: new hats, with fuller brims than last season. Ostrich feathers, for court presentations. Thelma had been presented last year—a triumph for Duke, as divorcées were rarely received. Silk shawls, hand-painted in the Orient.

She drifted into the men's section, walking past colorful displays of bow ties and cravats, gleaming loafers and ivory-topped canes. A glass case of cuff links caught her eye and she studied them, gold and silver, winking like coins beneath the glass.

An elegant man behind the counter rested his hand on the case. "Good afternoon, madam. Can I help you?"

Thelma pointed at a set of gold cuff links depicting a horse and rider, frozen in the act of jumping a hedgerow. "I'll take those, please," she said, and arranged for them to be delivered to York House.

NINETEEN

THELMA COULD HEAR THE STRAINS OF THE
evening's entertainment from the cloakroom at Ciro's, a high
feminine falsetto accompanied by the house orchestra, the combination of woodwinds and strings providing the musical depth
that, Thelma thought, the singer lacked. Still, it was an evening
out, and despite Thelma's reservations about the singer, Ciro's
boasted the best cabaret in London.

She draped her fox fur over one shoulder. Her dress, a sequined, backless shift, was too light to go without the added
weight of the fur, although she knew she would regret wearing it the moment she entered the overcrowded restaurant. She
pulled a compact out of her handbag and powdered her nose
before returning to the front room where Duke was waiting.

"I was beginning to think you might have gotten lost between
the coats," he said, taking her arm as they walked toward the
sound of the orchestra. Unlike the Embassy Club, Ciro's was
light and airy, decorated in greens and golds, immense white
pillars supporting a second-story gallery. Onstage, the house or-

chestra played a lively waltz, accompanying a trio of sequined dancers brandishing fans made of peacock feathers.

The maître d' led them to a small table near the orchestra, a bottle of wine already chilling in an ice bucket. "With our compliments, Lord Furness," he said.

"Very good," said Duke, reaching for the bottle. He handed a glass to Thelma, and raised his own in a toast before shifting his chair to watch the cabaret.

They had worked their way through half the bottle before a break was called and couples flooded the dance floor. Duke and Thelma stood, Thelma draping the fox fur over the back of her chair as she followed Duke to dance.

The floor was full to the point of bursting, couples turning in tight circles as the band played a slow, easy rendition of "Indian Summer." Thelma and Duke were content to stay near the edge, their movements an ebb and flow that responded to the footsteps of the couples surrounding them. Duke wrapped a hand around Thelma's waist, the claustrophobic atmosphere of the dance floor a fitting excuse for intimacy.

"It's been far too long since we've spent time together," said Duke. "Properly, I mean—no complications."

"It's nice," said Thelma. "Thank you."

Duke smiled. "For what? Taking my wife out on the town?" He lifted his arm, inviting Thelma to twirl under; she laughed as he pulled her close again, his movement looser, more carefree, as he led her in a fox-trot.

In the midst of the song, Thelma felt a warm hand on the back of her shoulder.

"May I?"

Thelma turned. The Prince of Wales standing behind her, the maître d' hovering at the edge of the dance floor.

Thelma sank into a curtsy and Duke bowed at the neck.

"Lord and Lady Furness. How wonderful to see you both."

"Your Highness," said Thelma, concealing her happiness behind a gentle smile. "We weren't expecting you for another hour."

The prince offered his arm to Thelma and they drifted back to the table. "I was able to slip away after cigars. The official bits were all said and done with." The maître d' jogged forward to pull out Thelma's chair as the prince sat down. "Three gins," said the prince, folding one leg over the other, "and a bottle of that cabernet franc you served me last time, it was a corker."

Duke followed, picking up his half-finished glass of wine. "It's an honor to have you join us, sir," he said.

The prince smiled. "Oh, the honor is entirely mine."

Thelma had expected Duke to drift away once the prince arrived—to melt into the crowd, handing Thelma over without a proper conversation, but he settled in to his chair and turned his attention to the cabaret dancers who had resumed the floor, a cigarette dangling loosely between his fingers.

The prince leaned closer to Thelma. "It's wonderful to see you," he said in a low voice. "You aren't angry with me? You must have been waiting ages."

"Not at all," said Thelma. "We've been dancing."

The prince winked and turned his attention to Duke. "Busy season in the shipyards, Furness?"

Duke looked over. "It's always busy in a shipyard, sir. We recently received a new contract to build a set of freighters, which should keep the workers happy for a few more months."

"What more can one ask for? It's always a pleasure to speak to a man of industry who's generating jobs for the common Englishman." Under cover of the tablecloth, the prince shifted, his leg brushing against Thelma's. "I understand there's something of a rivalry between shipbuilders on the Clyde and Newcastle—would you say there's a substantial expertise in one region over the other?"

Duke shrugged, tapping his cigarette against an ashtray. "Depends on the day—depends on the contract," he said. "My ship-

yard is in Hartlepool, so I'm partial to English talent as a matter
of principle."

Thelma knew she ought to feel stung by Duke's blasé attitude,
but she was relieved. Had she been with Junior, he would have
made a scene, but Duke simply smiled. He finished his drink
and, quite ostentatiously, yawned.

The prince reached for the bottle of wine. "One for the road,
Furness?"

Duke shook his head. "Very kind, but I ought to be moving on," he said. He looked at Thelma. "Terribly rude to make
you leave as well, my darling. Don't feel you need to come on
my account."

Under the table, the prince set his hand on Thelma's knee.
"I'm quite happy staying," she replied. "I'm sure His Highness
will see me home."

"I would consider it a privilege," said the prince.

Duke looked from Thelma to the prince and back. His expression changed; whether it connoted pleasure or sadness, Thelma
couldn't tell.

"Well," he said. "That's settled. Have a lovely evening."

The prince smiled as Duke melted into the crowd. "Good
sport," he said. "Shall we have a dance?"

The sun was rising over Mayfair when the prince called an
end to the night. He wrapped Thelma's fox fur around her shoulders as they left the club, offering her a lit cigarette.

"Jolly good band," he said. The prince's gleaming Daimler, its
heavy black bonnet muted to a soft gray in the predawn, pulled
to the curb, and Thelma stepped in, the prince's hand on the
small of her back.

"Nice to sit down," she said as the prince slid next to her.
"Have you got a busy day tomorrow?"

"Not in the morning, thankfully," he said, running a hand
through his hair, "but I've a few engagements in the afternoon.

And I've got to find time to speak to Sibyl Colefax at some point—she's helping me renovate my country estate."

"Is she? That's exciting," said Thelma.

The prince chuckled. "Perhaps if you've an aptitude for that sort of thing. I'm useless, I'm afraid—one wallpaper looks much the same as another to me." He stretched an arm along the top of the seat and Thelma nestled against his side.

"It can be fun," she said, resting her head against the lapel of his overcoat. She threaded her fingers through his, closing her eyes. "I enjoyed decorating Tony's nursery—seeing how it all comes together in the end."

"Perhaps you could help me," he replied. "It's not going to be anything fancy, mind. A place to bring friends."

"I would be honored," said Thelma. "I'll be in Cannes next month with my sister but otherwise—"

"Not a problem. I won't be able to get much done for quite some time regardless. When you return, I could take you there to see it yourself. It's an old pile, really, no indoor plumbing, no swimming pool. I may have bitten off more than I can chew."

Thelma pictured herself wandering through empty rooms with him, thrilled he was picturing life with her so far in advance. "If I can help at all, sir, I'd be delighted to," she said.

The car pulled up in front of Thelma's town house and the prince's chauffeur stepped out, leaving the engine idling while he turned to face the road. He lit a cigarette.

The prince clucked. "I think we can do away with the formalities, don't you, Thelma? 'Sir' and all that. Terribly stuffy."

Thelma smiled. "Oh? So, I'm to call you Edward?"

The prince brushed a lock of hair away from Thelma's face. "I go by David."

"David," said Thelma. It sounded solid: a workaday name that drew back the curtains on who he really was. "It suits you."

He looked at her, his expression earnest. "I hope you know, Thelma, how much I enjoy spending time with you. Would it be too forward if I asked to see you again tomorrow?" Before she could answer he kissed her softly, hesitantly, as though worried she would push him away, but she didn't.

When he looked up at her expectantly, she pulled her hand from his and reached for the handle of the car door. She stepped out, looking over her shoulder, smiling as she held his gaze, taking a petty sort of pleasure in keeping the Prince of Wales waiting for her answer.

TWENTY

August 1929
Cannes, France

THE SUNLIGHT IN CANNES SHONE BRIGHTER than it ever seemed to do in London, casting glittering light across the thousand blues of the Mediterranean and lending Thelma's pale arms a brief golden glow. The Croisette, a meandering promenade dividing the city from the beach, pulsed with movement: musicians played on street corners, vying for the attention of diners eating on patios along the sidewalk, the scent of grilled fish stronger than the petrol fumes from automobiles carrying people to and from the waterfront. Beyond the beach, small fishing boats darted between gleaming white yachts anchored in the harbor, matchstick men and women just visible on the decks. The houses, too, were prettier—as were the women, their flowing, patterned slacks giving them a languid glamour that reflected the stunning backdrop of the French Rivera.

"They're called pajamas, darling—aren't they a scream?" said Gloria, modeling a set of the wide-legged trousers in Thelma's bedroom at the Mountbattens' villa. She swept a hand along the top of her thigh, upsetting the tropical flowers painted on the silk. "So comfortable—it's as if you're walking around naked. Everyone here wears them."

Though Thelma had just arrived, Gloria had been living with George and Nada Mountbatten for two weeks in a spectacular flagstone villa with ten bedrooms and long, flowing curtains that breathed in and out with the breeze. Thelma's room overlooked a large backyard patio with steps that curved down to a rectangular swimming pool, beside which a five-piece band was setting up for the evening.

"They're very elegant," said Thelma, as Gloria sat on the bed and lit a cigarette. "They suit you."

"They'll suit you just as well. I bought six pairs—the Surrogates will be furious at the cost, but there you are. I was tempted by a set similar to these in greens…they'd look divine on you," said Gloria, sitting up and curling her legs beneath her. "And the best part is—you can wear them to bed. Truly! Nada and I—"

"Nada and I what?" The bedroom door opened and Nadejda Mountbatten, Lady Milford Haven, walked into the room, wheeling a trolley laden with bottles and glasses. "Don't go telling all our secrets, Gloria—life's no fun without a bit of mystery." She turned to Thelma and enveloped her in a hug, kissing her on both cheeks. "Welcome to Cannes."

Nada pulled back, a smile playing on her delicate features. Though she was Russian by birth, Nada was closely related to the British Royal Family, and was a prominent fixture in both court life and high society as a result. She was extraordinarily pretty, fine-boned and small, with arching eyebrows and full lips. She wore her hair loose, thick copper curls framing her round face.

"We get into rather a lot of trouble, your sister and me. It's been so exciting having a girlfriend about—I expect we'll have twice as much fun now that you're here." She had a husky, heavy voice entirely at odds with her appearance, but somehow the contrast suited her. She returned to the trolley and picked up a cut-glass decanter. "I thought we might begin early, seeing as it's a special occasion."

"What are we celebrating?" asked Thelma, fixing an earring in place.

Nada emptied the decanter into a cocktail shaker. "Your arrival. Gloria's spoken of nothing else for days. We're throwing a little party after dinner, I hope you don't mind."

"Of course not," said Thelma. She glanced at Nada's outfit—another set of silk pajamas. "But I worry I might be overdressed."

Gloria and Nada laughed in unison—one high, one low. "Oh, don't worry," she said, pouring the contents of the shaker into three glasses. She handed one to Thelma and the antiseptic tang of vodka hit her nose. "I'll find you something in my wardrobe. Gloria and I wear the same size. Now—" she settled on the bed next to Gloria, draping an arm around her "—a toast." She lifted her martini and tipped it back, finishing it in one. Gloria followed suit and Thelma took a sip, coughing slightly as the drink singed her throat.

"Welcome to Cannes," said Nada, rising from the bed. "I'll go see what I've got in my closet."

Thelma looked at Gloria, who pulled herself upright as Nada left. "She's something, isn't she?" she said, shifting nearer to the trolley. She knelt on the bed and began to mix a second set of drinks, ripping the foil from a fresh bottle of spirit. Thelma watched her, amused, and reached for a package of cigarettes.

"Is she always like that? I worry I won't be able to keep up."

Gloria smiled. "Nada's such fun—you'll love her," she said. "She's been an absolute angel to me, particularly since Friedel..." She drifted off, the smile fading from her face.

A few weeks after Gloria's last visit to Burrough Court, her engagement to Prince Friedel had fallen disastrously—spectacularly—apart.

After saying goodbye to Thelma, Gloria had returned to France, her daughter in tow, to find Mamma in the living room of their Paris town house, pacing and throwing pillows, accusing Gloria of conspiring to steal Little Gloria's inheritance.

"She was deranged," Gloria said, telephoning Thelma the day after the incident. "There's no other word for it. I haven't a clue where she came up with this—this fabrication, but we all know it's lunacy. I spoke to Friedel and he says I shouldn't let her upset me. Reggie's mother has given her blessing to our marriage, and the Surrogates have consented to allow Little Gloria to move to Germany. We'll be fine."

Several weeks later Thelma received another devastating telephone call: Mamma had repeated her accusations against Friedel to Mrs. Vanderbilt, who immediately withdrew her support for the marriage and notified Little Gloria's Surrogates of Mamma's concerns. Gloria had sailed to America to deal with the crisis in person, certain that she would be able to make Mrs. Vanderbilt see sense; however, when she next spoke to Thelma, her voice was dull.

"They agree that Little Gloria isn't in danger," she said, "but they've raised questions about how I'm using the income from Little Gloria's inheritance. Apparently, I'm spending too much on myself, and they're worried I'll use Little Gloria's money to finance my marriage to Friedel. They've given me an ultimatum. If I marry Friedel, I lose all rights to spend the interest from the inheritance." She paused. "That's all the money I have in the world. That's all I have to provide for my daughter."

"Can't Friedel support you?" asked Thelma.

"He can't afford the expense. He lost quite a lot during the war... He can't support us without some help, at least, from the interest." Gloria exhaled, tinny and resigned. "If I marry Friedel, I can't afford to keep Little Gloria. If I refuse to give up the money, I lose the man I love."

"What would happen if you married him regardless?"

"The Surrogates would take Little Gloria to live with her Vanderbilt relatives. It's what they wanted all along, really. They never approved of me raising Gloria in Europe. But how would it look if I foisted Gloria off on her relatives?"

"What about Mrs. Vanderbilt? Surely you can appeal—"

"I tried," said Gloria. "She won't consent to the marriage, not if there's any question about Little Gloria's safety—no matter how unfounded those questions are. If I marry Friedel, I doubt I'd be allowed to even see her."

Gloria had acceded to the Surrogates' wishes, breaking off the engagement with an announcement shamefully buried in the society pages.

Gloria looked up, recalling Thelma's attention to the room. "Nada was a rock throughout the whole mess. An absolute rock." She poured Thelma a martini and set it down on the vanity, then returned to the bed.

"How is Friedel?" asked Thelma.

Gloria shrugged. "Doing well, I think. We write."

Nada reentered the room, carrying a set of tangerine trousers and a silk blouse. "They'll look perfect. Gloria's worn them more times than I can count," she said. She sat down, lifting Gloria's cocktail out of her hand to take a sip. "Now…a little birdie tells me you've been making friends with my cousin David. You wicked girl. Tell me everything."

When the party started shortly after dinner, men and women flooded into the villa in languid beachwear—silk caftans and linen suits, anything to combat the relentless coastal heat. Thelma, dressed in Nada's pajamas, was thankful for her hostess's generosity: dotted here and there was the odd dark suit, the occasional evening dress, but those wearing them looked stiff and out of place amid the casual elegance of Nada and George's set.

Thelma recognized some familiar faces—a few friends of Duke's, several acquaintances she'd met in passing at the Embassy Club—but for the most part she was content to watch Gloria and Nada, who were, jointly, the undisputed life of the party.

Together they mixed drinks, passing bottles and shakers with familiar ease; they flirted with everyone, including Thelma, and Nada's husband, George Mountbatten—however George, pre-occupied as he was with a young artist in a paisley cravat, didn't pay much attention to their advances. When the party began to slacken, Nada pulled Gloria into the garden to dance the Black Bottom on the edge of the swimming pool, ending their performance by jumping, fully clothed, into the water.

Thelma watched Chips Channon and Cholly Knickerbocker fish Gloria out of the swimming pool. Floating on her back, Nada kicked into the center of the pool, demanding that the water be swapped out for champagne.

"They're quite the pair, aren't they?"

Thelma turned to find George Mountbatten, Marquess of Milford Haven, holding two cocktails.

Thelma smiled. "They certainly are," she said.

George offered her one of the drinks. "Is it odd?" he asked.

Thelma understood what he meant. For the past several years, Thelma and Gloria had been separated more often than they were together; and while they did their best to keep in touch, Thelma worried that she and her sister were growing apart. They had always been a pair—two sides of the same coin—but now Gloria had found a new half. While Thelma had struggled with this same question of intimacy when Gloria had first married Reggie, it was different knowing that Gloria was confiding in another woman. Could their lives become too separate to pair again?

Chips wrapped a blanket around Gloria as she attempted to coax Nada out of the pool. "I'm pleased she's found such good friends," said Thelma. "She's told me how much you and Nada mean to her."

"We get on, Gloria and me," said George, "but it's she and Nada who are thick as thieves. Some nights they get to talking and I can't get a word in edgewise." Behind him, Gloria

discarded her blanket and, spurred on by cheers from the assembled onlookers, dove back into the swimming pool to drag
Nada to shore. "Of course, those nights I'm obliged to go find
more entertaining company."

Thelma arched her eyebrows. "Indeed?" she said.

George laughed and glanced back at the artist. He set down
his empty glass and winked. "Enjoy the party."

Chips and Cholly had finally succeeded in pulling Nada from
the pool. She wrapped herself in a towel and linked arms with
Gloria; together they walked into the villa, leaving a dark trail
of matching footprints on the flagstones.

Thelma smiled. Despite her ambivalence, it was good to see
Gloria laugh.

Someone by the pool shouted: several partygoers—women,
mainly, no doubt hoping to bask in Nada's reflected glory—
had jumped into the swimming pool, shrieking with laughter
and attempting to shield their hair from errant splashes as their
beaux prowled the patio, catching unsuspecting victims and tossing them in the water. Thelma, not keen to ruin Nada's outfit,
turned to go back inside.

"Whoops!" A young man, his eyes rather bloodshot, bumped
into Thelma as she came through the doors, knocking her arm
and sending her cocktail cascading down the front of her shirt.

"Oh, bugger—terribly sorry," mumbled the young man as a
nearby footman came forward with a napkin. "So clumsy, can't
believe—"

"It's all right," said Thelma, dabbing at her front with the napkin. She climbed the stairs, the young man still making apolo-
gies behind her. Perhaps Nada would have a clean blouse handy.

Thelma knocked on the door to Nada's bedroom and heard
a scuffle of movement from within before Nada called out for
her to enter.

Nada's bedroom was larger than Thelma's, the four-poster bed
covered by pink-and-gold pillows. A Chinese dressing screen

dominated one corner of the room and a vanity, its top littered with tubes of makeup, trinket boxes and jewelry, dominated another.

Nada was slouching over the vanity mirror, half-dressed. She had changed into a new set of silk trousers, but her bare stomach folded in small rolls beneath her brassiere.

"Thelma," she said, straightening up. Gloria walked out from behind the dressing screen, toweling her hair; like Nada, she was half-dressed, her thin arms covered by a loose-fitting dressing gown. She smiled, her cheeks flushed, and dropped the towel on the bed.

"What happened?" said Nada.

"Someone spilled a drink," said Thelma.

"So they did. Gloria, there's a caftan somewhere in there. How are you enjoying the party?" asked Nada, opening a tub of rouge as Gloria began to sort through the wardrobe. The window was open; noise from the party floated into the room, shouts and laughter and music.

"It's wonderful," said Thelma.

Nada lit a cigarette. "Good," she said. "We have an awfully nice time here. One sometimes forgets London entirely." She tapped the lid of a small enameled box on the vanity. "Although, if you are finding the night a bit dull, I've got a little something to perk things up."

Gloria pulled a mauve dress out of the wardrobe, the fabric so light that it floated as the dress settled back on the hanger. "This one?" she asked.

"That's it," said Nada. "Just leave the blouse on my bed, Thelma, my maid will see to it."

Thelma took the hanger and ducked behind the dressing screen.

"Did you see Cholly?" asked Gloria.

Thelma slipped out of the blouse and draped it over the top

of the screen. "I did," she said. "He seems to be in good form—over for the season."

"He says society dies in New York this time of year. Nothing to write about for his column," said Gloria.

"Not much to write about," Thelma agreed, removing the silk trousers and folding them over a chair. She pulled on the dress, adjusting the neckline as she walked out from behind the screen. "Did you hear what he said about Millicent Hearst? Apparently, she—"

She stopped in her tracks. Nada's enameled box was open, revealing a pillow of fine white powder; Thelma looked at Gloria, whose hand was raised to her face, a line of powder balanced on the bridge of her thumb.

She inhaled delicately.

"Yes? What about Mrs. Hearst?" she asked, dabbing her nose.

Thelma missed a beat. "You know—I can't recall," she said. Nada held the box out to Thelma, smiling politely.

"No—thank you," said Thelma. "I'll see you back downstairs."

She wasn't sure why it shocked her so much, thought Thelma as she left the bedroom. She had used cocaine before, but not since marrying Duke—not since long before Reggie died. She had never seen Gloria bother with that sort of thing before—but perhaps she had. If anyone deserved something to help them unwind, surely it was Gloria.

No, it wasn't the cocaine that had troubled Thelma. It was that Gloria had been sitting on Nada's lap when she'd taken it.

TWENTY-ONE

THE NEXT AFTERNOON, NADA AND GEORGE WENT to the casino while Thelma and Gloria commandeered a set of lounge chairs on the back patio. Thelma had only just gotten warm when she was called back indoors to take a telephone call from David.

"You're enjoying yourself?" he said. "It's been so very dull here, hardly anyone to talk to. How do you like Nada and George?"

Thelma hesitated. Gloria hadn't said a word about last night and Thelma didn't feel right asking—not when the answer could open a box that was better left closed. Perhaps Thelma had misunderstood: it might have been the result of overindulgence, or maybe it was simply their rapport. Maybe Nada was just that affectionate with all her girlfriends.

"They're great fun," said Thelma. "And so generous. They threw quite the party last night."

David laughed. "I can imagine. Thelma, darling, I must

dash—tea with Bertie and Elizabeth in an hour. I can't wait for you to meet them, they're jolly good fun."

Thelma rang off and walked to the patio where Gloria, reclining on a lounge chair next to a tea table, rubbed coconut oil into her arms. "Chanel says a tan is the index of chic," she declared, her face half-obscured by a pair of sunglasses. Like Thelma, she wore a knit bathing suit, cut low over her thighs.

She held out the coconut oil as Thelma settled into a second lounger. "I can't imagine you get many chances to tan in London, so best to take advantage while you can. Who called?"

"The prince," said Thelma.

"Really? He's keen, isn't he?"

"Maybe a little," said Thelma, rubbing oil into her legs.

"I can't believe it. An affair with the Prince of Wales! How exciting."

"It's hardly an affair," said Thelma, though she enjoyed hearing Gloria say it. "Nothing's happened yet, we simply—"

"Go out dancing. Almost every night, from what I've heard."

"That's the trouble—you've *heard*," said Thelma. "That's one of the reasons it hasn't gone beyond dancing. London's far too small for anything exciting to happen."

"Do you want it to?" asked Gloria.

Thelma paused. "You know, you're the first person to ask me that."

"Could you go away with him? A country house party?"

"His country house is undergoing renovations, and I couldn't possibly bring him to Burrough Court without Duke," said Thelma. "My husband may be tolerant, but I doubt even he would be able to stand that."

Gloria removed her sunglasses, tapping them against the side of her mouth. "Where did you say his country house is?" she asked.

"Windsor Great Park," replied Thelma.

Gloria nodded. "I've been thinking about where I'll go after

Cannes," she said slowly. "I'd like to be in England, I think, closer to Nada... Little Gloria's doctors are constantly going on about her health. Perhaps they would sanction a few months in the countryside. I could rent a house."

"And if David and I were invited for a weekend..."

"Entirely innocent," finished Gloria. She rolled onto her side and stretched across the lounge chair, looking pleased at the idea. "Think about it. It would be nice to see more of you this autumn. Nada and George have a beautiful home in Berkshire."

The idea had merit. It would allow Thelma to see David on more intimate terms, without the potential for scandal. And the prospect of spending more time with him: two whole, uninterrupted days...

Thelma sat up.

"Oh dear," she said. "We'll have to find a way of keeping Mamma's mouth shut."

"We lock her in the nursery at Burrough Court and throw away the key," said Gloria as she reached over to share Thelma's cigarette. "She's coming over, by the way. Going to bring Little Gloria for a visit." She inhaled. "She's such a doll. Brown as a berry with all this sunshine, and so sweet. She'll be delighted to see you."

"And I her," said Thelma. "It's a shame I couldn't bring Tony along for her to play with."

Gloria crooked a finger round the arm of her sunglasses and slid them down her nose. "You think Mamma lets her play with other children?"

Thelma laughed as a footman opened the patio door and Mamma Morgan came out.

"Is that woman here?" she asked, looking out from beneath the wide brim of her hat. Thelma stood and gave her mother a kiss on the cheek, pulling back with the salty residue of sweat on her lips. No wonder she was in a mood, thought Thelma, looking at the heavy wool of Mamma's dress. She must be sweltering.

Gloria stretched farther, twisting her torso with the lithe movement of a cat. "*Nada* is at the casino," she said. "And I'd remind you that this is her house, and her hospitality."

Mamma exhaled through her nose. "So it is," she said. She looked at Thelma. "*Caro*. It's good to see you." She settled onto a chair next to Gloria, fanning herself. "Your daughter had to use the facilities after our walk over. I worry about her kidneys, I really do."

"Her kidneys are fine, Mother," said Gloria. "I wish you wouldn't coddle her."

"She deserves coddling," said Mamma. She turned to Thelma as the door opened once more. "You've not visited in weeks."

Little Gloria had grown in the three months since Thelma had last seen her, her arms and legs skinny after a growth spurt. She had Gloria's full lips and Reggie's dark eyes, her round face flushed in the summer sun. She stood uncertainly in the doorway, shifting her weight from foot to foot.

Beside her, Nurse Kieslich looked from Thelma to Gloria and back again, disapproving, no doubt, of the sight of them in bathing suits. Thelma was surprised that Gloria hadn't mentioned Little Gloria's visit earlier—she would have changed.

Gloria turned onto her side, peering over the lounger.

"*Querido*. Go say hello to your mother and auntie," said Mamma, beckoning to Little Gloria.

Little Gloria shuffled closer to Nurse Kieslich and reached for her hand. She looked uncertainly from Gloria to Thelma.

Kieslich gently prized Little Gloria's fingers from her own. "Go say how-do-you-do," she said.

Little Gloria walked forward, her white shoes scuffing across the flagstones. She paused, looking at Gloria and Thelma in turn. With a sinking feeling, Thelma realized that the child couldn't tell them apart.

She got out of her chair and crouched down. "Good gracious—that can't possibly be my niece," she said.

The child's face cleared; she walked to Thelma and curtsied. "How do you do, Auntie," she said.

"Very well," said Thelma. "Look at you. You can't possibly be four years old—you're far too big!"

"I'm not four," she said, a shy smile on her face. "I'm nearly six."

"Nearly six. Well, you're almost a lady," said Thelma. "Now go say hello to Mother."

Gloria swept her daughter into a hug, leaving a sheen of coconut oil on the child's arms. "Aren't you lovely," she said. "How was the beach? Did you enjoy the present Lady Milford Haven sent you?" Gloria patted the end of her lounge chair and Little Gloria perched, her feet brushing the ground; she looked at Nurse Kieslich, who nodded once, curtly.

"I've news for you, my darling—we're going to go live in England! What do you think of that?"

Mamma looked up. "When was this decided?"

Gloria gathered Little Gloria into her arms, her voice soft. "We'll live in the country, and have horses like Papa used to. What do you think of that?"

Little Gloria frowned. "Can't we stay here?" she said.

"Oh, no, darling. It's no fun once the summer's over. All our friends will leave. We want to go with them."

"To England? With that woman?" said Mamma. Thelma watched a bead of sweat work its way down her cheek.

"If you must know, Mamma, I think it would be a good thing for Little Gloria's health," said Gloria, stroking her daughter's hair. Little Gloria squirmed but stayed put, her pursed lips giving her an uncanny resemblance to Nurse Kieslich. "You're the one who's constantly telling me how sick she is. Won't the country air do her some good?"

Mamma's frown deepened as she exchanged a glance with Kieslich.

"And we'll see so much more of Auntie Thelma and Cousin

Tony and all of our friends in England. It will be a perfect autumn." She kissed Little Gloria on the top of her head. "A perfect end to the year."

When Thelma returned to London the town house was nearly empty, Williams greeting her in a quiet voice that echoed through the entrance hall. She walked to her dressing room, where a magnificent vase of red roses sat on the table, overpowering the small space with their scent.

She reached for the card set amid the blooms, smiling in anticipation of the prince's blockish handwriting.

Hope you enjoyed your week in Cannes—London wasn't the same without you.
 With great affection,
Duke.

She ran her finger along the edge of the card. Duke hadn't sent her flowers in ages—not since Tony was born, and he was nearly six months old now. Were things going poorly, perhaps, between him and his latest mistress? Was it a gesture born of jealousy?

Or perhaps, Thelma told herself, *it's a genuine gift from a husband to his wife.* She set the card down, staring absently at the roses before walking to her bedroom.

TWENTY-TWO

THE TREES HAD BEGUN TO TURN WHEN GLORIA invited Thelma for her first weekend party in the country. True to her word, Gloria had rented a house in Windsor Great Park: Three Gables, a Tudor-style home with large bedrooms and an unused stable at the back of the estate. When Thelma asked about the horses that Gloria had promised her daughter, Gloria frowned.

"It's the strangest thing—when I brought it up again Little Gloria burst into tears. Kieslich tells me she's terrified of the creatures, but remember how pleased she was at Burrough Court? In any case, I didn't want to press. Mamma can't stand the smell, and truthfully it's not worth the additional expense."

The expense, Thelma knew, was not insignificant. Along with the rent for the Paris town house, which Gloria had kept throughout their stay in Cannes, Three Gables would put Gloria at the upper limit of what she could afford on the income from Little Gloria's inheritance. It was reckless, and Thelma had said so—but Gloria waved off her concerns. "After losing Friedel," she said, "you can be sure I'll spend every last penny available."

When the weekend arrived, Thelma arrived early to help Gloria prepare. She found her in the dining room, flowers scattered across the table as she arranged bouquets. Without preamble, Thelma set down her handbag and removed her gloves, picking up a sprig of sweet pea and severing the end with a pair of garden shears.

"Consuelo and Benny are arriving on the 4:15…with Nada and George, that's all six accounted for," said Gloria, pushing a pile of discarded leaves aside to make room for a bunch of roses tied with twine. She tore the bouquet apart and began placing buds in a vase filled with baby's breath. "Little Gloria is in Berkshire—I thought it best, she won't get in the way. Do you think Consuelo will want to see her? Should I arrange for her to visit?"

Though Benny, Consuelo's husband, was stationed in Oslo, Consuelo had told Thelma that he would soon be transferred to the embassy in London. It would be a respectable promotion for Benny and a thrill for Thelma, to have one sister living in the same city. Along with Nada and George, Consuelo and Benny would serve as the weekend's chaperones—respectable married couples who could vouch for the propriety, real or imagined, of the company as a whole.

"I wouldn't bother," said Thelma. She lifted a finished vase from the dining room table and placed it on the sideboard for the help to move into the sitting room. "Where are we putting the prince?"

"In the second bedroom up the stairs. Yours is next to it—or should they be at opposite ends of the house? I don't know how these things are arranged—"

"Don't fret," said Thelma, amused at Gloria's sudden attack of nerves. "David doesn't stand much on ceremony."

"But I haven't met him yet. What if he's temperamental, you

know, like Mrs. Vanderbilt? What if he's friendly with you but ghastly to newcomers..."

"Really, Gloria—shouldn't I be the one worrying?" said Thelma. She pressed a set of ferns into Gloria's hand to trim, and the ends hit the table like pennies. "It will all be fine."

She was surprised, in fact, at how calm she felt. She knew what the weekend would hold, if she so wished. It hadn't gone far past hand-holding yet, murmured affections and kisses in the backs of cars, but after spending the night together, the tone between them would change, for good or ill. And despite Duke's continued permissiveness, an actual affair risked consequences beyond Thelma's control.

"A weekend with Gloria? How nice," Duke had said over drinks a few nights before Thelma was to leave. "Am I invited or is this strictly a family occasion?"

"Just me this time, I'm afraid," said Thelma, mixing Duke a whiskey and soda. "And a few other guests."

"Oh? Who?"

"Consuelo and Benny—you know them—and Nada and George Mountbatten, they're good friends with Gloria. I stayed with them in Cannes—"

"I know Nada and George," said Duke quietly.

"And the prince," Thelma finished, her voice faltering slightly as she handed Duke his drink.

"Oh?" he replied.

"You don't mind?" she said, brushing condensation from her empty hands.

"No...no, of course not. Why would I?" He tipped back his drink and finished it in two long, rolling swallows, his disapproval as present as an echo in the room. "Must be off. Meeting G," he said, standing.

"At this time? What for?" asked Thelma.

Duke pressed his fingers to his eyelids. "I don't ask your business—please don't inquire about mine," he said. He turned to leave but paused at the door. "Those—those flowers," he said, knocking his hand rhythmically against the doorjamb. "An apology, of sorts. We've gone off the rails, you and me."

An apology. There was something pathetic in the gesture—a sad return to the hearts and flowers of the past.

Thelma had all but admitted to her planned infidelity, while he strove to build a bridge back to her—and yet, she thought, musing on that bizarre exchange, she didn't feel guilty.

Gloria fixed a stray freesia into the last bouquet and transferred it to the sideboard. "Let's see we have all we need by way of cocktails," she said.

They left the dining room, their offcuts strewn across the table for the servants to clear.

David was the first to arrive, pulling up in a two-seat roadster ahead of his luggage and staff. He waved at Thelma and Gloria and opened his car door: two wiry dogs, frantic after being cooped up in the automobile, tumbled out and began running circles, barking at their sudden freedom.

"Your Royal Highness," said Gloria.

David removed his driving goggles and let out a sharp whistle. "Jaggs! Cora!" The terriers ignored him and shot past Thelma's legs. "I do hope you don't mind. They love the countryside."

Gloria smiled. "Not at all, sir," she replied, watching them tear through the flower bed. "Dear little things."

David looked at Thelma, a smile playing on his dusty face. "Hello, you," he said.

Thelma smiled back, pleased—absurdly so—that he'd truly come. "Hello yourself," she replied. "How was your drive?"

"It was perfect. Such a lovely day, it would have been a shame to spend it in a train carriage," he said, pocketing his driving gloves. "I thought I might check up on progress at the Fort tomorrow. I'm told the renovations are coming along nicely—plumbing in every bedroom." Gloria's butler stepped forward and David passed him his overcoat, looking up hopefully at the leaded windows of the Three Gables. Thelma could hear the terriers within, their nails scratching along the wooden floors.

"Not here yet, I'm afraid, sir," said Gloria, "but we've got electric lights and a working telephone."

The other guests arrived shortly after David. Consuelo and Benny, fresh from Oslo, came from the train station in a taxi-cab, their luggage tied to the roof of the motorcar. Nada and George, hoping for a more dramatic entrance, snuck through the servants' quarters to surprise Gloria as she led the others through for cocktails in the drawing room, jumping out from the staircase.

Despite her earlier composure, Thelma was excruciatingly aware of David's presence during dinner: where he sat, how he laughed. How on earth would she keep him entertained over forty-eight long hours?

After their meal, the women left the men to their cigars and went into the drawing room to set up a game of cards. They hadn't made it through the first hand of bridge before George and David came in, followed by Benny, casting a sheepish glance at Consuelo.

"The separation of the sexes after dinner is an antiquated practice," said George, lifting the deck of cards out of Thelma's hands.

Grinning, Nada turned on the gramophone. She chose a record Thelma hadn't heard before and grabbed Gloria's hand, leading her in a dance to a jumpy, offbeat tune as George sank into a nearby couch and lit a cigar.

"Do you know this one?" David asked, coming to stand beside Thelma.

"I don't," she said.

He took her hand. "Brilliant—neither do I. Let's give it a go, shall we?"

They began to dance, mirroring Gloria's and Nada's footsteps with clumsy success. Beside them, Consuelo laughed, resting a hand on Benny's chest.

After several more dances the prince relinquished his hold on Thelma in favor of a few turns around the drawing room with Gloria. Her face flushed, Thelma sat down next to Consuelo, who sent Benny to fix her a drink.

"Something new," called Consuelo. "I'm sick of martinis. And one for Thelma as well."

Benny jammed his cigar between his teeth, cracking his knuckles in mock anticipation of the challenge. Consuelo nudged Thelma as David glanced over his shoulder at her with a smile.

"He's enchanted by you," said Consuelo. "It's charming, really."

"Am I mad?" said Thelma in an undertone. "I keep thinking I must be, to go ahead like this."

Consuelo sighed, leaning back. "You're not mad," she replied. "Not so long as you keep your eyes open." She lowered her voice further. "At the risk of sounding like our mother, I hope you realize what an opportunity this could be. The most powerful man in the world is falling for you. This could open doors for you. For all of us."

"It's not about that," Thelma began, but Consuelo stopped her.

"I know—it's about love," she said. She glanced at Benny, who was making drinks at the cocktail table. "I understand that better than most."

David handed Gloria off to George for the next song. He looked over at Thelma before Nada, trailing a hand up the back of his suit jacket, distracted him.

"You're fond of him. I can see that," Consuelo continued, "but don't lose sight of the complications involved. You can't afford to mistake this for ordinary romance."

"There's hardly a chance of that," said Thelma. "He could never be mistaken for ordinary."

"But he wants to be," said Consuelo. "Don't you see? That—"

she nodded at the prince, who was allowing Nada to lead him in a tango "—is a man who craves normalcy in a world determined to prove he's different from the rest of us. Use that to your advantage."

Nada released David's hands and spun toward the couch, collapsing with a huff of exhaustion. Thelma met David's eyes, her heart thrumming as he walked over with a hopeful, careless but not-quite-carefree smile. She didn't say a word but held out her hand, allowing him to pull her close—closer than they could ever hope to be at the Embassy Club or Ciro's; close enough that she fancied she could feel the layers of his evening dress beneath her fingers: jacket, vest, shirt, undershirt, skin.

"You're in the room next to mine," she whispered, allowing the music to mask the sound of her voice.

She could feel him smile against her cheek. "Am I?" he said. "How nice."

Thelma's bedroom was dimly lit, an electric lamp on the nightstand illuminating the center of the room and casting the corners into darkness. She sat at her dressing table, twisting her hair into a low chignon: wearing nothing but a silk negligee, she was chilly, but refused to spoil the effect with a dressing gown. She ran a hand down her stomach; though she'd long since lost the baby weight, she still worried at what he would think of her. She worried about what she'd think of *herself*, in the morning. She listened for the sound of footsteps down the hall as she dabbed her pulse points with perfume, filling the room with the scent of jasmine.

David slipped into the room without knocking, carrying a bottle of champagne and two glasses. "Thank God," he said, "I was worried I'd chosen the wrong room. Would have been a sorry thing to have ended the night with Benny." He lingered in the doorway and Thelma stood, realizing he was just as nervous as she felt.

"It would have been a nasty shock for Benny, I bet," she said, moving to sit on the end of the bed. "If you'd found George and Nada's room, though, I'm sure they would have told you to climb on in."

He held up the champagne. "I pinched it from the bar," he said, sounding almost apologetic. "Thought we might do with a nightcap."

The champagne was already uncorked, and he poured two glasses before sitting next to Thelma. She shifted toward him and he rested his hand on her leg; somehow, the gesture put her more at ease.

"I like this," he said, rubbing the negligee with his thumb. "So elegant. You look like Marlene Dietrich."

"You look like—Nils Asther," she replied.

He looked genuinely pleased. "Do I really?" he asked, and Thelma laughed.

"No," she said. "You look like the Prince of Wales."

He leaned in. Thelma could smell his cologne—a musky, heavy smell that contrasted with his sharp features. Pulse quickening, she closed her eyes as his lips brushed against her cheek. "I've been told there's a passing resemblance," he murmured, and she lifted her chin to meet his kiss.

He ran his hand up her thigh; she could feel the skin beneath his fingers, electric, as if he were waking her one touch at a time. The silk bunched into waves as he raked the gown higher; her breath caught in her throat as his hand came to rest on bare skin, and he shifted, pulling Thelma beneath him.

She grasped the lapels of his dinner jacket, meeting his even blue gaze as she pulled him closer still. There was something intoxicating in his practiced touch that made her feel as though she was invincible: the simple fact that he was here, and wanted her. He was the subject of a million fantasies, the man women pictured to escape their dull lives—and tonight, he was hers.

He traveled down her neck, her collarbone, her breasts, her

stomach. Sinking into the bedsheets, Thelma moved toward the pillows as he shrugged out of his waistcoat and evening shirt. He was slim yet strong, his arms roped with wiry muscles, his torso taut as a board; his chest slightly caved, as though he hunched over the memory of an old wound. He was as fluid as dancing, his movements an effortless ebb and flow. She recalled the first night they met, marveling at the impossibility of it all. Who could have thought it would have ended up here?

TWENTY-THREE

THE NEXT DAY, THELMA AND DAVID SET OFF FOR Fort Belvedere, David's half-finished country home, after breakfast.

"It was originally built for the Duke of Cumberland," said David, raising his voice over the sound of the motor as he took bends in the road at top speed. "You know, Bonnie Prince Charlie and all that lot. It had been sitting vacant for years when I found it."

Thelma kept a secure hand on the scarf she'd tied around her hair. She and David had woken at first light, David collecting his collar studs in the early glow before slipping back to his assigned bedroom; last night could have all been a dream, but for her overwhelming happiness. "How long have you been working on it?" she asked.

"Father gave me the place in March. It's been tremendous fun. I'm looking forward to doing a bit of work on the grounds myself once the house is in order."

They turned down a drive marked by moss-covered gates.

"I'll be attacking those soon," David muttered, nodding at the crumbling stone—and the crenellated walls of Fort Belvedere came into view.

Fort Belvedere wasn't pretty: it was all blocks and austerity, too-small windows in sparse frames. Its main feature was a looming six-sided turret, so tall that it threw off the proportion of the rest of the building. A heavy brick wall obscured most of the first floor; newly planted ivy attempted to soften the masculine lines of the facade. The circular driveway was overlarge, paving stones in the middle of the pea-gravel forming a six-sided crest around which David drove and parked.

He pulled the hand brake, then rested his hand atop hers. "What do you think?"

Thelma was touched by his evident joy. "David, it's lovely," she replied.

He opened his door and jogged around to the other side of the motorcar to let Thelma out. "Wait until you see what I've done inside," he said. "The builders tell me I'll be able to move in by the New Year."

He took Thelma's hand and led her through the front entrance. As David had planned their visit there were no workers on-site, but buckets of plaster and drying paintbrushes had been left on canvas cloths lining the courtyard and front hallway. Fresh lines of mortar were visible between the bricks; David opened the door and the smell of dust and fresh-cut wood drifted out.

Thelma tucked her hand into the crook of his arm as they walked down the hallway. "Sibyl is helping me with the interior," he said, "And Freda, of course. And you, if you've a mind to."

Thelma smiled, her chest warming at the thought of helping David with the decorating.

He led her into the dining room, which was sharp with the smell of drying paint. "I had them do a faux-wood finish," he said, leaning close to the wall to examine the handiwork. "I'm told it's the latest thing. Freddie chose the wall sconces, what do you think?"

Thelma glanced at him, but his expression didn't change as he mentioned Freda Dudley Ward a second time. She turned her attention back to the room. It was small: once a table and buffet were brought in it wouldn't have much room for additional pieces.

"It's cozy," she said.

David beamed. "That's entirely by design," he said. "I don't want to conduct official business here. No courtiers, no blasted politics. This is going to be a room for friends."

"Excellent idea," she replied.

"I can't take credit. Freddie dreamed it up."

Thelma nodded carefully, recalling her conversation with Duke about David's beloved former mistress. *He's touchingly devoted,* the walls seemed to whisper. "And the furnishings?" she asked, taking David's arm as he led her through to an octagonal sitting room overlooking the back of the estate. "You must tell me about those."

"Burgundy in the dining room, mustard in the sitting room. Again, I can't take credit."

"Freddie?"

"Freddie," said David, as a numbness settled in the pit of Thelma's stomach. "Come take a look out these windows. Freddie says it's the best view from the ground floor."

David led Thelma through the rest of the Fort, showing off the renovations borne out of his dream of bringing the house into modernity. He showed her the kitchens, which had been outfitted with top-of-the-line cast-iron stoves, and the steam room, which he intended for use after tennis matches on the court he planned to build in the eastern part of the grounds. He dug out the blueprints for the central heating.

"Freddie recommended showers," he said, unrolling the papers across a table in the kitchen. "Plumbing in the bedrooms, now, that was *my* idea, but she thought a steam room—"

"Did she?" said Thelma carefully.

"Yes," David said. "She was most insistent on central heating. Says there's nothing less comfortable than a drafty bedroom."

"Freddie's had so many ideas for this place," Thelma replied, "I wonder you need my help at all."

David looked up. "I beg your pardon?"

She laid a hand over the blueprints. "I think you and Freda have this house entirely in order," she said. "You asked for my help, but given Mrs. Dudley Ward's involvement I don't see how I can be useful."

David's eyes widened. "Oh—you mustn't be jealous, darling," he said. "Is that what this is? Is it jealousy? Oh, dear..."

"David, she's in every room," said Thelma. In the city, David's relationship with Mrs. Dudley Ward was easy enough to put aside—the Fort, though, felt uneasily like a declaration of her prominence.

His face creased into well-worn worry lines as he rolled up the blueprints. "Oh, dear," he repeated. He sank into a nearby chair, the cane seat creaking.

"You must understand," he said. "Freddie and I—we've been through an awful lot together. An awful lot." He sighed, looking down. "And I won't lie to you. Yes, at one point I was in love with her."

Thelma nodded, but held her silence.

"It's difficult to explain. We—we share a bond, Freddie and me. I sometimes think she understands me better than I do myself. She has this knack, you see, for voicing what's already rattling about in my head."

He met Thelma's gaze, his expression strained.

"That's not what you want to hear," he said, "but it's the truth. There's nothing between Freda and me now but friendship. You have nothing to worry about, my darling, nothing at all."

Thelma sat down, not yet convinced. "After last night I thought... And then to see all this... It made me wonder, where does it leave me?"

David knelt and took Thelma's hands, raising one, then the other, to his lips. "It leaves you very high in my affections," he said. "Freddie will always be an important part of my life. And she is very much non-negotiable. But believe me—there's enough room for both of you in my heart."

Thelma sighed, feeling some of her frustration melt away.

"I've something to show you," he said.

He led Thelma upstairs and along a narrow hallway lined with oak wainscoting. They stopped in front of a door; David pushed it open to reveal an unfinished bedroom, the floors scuffed and worn, the four-poster bedframe covered by a dust sheet. The far wall was dominated by a lead-paneled window that over-looked the wild expanse of the Fort's back gardens, and a new wall cordoned off a section of the room—Freddie's en-suite bath, Thelma suspected.

She walked in, resting her hands on the window frame as she looked out at the cracked flagstone path in the garden below.

"This is your room," said David. "I want you to have a free hand—do what you like with it."

Thelma looked around. "Really?"

He smiled. "You must think of the Fort as your own. I want us to spend many happy days here, together."

For a moment, Thelma was speechless: she looked around the room again, taking in the wood trim, the plasterwork on the ceiling.

Her final feelings of bitterness toward Freda Dudley Ward melted away. Thelma was touched by David's gift—but even more so by the look of intense vulnerability on his face, as though he feared that Thelma would reject this grandest of gestures.

She crossed the room and put her arms around him. "It's too much," she said. "Thank you."

"Well, it's entirely selfish, really," said David, running a hand down Thelma's back. "I need a hostess to arrange my little parties. I wouldn't possibly make a good job of it on my own…"

Thelma slapped his arm, taking pleasure in David's happiness—his broad, sincere smile; his hands drumming a beat against her sides. Motes of dust caught in the light spilling in from the window, dancing in the small expanse between their bodies.

"I'll set up a meeting between you and Sibyl to start discussing what you'd like," he said, "but before we leave, I've one more room to show you."

He led Thelma back downstairs, to a room off the main hallway.

"Why the first floor?" Thelma asked, guessing at their destination.

David tapped a knuckle on the door's handle. "You ought to have looked closer at the blueprints. It's closest to the steam room. Given all the gardening I plan to do, it seemed like the sensible thing."

The room was fully furnished, large and lined with white wallpaper. Matching lamps sat on night tables next to a four-poster bed; an immense radio box stood in one corner, its design mirroring the smooth, modern lines of the teak dresser opposite. The room had clearly not been used: it was devoid of the clutter that generally accumulated in such places. The piles of books and the grooming products, the cuff links and collar studs that she would have expected to see were absent, giving the space a temporary polished glow.

"I had them finish this one first," he said, leading Thelma to the window and wrapping his arms around her as they looked out onto the back grounds. It was a similar view to Thelma's room but it looked more complete, somehow, framed by indigo satin curtains—more intimate, seen on the equal footing of the main floor as opposed to the lofty perspective of the second. She pictured what the grounds would look like in the winter, the treetops dusted with snow; how stark the view would be in the fall, when crisp air seeped through the windowpanes. "I wanted the first room to be my own. It's a funny thing. In York House, it feels like you're living with history—a very finicky housemate. It's difficult to make your mark on such a place— you're afraid to change anything at all lest it ruin the effect." He nestled his chin in the hollow between Thelma's neck and shoulder. "I think that's why this old place appeals to me. It's a blank canvas. I can make it entirely my own, exactly as I want it to be. Nothing to preserve—nothing to protect."

Thelma leaned her head against his, thinking about Freda Dudley Ward's influence on the living rooms; about her own bedroom, to be decorated as she liked. If the Fort was to be a reflection of David, what, exactly, did it say about him that the women in his life had such a role in building it?

Thelma returned to Arlington Place late Sunday afternoon, hoping, somewhat shamefully, that Duke would be out of the house—attending a late luncheon, perhaps, or early drinks at the club—but when Williams opened the front door he informed her that Duke was in the sitting room.

"Of course," said Thelma, avoiding Williams's gaze as she removed her hat. She loathed the thought of a confrontation with Duke; she wished she'd lingered at Harrods on her way home. "Let Lord Furness know that I'll be in as soon as I've had a chance to change."

She went upstairs and opened the bedroom door to find Elise sorting through her weekend valise, Thelma's gray negligee folded over her arm.

"Haven't you finished that yet?" said Thelma, and Elise looked up in surprise.

"I'm sorry, my lady—you only just got in, and—"

"I don't want excuses. I need something to wear."

Thelma sat at her vanity and Elise, her hands full of Thelma's effects, looked down at the valise.

"Now, please," snapped Thelma and Elise jumped as if she'd been bitten; she rushed out the door, but not before Thelma saw her hurt expression. Thelma immediately regretted her tone— Elise had been with her since New York.

Thelma unzipped the back of her day dress, letting it fall in a heap to the floor.

Would Duke know—would there be some tell, perhaps, like in a card game, to advertise Thelma's infidelity? She looked down at her wedding ring, the overlarge diamond shining an accusation, and she twisted it around so the stone bit into the flesh of her palm.

She wondered whether she ought to admit to the affair, and hope that Duke's blasé attitude toward his own transgressions would extend to her—but then she recalled the belated roses. Perhaps Duke would have the tact not to ask.

Thelma turned the ring back around as Elise came back in, a fresh dress draped over her arm.

"That's fine, Elise, thank you," said Thelma. She put the dress on and Elise tugged it straight, fussing with the hemline.

"I'll find you the right shoes, my lady, and perhaps you might consider the pearls…"

"Elise—I'm sorry," said Thelma.

Elise met Thelma's gaze in the mirror, bright and guileless.

"Whatever for?" she said.

Duke stood as Thelma entered the sitting room and went to the sideboard to mix a drink. "Back, then, are you? How was the party?"

"Lovely," said Thelma. "Gloria says hello."

"Does she?" said Duke, as he poured her a glass of sherry. He'd turned on the radio; the six o'clock news was playing, the announcer's voice tinny and jarring. "I've been thinking we ought to plan a country party of our own, up at Burrough Court. I was shooting there the other day with G—Tony's well, by the way—and it seemed so empty. Couldn't put a guest list together, could you? Ten or so, maybe, sometime next month?"

"Of course," said Thelma. "I didn't realize you went to Leicestershire. How was it?"

Duke lit a cigarette. "Last-minute plan," he said. Late afternoon light spilled into the room; if they opened the window, Thelma knew they would be able to hear couples walking through Green Park. "Averill was there. Berated me for not coming more often—hasn't seen either of us in a while. Dickie came down from Oxford, his term's started. Said to say hello."

Thelma sipped her drink. "I'm pleased to hear it," she said. "I wrote him last week and he mentioned that his tutor was ill. Has he recovered?"

Duke frowned. "I hadn't thought to ask," he said, knocking ash into a chrome ashtray.

Thelma opened her cigarette case and Duke rummaged in his jacket pocket for his lighter. She leaned forward as Duke struck the flint.

Smoke rose in a thin column between them.

"Did the prince enjoy himself?" asked Duke.

Thelma held her cigarette aloft and looked out the window. "I think so," she said, watching couples walk arm in arm along the park pathways.

"With you?"

Thelma exhaled. She knew she could avoid the question—but a lie by omission was still a lie. "Yes."

Duke stubbed out his cigarette and eased out of his chair. He walked across the room to the radio and turned a knob. The announcer's voice grew louder, crackling sharply across the couch cushions, the books, the paintings, the bottles.

TWENTY-FOUR

October 10, 1934
RMS Empress of Britain

THE FIRST-CLASS LOUNGE WAS A LARGE, OPULENT
space with an illuminated stained-glass ceiling and overstuffed
damask armchairs. A pianist, seated at a glossy Steinway, played
music that muted the voices of the other passengers. Across the
room, Thelma watched a trim woman in a tweed suit lean forward, raising her eyebrows as she whispered something to her
dining companion; a few tables over, a couple faced the window, clasping hands on the tabletop as they watched the water.

She glanced at the empty seat across from her, thinking of
David and Gloria. They did get along, the pair of them—how
many people could say that about the two people they loved
most? Like Reggie, David found it amusing to take Gloria and
Thelma out together, one on each arm. Even at thirty, with
marriage and children behind them, they could still turn heads,
Thelma thought with quiet satisfaction—though recently she'd
noticed a set of fine lines, thin as spider's silk, tracing through
the soft skin under her eyes.

After her rental on Three Gables ended Gloria had hoped

to stay on in London but there had been some complication or other that had sent her back to the States. Thelma pursed her lips, attempting to recall…she had been called back to New York to discuss Little Gloria's education with the Surrogates—of course that was it.

If Thelma had chosen to let Tony muddle along with a piece-meal education, no one would have stopped her from doing so. It was her right as a mother, to choose how to raise her son. Gloria hadn't proposed anything nearly so drastic: she'd planned to enroll Little Gloria in a French boarding school. But the Surrogates, as usual, had had their own ideas.

Gloria had managed to convince them to allow her to remain in Europe for another year, and quietly began to explore the possibility of taking full guardianship over Little Gloria's estate. She was of age, after all, and the Surrogacy had only been intended as a stopgap until Gloria turned twenty-one. If Gloria had managed to secure control over Little Gloria's estate, she would have had full authority over her daughter's life, just the same as any other mother in America. She would never have been subjected to the tyranny by council that had led to this courtroom farce.

The pair of women across from Thelma burst into laughter. They quietened immediately, stifling their smiles as they dabbed their mouths with napkins. The one in the tweed suit scanned the room and met Thelma's eye; her smile broadened further as she turned back to her companion.

Mamma should have let Gloria marry Friedel.

She had destroyed Gloria's chance at happiness—she would have done anything to preserve her own brittle grip on her granddaughter's kingdom, would have driven away any of Gloria's suitors, European or American alike. With Nada, at least, there was no question of marriage, nor of Nada influencing Little Gloria's inheritance. Nor was there much of a question of scandal, in the right circles—half the aristocracy, Thelma knew, carried on extramarital affairs, many of them homosexual, including David's brother George. It was only here, under these circumstances, that the friendship between Gloria and Nada was seen as abhorrent.

Thelma looked out at the sea, iron waves churning endlessly, and wondered whether Nada would come to Gloria's aid. *Come to America and deny it all,* she thought, sending her plea back across the water. *Hold her hand in private but deny it all for Gloria's sake. For your own.*

Thelma left the lounge and walked down the narrow hallway toward her stateroom.

She rounded a corner and bumped into Harry, who slumped back against the wall.

"I'm sorry," said Thelma. The collision had brought on a bout of tremors, and Thelma held his arm as he shuddered into stillness.

Thelma never felt entirely at ease with Harry: they didn't share the same easy camaraderie that Thelma had with Consuelo, nor the intense intimacy she had with Gloria. Throughout her childhood, Harry had been largely absent: away at boarding school, training for a career in the diplomatic services like Papa. Perhaps they might have gotten closer but for the war, which had left Harry with permanent nerve damage. It grated on him, she knew, to be so affected by his injuries. It was the reason he refused to accept weekend invitations.

"I was just going to my rooms," said Thelma.

"Yes, I know—I was looking for you."

"Would you like to come in?"

"Thank you, but no," he said. "I'm meeting Edith for a turn around the deck, but wanted to stop in on my way. I met someone on board with an interest in the case."

"Not a reporter?"

Harry shook his head as Thelma opened the door to her berth. "An attorney," he said. "Nada sent him. He's asked if we'll meet him after dinner."

Thelma's heart lifted. "Really? I knew she was sending some-one but didn't dream he was on the same boat. Did you tell him to meet us here? Best to keep these things private." She smiled. "Did he say whether Nada's coming?"

"He didn't," said Harry. "I really must run, Edith will be waiting. Eight o'clock? I think…" He paused. "I think he might be useful."

Thelma unpinned her hat. The news had given her renewed hope: Gloria wouldn't be fighting alone. She thought of Nada's spirited demeanor and smiled. "If Nada sent him," she said, "he's bound to be."

TWENTY-FIVE

November 1929
York House

THELMA'S MOTORCAR PULLED UP OUTSIDE YORK House, chill rain streaming in heavy curtains from the overhanging arches of the portico. She straightened her hat as Finch, David's butler, emerged in the gloom, his breath clouding in the cold.

She stepped out of the car and ducked under his umbrella. "Good afternoon, Lady Furness," he said.

Thelma had come to York House at David's invitation so many times now that she knew his apartment blindfolded. She needed no assistance from Finch as she walked the familiar route past the palace's formal rooms to its cozy private quarters, toward the sound of the perpetually playing gramophone.

She found David immersed in a book at his desk, the wordless peace of a classical record playing softly in the background. He was dressed in dark bagged trousers and a cable-knit sweater over a collared shirt and cravat. Surrounded by stacks of paper at the desk, he looked like a student at Cambridge aiming for a first.

"Goodness," she said. David looked up, folding down the

edge of his page. "I can see why you telephoned—you must be bored to tears. What are you reading?"

"A biography of Charles Lindbergh. Rather a good read, actually." He stood. "How are you, darling?"

"I'm well. What happened to your appointment?" asked Thelma, and David moved to sit next to her on the couch. "I didn't expect to see you."

"An outbreak of typhoid. I was meant to be opening a new hospital wing," he murmured, his lips brushing against her neck. "Didn't want to risk it. Can't say I'm sorry..." He crept a hand up Thelma's front.

There was a knock at the door and David started, cursing.

"What? *What?* Blast it, man—the bloody nerve, damn it!"

Thelma giggled, lifting a hand to her mouth to hide her amusement. In his fury, the prince looked like a terrier.

"Terribly sorry, sir," said Finch. "But it's Mrs. Dudley Ward on the telephone. You were most clear in your instructions, sir, to put her calls through—"

David's anger melted. He went to the desk, nearly knocking over a side table as he picked up the telephone.

"Freddie?... Yes, it got canceled. Thankfully. You know how much I loathe... What? Yes, I am." He gripped the receiver and glanced at Thelma. "No, as a matter of fact, I'm—yes. Yes, exactly." He listened. "Of course. Jolly good. Yes, I will. Shall we say three o' clock? Good. Righto, see you soon." He hung up and smoothed back his hair.

"That was Freddie," he said, circling back to the couch. He grabbed a gold cigarette case on the coffee table and flipped it open. "She's going to come for tea in an hour." He lit a cigarette, avoiding Thelma's eye. "She's awfully keen to meet you, I hope you don't mind."

"Of course," said Thelma, who was curious herself.

"Good," he said. "I hope you like her. She's—" He stopped, his ear cocked. The record had shifted into a slow, mournful song, a string-and-piano combination, and he shook his head. He pulled the record off, tossing it aside to hit the baseboard with a thud. "She hates this sort of music," he murmured, and bent down to search through a collection of records on the bottommost shelf of a bookcase. "Prefers more modern stuff...so do I, truth be told..."

"David, she's not coming for an hour," said Thelma. "Why change the record now?"

"So I don't forget," he replied, his cigarette clamped between his teeth.

Of course, David would know the sort of music that Freda Dudley Ward enjoyed. Freda, no doubt, also knew the path to David's drawing room blindfolded—and to other rooms besides.

Thelma wrapped her arms around his waist, kissing the back of his neck.

"If Freddie isn't coming for ages," she said, "I think we might find a better way to pass the time."

David stilled. "Oh?" He turned; she trailed her fingers down his shoulders, her hand coming to rest in his. She nodded and he pulled her out of the drawing room, down the hallway and into his bedroom—where, for a short while, Thelma knew she could put Mrs. Freda Dudley Ward out of David's mind entirely.

When they returned to the drawing room the butler had turned the record over and set up the bar, crystal decanters and chrome shakers lined up like chess pieces behind rock glass pawns. David walked to the window, resting a hand on one of the decanters as he stared out, though Thelma wasn't sure what he hoped to see: rain continued to fall in thick sheets. He moved to the fireplace, then back to the window, his hands clasped behind his back.

"You'll wear a hole in the floor," said Thelma. "Stop worrying."

He exhaled. "I hope you will—it's just—you both mean so very much to me. I don't think I could stand it if you didn't get on."

Thelma smiled. She would make an effort with Mrs. Dudley Ward, for David's sake—but she worried about the influence that Freda had already wielded over the afternoon, without even being present.

David looked up at the sound of footsteps.

A small woman walked into the room, preceded by Finch who announced her. Freda Dudley Ward, however, needed no introduction: her familiarity with York House was obvious in the way she dropped her handbag on David's desk and swept into a perfunctory curtsy, rising with an amused expression on her face.

"Your Royal Highness," she said.

David stuffed his hands in his trouser pockets. "Come now, Freddie, let's not stand on ceremony." Mrs. Dudley Ward rose and kissed his cheek, resting her hands on his shoulders.

Though Thelma had seen Freda Dudley Ward at a distance many times before, she was struck, up close, by her delicate beauty: she had extremely fine features, as if they'd been drawn on the head of a pin. Even standing next to David, Mrs. Dudley Ward was small. She looked proportionate to his slender figure in a way that most women, with their heels and hats, their bulky shawls, did not.

"David," she said. "I'm so glad you could make time for me on such short notice. How are you? Have you been eating?"

David guided Mrs. Dudley Ward toward Thelma. "Freddie, I'd like to introduce you to Lady Thelma Furness."

Thelma hadn't expected to find warmth in Mrs. Dudley Ward's smile. "Lady Furness, I'm so pleased to meet you. David speaks of nothing else these days."

Thelma inclined her head. "Good things, I hope. Shall we?" She and Mrs. Dudley Ward sat down as David went to the bar.

"Cocktails, at this hour... David, have you ordered tea? You're looking peaky, I do hope you ate breakfast. Finch," she said, raising her voice for the butler, "A tea tray, please, with a plate of sandwiches. I don't know whether you've noticed, Lady Furness," she said to Thelma in a confidential tone, "David eats like a bird. I've seen him go an entire day on nothing more than an apple. He'll collapse of exhaustion if he's not careful."

"Any collapse would be purely the result of my public duties, not my diet," said David, handing martinis to them both. "I'm fit as a fiddle. I do my—"

"Your exercises every morning, yes," She winked and his smile broadened in the light of her approval. "Lady Furness, David tells me you visited his work-in-progress in the countryside."

"From what David tells me, it's as much your work as it is his," said Thelma.

Mrs. Dudley Ward waved off Thelma's compliment. "I provided a few small suggestions—it's all him, really. But Lady Furness, I hear you'll be making a few changes there yourself. How exciting. Thank you, Finch," she added as the butler returned. "David, please have a sandwich. For me."

Mrs. Dudley Ward leaned forward to take a sandwich from the tea tray and David leaned back in his chair as if in response, their movements an unconscious dance—a muscle memory born of years of intimacy. Thelma was struck: she had expected familiarity between them, but Mrs. Dudley Ward's complete and utter comfort in David's world was unsettling.

"David tells me you're American?" Mrs. Dudley Ward was saying.

"American and Chilean, Mrs. Dudley Ward."

"Call me Freddie, please," she responded.

"Thelma has a son, and an estate in Leicestershire," said David. He sank back into his chair and smiled at Thelma.

"Perhaps you know my sister Consuelo Thaw?" asked Thelma.

"I've not yet had the pleasure, but I've heard of Gloria—she's become a dear friend of Lady Milford Haven's, hasn't she?"

"Thelma's sister was kind enough to have us stay with her in the country sometime ago. I look forward to returning the favor," said David. "And Mr. and Mrs. Thaw will be joining

us in London in the New Year—Benny's taken a position with
the American embassy."

"Has he?" said Freda. She sipped her cocktail. "The entire
family. How charming."

The telephone rang once more and the butler came in. "Major
Metcalfe, sir," he said, "asking for a moment of your time."

David stood. "I'll take the call in the library, I think." He
strode out of the room. "Won't be a minute."

"He seems very taken with you," said Freda, after the door
clicked shut. "I must say, I've not seen him smile like that in a
long time."

"Quite simple, really," replied Thelma, with more edge than
she'd intended. "Just a matter of knowing how to make him smile."

Freda laughed—a low, soft noise, delicate and deliberate. "I've
upset you," she said, setting down her drink.

"I don't know what you mean," said Thelma.

Freda raised her eyebrow. "Of course you do," she said.
"David and I… We've known each other a long time. We were
practically children, then." She folded her hands in her lap. "He
proposed to me once—did he tell you that? I turned him down."

Thelma let out a breath and looked up at the portrait above
the mantel: David's mother, resplendent in her court dress.

"He's not an easy man to love. The pressure of his station
weighs so heavily on him…and his temperament." Freda raised
her eyebrows. "And then there were the implications for me.
What sort of life would it be, being married to a king?"

"And you were already married," said Thelma.

"Yes. I was," said Freda. She touched the soft gold of her wedding ring, a slight smile playing on her lips. "I'm not telling you
this to upset you, or to put you off, but to give you a better idea
of where David and I stand. I love David—I always will—but I
couldn't sacrifice my own happiness for his." She sat back. "So,
you see. You've nothing to worry about on my account."

TWENTY-SIX

Christmas 1929
Burrough Court

THELMA REMOVED HER OVERCOAT, FEELING A childish sort of pleasure at seeing Burrough Court's front hall decorated for Christmas—Averill's doing, no doubt, she thought, brushing a hand against a pine bough adorning the staircase. Cedar garlands hung from the chandeliers, spicing the room with a woodsy perfume; on side tables, nestled amid pine cones and dried pomegranates and oranges, stood white taper candles, unlit but ready to suffuse the foyer with a soft glow.

Webb, Burrough Court's ancient butler, took Thelma's coat, sodden around the hem from the slushy rainfall. "Miserable weather, this, my lady, miserable..."

"Is Averill in?" asked Thelma.

"She's in the stables with Rattray," said Webb. Several weeks ago, Duke had returned from a Kenyan safari with two wild zebra foals, hoping they could be trained to pull Averill's pony trap. He'd convinced Andrew Rattray, his white hunter, to come to Burrough Court to break the creatures in properly; to no one's surprise, Averill had taken to the project immediately.

She passed the butler her gloves. "And Tony?"

"He's in the nursery, ma'am. I believe he's woken from his nap."

Thelma went upstairs to find Tony in his nurse's arms, grizzling for a bottle. The nurse obliged, nudging a bottle of milk gently between the child's lips, singing a nursery rhyme under her breath.

"He's gotten so big," said Thelma.

"My lady! We didn't expect you until this afternoon," said the nurse. "I'd hoped to have him all fed and rested for a visit at teatime."

Thelma smiled at Tony, who was gripping the glass bottle with pudgy fingers. The nurse held him out but Thelma stepped back.

"I wouldn't want to interrupt," she said, thinking of the mess he might make of her dress, but she watched him nonetheless, admiring the subtle changes since she'd seen him a month ago.

"He'll be livelier in a few hours, my lady," said the nurse. She set the bottle on the nursery table and hugged Tony to her chest, patting his back. He blinked heavily, twice, three times.

"Did you receive my parcel?" said Thelma, thinking of the new clothing she had sent last week: sailor suits and pajamas with sewn-in feet.

"Indeed, we did, ma'am. They're a bit too big, but he'll grow into them soon enough."

Tony burped and the nurse wiped his mouth; he scrunched his face in a look of intense concentration and nurse laughed as the room began to smell.

"I'll take care of this, my lady," she said.

Thelma slipped out the door. Though she tried to come to Burrough Court frequently, she worried she didn't see Tony as often as she should—surely she should have known the clothes would be too big for a nine-month-old? But the constraints on her time—particularly now—meant that she was in London more than she anticipated.

She wandered back downstairs, admiring Averill's handiwork. Nearly every room had received its share of Christmas decorations: sprigs of holly and hothouse flowers adorned almost every surface, tables and mantels creaking under the weight of greenery. Thelma paused in the drawing room. For the last four years they had opened presents under a magnificent Christmas tree decorated with electric lights and colored ornaments, but this year presents sat in a pile by the fireplace. Had Averill moved the tree? She did a second circuit of the rooms.

Thelma hoped that Averill might have come in from the stables during her visit to the nursery, but the house was quiet. She changed into Wellington boots and an old mackintosh of Duke's at the back door and made her way toward the stables.

Though Thelma wasn't much of a rider she appreciated the stables at Burrough Court as a masterpiece of overengineering. With a footprint nearly as sprawling as that of the main house, the stables had stalls enough for an entire cavalry, paved with level flagstones hidden beneath trampled hay and sawdust. Horses nickered as she passed, hoping, no doubt, for attention, but Thelma ignored them and walked through to the training ring.

In the center of the ring, Averill held a long rope attached to a zebra's halter. Beside her, a man in a dust-covered khaki shirt—Rattray—watched the zebra's progress, his fingers wrapped around a long leather riding crop. Afraid of breaking Averill's concentration, Thelma didn't call out. She rested her elbows on the top of the gate and watched the zebra thunder past.

Small and bow-backed compared to the Arabian horses Averill kept in the stables, the zebra put up a fight, straining against the halter, running as far as the length of lead would let him. Averill pulled on the lead and the zebra reared, whickering in protest, but Averill stood her ground. She yanked on the rope and the zebra dropped its head, kicking up a cloud of dust from the sawdust-strewn floor.

"Good lass," said Rattray. He tucked the crop beneath his arm as Averill, cheeks flushed, passed him the lead. Thelma couldn't hear what he said but Averill laughed, the sound ringing off the rafters. Though she was as dusty as the zebra itself, Averill seemed to shine. She was in her element: entirely unguarded, completely at ease.

"Averill!"

Averill looked up, her expression cooling as she began to jog to the edge of the training ring. Rattray nudged the zebra's hindquarters with the end of the crop and it started trotting.

"Good afternoon," said Averill. She took off her gloves, looking down as she shook dust out of her newly bobbed hair.

Thelma nodded at Rattray. "Is that whip really necessary?"

"Have you ever been kicked by a zebra?" said Averill. "Rattray's seen them trample lions to death. Why are you here so early? I didn't expect you for another hour."

"I was able to sneak out on an earlier train. I thought we might have tea before the men arrive, what do you think?"

Averill hesitated. "I was hoping to spend the afternoon here," she said. "We're only halfway through this zebra's paces, and then we really ought to take some time with the other..."

"Oh—of course." Thelma tapped the edge of the training ring. "How are they getting along? That one looks magnificent."

"They're fine. Rattray's been wonderful. We're hoping to have them pulling the coach in a month or so."

Behind her, Rattray had brought the zebra back up to a trot, flicking at its hooves with the whip. "Will he return to Africa once he's done?"

"I suppose so."

She didn't elaborate. Something as exciting as horse-breaking ought to have provoked an uninterrupted stream of conversation from Averill, but she was quiet—almost sullen—as she watched the slush fall from the stable windows.

'You've done a magnificent job with the decorations," Thelma tried. "Really, the house looks wonderful. Thank you so much for taking it all on, I'm so pleased—"

"Mum used to do the Christmas decorations. I just copied what she would have done," said Averill. "Can we talk later? Rattray looks ready to get back to it…"

"Oh—of course," said Thelma but Averill had already begun to jog away.

Duke arrived later that afternoon with Dickie in tow, the pair of them identical in long overcoats and hats.

"Ho, ho, ho," said Dickie, unfurling a scarf from around his neck. Averill ran into his arms and he wrapped her in a hug that lifted her off her feet. "Miss me?" he said.

Averill laced her hand through Dickie's and led him through to the sitting room. "You'll be glad to know you've already gotten me a Christmas present, I couldn't count on you choosing the right one yourself. It's in your room…"

"Terrible ride up from London," said Duke, handing his hat to Webb. "The rails were nearly washed out with all this sleet."

"Sunshine tomorrow, perhaps?" said Thelma.

"Perhaps."

"Averill's been working with the zebras," said Thelma. "She was in the stables all afternoon."

"Was she?" said Duke. "I'm glad to hear she's taking an interest."

"Rattray's been good to let her help. She needed a project."

"I was thinking Rattray might join us for dinner," said Duke. "We've not got anyone coming, do we? He's an interesting fellow."

"I'll ask Webb to set him a place."

Duke cleared his throat. "Good. Tell Nurse to bring Tony down for tea, would you? Must go change."

When Rattray came in for dinner, Duke welcomed him as an old friend.

"We've hunted together—oh, ten years, now?" said Duke. It was a quiet dinner, by Burrough Court standards. Most evenings they were joined by friends and fellow fox hunters—tomorrow, Thelma's family would descend upon the house—but this evening the dining room felt empty. The five of them—Duke and Thelma, Averill and Dickie and Rattray, wearing a well-worn suit—sat in the middle of the long table.

"Ten years, maybe more," said Rattray. He was a slender Scotsman with a trim mustache and sun-seasoned cheeks. Though not quite as old as Duke, he'd amassed a fine collection of lines around his eyes: the result, no doubt, of squinting through binoculars. "Since the war, no?"

"He's the finest white hunter I've had the pleasure of working with," said Duke, raising his glass.

Rattray reddened. "That's very kind of you to say, Lord Furness," he replied.

"It's true," said Duke. "I never want for a thing when I'm on safari with you. Guns, food, wine…"

Rattray tugged at his collar. How often did he wear black tie in the Serengeti? Thelma disapproved of Duke's insistence on having Rattray dine with them: he would be more comfortable, surely, eating with the help, rather than sitting up here as some sort of oddity.

Dickie leaned back as Webb filled his wineglass. "Tell me, Rattray, how did you come into your line of work?"

He shrugged, resting a wiry arm on the table. "I suppose by chance," he said, with an air that suggested to Thelma he'd told this story many times before. "I grew up with nine brothers. There was never enough space for us all on the farm, so I suppose that gave me a restless side. I served in South Africa during the Boer War, and fell in love with the continent. Knocked about a bit afterward, made a living breaking horses here and there, but I was posted to Kenya during the Great War and stayed."

"I've always wanted to go to Africa," said Averill. "Father keeps promising to take us."

"I hope you do," said Rattray. "It's a profound place."

"If I were to go, I suppose you'd be our guide?"

Rattray smiled, the corners of his eyes crinkling. "I suppose so, my lady," he said.

Averill glanced at Rattray, her expression almost daring. Really, thought Thelma, it was unkind of her to tease him.

"Tell me, Rattray," she said. "How long do you plan to stay in England?"

Rattray shrugged. "As long as it takes to break in the zebras— assuming, that is, they take to being broken," he said. "Not all of them do, as I warned you, Lord Furness."

"Is there anything you can do to increase the odds?" said Dickie.

"Be consistent," Rattray replied. "I've done it before, but failed half as many times as I've succeeded. They're wild animals—can be very aggressive when they feel threatened. Building trust is the key." He nodded at Averill. "I'm lucky to have such a competent horsewoman helping me."

"She's certainly that," said Duke, and Averill beamed.

"Do you plan to visit home while you're here?" said Thelma.

Rattray set down his glass. "Perthshire?" he said. "I doubt it. I've not been back since my father died. Ten—twelve?—years ago."

Thelma recalled the light at Glen Affric, and the long, slow days spent by the loch when she and Duke were first engaged. What might have happened to Rattray, had he not given in to his restless side? He might have ended up a banker: she could picture him behind a brass screen at an Edinburgh bank, his worn khaki replaced by a crisp suit, holding a check to the light to inspect for a watermark.

"Do you miss it?" she asked, her tone softer than before.

Rattray considered. "The thing I used to resent as a boy were the walls," he said. "We lived in a small farmhouse—too cold in the winter, too warm in the summer. Damp, always damp. Oh, you could go outside, breathe the fresh air, but it was always for a purpose—muck out the stables, collect the eggs." He winked at Averill. "Now, don't go thinking, my lady, that I resent a bit of hard work—but in Kenya it's *my* work. I've space there, and friendships. It's modest enough, but it's all I need." He looked at the stag's head, hung in place of pride over the head of the table. "Kenya's my home. It has my heart—one day it will have my bones."

After dinner, they moved into the drawing room. Someone had set a roaring fire in the hearth, and Rattray knelt to add another log.

"I'd rather hoped you and I could go sledging tomorrow, Averill, but I think we might be in for a green Christmas," said Dickie.

Averill looked out the windows onto the dark ground. "A gray one, more like," she said. "Coffee, Rattray?"

"We'll find other ways to keep busy," said Duke. He took Averill's offered cup and passed it to Thelma. "Perhaps a ride, if the ground isn't too soft."

"You ought to find a tree," said Thelma, balancing the cup and saucer on her knee. "Averill's done such a lovely job decorating but we're missing the tree. Tony would love the ornaments."

"Mamma didn't like having one in the house—not after the war," said Averill, pouring another cup. "She thought they were a German tradition. Said she felt disloyal, having one in the parlor. We only started doing them again for your benefit."

Though Averill's tone had been light enough, Thelma felt the edge. "They're an American tradition as well," she said. "I've had one my whole life."

Averill leaned against the sideboard, smiling. "Well," she said quietly. "We know how all things American are in vogue these days."

Thelma blushed. She looked at Duke, who was staring intently at his coffee cup; beside him, Dickie's perpetual smile faltered. Rattray placed another log on the fire, sparks hissing up the chimney.

"Particularly among high society," Averill continued, her tone hardening. "Why, I'm told the Prince of Wales admires just about anything American. Cars, music, even women—"

"That's enough, Averill," said Duke. He stared into the fire, his expression clouded.

"But surely you should put up a tree," said Rattray. He straightened, the joints in his knees cracking as he stood. "We put them up in Kenya, even, at the Mugaitha Club. It isn't Christmas without a tree, really, is it?"

His words fell heavily on the quiet room and he glanced at Thelma, pity in his smile. Was that it, then? Rattray, the only one willing to stand up for her?

Dickie cleared his throat. "Webb, I think I'll have a splash more, if it's not too much trouble," he said quietly, and the butler came forward with a bottle of port, wine splashing up the sides of the glass as it filled.

TWENTY-SEVEN

WITH ITS WIDE WINDOWS AND CREAM-COLORED walls, the morning room at Burrough Court was Thelma's favorite, better suited to the summer months but pleasant in December nonetheless. With plaid blankets on the backs of all the chairs and a fire in the grate, the light streaming through the fogged windows was gentler than Thelma expected, the fields beyond looking a little less cold.

Gloria was at the chess table, its ivory playing pieces replaced by magazines and small boxes, a pair of small scissors and a pot of glue resting on a linen napkin. She and Mamma had arrived on the first train from King's Cross along with Little Gloria and Kieslich, now ensconced in the nursery with Tony. Mamma, in an armchair by the fire, read a cloth-bound book; Thelma didn't need to look at the worn spine to know it was an anthology of Napoleon Bonaparte's correspondences, the pages well-thumbed over years of perusal.

Thelma joined Gloria and picked up a half-cut-out illustration of a rose. "What's this?" she said.

"Decoupage," said Gloria. She took the rose from Thelma and finished cutting it out. "Nada taught me. I'm decorating cigarette boxes as Christmas gifts." She affixed the rose to the top of one of the boxes with a swipe of glue.

"Very clever," said Thelma. Gloria had finished two already: a mahogany box pasted with flowers that curled down the sides and under the base; one with a magnificent geometric starburst in shades of yellow.

"It's a wonderful hobby," said Gloria. "Very relaxing. I've got all sorts of different designs—horses for Averill, steamships for Duke. It's not that difficult. Cutting the pictures is the tricky part."

From her seat by the fire, Mamma huffed. "You ought to give proper gifts, not handicrafts. I hope you aren't sending one to Mrs. Vanderbilt."

"Oh, you don't know the first thing about it," said Gloria. "Everyone loves my gifts."

"They're unsuitable," said Mamma. "You're the mother of an heiress. If you don't give proper presents, people will talk."

Gloria shook her head "I can't win, can I?" she said. "Either I'm spending Little Gloria's inheritance recklessly, or else I'm too tightfisted. What should I do, Mother? Spend her money on presents instead of food?"

"Don't be childish. It isn't your money to spend. You're giving these gifts on behalf of your daughter. What will they think, if you can't afford to give nice things? It makes sense, to give proper presents to the people who care for her."

"Ignore her," said Gloria. "She's sulking because I rented a new house in Paris. A house with fewer bedrooms," she continued, raising her voice, "Not enough space for you, Mamma— but that's an economy, isn't it? I'm saving Little Gloria's money."

"And yet, you always have room for friends," said Mamma. "I don't approve of you using her inheritance to host parties— but a few gifts here and there, an investment—"

Thelma smirked. Mamma would have spent Little Gloria's inheritance ten times over, if she'd had the chance.

"I ought to enjoy the parties while they last, Mamma," said Gloria. "The Surrogates want me to return to New York for Gloria's school year. After I signed a three-year lease in Paris, no less."

"Can't you put them off until the lease ends?" asked Thelma. "Surely she could attend an academy in Paris."

"I've already tried to persuade them," said Gloria, "but they feel that, as an American—"

"She ought to have an American education. And I quite agree," said Mamma. She set down her book, saving her place between the pages with her finger. "It's a better schooling system."

"You've changed your tune," said Thelma. "When we were young you had us at schools in London, Paris, Switzerland…"

"I couldn't afford to send you to America," said Mamma. "Not on your father's salary. And then the war…"

"All the same," said Gloria, "I don't understand why Little Gloria wouldn't benefit from an education in Paris."

Mamma pointed at her. "You want to stay in Europe for your friends."

"Of course I do," said Gloria, without missing a beat. "Why wouldn't I? My life is here—my friends are here. I don't want to go to New York and be Reggie's widow again."

"It's not your life that matters," said Mamma. "She is a Vanderbilt. She should be treated like one—not living in the attic of a rat-filled flat in Paris—"

"Rats," scoffed Gloria, pressing a paper doll onto another box.

"And how would you know there aren't any rats in the nursery? You never go there!" said Mamma.

Gloria brushed glue onto the lid. "You know, Mamma, I don't think it would be healthy to move. In America, Gloria will be treated differently for being a Vanderbilt."

"Of course she should be treated differently," said Mamma. "She's wealthy—she has an American pedigree—"

"All the more reason for her to be raised here," said Gloria. Mamma huffed, a flush rising in her cheeks; Thelma realized that Gloria was taunting Mamma, and wondered how many times this same argument had played itself out in France, Germany, America. Gloria brushed more glue across the top of the cigarette box, smiling—not looking at Thelma, Thelma knew, for fear of laughing. "In America she's too recognizable. She should grow up in Paris, where she can be like any other common child."

Mamma's face was suffused with fury. "My granddaughter will never—never!—be European!" She pointed a shaking finger at Gloria. "I swear to God," she said, "I will do everything in my power to keep you from ruining that little girl's life."

She stalked out of the room, and Gloria burst into laughter. Thelma couldn't bring herself to join. She'd seen Mamma lose her temper before, but not to such an extent—and not at such a slight provocation. Gloria, however, seemed unconcerned—perhaps because in pushing Friedel away, Mamma had already done her worst.

"Crazy," she said, presenting Thelma with the finished box.

Thelma ran a nail along a creased fold of wrapping paper, bisecting the pattern of painted carolers down the middle as she ran the paper up the side of the box and secured it with a piece of Scotch tape. It was a cozy afternoon to be wrapping presents: a furious downpour had driven Duke, Averill and Dickie indoors after luncheon and the entire family was gathered in the sitting room. Mamma and Duke were caught up in books; Averill and Little Gloria were gathering cast-off scraps of wrapping paper and folding them into paper chains and birds. Gloria turned the wireless on, and the room filled with Christmas carols.

Thelma leaned over the arm of her chair to place the wrapped gift—a celluloid fountain pen for Averill—under the Christmas tree. Nearby, Dickie stretched out on the carpet next to Tony, lining up toy soldiers.

"Is that one for me?" he asked. He propped himself up on one elbow and reached for Tony, pulling him into a tight hug.

"Not too close to the fireplace," said Thelma, as Tony's shoe caught one of the toy soldiers and sent it toppling from the edge of the carpet onto the lintel. Dickie rolled onto his side and released Tony onto the safety of the rug.

"Come on. Is it for me?" Dickie repeated, grinning.

Thelma smiled. "Ask me no questions, and I'll tell you no lies," she said. From the front of the house, she heard the doorbell.

Dickie slid across the carpet and picked up the package, inspecting the card; Tony crawled toward Thelma and, using the leg of her chair, pulled himself upright. He swayed precariously and took one step, then another, before falling to the floor with a thump.

"Well done, Tony!" said Thelma. She picked him up, inhaling his baby-sweet scent as she cuddled him close. "Did you see that, Duke? I've not seen him walk before."

Duke set down the book. "Well done, lad." He walked toward Thelma and Tony, holding out his hand; Tony curled his chubby fingers around Duke's thumb and yawned, resting his head against Thelma's shoulder. "Now we're coming to the tricky part. His poor nurse won't be able to keep up."

Pressing a kiss to Tony's forehead, Thelma met Duke's proud gaze and smiled. With a jolt, she realized they were closer than they had been in months.

Duke, too, seemed to realize they'd forged some small bridge across the invisible breach between them. With one hand still trapped in Tony's grasp, he rested the other on Thelma's arm.

A voice from the hallway broke through the calm. "Good afternoon—ho, ho, ho! Not interrupting anything, am I?"

Thelma blushed and looked up, registering Averill's surprise and Mamma's suspicion, Gloria's wide eyes and Dickie's smiling complicity. Duke's expression hardened; Thelma stepped away, placed Tony back on the floor and curtsied, deeply, to the Prince of Wales.

David wasn't expected. He hadn't called ahead, nor had Thelma invited him, but here he was, cheeks red from the cold, his overcoat unbuttoned and a tartan scarf hanging limply from his shoulders. His usually smooth hair was ruffled; he had a canvas bag slung over one shoulder, giving him the impression of a slim Father Christmas.

"Don't get up on my account," he said, as Mamma gripped the arms of her chair to heft herself to her feet, her eyes wide. "Only a stop-in, I'm afraid. I meant to ask Finch to send these along but it slipped my mind entirely. Thought I'd drop them off on my way to Sandringham. Good afternoon, Lady Furness, how are you?"

"What a pleasant surprise," said Thelma, and David's smile broadened. She was absurdly happy to see him; she hadn't expected to, not until long after the Christmas season ended and David's responsibilities, his church services and Christmas cards, faded into the New Year. She resisted the urge to smooth his hair back into place as he hefted the bag onto an empty armchair and began to rummage through it.

Duke smiled. "Your Royal Highness. What an honor."

David pulled out a box of cigars and handed them to Duke.

"A Christmas present," he said, "To thank you for your hospitality over these past few months."

Duke raised his eyebrows. "How kind of you, sir," he said. "But entirely unnecessary, I assure you."

"Nonsense," said David, and dove into the bag once more. "Presents for the little ones—Gloria, Tony, here you are." He handed the children toy airplanes, little model men sitting in the pilots' seats with tiny glass goggles.

Little Gloria stared solemnly at David as she accepted the airplane. "You're not wearing a crown," she said.

David glanced at Thelma, suppressing a smile. "No, I'm not," he said. He patted the top of his head, as if calling attention to the lapse. "I should beg your pardon."

"Naney told me you wear a crown," she said.

"Well, it's only for special occasions," said David. He lowered his voice. "And to tell you the truth, it isn't very comfortable."

Little Gloria giggled. "Naney said you'd be wearing a crown, and that I had to be on my best behavior if you came."

"I suppose if I'm not in my crown, then you don't have to be on your best behavior, do you?" he said. "Now, can you help me give this gift to Averill?"

With Little Gloria's help, David passed out gifts to them all—a book on animal husbandry to Averill, a bottle of single malt for Dickie; silk scarves for Gloria and Mamma.

"Are you sure we can't persuade you to stay for tea?" said Duke.

David shook his head. "I'm afraid I really must dash—Father will have my hide if I'm late. Lady Furness, would you show me out?"

Thelma walked David down the hall. "All a bit on the nose, I know," he said in an undertone as they walked toward the door. "I hope you don't mind."

Thelma glanced back toward the sitting room. "Of course not," she said. "I'm pleased, really. Won't your family be upset?"

David sniffed, pulling on a pair of calfskin gloves. "Father will be upset no matter what I do," he said. They reached the front door and Thelma grabbed a shawl from the front closet. "I might as well earn my criticisms."

Thelma followed him out to his car, wind biting at her ankles. His roadster had its top up against the wind; she could see the prince's terriers in the passenger seat, jumping at the windows.

David rested an arm across the top of the motorcar: with his task complete, he seemed to want to linger.

"Next time, you ought to call ahead," said Thelma lightly. "Give Duke some warning."

"He did look a bit taken off guard," said David. "You don't mind, do you? I needed to see you before I get swallowed by my family."

"You make it sound so grim," said Thelma. "Don't worry. You'll enjoy yourself once you get there."

David snorted, but didn't say anything. He squinted down the puddled drive: though the rain had ceased, black clouds still hung heavy over the house, threatening another downpour. Thelma's skirt whipped round her legs. She hugged her elbows, the thin shawl doing little to keep her from the cold, and David moved to better shield her from the wind.

"You are pleased I came?" he said. He glanced up at the house, scanning the windows. Thelma looked, too, half expecting to see Mamma's face pressed against the glass.

She slid her hand into his. "Of course, I am," she said. "I just wish it weren't all so tangled. I feel sorry for Duke, really."

He chuckled. "Don't we all," he said. He reached into the inside pocket of his overcoat and pulled out a small velvet box. He handed it to her, then kissed her on the cheek.

"Happy Christmas," he said softly.

She opened it. Inside, a pair of opal earrings, each stone the size of her nail, shimmered in gold settings.

"They're beautiful," she said. "Thank you, David."

"These past few months…" said David. "They've been so— so peaceful, with you. I feel like I can breathe better, somehow. Does that make sense?"

"It does," said Thelma. She knew what he meant. She felt a slow, steady joy when she was around him: a peaceful happiness, a release from reality.

David smiled. "Good," he said. "I really must go now," he said. "I'll call you tomorrow. Happy Christmas, my darling."

He got into the car and drove off, but Thelma waited, watching as the car shrank down the drive, wishing she was in the passenger's seat, traveling to Fort Belvedere or London or Scotland—anywhere, so long as it was with him.

She returned to the house, folding the shawl over a coat hanger in the closet. She passed the velvet box from one hand to the other, then slid it into the pocket of her overcoat.

"He's gone, then?"

Thelma turned. Averill had come out from the drawing room, and was leaning against the newel post at the foot of the staircase.

She brushed past Averill to climb to the second floor.

"He's quite the showman, isn't he?" said Averill. "I wonder that he had the nerve to come. Though, I am glad he continued on to Sandringham, didn't try to budge in for dinner. It would have made for a rather awkward Christmas, wouldn't it? Awkward questions."

She was so like her father when angry: the same brittle fury, a fire stoked over hours—months—of resentment.

"This has nothing to do with you," said Thelma. She wasn't surprised—but she didn't feel guilty.

"And Father? Does it have nothing to do with him, either?"

"Your father and I have an understanding," said Thelma.

"An understanding—is that what you call it? And what, exactly, has His Highness offered him in exchange for his wife? Not money, clearly. I hope you've arranged for a share of the commission, it would be a shame if the men reaped all the benefits of your hard work."

Averill might as well have slapped her. Thelma froze, lowering her own voice in the fervent hope that Averill's words hadn't carried.

"How dare you," she said. "You know I did everything I

could to repair things with your father. You were *there*, you know—"

Averill deflated. "That's what I don't understand," she said. "You tried so hard…" She sat on the bottommost step, her back to Thelma: she looked so young, her cropped hair barely covering the back of her pale neck. "You were so upset with Father—and now you're parading *him*, here. It's as if you're determined to make a laughingstock of him. Of all of us."

Thelma joined Averill on the stair. "That isn't fair," she said, her own anger dissolving. "It all happened so fast—and of course I was angry—"

"And that makes it all right? Poor Thelma?" said Averill, bristling once more. "Don't pretend this wasn't as much your choice as his. You could have said no. You could have been there when Father finally saw sense."

"And I'm meant to wait around until that happens? Sit and watch Duke take his latest mistress to Paris?"

Averill's blue eyes were hard. "Don't think I approve of what Father did."

The seconds stretched between them.

"Tell me this," said Thelma finally. "Do you honestly think I should have waited for Duke to see sense?"

Averill sighed. "I think he sees sense now," she said. "He took you for granted, and now he regrets it. Father—he's a fighter." She sighed. "He would have fought to win you back, you know. It's what he used to do with Mother—seek her forgiveness. She wasn't a weak woman, and neither are you." She looked at Thelma with faint acknowledgement, weary, now, without anger to sustain her. "I don't know if Mother ever—did what you've done… She would be so mad when Father finally came home, but he always won her round, no matter how far he'd strayed. Bring her flowers, take her out to dinner…he's a romantic. If Mother had ever gone with another man, Father would have fought for her."

Thelma was surprised by Averill's honesty. Was that truly how Duke saw it all: relationships as an ebb and flow of transgressions, past hurts and current remorse and future joy all bound together, over and over again in a tangled, torturous cycle?

"It upsets him, I know it does. He hides it well—tries to ingratiate himself, but he's horrified, I think." Averill crossed her legs at the ankle, one over the other. "If it had been any other man he would be able to win you back. But the Prince of Wales…" She smiled sadly, resting against the newel post. "How can he possibly compete with that?"

When Thelma returned to the sitting room, she wasn't surprised to find that Duke had disappeared—some excuse about a telephone call, Dickie had said, covering his father's embarrassment with a young man's bravado. By three o'clock, the rain-laden clouds had passed on, the sky lightening enough for Averill and Dickie to chance a ride through the fields; shortly afterward, Kieslich came to take the children for their naps and Mamma followed, clutching her prize from David as she climbed the staircase.

Gloria, curled on the sofa with a copy of *Tatler*, looked up.

"Will you have a lie-down, too?" she said with a grin. "It must be exhausting, after all, juggling two men…"

"Oh, ha ha," said Thelma. "I didn't know he was going to come today. I feel rather bad about it, for Duke's sake."

"What did he give you? Something naughty, for him to have given it privately." Gloria flipped to a new page, her attention only half-given.

Thelma glanced at the sitting room door. "Earrings," she said in a low voice. "Opals."

"Lucky you. I knew he had taste."

Gloria flipped through the magazine. Was she searching for a mention of Nada, ensconced in Lynden Manor for the holiday season? Or of Friedel, whose engagement to Princess Margarita of Greece had been announced earlier that month?

"You know, I think I will go have a lie-down," said Thelma. Gloria nodded without looking up, and Thelma retrieved her earrings from the entrance hall.

For months now, Thelma had been sleeping separately from Duke, both in London and at Burrough Court—if they went to Affric Lodge together, Thelma supposed, the arrangement would continue, Thelma choosing the best of the guest suites with a long view over the loch. The arrangement suited her—she preferred a room without memories. Of them all, though, Thelma was saddest to have lost the master bedroom at Burrough Court: it was where she'd spent her honeymoon with Duke—where Tony, she suspected, had been conceived. She was now staying in a bedroom at the far end of the hallway, with airy curtains and a view of the manicured gardens to the east of the house.

As she passed the master bedroom, she realized the door was ajar.

"Is that you, Thelma?"

Duke's voice was gruff. He might have been drinking—or simply on the edge of a cold.

Thelma wished she didn't have the jewelry box in hand, but there was nowhere to leave it so she concealed it behind her back.

Duke was sitting in one of the armchairs by the window, an unopened book in his lap, pearl gray clouds illuminating the room with soft light. Thelma hadn't been here in months: even when Duke was away, she respected his privacy enough not to enter. His suit jacket hung on the back of the wardrobe door, where Thelma's dress used to be.

"He's left?" said Duke. He nodded to the chair opposite and Thelma sat. She'd always thought of the chair as hers: the one she used to sit in, reading, when Duke slept late, his mouth twitching as he dreamed.

"To Sandringham, yes," said Thelma. "He's hoping to arrive before teatime—hates to be late."

"Does he," said Duke without enthusiasm. "What have you got there?"

Thelma had hoped to spare him, but she showed him the box. It was easier to look elsewhere: the pattern in the bedspread, the grooves in the floor.

"A Christmas present," she said, playing with the clasp. "Earrings."

Duke nodded. "How generous." He set down his book and exhaled heavily. "I don't quite know how it all…" he said, drumming a finger on the book's spine, "When I think of everything between us… It didn't truly hit me, Thelma, how far gone we were until you came back from that weekend party."

Thelma's heart broke, wishing, in some small part, that she shared his sadness. "Oh, Duke," she said, "We were long gone before that."

He nodded, pursing his lips. "If I'd been more…if I'd been warier, when you said you were joining him for dinner—"

Thelma looked up, genuinely surprised. "You think we fell apart because of David?"

"Didn't we?"

Thelma could have listed off the names of the women Duke had had affairs with in the past year. But what would that solve?

She shook her head, and Duke sighed once more.

"Perhaps not," he said. He stood, his square shoulders rounded. "I can't have this, Thelma."

"I know," she said.

"Coming into my house, making friends with my children—what sort of man allows that?" he said. He seemed to be on the verge of saying something else, but held back, his cheeks reddening. "I can't," he said, quite simply.

Thelma looked at him, pity and anger fighting for prominence in her mind. She could have apologized—it would have felt appropriate—but what, exactly, would she be apologizing for? Duke had won the prince's friendship. Cigar boxes and club tables in London. She might have pitied him, but for his calculated approval of the arrangement in the first place.

She could hear Averill's voice, defeated. *He regrets it now.*

Thelma turned the jewelry box over in her hands. "He's the Prince of Wales," she said quietly.

Duke turned to look out the window. "Yes," he said. "He is."

Thelma knew what Duke wanted her to say—that she wouldn't see him again. That David had finally overstepped himself, encroaching on their family time. That she would refuse his calls.

That she'd fallen in love with Duke once more.

Thelma stood. "I want a separate apartment in London."

"I think that would be best."

She turned to leave, but lingered at the door, wishing she could say something to make right an impossible situation.

Duke continued to stare out the window. "Tell me one thing," he said. "If he weren't the Prince of Wales, would you still be in love with him?"

So he knew. She hadn't said it before—she hadn't admitted it to herself, even, before now.

She thought about lying to him. *Tell him what he wants to hear,* she could hear Mamma say. *You'll need him one day.*

"Yes," she said.

"I see," Duke clasped his hands behind his back. He didn't sound particularly angry, nor particularly crushed. He'd retreated behind a veneer of civility, as though a promising business arrangement had fallen through. "I'll speak to my solicitor after the New Year."

It should have felt like a victory: a clearing of the ledger, a disentanglement that would make her life—David's life—simpler. Perhaps she would feel triumphant, once it all sank in. For the moment, she felt empty.

"Happy Christmas, Thelma."

TWENTY-EIGHT

October 10, 1934
RMS *Empress of Britain*

THELMA PACED HER LIVING QUARTERS. SHE HAD left the ship's dining room before the dessert course, ostensibly to prepare for her meeting with Harry and Nada's lawyer, but in truth, she didn't have much to do. She glanced at the secretary table, hoping to find a telegram from David. He liked to send notes at odd hours, but tonight she was unlucky: there was no new envelope waiting for her.

She picked up the silver-backed cigarette case and lighter she'd borrowed from David's shaving kit. He always kept a few lighters handy, burrowing them away like a squirrel hoarding nuts for the winter. He smoked too much. So did she, she knew, eyeing the ember at the end of her cigarette.

A knock came at the door and Thelma stood as Harry entered the room, followed by a man with a blond mustache.

"Good evening, Thelma," said Harry. "Might I introduce Theobald Mathew? Mr. Mathew—my sister, Lady Furness."

"Lady Furness," said Mathew. He was tall and handsome, his face scored with deep lines that might have once been dimples.

Like Harry, he was dressed in black tie, but where Harry's suit fell loose across his shoulders Mathew looked impeccable, as though he lived in formal wear.

Thelma sat and Mathew followed suit, pulling a cigar from his breast pocket. Thelma handed him David's lighter, watching as he studied the monogram briefly before snapping it open.

Thelma smiled as the sweet smell of cigar smoke plumed into the room. *Nada's vanguard,* she thought.

Harry went to the liquor cabinet. "Thelma—Mathew—a drink?"

"Whiskey—neat," said Mathew, in a clipped English accent.

"Sherry, thank you," said Thelma. "My brother tells me you've come for the trial."

"I have," said Mathew. "Lady Furness, I represent the interests of Lady Milford Haven. A friend of yours, I understand."

"Dear Nada," said Thelma, accepting her glass from Harry. "How is she?"

Mathew set down his drink untouched. "Lady Milford Haven is very upset. For Mrs. Vanderbilt's sake as well as her own." He paused. "Lady Furness, we arrive in Montreal tomorrow, so I'll not mince words. While your brother has apprised me of your resolve to defend your sister, I feel you underestimate how serious this case has become."

Thelma glanced at Harry. Doubt settled, fetid, in the pit of her stomach.

"Enlighten me, then," she said.

"Lord and Lady Milford Haven are extremely concerned," Mathew said. "Naturally, Lady Milford Haven denies all allegations made against her in the strongest possible terms—"

"She'll come?" said Thelma.

Mathew smiled thinly. "I have advised against that particular course of action."

"But she must," said Thelma. "She has to defend herself, to

testify..." She faltered into silence at Mathew's patient, professional disapproval.

"Let me make myself clear, Lady Furness," he said. "I have been retained to defend the interests of my client, insofar as they pertain to the case against your sister. In this, our objectives will generally coincide—in a perfect world, your sister's lawyers would refute the allegations made against Mrs. Vanderbilt and the stain on Lady Milford Haven's reputation would, naturally, clear. However, given the breadth of evidence given against your sister—"

"False evidence," said Harry.

"—I count it a rare chance that she will succeed in regaining custody of her child. A rare chance indeed."

His words fell heavily on the room and Thelma glanced at Harry. Neither of them, it seemed, had the conviction to disagree.

"I have not been sent to argue Mrs. Vanderbilt's case, nor to attest to her abilities as a mother," said Mathew. He set down his cigar and leaned forward, clasping his hands. "I am only concerned with the allegations levied against Mrs. Vanderbilt as they pertain to Lady Milford Haven."

"But surely Nada ought to defend herself," Thelma repeated. "She would clear her name by testifying."

"Lady Milford Haven is not on trial," said Mathew, "and it is my belief that to interject herself further into this case would be of no benefit to her, nor anyone else."

Thelma stiffened. "It would be to Gloria's benefit."

Mathew raised his eyebrows. "Would it?"

Thelma hesitated. Nada was unpredictable at the best of times. She thought of Nada, swimming at midnight in Cannes; Nada holding court while soaking her feet in a bathtub of champagne.

"All right," she said. "So why send you at all?"

"Lady Furness," he said slowly, "I hope you'll forgive my candor, but there is some concern that your—friendship—with the

Prince of Wales might be raised in the courtroom. The connection between Mrs. Vanderbilt and His Royal Highness appears, as yet, to have escaped notice in the American papers..."

"Why shouldn't he be called upon to testify on Gloria's behalf?" said Thelma. She could picture it now: David, coming to America, putting the judge at ease with a personal assurance of Gloria's good character. He had offered his help. Why had Thelma told him to stay behind? "Surely a word from David could settle the matter? A degree of respectability, surely—"

"Under normal circumstances, your sister's friendship with His Royal Highness would be inconsequential," said Mathew. "Perhaps his name would arise on a list of guests to Mrs. Vanderbilt's home—His Royal Highness, after all, has many friends— but the allegations concerning Lady Milford Haven... Should His Royal Highness's name arise in connection to such scandal, it would cause a great deal of embarrassment to the Royal Family. A great deal of embarrassment indeed."

"Friedel is coming," Harry pointed out. "His family doesn't seem to have an issue defending Gloria's reputation."

"Forgive me for saying so, but Prince Gottfried zu Hohenlohe is not the Prince of Wales, nor is he the future Head of the Church of England. For His Royal Highness to be called to testify on behalf a woman with Mrs. Vanderbilt's alleged proclivities—"

"I see," said Thelma, her cheeks starting to burn. "And the fact that the prince's cousin-in-law is the woman with whom my sister is accused of indulging these *alleged* proclivities is beside the point."

Mathew conceded with a shrug, spreading his hands wide across the arms of his chair. "Should the press realize the connection between Lady Milford Haven and the Prince of Wales... that is what I am attempting to prevent. The Royal Family must remain above reproach."

Thelma stood. "So Nada will hide behind a lawyer."

Mathew picked up his cigar. "You know, Lady Furness, as well as I do, what the Royal Family is. The Prince of Wales is an invaluable asset to the institution, to Great Britain—"

Thelma knew, now, she was arguing for argument's sake, but she couldn't help it. She bristled at the thought of David, trapped within the confines of his crown. "He's a symbol, is that it? Nothing more?"

"He's a symbol because he has to be," said Mathew sharply. "The Commonwealth has survived over generations because the Royal Family is a uniting force. Surely you can see that his duty to his people comes before his friendship with Mrs. Vanderbilt?"

Though he didn't say it, Thelma and Mathew both knew the words that he left unsaid. *His friendship with you, Lady Furness.*

"So you've not come for Nada," she said, sinking back into her chair. "You've come to keep David's name out of the trial."

"I've come on behalf of the Royal Family," said Mathew. "To repudiate the charges against Lady Milford Haven—and to keep scandal from staining the House of Windsor."

"I see." Thelma felt an overwhelming sadness. She never expected David to come—she herself had advised against it. But to know that Gloria would receive no support from Nada…

And that one word from David might make the difference.

Thelma stood, avoiding Mathew's eye.

"Mr. Mathew, I'm afraid you must excuse me," she said. "I'm very tired."

Mathew and Harry rose. "Of course," said Mathew. "I'll come to you in the morning before the ship docks to discuss particulars—suggest a few suitable words for the reporters in Montreal."

Thelma nodded and Harry escorted Mathew out. She leaned across the table and stubbed out Mathew's cigar, which he'd left burning on the edge of the ashtray: the smoke would linger in the fabric of the chairs like a bad perfume.

She rang for Elise and moved to the bedroom, patting her cheeks dry before the maid walked in.

TWENTY-NINE

May 1930
London

AFTER CHRISTMAS, DUKE HAD BEEN QUICK TO find Thelma an apartment in Mayfair. Her new flat was near the American embassy where Benny was now an attaché to the Court of St. James.

"Among your own people once more," Duke said, smiling tightly as he and Thelma reviewed the lease in his study at Arlington Place.

"Lady Furness, you'll notice that your husband is providing you with an additional stipend to hire household staff," said Duke's lawyer, passing her a sheet of paper. "You'll be taking your lady's maid with you, I presume—"

"Yes."

"…but I've taken the liberty of having my office arrange the services of a domestic search agency to help you find the other staff you'll require. Cook, butler, so forth."

"Thank you," said Thelma, scanning the document without reading it. She had been outraged when Duke's lawyer had made her sign a settlement before her wedding to Duke, to provide a stipend for her in the case of a separation; now, she was grateful for his foresight.

"You will, of course, retain full rights to Lord Furness's other estates, Burrough Court and Affric Lodge, subject to Lord Furness's approval—a simple telephone call, I'm sure, will suffice." The lawyer smiled, cheeks pouching under bagged eyes.

"Of course it will, it's not a bloody divorce." Duke signed the lease, a spot of ink pooling in a glossy stain at the end of his signature before it dried flat. "Is that it, then?"

The lawyer picked up the sheets and shuffled them back into his briefcase and slipped out of the room as Duke moved to the window.

Thelma stood beside him. "We'll still see each other," she said, knowing how contrived she sounded. "I'll come to dinners— we'll go dancing. You're still my husband."

Duke snorted. "I'm something, all right," he said. He planted his hands on the windowsill. "No," he said, more softly. "I understand. Truly, I do. Just—promise you won't lose sight of me." He paused, and Thelma looked away. "You've still got a home here, if you ever want it."

The apartment was more than Thelma deserved: spacious and light, with large windows that overlooked Grosvenor Square, a spare bedroom and a dining room large enough to seat ten. Thelma found a decent cook and a housemaid, as well as a stately butler and a chauffeur for the new Daimler that Duke had purchased—not without a sense of humor. The immense car matched David's exactly.

On her first night in the new flat, Thelma walked through the rooms, running her hands along the sleek buffet in the dining room, admiring the palm-frond chandelier and gleaming Wedgwood china. For the first time in her life, Thelma had a place entirely her own, along with the income required to furnish it. She'd taken complete advantage of the opportunity, rejecting Duke's stately, antiques-filled aesthetic and David's comfortable, homey chintz in favor of a clean, modern look: chrome and brushed metal and glass, sleek and expensive.

Two weeks later, David came to Thelma's flat unannounced.

"I just came back from the Fort. It's a marvel, darling, an absolute marvel," he said, striding through the front door. He allowed Thelma's butler to help him with his overcoat, then leaned forward to kiss Thelma's cheek. "They finished two weeks ahead of schedule. Entirely state-of-the-art, top to bottom. Mind if I telephone Freddie?"

"Not at all," said Thelma, though David was already halfway to the study. She followed, stepping into the room as he picked up the receiver. Loosening the knot of his tie, David put Thelma in mind of a child freed from church. "Freddie? I just got back from the Fort. You'll be thrilled..."

Thelma shut the door and moved into the drawing room, pouring tea as she waited for David to finish. He entered a few minutes later, still beaming.

"Freddie's so pleased," he said, taking a cup. "Told her she'll have to bring her daughters along to see it—after you, of course."

David took Thelma's hand in his, absently twisting her wedding ring around the base of her finger. Thelma could tell he was thinking about the Fort: the tennis court, strung up with a white net; the octagonal drawing room, finally filled with furniture.

"I've asked my brothers to come Friday. Piers, too—Piers Legh, my equerry. You'll enjoy him immensely if I can pull him away from work. You'll organize it for me, won't you?"

"Of course," said Thelma. "It sounds like quite the boys' trip."

David unbuttoned his jacket. "Actually, I was rather hoping you'd come and organize the menus, spend time with Elizabeth when I take the boys shooting. I doubt even she has the constitution to handle us all on her own."

"Bertie's wife?" said Thelma. Though she'd become friendly with George and Harry, David's two youngest brothers, she hadn't yet met the Duke and Duchess of York. She'd seen them before at court presentations, the tall prince and his apple-cheeked wife, standing in long receiving lines next to wizened lords and ladies with close-lipped smiles.

David pulled Thelma into his lap. "I think you two will get along, as a matter of fact. You don't think I'd plan my first party at the Fort without you? What do you imagine I'd do all night, play checkers?"

Thelma batted David's hand away. "David, I can't possibly host a weekend for your family." Nada had once told Thelma that the Duchess of York had a warm friendship with the king: Thelma could only imagine what she might think of being asked to spend time in the company of her brother-in-law's married mistress. "What would your parents say?"

"It's not their house—not their decision," said David. He kissed Thelma's neck, the chain of her necklace brushing against his lips. "You'll do it, won't you? I'm rubbish at organizing these things." He slid his hand beneath the collar of her jacket, nudging it off her shoulder; she ran her fingers up David's back, playing with the soft hair at the nape of his neck.

He could be so obtuse. It was one thing for Thelma to host parties for their friends—a casual, glittering crowd that barely batted an eyelid at infidelity. She could even wrap her head around the idea of hosting a dinner for David's brothers in London, where she could retreat to a respectable distance at the end of the night—but to spend the weekend with his family in the country? Without her husband?

"I'm sorry, darling, I just don't think it's a good idea. If the newspapers caught wind..."

David nudged Thelma off his lap. "The newspapers won't print a damn thing if I don't want them to," he said.

Thelma pictured herself and the Duchess of York, trading icy pleasantries across the dining table. "I don't know, I really don't."

"I see." David straightened, the thin lines of his face drawn tight as he buttoned his jacket. "Fine—I'll cancel it."

"That's not fair. Surely you could ask someone else. Freddie—"

"I don't want Freddie. I want you." He stood. "I don't see the problem. I want a weekend with my brothers, and I want you there. If you can't come, there's really no point."

Thelma knew David wasn't bluffing: he would follow through on his threat to cancel the party altogether if Thelma stood her ground.

And all because you're afraid to meet his sister-in-law. Was her discomfort really worth spoiling David's first party at the home he'd worked so hard to build?

"It really means that much to you, if I come?" she said.

"Yes," said David. He returned to the sofa and sat beside her, resting his elbows on his knees. "I don't want to go it alone," he said. "Bertie and Elizabeth, they always look so *happy*...and Father makes no secret of the fact that he prefers Bertie. I want to show them all that I can do something right."

"All right," she said.

David looked up. "You promise?"

Thelma sighed. "I suppose I do," she said, "although I'm not so sure the duchess and I will get along as well as you think."

He kissed her firmly on the lips. "You're so good to me," he said. "I would be hopeless without you, truly I would."

THIRTY

THEY LEFT FOR THE FORT IN DAVID'S CONVERT-
ible early on Friday morning, Thelma half sleeping in the passenger seat, a silk scarf bundled like a pillow between her cheek and
the window. She'd barely slept the night before—despite David's
assurances that he wanted the weekend to be informal, Thelma
fretted over the menus, the weather, the room assignments.

She now understood why Gloria had been so nervous about
hosting David at Three Gables. Though she could win over David's brothers with charm and good humor, Thelma knew she
was at a distinct disadvantage with the Duchess of York. Thelma
suspected she would be reporting back to the king and queen
on David's new home—and on his mistress.

David, thankfully, let her doze. He drove at a leisurely enough
speed for Thelma to enjoy the sun on her face, the gentle movement of the car pulling her into occasional wakefulness.

"We're here," said David, patting Thelma's leg as they passed
the newly restored gates.

The car crept up the drive, and Thelma marveled as Fort Belvedere came into view. The front entrance, which had once been a courtyard overrun with weeds and piles of loose cobblestones, was now a pristine drive centered on an elegant wrought-iron sundial. Ivy climbed attractively along the Fort's brick walls and the Gothic windows gleamed in the sunlight. For the first time, Thelma could see what David had seen in the place so many months ago: it looked liveable—comfortable. A ruin brought back to life.

David parked and stepped out of the car as two small blurs came shooting onto the drive—his terriers—followed by a butler in a dark tailcoat.

"Your Royal Highness," he said, bowing as David opened Thelma's door.

"Kept the place standing, I see," said David. He held out a hand for Thelma and she stepped onto the pea-gravel drive, shielding her eyes from the sun. "Osborne, this is Lady Furness," David said.

"How do you do, Lady Furness?" said Osborne. "Welcome to Fort Belvedere."

"Thank you," said Thelma. She had spoken to the butler several times over the past few days, telephoning him when she changed her mind about what to serve for dinner. Osborne looked much as Thelma expected—young enough to indulge David's extravagances, but with the composure required of a butler in service to the Prince of Wales.

"Well?" said David, hugging Thelma to his side. "What do you think?"

Thelma cast an appraising eye over the newly planted greenery. "Very nice," she said. "Though the tour's far from over."

David looked up at the tower with pride. "Let's see if the rest of the house passes muster."

David had done everything he said he would, and more besides, to make the Fort a comfortable country retreat. Every room had modern conveniences: call buttons in the bedrooms to the servants' quarters; hot water in every bathroom.

"I think we may lose you to this place," Thelma murmured, sweeping aside a heavy curtain in the drawing room to look at the vast grounds beyond. The drawing room was the heart of the Fort: a cozy octagonal space with wood-paneled walls and windows on five sides that flooded the dark space with light.

"Marvelous, isn't it?" said David, wrapping his arms around her waist. He nestled his chin in the hollow of her shoulder.

"Too marvelous. I worry I'll never see you in London again," said Thelma. She could see the top of the tennis court, its posts just visible past the ramparts that hemmed the lawn into a wide semicircle. "I'll know where to look if I lose you at the Ritz."

He pointed to the treetops beyond the lawn. "I've an aerodrome just past there," he said, his breath spiced with tobacco, "so I can get here from anywhere in Britain. And from most places in Europe, too. I'll be able to bypass London entirely."

"Your father let you put an aerodrome in Windsor Great Park?" said Thelma, but even the mention of the king couldn't put David in a bad mood.

"He wasn't exactly part of the decision. I had my men clear a landing strip weeks ago. Father's not caught wind yet, but better to beg for forgiveness than ask permission."

"So you've an *airplane*, now?"

"A little Gypsy Moth. I had Legh arrange it. I pick it up in a few weeks—won't be flying solo yet, but it's only a matter of time. I'll take you up one day, it's the most incredible feeling."

Thelma laughed, thinking of herself in the back of an airplane piloted by David, her face hidden beneath a bulky helmet and goggles.

"How very unconventional," she said. "Just like you."

"Just like *us*. I plan to have you here with me, as often as you can come. I need you."

She watched a goshawk soar over the woods. "A married

woman, hosting your parties," she said. "Won't the neighbors talk?"

David kissed her. "So leave your husband. Marry me."

The goshawk circled a copse of pine trees, its small body stiffening as it saw something on the forest floor. It pulled in its wings and dove, disappearing into the green. "Just like that?" she said, attempting to match David's levity.

David kissed her neck. "Just like that. Why not?"

Thelma was silent. She could hear footsteps in the hallway outside—Osborne, perhaps, putting his ear to the door to see if David needed anything. "I'm married," she said in an undertone. "I'm a divorcée, David, I—I'm American, for goodness' sake."

"So?" said David. "It wouldn't matter. Not really—not once I'm king."

She ought to have felt something—elation, joy—but she was numbed by sheer incredulity. She twisted out of David's grasp and faced him head-on.

"Do you really mean it?" she said.

David smiled, his tired eyes twinkling. "Well, not today," he replied. "There are complications to consider—your husband, my father... It would take time, but I'm mad about you, darling. Think of it—you and me, taking on the Fort. Taking on the *country*..."

Thelma sat, warmth—panic—seeping into her chest. "Did you just propose?" she said. "Was that your plan all morning?"

David's smile faltered. "Well—no," he said, and Thelma fought a dark urge to laugh. "It was—more of a suggestion, really. It certainly couldn't happen until after Father goes..." He trailed off, and took Thelma's hand. "I can see I've upset you. Perhaps it's something to think about?"

"David, I'm not ready to think about it," said Thelma. "I've got my family. I've got *Tony*—"

"But what about me?" said David.

The thought of a life with David was a good one. David as

he was here, now, at the home he'd built—a home they might share together, if reality, plain reality, weren't to intervene.

"If you were my only consideration, I'd marry you tomorrow," said Thelma, and the concern on David's face melted away. "But I've got responsibilities—and so do you."

He exhaled, nodding. "So we do," he said, and Thelma wondered if some part of him was relieved. "I'm sorry, darling. I got carried away. Let's not mention it again." He glanced over his shoulder at the brilliant morning outside. "What do you say we go for a walk in the grounds? I can go down to the kitchens, ask them to pack us a picnic lunch."

Thelma nodded and David jogged out of the room. Thelma relaxed her hold on the cushion and stood, her heart sinking back into her chest.

Thelma and David walked back from Great Windsor Park in the long shadow of the Fort, thrown across the grounds by the deepening sunlight, the last reminder of a brilliant spring day. They'd spent their afternoon well, wandering along the banks of Virginia Water, stopping to picnic at a curious set of Roman ruins, mottled and discolored with age.

They talked about David's brothers; about Gloria's most recent letter, sent from Cannes where she was holidaying with Nada. It felt right, after David's careless proposal and Thelma's delicate refusal, to keep to lighthearted topics—to pull back from the edge toward which they'd strayed.

They reached the lawn leading to the back door and David, holding the picnic basket in the crook of one arm, gave his free hand to Thelma. Like the rest of the house, the lawn had undergone a transformation: it was level with fresh sod, a dozen newly painted sun chairs standing in a neat row.

"You've done really well," said Thelma, looking up at the tower as they passed. "I'm impressed."

"It's all exactly how I want it," said David. He knocked dust from his shoes and opened the back door. "Informal, homey—that's how I want to feel when I'm here." They walked toward the staircase and David glanced at his watch. "The others will be arriving soon—best get dressed. You remember where your room is? You'll be pleased with it, I think."

He kissed her on the cheek and set off down toward the kitchen with the picnic basket. Thelma knew Osborne would have gladly taken it if David had left it at the back door, but she suspected David was keen to see the kitchen once more, with its gleaming new stoves and counters.

She went up to the guest bedrooms, opening each door in turn to see the changes made, saving her own room until last.

It looked exactly as she'd hoped, its gay shades of pink and cream providing a bright, feminine contrast to the rest of the house. She walked to the window, toying with the curtains as she searched for their picnic site.

Elise had already unpacked Thelma's suitcase and had hung a satin evening dress on the wardrobe door, but the buttons down the back of her day dress were tricky to undo alone. She pressed the call button on the wall before opening a jar of scent, setting it on the corner of the table: the room still smelled of new paint, clean yet chemical, and the perfume filled the room with the rich, flowery scent of jasmine.

Is he mad? she wondered. Surely, he understood the obstacles involved; the opposition that he—they—would face.

A divorcée as queen. She rouged her cheeks, coaxing color from cream. He couldn't have meant it seriously. Once he had time to think about it he would come to the same conclusion that Thelma, immediately, had made. It was impractical, unconscionable, to think that theirs was a relationship that would be anything more than an affair. A loving affair—long-lasting—but an affair nevertheless.

There was a knock at the door and Thelma called out an invitation to enter.

It was David, dressed splendidly in a Balmoral kilt and barathea coat, silver buttons studding two broad lines down his front.

"Are you coming in or staying out?" said Thelma, admiring his attire. David had specified more casual wear for the weekend, but Thelma suspected that he would be the only one wearing Highland dress as opposed to black tie. His eye for clothing was a trait not shared, Thelma knew, by his brothers.

"I was walking through the servants' hall when the bell rang, and I told Elise to stay and finish her tea," he said. "Your room looks nice." He stepped inside and shut the door.

"It does, doesn't it?" said Thelma as she leaned forward to apply her lipstick. "A bit too feminine, perhaps, for a bachelor's home?"

Thelma caught his expression in the mirror. "It's perfect," he said. He rested his hands on Thelma's shoulders, his thumbs brushing against the cloth–covered buttons on the back of Thelma's dress. "May I?"

Thelma nodded, lifting her hair from the nape of her neck and David began to loosen the buttons, his fingers grazing against the silk of her slip. She held her breath, watching his reflected progress in the mirror.

He stepped back and Thelma stood, letting the dress fall to the floor.

She turned to face him. "The slip," she said. "In the wardrobe."

David went to retrieve it. Thelma could feel her face reddening; they had been together nearly a year now, but it was thrilling, and wonderfully intimate, to watch him sort through her underclothes.

"This one?" he said. Thelma nodded, removing her slip as David came forward with the new one. She put in on, letting the silk slide down her body.

"The dress now," she said, and David retrieved the evening gown from its hanger as Thelma changed her earrings. David bundled the dress in his hands and helped Thelma step into it, pulling it up inch by inch before settling the straps on her shoulders.

"There," he said quietly. He pulled her close and ran his hand down her shoulders; the dress was high in the front and low in the back, gathering in folds around her waist before falling to the floor, and his touch made her want to leave David's brothers to fend for themselves until Monday.

If they were married, this is what they would do: dress together, host weekend parties, walk the grounds. Make love, leaving dirty breakfast trays in the halls, playing hide-and-seek through the empty bedrooms. Would it really be so different, if they were married? Would it really matter?

Unbeknownst to Thelma and David, Prince George had arrived while they were dressing. He was bent over the cocktail table when they entered the drawing room.

"Osborne let me in. Is that his name, Osborne?" he said, stirring a lethal-looking concoction with a toothpick. He dropped onto the sofa, crossing one leg over the other. "Thelma, darling, you look smashing. And the Fort, quite the transformation. One could almost forget this room was once—a barracks?"

"A watchtower," said David, examining a box of records next to the phonograph-radio.

"Watchtower," said George, raising his eyebrows in mock interest. The white noise of the phonograph filled the room and David dropped the needle on a Fred Astaire record. "And its function now?"

"Used solely for the purposes of drinking." David replied. "Thelma? Gin and tonic?"

"Please," she said.

Osborne came in and cleared his throat. "Sir, Colonel Legh has arrived," he said, and David whirled around.

"Excellent! I'll go show him in, shall I?" he said, halfway down the hall before the butler could answer.

"I *think*," said George, smirking, "he's excited about playing house."

"I've never seen him so happy," said Thelma, rising to finish the drinks David had abandoned. "He'll want to show you the kitchens."

"The poor cook. Well, we all need our hobbies," George replied. "David's got this place—you've got David."

"And yours?" asked Thelma.

George examined the crystal cut of his cocktail glass. "Hardly a subject for polite society."

David returned to the room a quarter of an hour later, looking flushed. "It was Piers," he said. "He's upstairs getting changed. I put him in the blue room, darling. I hope that's all right. I helped him with his bags," he said, with something of a boast. "Osborne turned on the electric lights in the front drive, did you see them?"

"How do they look?" asked Thelma, handing him a martini.

"Like lights," George muttered.

"They're wonderful, come see."

"I'll entertain myself, shall I?" called George, his voice carrying as David led Thelma out to the front drive.

The lights, in Thelma's opinion, were slightly excessive: the Fort had been lit by low floodlights, placed every few feet in the gardens to give the building a ghostly glow in the mist.

"See the effect on the tower?" said David. He held up his hand, sweeping it along the Fort's silhouette. "The lights illuminate it, just so. Really gives you a sense of the atmosphere, doesn't it?"

"You've got them around the back as well?"

"I'll have them at the swimming pool and tennis court, so we can use them in the evenings," he said, looking around as a car turned onto the drive. "There they are! I was beginning to worry."

Thelma's heart sank. She had hoped to meet the duke and duchess in the comfort of the drawing room—not lurking on the front drive like some vagrant. She hesitated, wondering whether she could slip inside unnoticed, but the car wheeled round the sundial, catching David and Thelma in its headlight glare.

David stepped forward and opened the passenger-side door. "Trust you to be late, Elizabeth."

The duchess was small, made smaller still by the profusion of furs and fabrics which, despite the warmth of the season, she had worn for the drive over. She stepped out and tilted her chin, offering her cheek for David to kiss.

"I know." She clasped David's arm. "It takes me so long to go anywhere these days, me the size of a Spanish galleon."

"C-come now, darling." The Duke of York, taller than David by several inches, tucked his hands in the pockets of his over-coat as he came round the front of the motorcar. "You move so s-slow, you'll be the l-last one left on Judgment Day."

The duchess smirked. "You're impossible," she said warmly, before turning her blue gaze onto Thelma.

"Elizabeth, I'd like you to meet Thelma, Lady Furness," said David.

Though Thelma knew she was only three or four years older than herself, there was something matronly about the Duchess of York: she was short, with plain features and heavy eyebrows, her hair bound up in a diamond headpiece.

She inclined her head. "I'm delighted to meet you," she said. "David tells me you're the one to thank for organizing this lit-tle get-together."

"Oh, we'll see," said Thelma. "Thank me once the week-end is over."

The duchess laughed. "I'm sure it will all be perfectly lovely," she said. With one arm on each of the princes, she moved toward the front door, leaving Thelma in her wake.

Perhaps to make up for their tardiness, the Duke and Duchess of York had come dressed for dinner: once indoors, the duchess removed her cape to reveal a loose-fitting periwinkle evening gown. When she turned, Thelma saw that the dated cut was intended to hide the duchess's advanced pregnancy.

"Look at you—Lilibet must be getting excited for a little brother or sister," said David, with genuine fondness.

The duchess wrinkled her nose. "Isn't it dreadful? I try to keep to myself this far along, but I wanted to see you." She handed her cape to Osborne, taking in the entrance hall. "Why, David, it's charming!" she said. "Bertie, isn't it lovely? And to think you're just across the Park…if we could convince Papa to give us Royal Lodge, we would be neighbors." Her voice was high and bright, ringing off the marble as David led her in. "Now, I'm sure you had something to do with the chandeliers, Lady Furness," she said. "They're far too pretty to have been chosen by David."

David looked over his shoulder at Thelma, who, given Freddie's outsize influence on the house, had limited her decorative contributions to her bedroom. "She's got an eye for this sort of thing," he said, gallantly allowing the duchess's misconception to stand. "If it had been left to me, all the furniture would still be in boxes."

"I f-find that rather hard to believe," said the duke. David had warned her about his brother's speech impediment, but Thelma was surprised by how pronounced it was—his sentence stalled midway through, but David and the duchess, no doubt used to the duke's peculiar cadence, didn't attempt to finish it. "For a man as f-f-fastidious—" he caught the word on the edge of his teeth before tugging it loose in a rush "—as you, I'd expect you to w-worry over each d-d-decorative pillow."

David shrugged, conceding the point. Thelma was used to seeing David charm people, but his easy manner with the duke and duchess was something new: he was relaxed, the nervous energy that had propelled him all day finally at rest.

They entered the drawing room, interrupting George and Piers Legh mid-conversation. The duchess released David to pull George into a tight embrace.

"How are you? How goes the conquest?" the duchess asked George in a low voice. George grinned, pressing a finger to his lips; with a pointed glance at Thelma, the duchess pulled George close to continue their conversation in whispers.

Thelma broke away from the huddle and moved toward David, feeling out of place amid Elizabeth's easy camaraderie with the men.

"Bertie—Elizabeth? A drink?" said David.

"Nothing for me, thank you, but Bertie will have a cigarette. Doctor's orders," said the duchess, and David pulled a case from his sporran. "We're told it helps relax the vocal chords."

"I like the sound of that doctor," said Legh, letting a plume of smoke escape from his mouth. He was tall, with receding dark hair and heavy eyebrows, his prominent features out of place compared to the handsome Windsor brothers. He sat backward on the piano bench, the key guard turned down to use as an armrest. "Is he taking patients?"

The Duke of York lit a cigarette, chuckling. Like his eldest brother, the duke was fit and handsome, with aquiline good looks and an intensity that David, with his easy charm and mournful smile, lacked. He sat down and David perched on the armrest: side by side, they looked like a photo and its negative. The duke was dark where David was light, tall where David was short; staid, in his black tie, while David was flamboyant in plaid.

Thelma sat next to the fireplace, watching David's smile broaden as he surveyed his family.

Over dinner, Thelma gained a new appreciation for David's relationship with his brothers. She felt as though she'd walked into the midst of a conversation started years ago, listening to jokes half explained, stories recounted in fits and starts, interrupted by irresistible tangents, raised arms and shouts of laughter, hands loosely clasped around the stems of wineglasses.

David, without question, was the ringleader, goading George and Bertie—and Legh, who had known them all so long he was practically a brother himself—with boyhood insults. There was something gleeful in his conduct: an uncomplicated loosening, children liberated from their parents' gaze.

George, unsurprisingly, was equally exuberant: the handsomest and most outgoing of the brothers, he didn't seem to begrudge David the accident of birth that put him next to the throne and first in the minds of the women who followed their antics in the society pages. No, Thelma suspected that George was content to follow David's lead, enjoying the benefits afforded by a royal title without the accompanying responsibility.

Of the three brothers present, though, Thelma was most intrigued by the Duke of York. In Bertie, David's constant restlessness was transformed into a nervous rigidity. He seemed to have his mind on everyone's comfort but his own, deferring to his wife and briefing Thelma on George and David's long-winded reminiscences. Thelma thought back to the first time she met David at Lady Londonderry's ball, recalling her overwhelming impulse to care for him, to smooth out the troubles in his face. She felt the same solicitousness toward Bertie, wanting to will the tension out of his shoulders, his clenched jaw. With his stammer, it would be easy to dismiss Bertie as a slouch—a slow mouth attached to a slow mind—but he was sly and witty, responding to David's humor with subtle asides, a wry smile on his lined face.

As they finished dessert, David set down his spoon and glanced at Thelma. Recognizing the unspoken gesture, Thelma made to rise from her chair but the Duchess of York stood first.

"Well, gentlemen, I think we shall leave you to your brandy," she said. "Lady Furness, perhaps you'd be so kind as to join me in a game of cards?"

"Of course," said Thelma, putting a gentle hand on David's shoulder. The duchess narrowed her eyes as David patted Thelma's hand.

It was petty, perhaps, to have goaded her, but it irked Thelma, the way the duchess had come into the Fort and treated it as her own. She had all but ignored Thelma throughout dinner, telling lively stories that had the men in an uproar while blithely deflecting Thelma's attempts to pull her into conversation. Had she been so lofty with Freddie, when David had first brought her to a family dinner?

The drawing room was warm. In their absence, someone had stoked the fire to a merry roar, and it cast flickering light up the walls to animate the portrait hanging above the mantel—some relative of David's, Thelma assumed, with a heavy periwig and ornate robes. He sneered at Thelma as she sat down, and she turned on a nearby table-lamp to dispel the flicker of flames from his face.

The duchess sank into the chair opposite Thelma with a sigh, her merry face slack with exhaustion. She seemed to have left all her energy in the dining room, the sparkling wit she had shown in front of the men replaced by a fatigue that seemed to reach for Thelma across the room. Thelma's frustration rose again: Would she even make an effort, now that she and Thelma were alone?

As though recalling she was in company, the duchess looked at Thelma with a half-hearted smile.

"Bertie's so been looking forward to an opportunity to see David," she said.

"And David," said Thelma. "He's talked of nothing else for days."

The duchess blinked heavily. "Isn't that sweet," she said.

"May I offer you a drink?"

The duchess opened her eyes. "No, thank you," she said,

resting a hand on her swollen stomach. "But don't abstain on my account."

They lapsed into silence once again, and Thelma fancied she could hear laughter from the other room. She wasn't entirely sure what to do: whether she, as hostess, was responsible for starting a conversation or whether the duchess should be allowed to sit in silence if she felt like it. With David, Thelma had thrown protocol entirely out the window, but with the duchess questions of propriety seemed so much more demanding.

She was on the verge of ringing Osborne for tea when the duchess shifted in her chair, wincing as she tightened her hand over her belly.

Thelma's irritation faded. "Is it kicking?" she asked.

The duchess looked up. "Oh? Yes. I don't know why he's so upset. The drive must have jostled him out of sorts. He's been shifting about all evening."

Thelma smiled. "I remember that feeling," she said. "When they decide to do the Charleston. Can I get you anything for it?"

She pursed her lips. "I would say a glass of champagne, but the pregnancy has put me off cocktails entirely. It's making for a very long nine months." She looked at Thelma with renewed interest. "You've one of your own, then?"

"I do. A little boy. He's just over a year."

Elizabeth smiled. "They're lovely at that age. My Lilibet just turned four. It's remarkable how much they change." She caressed the rise of her stomach, a slow, circular motion. "This one though—I've a feeling it's a boy. Bertie thinks so, too."

"And I thought my Tony would be a girl." Thelma recalled the sheer terror of her own pregnancy. "Will you have more?"

Elizabeth glanced at Thelma, who worried she'd gotten too familiar.

"I don't think so," she said, after a moment's excruciating silence. "The toll it takes…no, I've done my duty by Bertie, I think. Will you?"

Thelma deserved the question after asking it herself. She'd never really considered whether she wanted another child—she wasn't entirely sure she was capable of it. David never seemed particularly concerned about the possibility of a pregnancy, which led Thelma to believe that, perhaps, he was incapable, too—but she'd never asked, and David had never explained.

But if circumstances were different?

"I don't know...the toll it takes," she echoed. She recalled standing over Tony's crib, watching him sleep with the same detached interest she would have shown to one of Averill's foals. "It took time for me to love him, after he was born. I didn't know what to do. How to talk to him. I suppose you think that's monstrous—a mother's supposed to love their child—but it didn't happen. Not right away."

The duchess was looking at Thelma with the most curious expression. "No," she replied. "I don't think that's monstrous at all."

Thelma sniffed, wishing she'd poured herself that drink after all. "Well, it all came right in the end," she said. "He's a lovely little boy—I adore him. But to your question: I don't know whether I would have another child. Not unless I knew I was ready to be a mother again. I suppose I would, if the stars aligned."

The duchess shifted forward and patted Thelma's hand. "You're young—there's time," she said, and Thelma felt as though something hopeful had fallen into place.

THIRTY-ONE

THE NEXT MORNING THELMA WAS JARRED OUT of sleep by the sound of bagpipes. She turned over in bed, feeling for David, then shifted the tangle of bedsheets and walked to the window.

It was a cool day, with heavy clouds hanging low over the forest and the smell of rain in the air. The bagpipes grew louder as the player reached a crescendo and she pushed the window open, letting the noise force itself into the room.

David was standing to attention on the terrace below, the offending instrument slung over his shoulder. He took a breath, his fingers running up and down the pipe as he played a tune that jumped from high to low. He took the finale at a run, then lifted his fingers; the bag ran out of air in a dissonant squeal and Thelma leaned out the window, feeling the first few droplets of rain on her face.

"Is this your way of telling us we've slept too long?" she said.

David looked up. "Good morning! I hope you don't mind—have I woken the others?"

Thelma squinted along the row of second-story windows. "I would say so. Is it meant to rain all day?"

"Wireless says it will stop this afternoon. I've made some progress on a path through the wood."

"Already? What time is it? I'm coming down now." She pushed the button on the wall to call for Elise, hoping she hadn't been the only one to sleep the morning away.

She hadn't—David, it transpired, had been up since daybreak. It was a change from his habits in London: at York House, David never woke before ten.

As promised, the rain stopped midafternoon, leaving a pearl sky. After luncheon, they went out on the terrace for fresh air, David's terriers leading the way.

"Shall I show you how to hit a hole in one?" David asked Thelma, picking up a golf club as they trooped outdoors. He set up a tee by the lawn chairs while George and Piers pegged croquet wickets in the green.

"Careful now," said George, driving the last wicket into place with the heel of his shoe. "You don't want to go telling her all your secrets—you'll never win a game again. Ten pounds on the outcome, Legh?"

David handed Thelma the club. "I don't know about secrets—skill's what makes it. Now, if you hold it like so…" He wrapped his arms around her to illustrate the proper stance, and she swung the club, sending the ball soaring past the cannon-lined rampart.

"Well done! Did you see that, Bertie? She's a natural!" He lowered his voice and dug another ball out of the basket. "What do you think of them?" he whispered.

"They're lovely," said Thelma. David snorted, glancing at lawn chairs where Bertie and Elizabeth were seated side by side, reading. Bertie, a cigarette clamped between his lips, reached absently for Elizabeth's hand; she took it, resting the book on the rise of her stomach as she turned a page.

"Even Elizabeth? I'm impressed. She generally spits people out before deciding they're friends."

"I can't believe it of her."

"You should. She comes across as sweetness and light, but she's a core of steel."

As if on cue, Elizabeth called out, "What are you two whispering about?"

David grinned. "We're putting money on that belly of yours." He stood behind Thelma once more to help her line up the club and ball. "Two pounds to me if it's a girl, three to Thelma if it's a boy."

"You w-w-wouldn't," said Bertie. He smiled at Elizabeth, her hand still in his. "Not without my—" He paused, exhaling as he forced out the next few words, "my fiver on a boy. Lilibet wants a b-brother."

Though his stance didn't change, David stiffened, watching Bertie and Elizabeth through narrowed eyes.

"Looking to secure the bloodline are you?" he said. His fingers, still wrapped around Thelma's on the golf club, began to dance, drumming a restless, unceasing rhythm. "The heir and the spare?"

Bertie's ears reddened. "D-d-don't be—" he said, dropping Elizabeth's hand. "Stupid."

David held his silence, a thin smile curling on his lips; from the croquet wickets, George looked up.

Thelma stepped out of David's grasp and swung her club; she missed, and the ball rolled limply along the grass.

Elizabeth closed her book. "Well, someone has to work on the next generation," she said, attempting to steer the conversation back to the playful tone it had begun with. "In any case, David, you ought to thank us—Papa's so taken with Lilibet that he's stopped hounding you."

Thelma handed the golf club back to David. "How about you show me how it's done?" she said.

"No, I'd rather a game of croquet," he said. "Shall we make it a foursome? Bertie's looking like he could use some sport."

Bertie glanced at Elizabeth, then stubbed out his cigarette.

"All right," he said. He stood and David handed him a mallet as Piers and George returned their balls to the starting wicket. Thelma took Bertie's vacant seat next to Elizabeth, who was watching the brothers with an expression that told Thelma the storm had not yet passed.

Piers struck first, his ball rolling through the first hoop and coming to rest slightly off course. His second shot came short; he moved aside to let David strike next, but David deferred.

"Let Bertie go," he said.

Bertie came forward, lining up his shot with careful precision. He looked down at the wicket, swinging the mallet experimentally.

"Come now, Bertie," said David. He raised his voice so that it carried across the lawn with cutting clarity. "If you play as slowly as you speak, we'll b-b-be here all d-d-day."

Thelma's heart dropped and she willed herself not to look at Elizabeth as the idyllic quiet of the day congealed. Still bent over his mallet, Bertie tensed; he struck the ball and it hit the side of the wicket, rolling off into the sloping grass.

He straightened. Without looking at anyone, he set his mallet back on the croquet rack and walked off.

"Oh, don't be like that," called David. He lifted his mallet to his shoulder and looked at George with a smirk.

Bertie walked across the green, his shoulders slumped. For a moment, Thelma thought he had broken into tears—but then he turned, and she could see he was lighting a cigarette.

"Should you go to him?" she whispered.

Elizabeth's expression was inscrutable. "No," she said. "Best leave him alone." She marked her place in her book. "In fact, the baby's kicking. Would you be kind enough to walk with me?"

Thelma nodded, avoiding David's eye as she helped Elizabeth

to her feet. To one side, Bertie threw his cigarette on the lawn and returned to the croquet game.

"I'm sorry," said Thelma as they walked down the green.

"Why? It's not your fault," she said.

They walked along the stone rampart that separated the lower garden from the upper terrace, a sweeping lawn punctuated every few feet by decommissioned cannons on a crumbling battlement, relics from some bygone redcoat feud.

"He's awfully hard on Bertie," said Elizabeth. "They're the best of friends, until something puts David out of sorts. He's so like his father."

Thelma glanced at Elizabeth, noting, as she had last night, how drawn the duchess looked. Under the guise of pulling a stone from her shoe Thelma sat on a nearby cannon, the iron gone red with age. Elizabeth lowered next to her with a sigh, her hand on her belly.

"I love David, but he can be so terribly self-indulgent," she continued, staring off into the grounds. "He labors under the assumption that if Bertie—if any of his brothers—has something he doesn't, he's been cheated. Never mind that he's never shown the slightest interest in wanting a family."

Thelma's mind turned to David's proposal. "I think he does, one day," she said.

"He might," said Elizabeth, "but on his own terms. On the one hand, he wants a family, children, a wife—on the other, he wants to continue going out with his friends until all hours, flitting to Europe every month for a holiday. He's a bit of a fantasist, I'm afraid—he wants what he can't have. He'd live twelve different lives if he could."

Thelma pictured twelve different Davids, living twelve different lives, sitting one inside the other like nesting dolls: in one, he had a wife, comely and gracious like Elizabeth, clutching four happy children; in another, he lived as the country gardener he always claimed to be, felling trees with a dog at his side. David as the night owl, dancing his way from club to club with a different woman for each night of the week; David as an RAF pilot, flying the fighter plane his father would never permit him to have.

And the life that superseded all the others—the one at the heart of it all—David as king.

"That's the trouble," she said softly. "Bertie's got the freedom David doesn't have. He isn't…predetermined. Not like David. That's what he envies."

Elizabeth nodded; wincing, she tightened her hand over her stomach and Thelma knew the baby was kicking, turning like a butter churn. "I know he struggles," she said. "Particularly with Papa." She got to her feet, her palm pressed against the cannon for support as she straightened.

"David's got his merits," she continued, "I'm sure you've found them or you wouldn't be with him, but he has a tendency toward crippling selfishness. Perhaps he thinks it's his due—or perhaps he hasn't found someone to help him improve upon his shortcomings. I wonder—did he tell you why Harry couldn't join us?"

He hadn't; Thelma hadn't given much thought to the Duke of Gloucester's absence, though he was the only one of David's brothers not present.

"He had to attend an opening of a new shipyard in Clydesdale. It was David's responsibility, originally, but he passed it off to Harry. It's not the first time he's shirked his duties—there's always an excuse, some sudden illness. Bertie and I are usually the ones to pick up the slack."

Thelma wasn't altogether surprised. How many times had he rung her claiming that his evening engagement had been rescheduled? She only hoped Elizabeth didn't see her as the genesis of David's bad behavior.

They had wandered the length of the cannons and were now

on the far side of the Fort, looking down on the muddy pit that, David said, would soon become the swimming pool.

"I worry about him," said Elizabeth. "He needs someone strong by his side. Someone to help him live the life he's got, not the one he wishes he had."

Thelma squinted into the gray sky. "You think I should give him up?"

"Quite the contrary," said Elizabeth. "I think you're rather good for him. He has a heavy burden, and one can hardly blame him for wanting someone to help him carry it. Bertie and I, George and Harry—Piers, even—we all help, in what way we can, but David needs a partner." She looked up at the Fort, its gleaming windows blanked by reflected clouds. "David's done so very well, but I worry about him."

Thelma and Elizabeth waited in the drawing room for the men to come in, listening for the stomp of boots as the men came to the back door. Thelma looked out the window: Bertie was still near the croquet set, another cigarette between his lips.

David opened the door, laughing. He had removed his sweater and knotted it about his shoulders, making him look as if he'd come in from punting on a river.

"I'm for the steam room, I think… Anyone care to join? Legh? George?" He set off for his bedroom, and Thelma followed.

"I want you to apologize to Bertie," she said, once they were out of earshot.

David opened his bedroom door. "I know," he said as Thelma walked in. "I was out of line. I always seem to be, when it comes to him."

"It was cruel," she said as David tugged his sweater free. "I wouldn't be surprised if they packed up and left."

He tossed the sweater in a corner and unbuttoned his shirt, looking up at Thelma with sudden concern. "You don't really think they would?"

"Why? Afraid they'll ruin your party?"

"Of course not." David sat on the bed. "I don't know why I fly off the handle. Not enough sleep, I suppose."

"Whatever the reason, you were a bully."

David winced.

"I know," he said. He laid back on the bed, one hand beneath his head as he stared at the ceiling, eyes deep with remorse. "I feel terrible but I can't help myself. Flaunting his marriage, his children in front of the rest of us... Perfect Bertie. He can be so *frustrating*..."

Thelma sat down. "So can you," she said, more gently, as his hand found hers across the coverlet, "but you're brothers, and you owe it to him to be kinder."

He sat up. "You don't really think they'd leave?"

"I wouldn't blame them. Think of what Gloria would say if I mocked her the way you did Bertie."

David sighed. "I suppose." He ran his hand up her arm, kissing her neck—but Thelma stood.

"Apologize, David," she said, and left the room.

Thelma was the last to come down for cocktails. David and Bertie were at opposite ends of the drawing room, Bertie next to Elizabeth by the fireplace, David by the phonograph, leafing through a wooden box of records. At the cocktail table, Piers and George mixed drinks, George's idle conversation louder than usual in the absence of music.

"Gin and Dubonnet, Thelma?" said Piers. David looked up, his expression wary, and Thelma knew he hadn't yet asked Bertie's forgiveness.

"Whiskey and soda, please," said Thelma. She sat next to Elizabeth. "No music tonight, David?"

David pulled a record from the box, frowning as he turned the jacket over to look at the cover.

"Did you know these are meant to be unbreakable?" he said.

"I had this entire box sent from London. It says on the label they're indestructible." He pulled the record from its sleeve, inspecting the vinyl up close. "Remarkable, what they can do with technology."

Bertie puffed on his cigarette. "Well, are they?" he asked, and David looked up in surprise. "Unb-breakable. That's a b-bold claim."

David held Bertie's gaze, his fingers playing with the edge of the record. Suddenly he whipped the record across the room; it whizzed through the air and hit the wall, then fell to the floor with a clatter.

George picked it up, inspecting it for signs of damage. "The record's survived—can't say the same for the wallpaper," he said.

Bertie snatched the record and threw it back. David reached for it, but it veered off course, hitting a lamp on a nearby table.

The lamp teetered once, twice, then toppled from its perch and shattered to pieces.

Elizabeth gasped. Bertie looked up, horrified—but then David nudged a shard of lamp with his shoe. "I always hated that one," he said. "One of Father's, I think."

"Perhaps we ought to continue this experiment outside?" said Piers.

David hefted the box of records into his arms. "I've a better idea." He walked through a small, wood-paneled doorway and Thelma followed, George grabbing the bottle of gin as they tailed David up the spiral stairs of the Fort's tower.

They came out at the top, laughing as they spilled into the cool evening air. David's dogs were barking ecstatically at the commotion, nipping at heels and running in circles. The view was spectacular: Thelma inhaled deeply, looking out along the sloping grounds to Virginia Water. The clouds had lifted, leaving low, rolling fog along the water and the sun finally, spectacularly visible as it descended into the trees.

David set the box down and pulled out a handful of records, the lapels of his jacket lifting in the wind.

"Ten pounds to the first person to break one?" suggested George, as David handed him a record. He tossed his record like a discus and it spiraled into the empty air, catching on an updraft before arcing slowly toward the ground.

"You're not giving it enough force," said Elizabeth. She went to the edge of the tower and whipped her record straight down; Thelma ran over, watching the record's progress as it knocked against the side of the tower and shattered on the flagstones below.

They all cheered.

"Ten pounds to Elizabeth!" shouted David.

"You'll have to write to the record label—false advertising!" said Piers, and he threw his record, not bothering to watch its progress as he reached for more.

David took a stack in his arms and threw them one by one. They watched, laughing, as the records caught the light, gleaming leaves in autumn, before falling to earth.

THIRTY-TWO

November 1930
London

THELMA WALKED OUT OF HER FLAT, NODDING TO
the doorman as she stepped onto the sidewalk. Across the road,
gray branches formed a latticework canopy above Grosvenor
Square; though still early in the day, people wandered through
the park, shoulders rounded against the chill. She crossed the street,
quickening her pace as she made her way toward Claridge's Hotel.

Seven months had passed since Thelma had left Duke, and
the freedom afforded by having her own apartment had fundamentally changed the nature of her relationship with David.
The move served, for all intents and purposes, as a public declaration: whereas before, Thelma had to be content with the few
hours David could spare between his royal duties, now she was
hosting dinner parties on his behalf.

The weekends, David insisted, were to be spent out of the city.
Nearly every Friday night, Thelma met David at Fort Belvedere or Burrough Court, which Duke continued to let Thelma
use when he was away. As promised, Duke hadn't fallen out of

Thelma's life completely. They met for luncheon and telephoned most weeks to discuss the houses and the children.

Thelma and Averill, too, had patched up their differences. Now that Thelma had moved out of Arlington Place, Averill had withdrawn her opposition to David. She had even agreed to be at Burrough Court for a weekend party, where Thelma was hosting David and George for the Belvoir Hunt.

The party was, Thelma supposed, the reason Consuelo had asked her to lunch. Though Thelma and David were, for all intents and purposes, a couple, appearances had to be maintained: accordingly, Consuelo and Benny had agreed to chaperone the weekend, as they had done at Three Gables over a year ago.

Thelma stepped into Claridge's, crossing the checkerboard lobby into the foyer.

Consuelo was at a table near the entrance, dressed in a tweed suit and matching hat, a tiered tea tray in front of her.

"I ordered already. I hope you don't mind," she said. "I can't stay long."

Thelma sat, and Consuelo poured her a cup of tea. "How are you?" asked Thelma.

Consuelo transferred a tea sandwich onto her plate. "Bad news first, I'm afraid. Benny's mother is ill," she said. "I've got to go to Paris tomorrow to take care of her."

"Tomorrow? For how long?" said Thelma.

"As long as I'm needed," said Consuelo. She finished the sandwich and dabbed at her lips with a cream-colored napkin. "Benny can still come—he's in the midst of some entanglement at the embassy and doesn't dare leave the country until it's finished. But he's so anxious about her, I know it would be a comfort if I were to go."

"I understand, of course I do—but that does leave me in a fix," said Thelma. "Where will I find another couple on such short notice?"

"I've already thought of someone," said Consuelo. "You re-call Maud Kerr-Smiley?"

Thelma did: Maud was a friend of Lady Sarah's. A bit aus-tere, but gracious enough on the few occasions that Thelma had met her.

"Her brother and his wife have become friends. She's Amer-ican—he pretends not to be, but everyone knows he was born in New York." Consuelo smirked. "They've lived here nearly two years but I only got to know them a few months ago. Maud tells me they're looking to make friends. I've lunched with the wife. You'll like her, I think. They'd be happy to take my place. I can't imagine they've any other engagements."

Thelma hesitated. "I don't know," she said. "David can be so particular about strangers."

"I know it's not ideal but it's the best I can do," replied Con-suelo. "They'll be fine—Ernest Simpson is terrifically dull, but you can count on him not making a scene. As for Wallis...well, I'll let you draw your own conclusions. I really do think you'll get along."

Thelma hesitated a moment longer, then reached into her handbag for her address book. Consuelo wrote down the num-ber for the Simpsons, who, when Thelma telephoned later that afternoon, said they'd be delighted to join.

David fiddled with his tie in Thelma's dressing room, in-specting the red silk against the gray check of his unbuttoned waistcoat.

"I live in suits," he grumbled, frowning at his reflection in the mirror.

David was in a black mood. Thelma had arrived at Burrough Court on Thursday, and while David had planned to join her Friday morning, an impromptu summons from Buckingham Pal-ace had pushed back his departure to noon. To David, Thelma knew that the delay alone was reason enough to frown, but his meeting with the king had pushed him even further into a sulk.

"But you look so handsome in them," said Thelma. She resisted the temptation to look at her watch: they were twenty minutes late for tea at Craven Lodge Club, but she knew better than to say so. She pulled at the clasp of a pearl bracelet, attempting to look busy while David finished dressing.

He grunted, pulling the knot of his tie apart. "Who are these people you invited?" he said, letting the tie fall to the floor. His valet stooped to catch it before handing him a different one.

"The Simpsons. They're friends of Consuelo's. Americans—Connie tells me they're good fun."

David passed the second tie back to the valet with an irritable shake of his head. He looked over the drawer of ties and pocket scarves the valet had brought in, indicating the one he wanted with a flick of his wrist. "And I suppose you'll want me to be charming to them, do you?"

"What do you mean by that?"

The valet gave David the tie and he fashioned an asymmetrical knot, over under.

"Nothing," he said. He folded his collar down and fastened the buttons of his waistcoat.

"David, please," said Thelma. "They're friends of Consuelo's."

David put on his jacket and Thelma tucked the pocket square into his breast pocket, smoothing the lapels of his jacket. Craven Lodge Club wasn't far away; if they left in five minutes and stayed for forty, they would be back by the time the Simpsons' train came in. She hoped David and George weren't feeling too chatty—she didn't want the Simpsons to feel snubbed. Thankfully, Averill was here: if they didn't get back on time, she could keep them entertained.

"I just don't see why you had to invite strangers," said David as they walked down to the car. The sky was a deepening blue-gray, clouds rolling heavy over dull fields. Before getting into the car, David lit a cigarette, its glowing end the only spot of color in the drab landscape. "I've had an exhausting week—has anyone ever heard of the Simpsons? I doubt anyone we know has even met them."

"They're friends of Consuelo's," Thelma repeated as David settled beside her. He let out a breath, filling the back of the car with smoke. "Do you really think Consuelo would send boring people?"

David shrugged as the car pulled out of the drive. "I wouldn't know," he said. "What's to say they're not here to…"

"To what?"

"To *gawk*," he said. He looked away, his face sharp in profile as he stared out at the passing hedgerows. "It happens all the time, you know. Hangers-on. Social climbers."

"That's not fair. You're being terribly snobbish," Thelma replied.

"Aren't I allowed to be? I spend all my days meeting strangers, shaking hands…is it too much to ask that I spend my weekends with friends?"

Thelma ought to have expected this. David did well when things went according to plan, but he loathed surprises. "You might make new friends," she said.

"I don't want new friends." He reached across the seat and put his hand on Thelma's thigh. She considered slapping it away— it would serve him right—but he moved closer. "I want to be alone. With you."

The motorcar turned onto a laneway flanked by brick pillars and a modest wrought-iron gate. He kissed her neck, his breath warm against her chest.

"David…" Thelma could see Craven Lodge Club through the trees: a two-story brick building with warm light in the windows. She shifted away, tucking a loose lock of hair back into place.

David slumped, and Thelma wanted to scream: How would it look, arriving entwined like sixteen-year-olds? He could be so *petulant*… But he squeezed her hand all the same.

All he wanted was to spend time with her. Was that so terrible?

The car rolled to a stop and a footman came forward to open David's door. Framed by the mullioned picture windows at the front of the Club, Thelma could see people milling about, laughing and talking.

"All right," she said. David brightened; he kissed Thelma on the cheek, then on the lips, and the footman lifted his hand from the handle and turned his back to the door.

Thelma smiled, amused by how close David's emotions were to the surface. He was predictable, really, in a charming sort of way: easy to put out of sorts, and easy to please. She opened her door to slip out of David's grasp and leaned down, resting her arm on the frame of the motorcar as David shifted out. "But I won't have you being rude to my guests. All right?"

He touched the knot of his tie and held out his arm. "Of course," he said smoothly. "For you, my darling, anything. Anything at all."

Thelma stared out the window, tapping a finger against her crossed arm. She set down her teacup and walked to the front hall, glancing at an austere grandfather clock. She and David had only planned to be at Craven Lodge Club for an hour but the weather, it seemed, had different plans: minutes after they arrived fog had rolled through Melton Mowbray, thick as cement, obscuring the laneway and the line of cars in the drive. She asked a footman to find her chauffeur and he disappeared down the drive, his tailcoat flapping as he plunged into the mist.

Unless the fog delayed their train, the Simpsons would have long since arrived at Burrough Court. They would be in the front room with Averill and Benny—excited and nervous at the prospect of meeting the Prince of Wales, and wondering, no doubt, at their hostess's absence.

The footman rematerialized with Thelma's chauffeur in tow.

"Is there really no way we can leave?" she asked.

The chauffeur touched the brim of his cap. "Begging your pardon, my lady, not without risk. Best to let the fog slacken a bit. Go back inside before you catch a chill."

Frustrated, Thelma retreated to the sitting room, where David was sitting with George and Piers Legh.

"We're stranded a little while longer yet," she said to David, trying to sound as though the timing was nothing of consequence. "Safety first, Mills tells me."

"We ought to have a cocktail, then," he replied, and beckoned for a footman. "We've moved long past teatime."

Forty minutes later, the butler told Thelma in an undertone that the chauffeur had deemed it safe to go.

"Finally," said George. Thelma and David stood, but George slipped between them to take Thelma's hand. Laughing, Thelma let George lead her toward the front door.

"Tell me you've a decent cook," he said as he helped Thelma with her overcoat. "And a decent bar."

"Georgie, you've been eating sandwiches all afternoon," said David as he followed them into the deepening night. "Any more and we'll have to roll you to Thelma's house."

George released Thelma's hand as she climbed into the motorcar; he slid next to her, sitting a shade too close, and murmured into her ear. "My dear, have you any American bourbon? I've a cocktail I want to try. It's got bitters and orange peel and I got squiffed on the stuff in Malta..."

"It's called an old-fashioned, and yes, I do," said Thelma. "Provided the Simpsons haven't finished the bottle by the time we arrive. I wouldn't blame them..."

They arrived at Burrough Court at seven o'clock and Thelma, flinging her coat at the butler, rushed to the drawing room as David and George, idly unwrapping their scarves, continued an animated discussion they'd begun in the car about the upcoming fox hunt.

"I'm so very sorry," said Thelma, clasping her chilled hands together as she met Averill's expression of evident relief. She smiled at the dark-haired couple on the sofa sitting next to Benny. "We got stranded in this awful fog."

Though Mrs. Simpson had little in the way of natural beauty, Thelma was impressed by her striking sense of style: she was rail-thin and impeccably put together, her sharp features smoothed under a layer of porcelain makeup. Like Thelma, she was dressed in day clothes—a blue-gray tweed dress and a tidy gray hat over thick, glossy curls.

She stood, arms outstretched, and pulled Thelma into a bony hug. "No matter," she said, her Baltimore accent warm. "You're here now. It's lovely to meet you, Thelma. Thank you so much for including Ernest and me in your little soiree."

Ernest Simpson nodded. He held out his hand, bending forward to kiss the backs of Thelma's fingers with Prussian decorum. "Lady Furness," he said, "What a pleasure to meet you." He had a British coloring to his voice, and Thelma could see what Consuelo had meant about him trying to hide his American roots.

Mrs. Simpson laid a hand on Thelma's arm. "I must warn you, I've the most terrible cold," she said. "I do hope you don't mind if I pop upstairs before Their Highnesses arrive, to pull myself together. Your stepdaughter has been the most wonderful hostess, I couldn't bear to pull myself away before now."

"I'm afraid you're too late," she replied. "Their Highnesses are already here, just in the hall."

Mrs. Simpson's composure slipped for the briefest of seconds and Thelma saw, despite her heavy makeup, how chapped her nose looked. She recalled her first date with David—how nervous he had made her; how determined she'd been to present herself at her best.

"I tell you what," said Thelma. "I'll take David and George upstairs to change. You and Ernest can run up after us for a quick lie-down."

"Oh, would you?" said Mrs. Simpson. "You're an angel. I can see why Consuelo thinks so highly of you."

"It's no trouble," she said, enjoying the moment of friendly collusion. "I'll go out now."

She returned to front hall, where David and George were still arguing about the fox hunt.

"Darling, let's change for dinner. We're running late, and our guests will be arriving soon," said Thelma. "You best come, too, George, if you want that old-fashioned before midnight."

Thelma chivvied the brothers, still arguing, up the stairs, and Mr. and Mrs. Simpson hurried forward as the princes drifted away.

"You're an absolute doll," said Mrs. Simpson, gripping Thelma's arm as she passed.

"Really, Mrs. Simpson, it's no trouble," said Thelma.

Wallis's voice floated back down the stairs. "Call me Wallis. Mrs. Simpson is Ernest's *mother.*"

The next day David and George left the house early to join the hunt. Ernest and Benny, neither of them sportsmen, remained at Burrough Court, but Wallis was too restless to sit.

"Show me the grounds?" she asked as Benny and Ernest began to read through a stack of newspapers. Thelma lent Wallis a pair of Wellington boots and they set off.

Although the fog had lifted, the countryside was muddy and brown, and a light drizzle misted onto Thelma's woolen coat as they walked along the hedgerows.

"You're so lucky, to have all this," Wallis said. Rather than venturing into the fields behind Burrough Court, Wallis had suggested wandering toward town and Thelma agreed—the hard-packed ground on either side of the road was easier going than the muddy pathways Thelma and Averill usually took. "This air—what a change from London."

"Do you like living there?" asked Thelma.

Wallis smirked. "The drafty house, the perpetual drizzle and the cold company? It's a scream. When I think of all those times I complained about Washington summers... I'd take the humidity any day of the week. How do you stand it?"

Thelma shrugged. "London has its merits," she said.

"So says the woman romancing the Prince of Wales." She wrapped her arm through Thelma's. "Really, though—how do you stand it?"

"It was an adjustment," said Thelma. "I'd been living all over the place, before I met Duke—Paris, Los Angeles, New York... more than anything, it was nice to make a home. A real home."

"How romantic," said Wallis, looking across the field.

"It was, at the time," said Thelma.

Wallis nudged her. "But now—the prince! What a thrill. You know, he's shorter than I thought he'd be. You see all these photographs and would swear he's ten feet tall. Do many people tell you that? Goes to show, I suppose."

"I suppose," said Thelma, "though I don't particularly notice anymore. He's just David."

"To you," said Wallis. "To the rest of the world, he's something else entirely." She looked up and Thelma followed her gaze: there, tiny on the rise of the hill, a cluster of horsemen galloped out from a copse of trees, preceded by a contingent of hounds. They looked like something out of a painting, their scarlet coats bright against the gray sky.

"That will be the Belvoir?" asked Wallis.

Thelma nodded as the thin sound of a hunting horn broke through the still air. One of the horsemen pulled away from the rest, galloping toward the running hounds. As they watched, his horse faltered; Thelma screamed as it somersaulted, the rider flying from its back and hitting the ground with sickening finality. Unable to rein in, several riders thundered past the fallen man.

Thelma gripped Wallis's arm.

"Oh, God," she whispered.

The riders came to a ragged halt. One small figure jumped down from his mount as the fallen horse struggled to its feet and bolted, leaving its rider motionless on the muddy field.

"Is it him?" said Wallis, her voice hushed.

Thelma felt sick. "I don't know," she said. "Oh, God, what if it's him?" She was trembling: Hadn't David's father prohibited him from riding for this very reason?

Several other riders were off their horses now, crouching next to the fallen man. Thelma could have counted the space between seconds as she willed the figure on the ground to move.

Wallis started. "He's up," she said, as the figure rose unsteadily to his feet. "Oh, thank God, he's up."

He bent double and vomited, then straightened once more, assisted by two others.

Thelma let out a shuddering breath.

"There we go. Whoever it was just had the wind knocked out of him." Wallis sighed, and patted Thelma's back. "The dangers of the sport, I suppose—it's a blessing Ernest isn't outdoorsy. Should we go back to the house? If it's one of ours, he'll be wanting a brandy."

Thelma allowed Wallis to steer her back toward Burrough Court. If it was David—if he'd seriously hurt himself—she wouldn't have known what to do. What would have happened, if the future king had crippled himself in her company? The papers, blessedly, kept quiet about their relationship. But even putting aside the consequences to her reputation, to her heart, to Duke…if something had happened to David, it would have been disastrous.

Only once they got back to Burrough Court did Thelma realize that Wallis had been gripping Thelma's arm just as tightly as Thelma had been gripping hers.

THIRTY-THREE

October 12, 1934
Grand Central Station

THE TRAIN CAME SLOWLY TO REST. THE JOURNEY from Montreal had taken nearly twelve hours: night had fallen once more, and the lights of Grand Central Station provided a welcome refuge from the evening gloom. In her compartment, Thelma rubbed a finger across the windowpane, hoping for a clear view, but steam obscured the platform and the reporters crowding it. She could already hear what they were shouting— they were waiting for her. She turned to Mathew.

"I shan't come with you. I'll have enough trouble finding my driver without the commotion of your arrival," he said, sharing a thin smile between Thelma and Harry. "Remember what I told you—it will be you, Lady Furness, that the reporters want. You mustn't allow them to provoke you into making an unwise statement. Don't say a word beyond 'no comment.' Not until tomorrow—not until you've spoken to Mrs. Vanderbilt's lawyer."

Thelma wound her fur around her neck.

"Thank you, Mr. Mathew, for your advice," said Harry. He held out his hand and the lawyer took it, nodding.

"Good luck to you," he said, and opened the compartment door.

Noise from the platform grew louder as Thelma walked down the corridor. Her heart hammered at the thought of them so close, but she couldn't turn back; not when Gloria needed her. She gripped Harry's hand, then moved into view.

"Lady Furness! What do you think of your sister's troubles?"

"Were you aware Mrs. Vanderbilt is a lesbian?"

"Lookee this way, Thelma! Smile for the camera!"

Thelma blinked as dozens of reporters, holding notepads and cameras, pooled around the carriage door, jostling for position, obstructing other passengers who were attempting to disembark from the train. Flashbulbs popped left and right, filling the air with a sulfurous stench.

Two policemen stood at the carriage steps, and one held out his hand with a reassuring nod.

"With me, Lady Furness," he said, and she took his arm to step down onto the platform. He began to push forward and Thelma looked back to see the other officer assisting Edith and Harry into the fray. She worried for a moment about Elise, but the maid was staying behind to help with the luggage—grateful, no doubt, that she wasn't subject to her mistress's troubles.

The reporters followed Thelma through to the main concourse, shouts echoing through the cavernous space. The noise was such that Thelma pictured it bringing down the marble pillars, startling the serene constellations painted on the ceiling above.

"No comment," she said, attempting to quell the noise. A sleepy attendant jumped up as she passed the ticket desk, startled into action. "*No comment,*" she repeated, vaulting up the staircase as the crowd seemed to multiply below.

With the police officer forging the path, Thelma exited the front doors at a run. The reporters poured outside, too, forming a scrum past which Thelma could see a gleaming Rolls Royce, its driver at the ready.

The reporters seemed to lose heart as Thelma neared the automobile, their questions slackening as the cameramen ran short of flashbulbs. She was still a few yards away from the car when a reporter attempted one final bait:

"Lady Furness! Do you think your sister ought to lose custody of Little Gloria? Is she as unfit as your ma says she is?"

Thelma halted. Perhaps it was the exhaustion of travel, but the reporter's words stopped her in her tracks. Panic turned to indignation—she let go of the policeman's arm and looked back, attempting to find the man who had asked the question. Gloria, unfit?

"The charges are ridiculous," she said. "It's all lies. It's a gross injustice."

Encouraged by her answer, another reporter raised his arm. "What do you think of your mother testifying for Mrs. Whitney?"

"I have no idea what she is doing," Thelma replied, louder. "I'm positively amazed that she has sided with Mrs. Whitney."

The reporters scribbled furiously, heads bowed as though in reverence. Thelma took a breath and moved forward, the crowd parting before her as she made her way to the idling motorcar.

"Do you think your sister should have charge of Little Gloria?"

"Certainly she should," said Thelma. "Little Gloria should be with her own mother. I'm a mother myself, you know—I dare anybody to try to take my baby from me. It's too outrageous to talk about."

"Will you testify to that?"

"I certainly will."

They reached the motorcar and the driver opened the passenger door. Thelma was on the verge of getting in when a final reporter pushed his way forward.

"Your mother thinks you're crazy," he said, his eyes darting to meet hers.

Thelma's ears rang with sudden fury. In her mind's eye, she could see Mathew, urging her to remember what they had practiced in the train. She could laugh at Mamma's shameless hypocrisy; she could lash out—but what would that accomplish?

You're here for Gloria. She settled the fox fur more snugly around her neck and faced the crowd once more.

"It is beyond my comprehension," she said, shaking, "how people in glass houses can sling mud."

She entered the car and slammed the door behind her.

"That was quite the performance," said Harry, craning to look past Edith, who was sandwiched between them in the back of the motorcar. He didn't look altogether pleased; his face was pale, fingers twitching against Edith's like the legs of a pinned spider. "I hope you knew what you were doing."

Thelma looked out the window, though there wasn't much to see: the lamp-lit bottoms of illuminated buildings; dark figures walking past parked automobiles.

"Of course I did," she said, still shaking. She wished she hadn't ended on such a nonsensical note, glass houses and mud-slinging. "It's unconscionable, really. The nerve…"

"I don't think Mr. Mathew will be impressed," said Edith.

"Mr. Mathew doesn't have Gloria's best interests at heart," said Thelma. "You heard him. He's here for Nada."

She continued to stare pointedly out the window, and Harry held up his hands in defeat.

Thelma closed her eyes, the space between her and Gloria shrinking smaller. It had been too long; Thelma ought to have been here weeks ago. She would have come, if Gloria hadn't kept the gravity of her predicament closeted away for so long.

"I want you to promise me something," said Thelma. "When we arrive, don't tell Gloria about Mathew. I'll tell her about Nada, but the rest of it—it's not relevant. Not now. She has enough of us coming to speak to her character—it won't matter that we don't have David and Nada."

"Won't it?" said Harry. "She ought to have the facts. As unpleasant as they might be."

"You weren't with her when she lost Reggie," Thelma replied. "She's not strong enough to hear it all at once. Mathew's right—David doesn't need to be brought into this, but Nada chose not to come. She chose that." She sat back, arms crossed.

Harry and Edith exchanged a glance but said nothing more.

Brick apartments became limestone buildings as they crawled into the Upper East Side. Gloria's brownstone was on Seventy-Seventh Street, just past Park Avenue. She'd been so pleased with it when she first signed the lease: she'd chosen it because of its proximity to Central Park, how easy it would be for Kieslich to take Little Gloria to feed the ducks when they moved home from Paris—but mere days after arriving, Kieslich had walked Little Gloria out to Central Park and into a waiting car that took them to Gertrude Payne Whitney's art studio in Greenwich Village.

Gloria hadn't seen her daughter since.

The car stopped half a block from Gloria's house and the chauffeur let out a low whistle. "Will you look at that?"

The lamp-lit street was filled with reporters camped out on either side of the narrow town house; some were standing in small clusters next to Gloria's front steps, while others crouched on the steps of the houses opposite or sat on the curb. Clearly, they had been waiting for some time: one man, lolling against a lamppost, started into wakefulness as the people around him surged up from their roosts.

They poured into the street, pushing each other aside and shouting as the car inched forward. Thelma held a hand over her face as a flashbulb burst outside her window; Harry swore, putting his arm around Edith's shoulders.

The car moved another foot. "I'll get you within spitting distance," said the chauffeur, pushing his cap up on his forehead.

Thelma felt a small pressure on her leg and looked down: Edith was holding out her hand, palm open like a clamshell. Thelma took it and squeezed.

"I'd recommend, perhaps, that we keep quiet this time," said Edith. "They've more than enough to write about for the morning's papers."

The car finally stopped its slow progression. The chauffeur dove out of the car, fighting against the sea of bodies; Thelma could hear him pleading for space, and the crowd grudgingly moved to form a narrow pathway.

Harry was closest to the door. "Are you all right?" Edith whispered.

"Yes," he replied, his face shiny as he brushed dust off the brim of his hat. He jammed the hat on his head and nodded to the chauffeur.

Ignoring the cameras, he stepped out, then turned to assist Edith.

Striving to match Harry's courage, Thelma smiled as she stepped out, looking blindly above the crowd. Even if she wanted to make a statement Thelma doubted anyone would be able to hear her over the noise. In the town house beside Gloria's, curtains twitched in the parlor windows: she felt a moment's pity for the family trapped inside, caught up in Gloria's circus for no reason other than proximity.

The commotion died down as they were shuttled inside by a waiting butler. The front hall was dim and comforting, mahogany trim and violet wallpaper, sconces casting yellow light up the staircase. Thelma squinted as her eyes adjusted to the dark; Edith let out a nervous giggle and Harry removed his coat with a curse.

"Sorry about all that." The butler, a broad young man built like a wrestler, gave Thelma a fleshy-cheeked smile. Thelma wondered whether he doubled as Gloria's bodyguard or whether he'd been hired simply to give the impression of bulk at the door. "Things are a little wild around here. Lady Furness, may I take your coat?"

Thelma unbundled herself from her coat and furs, handing them to the butler who flung them over his arm. "You've got some letters, Lady Furness—I had them taken up to your room."

Thelma's heart lifted. She followed Harry and Edith into a drawing room where Consuelo stood waiting.

"Thank God," she said, wrapping Thelma in a hug. She stepped back, unsmiling; beside her was a man Thelma didn't recognize. "I hope it wasn't too much trouble getting in. We've asked policemen to keep them from the front doors, but it's proving more difficult than we anticipated. Harry, Edith, thank you for coming." She gestured to the man at her side. "This is Gloria's solicitor, Nathan Burkan."

Burkan was small and gray and sensible-looking, dressed in a single-breasted suit. Thelma recalled how highly Gloria had spoken about her lawyer in the past; taking his hand now, Thelma could see why. Behind his wire-rimmed glasses, Burkan scrutinized Thelma with a sharp, unwavering gaze.

"Lady Furness, we're so pleased you've come," he said. "Your sister needs all the support she can get—and from what she tells me, you're the strongest support of all."

"Well, she's lucky to have good representation," Thelma replied. She looked at Consuelo. "Where is she? Surely she hasn't gone out?"

Consuelo lowered her voice. "In bed, poor thing," she said. "I'm worried about her health. Her former butler testified in court today, and she's in a complete state about whether the rest of her staff has been bought by Mrs. Whitney, too. She hardly eats a thing. The strain of it all… It's nerves, of course, but something else, too, I think."

"She's distraught—absolutely distraught," said Burkan, nodding with fatherly concern. "Who can blame her? It would be a strain on anyone, let alone someone with her disposition."

★ ★ ★

The last time Thelma had visited, Gloria's bedroom had been at the front of the house.

I love watching the street go by, Gloria had told her, opening the curtains and curling up in a window seat. Together, they watched nurses walk by with babies in oversized perambulators; suited businessmen, walking too quickly because they'd lingered over their morning newspaper. Women like Thelma and Gloria themselves, in fashionable outfits.

Tonight, Thelma strode down the second-floor hallway toward the back of the house, to the bedroom farthest from the street. The door was shut, but light spilled a sliver onto the hallway floorboards. She knocked, then turned the handle.

Gloria was lying in bed, her hair bound up in a peach turban.

"Thelma," she said, halfway between a laugh and a sob. She held out her arms and Thelma sat on the bed, collecting her into a hug.

Gloria pulled away. "I knew you'd come. Harry and Edith?"

"They're here, too. We all made the trip together," said Thelma.

"I knew you would. Mamma's going to be furious, but Nathan is so pleased. He says it will be a real show of force, all of us together. It's going to be a real boost, he says."

Thelma nodded, her hand on Gloria's back. Beneath the robe, Thelma could feel Gloria's bones: spine and shoulder blades and ribs. "How are you?" she asked.

Gloria sighed. "They took my baby," she said in a hollow voice. "I don't understand any of it. Nothing... I keep running over it all. Gertrude offered to take Little Gloria to Old Westbury so that I could close up the Paris house. I thought, why not? Gloria could stand to spend some time with Reggie's family—better, surely, than coming back to Europe with me to pack boxes..."

Thelma wondered how many times she'd circled through the

same sequence of events in her head—whether the story was as Gloria truly understood it or whether, even now, she was reciting what she would tell the judge.

"...so I returned to New York and leased this place, but then Little Gloria got tonsillitis and the doctors recommended that she stay with Gertrude in the country for fresh air—and who was I to argue? Then she started her schooling, and the doctors didn't think I should upset her by moving her back to New York when she'd met new friends. It was so *gradual*, Thelma. A little piece here, a little piece there..."

She trailed off and Thelma looked around the room, seeing further evidence of Gloria's decline: jars of heavy makeup; cigarettes scattered across a table. An empty medicine bottle, missed by the maid, under the armchair.

"When I finally demanded that Gloria come home, she threw a tantrum...*such* a tantrum." Gloria looked older than her thirty years. "They say I only want her for the money, but what kind of mother would do that? I'd want her with me if we were penniless... We *will* be penniless if this continues."

The expression on Gloria's face was such that Thelma regretted thinking, even for a moment, that her story was anything other than true. She stayed silent, letting Gloria speak her fill: perhaps it was good for her to let it out. To excise it, like a tumor, from her mind.

Gloria lifted her chin, genuinely bewildered. "I haven't been any less of a mother than Mamma was to us," she said. "And she's saying I'm irresponsible? I'm neglectful?"

Your mother thinks you're crazy. "She's unstable," Thelma replied. "We've always known that."

"That's just it," said Gloria. She reached for a bottle of mineral water on the bedside table, unscrewing the lid with trembling hands. "I'm her daughter—*we're* her daughters. What if I'm just as unstable? What if they're right, to want to take her away?"

"You can't start thinking like that," said Thelma. "It's not helpful—not to you, and certainly not to Little Gloria."

"Perhaps." Gloria retreated into silence once more; Thelma extricated herself from the bed and picked up a pair of cigarettes from a pile on a nearby table. Gloria waved away the offer and Thelma found the carton, replacing the spilled cigarettes back in their box one by one.

Gloria leaned back against Thelma's shoulder once more and Thelma stroked her forehead, surreptitiously feeling for a fever; Gloria shifted, reaching for the mineral water and a dish of tablets.

"What are those?" asked Thelma, as Gloria swallowed the pills one by one.

"For nerves," she said, wiping her mouth with the back of her hand. "It's been exhausting. But Nathan says it will all turn around when we start our defense. I'll be able to respond to these horrible—" She shook her head, as though reorganizing her thoughts.

"Nathan says it's important to focus on our defense," she continued. "With you and Harry and Consuelo, I've three witnesses. Connie Bennett said she'll come—and Friedel and Nada, of course. Have you spoken to Nada? I've so much to tell her. She must be horrified, I really must apologize for all the confusion…"

Thelma's heart sank. Gloria looked so hopeful, going on about how people could, of course, misconstrue a close friendship; that she and Nada would simply explain to the judge that their friendship was entirely proper; that Nada's relationship with George was, thankfully, strong enough to withstand the rumors of impropriety.

Thelma looked at Gloria's shaking hands.

"Nada isn't coming," she said gently.

Gloria's veneer of composure cracked with a delicate, miserable upturn of her lips. She let out a single, empty laugh, running her fingers along the hem of her coverlet. "Did—did she give you a letter for me? A message?"

Thelma shook her head. "Friedel's coming," she said. "He'll support you, you know he'll say anything."

Gloria pulled away, dabbing her eyes as tears fell down her cheeks, unwanted, uncontrollable.

"Silly, I know. I can hardly blame her for wanting to keep out of this mess. Her reputation—"

"You loved her," said Thelma.

Gloria looked at Thelma sharply; Thelma was heartbroken at the suspicion on her face.

She took Gloria's hands in her own once more, and Gloria's eyes filled with tears.

"I loved them both," said Gloria. "May God forgive me. I loved them both."

"How is she?" asked Edith, when Thelma returned to the sitting room. Harry, perched on the edge of an ottoman, looked up.

"Much the same, I expect," said Thelma. "She took a sleeping pill. Hopefully that will do her some good."

"The best thing for her right now is sleep," said Burkan, handing Thelma a glass of sherry, "but it's imperative that we work together in her absence. Gloria's best chance is if we present a united front—a party seeking nothing more than the return of a child to its mother."

"That's exactly what we're doing, isn't it?" said Thelma.

"Certainly," said Burkan, "but we can't be the only ones who know it." He placed his drink on the fireplace mantel. "I don't know what Gloria has told you about me, Lady Furness, but I've built a long and successful career on one simple fact: knowing that what goes on outside the courtroom is as important as what happens inside it."

"The public?" said Consuelo.

Burkan nodded. "Precisely," he said. "I won't lie to you. Right now, Gertrude Whitney has the upper hand. Lady Furness, Mr. Morgan—I know you've not been privy to the past few days in court but the Whitney lawyers have been merciless. They've called just about everyone in Manhattan to testify to the fact that Gloria is a lying, selfish woman with loose morals." He held up a hand, as if to tick off the witness one by one. "Nurse Kieslich—an openly hostile witness, even the judge agreed to that. She named Prince Hohenlohe as Gloria's lover, and said that Gloria kept dirty magazines in the house. I believe the judge recognizes the nurse's antagonism and will take it into account, but her testimony raised questions about Gloria's conduct, which were later corroborated."

Thelma and Consuelo exchanged glances.

"Gloria's maid testified that she found Gloria in bed with Lady Milford Haven. Now, I think I've done a fair job refuting that evidence, but publicly, the damage is serious. Very serious. Your brother, Lady Furness, tells me that Lady Milford Haven won't be coming to testify." Burkan frowned. "That's unfortunate, but we'll have to move forward without her. I'm working on a strategy to control the damage."

"Which is?" asked Thelma.

Burkan smiled grimly. "Let's just say that Justice Carew would be very interested to know the sort of company that Mrs. Whitney keeps in her art studio."

Thelma raised her eyebrows. "You mean…?"

"Lovers," said Burkan, nodding. "She prides herself on living a bohemian life—as bohemian a life as a trust fund can give you, but bohemian in the essentials. There's little enough we can do with that information right now, though, until Whitney's lawyers have finished presenting their case."

"But that's it, isn't it? If their case against Gloria relies on the fact that Gloria had a—a liaison…"

"You forget, Lady Furness, that Mrs. Whitney is well respected and well-known," said Burkan. "She has a great deal of money and influence. You can bet her lawyers have already developed a counterstrategy."

Burkan took out a cigar; he held it up, eyebrows raised, in deference to Thelma, Edith and Consuelo; Edith nodded and Burkan trimmed it, marshaling his thoughts.

"Mrs. Whitney may be a bohemian but she's a Vanderbilt, first and foremost. She has power and influence on her side. We, on the other hand, have public opinion."

The room was silent, but for the hissing of condensation off a log in the fireplace.

"Public opinion." Harry sat up, pinching the bridge of his nose between two fingers. "Forgive me, Mr. Burkan, but this seems to be a David and Goliath scenario to me."

Thelma couldn't help sharing Harry's disappointment. For a moment, she thought they had found the key—if extramarital relationships were the reason Gloria was considered unfit and Gertrude engaged in extramarital relationships herself, the judge could hardly grant her custody.

But then, if both Gloria and Gertrude were ruled unfit, who would take guardianship of Little Gloria? Mamma? Kieslich?

Thelma?

"Consider this."

She returned her attention to Burkan, leaning against the fireplace mantel.

"You're a housewife in rural Ohio," he said. "Two kids, a husband who works in a factory—not his own factory, mind, he makes the widgets that fire the thing that makes the machine run. It's not a good job but it's a job—it pays enough to feed the kids, but not much else." His eyes flicked, almost involuntarily, to Thelma: she was in a tweed traveling suit, custom-made on her last trip to Paris; diamond earrings, a matching necklace.

"Your husband comes home one day and tells you he's lost his job. Well, so have all the other men in town. There's little enough to be done for it but tighten your belt and hope that little garden patch in the backyard keeps you all fed until good times come again. He's on the dole, out every day knocking on doors, looking for work. He finds a newspaper in the bin and brings it home. You start to read the front-page story: *Vanderbilt sues widow for custody of child.*

"A wealthy woman—wealthy beyond your wildest dreams, money enough to keep not only you, but your whole town, in the black for the rest of your lives—is trying to take a baby from a widow. A *widow*. Nothing left of her beloved husband but the child in her arms. And Mrs. Whitney isn't just any rich old lady—she has children of her own! She's had her share of motherhood, and here she is, trying to take a widow's only child— her one tie to her dead husband, her only source of happiness in this grim, cold world that has taken your husband's job, your kids' food off the table..."

Burkan bit the cigar between his teeth. "Now tell me," he said. "Who do you think that woman's going to support?"

Consuelo leaned forward. "I see," she said.

"I don't." Edith looked from Burkan to Consuelo. "It's the judge who needs convincing—not the public. Why would their opinion matter?"

Burkan's briefcase was resting next to Thelma's seat; he opened it, pulling out a handful of letters. "These are from mothers across the country—letters of support. We've already got public sympathy on our side, and you can bet that if these women are writing to us, they're writing to the judge as well." He pulled one of the letters out of its envelope and read aloud: "*I think it's appalling what Mrs. Whitney is doing to you—she ought to leave well enough alone. A child belongs with its mother.*" He folded the letter back in its envelope. "I've got hundreds more."

"And have these letters continued to pour in since Gloria's maid accused her of improprieties with Lady Milford Haven?" asked Edith.

"They've slowed," Burkan admitted, "but it's all slander, which works to our benefit. We need to shape how people see this story. We need to keep public sympathy on our side. We need them to see that Gloria's being unfairly treated by a woman with a lot more money and a lot more influence."

"And how, exactly, do we do that?"

Burkan seemed energized by Edith's relentless questioning. "We make Gloria into a symbol. The only way to counteract personal accusations is to make her into a public figure. We turn her into a rallying point. That mother in Ohio? She's mad as hell at the wealthy businessman who's shut his plant, who's laid off her husband—she's furious that she has to scrimp to get by. You can bet she'll feel the injustice of some rich bitch taking away a mother's God-given right to her child."

THIRTY-FOUR

January 1931
London

THELMA WALKED THROUGH THE FRONT STEPS AT York House, trying to look unhurried as she discarded her overcoat in one fluid motion and handed it to the butler. He passed it to a footman, quickening his steps to match hers as she vaulted up the staircase.

"He's in the drawing room, my lady," he said.

"Is he upset?" asked Thelma.

"His Royal Highness has been terribly busy," he said, escorting her through the double doors at the top of the stairs and along the corridor. She could hear rustling in the rooms on either side, maids and footmen darting back and forth with clothing and books, dust sheets and gramophone records. David was leaving on a four-month trade mission to South America in two days' time: reluctant as he was to go at all—and doubtful of the amenities he'd find there—he'd flatly refused to travel without the modern conveniences of his day-to-day life. The newspapers were reporting that David planned to take ninety-six pieces of luggage: watching a footman push past with a trunk-laden hand trolley, Thelma was inclined to believe it.

The butler paused outside the drawing room and knocked before Thelma entered. David was sitting in an armchair beneath the austere portrait of his mother, a half-finished piece of embroidery in his lap.

"You're late," he said. He jabbed his needle into the fabric and stood, setting the hoop on a side table.

"I'm so sorry," she said. "The morning got away from me."

"As mine so often do."

"I really am sorry," Thelma said, sinking into the seat beside him; David waved away her apology as he lit a cigarette. His hand shook, making the flame dance before he flicked the lighter shut. "Have you finished packing?"

The prince tapped his cigarette against the ashtray. "Have you seen the place? It's Paddington bloody station out there, and I know they'll forget something important." He frowned. "I ought to remind Finch to put in the bagpipes. After all the practice I've put in…"

"I'll tell him," said Thelma, taking his hand in hers.

"I know I'm being difficult," he said, resting his head against the back of the couch. "It's just the effort of it. I couldn't begin to tell you why they're sending me for such a long time—Father's keen to get rid of me…"

"*A mal tiempo, buena cara,*" said Thelma, *At bad times, put on a good face.* David chuckled. Thelma had been helping him practice his Spanish for weeks, and he'd become surprisingly proficient.

"Well, quite." He picked up the needlepoint and scrutinized a stitch. "It's going to be a bore without you. Weeks and weeks of speeches and shaking hands… I so wish you were coming."

Thelma wished she were going, too, if only to lift him out of the moods he so often sank into. He was sinking now: she could see it in his creased forehead, his hunched shoulders.

This time, at least, Thelma could handle it. She reached into her handbag and pulled out four miniature teddy bears. She'd been shopping at Claridge's when she saw them: they stood two inches tall, with wired limbs. She'd bought two sets, one in pink and one in green, thinking they could sit on Tony's windowsill—but David looked so forlorn she changed her mind. "Well, I can't fit in your suitcase, but perhaps these might. They'll keep you company," she said.

He brightened. "How charming!" he said, taking the bears in hand. "Lovely little chaps, aren't they? The green ones are mine and the pink ones are yours, how about that?" He held the bears up, two in each hand. "I've an idea. When I'm gone, I'll take your pink bears with me, and you'll keep my green ones. That way we'll have a little something of each other even though we're apart."

He handed her the green bears and Thelma smiled, pleased at her stroke of inspiration. She hadn't expected him to be so charmed by the silly things, but it was touching to know that he'd have her bears sitting on his nightstand before he went to bed.

David picked one up, lifting its arms before setting it on the arm of his chair. He looked at Thelma, beaming, and she laughed. Together, they arranged the bears on the top of the couch where they surveyed the room with glassy eyes.

"There," she said. "Now we're a proper party."

David put his arm around Thelma and she leaned in, closing her eyes to better relish the warmth of the fire on her face, the feel of his chest against her back.

"I'll miss you terribly, you know," he said, lifting his free hand to curl a tendril of her hair around his finger. "Four months is such a long time to be on one's own."

"George will be with you," Thelma murmured. She thought of the two of them getting into trouble, charming the South American elite. The newspapers wouldn't be able to resist them.

David ran his hand along Thelma's shoulder. "George is all

well and good…but he's not you. Not to sound crass, but he lacks certain qualities of yours that I will sorely miss."

Thelma savored the feel of his fingers, watching the fire dance in the grate. "I want you to know," she said slowly, "that I don't mind if—if you—spend time with other women. While you're gone."

He paused. "Truly?"

He asked as though Thelma was leading him into a trap. She'd given the matter a lot of thought over the past several weeks, swinging between principled outrage and reasoned calm, but she knew David: his appetite would not withstand four months of abstinence. Although she recoiled at the thought of him with other women, she knew, with a sort of twisted logic, that her blessing—and his honesty—would stand them in better stead on his return.

He stilled. Resisting the urge to turn and look at him, Thelma frowned, thinking she might have misjudged him—but then he pressed his lips to her forehead. "That's awfully considerate of you, darling. I had no idea you were so modern."

He continued kissing her, traveling downward from her lips to her neck, knocking the bears from their perch.

He stopped. "What's wrong?"

Thelma sat upright, pulling her blouse straight, not trusting herself to speak. David exhaled, the root of a smile playing at his lips.

"They won't mean a thing," he said, ducking to meet Thelma's lowered gaze. "It's—it's a need, you understand. Purely biological. There's nothing in it—there *will be* nothing in it," he corrected himself swiftly, and Thelma pretended not to notice. "It's—" he stopped. "What you and I have is so much more than anything I could find with someone else. And you know I'll be so damned busy with the tour. Do you really think some dalliance could come between us?" He took Thelma's hands in his, and she attempted a smile.

"I know," she said. "But even so."

David sighed, flicking his cigarette into an ashtray. Even in this delicate moment, Thelma couldn't help feeling that familiar pull of attraction—other women felt it, too: she saw it every night they went out together, in the sidelong glances, the whispered conversations hidden behind the stems of wineglasses. How could either of them fool themselves into thinking he could resist?

"You know I don't want to go—it's my father. It's the damned government, thinking I can boost tea shipments or some rot by charming the locals. A silly idea, and a complete nuisance. And it's upsetting you to boot.

"I love you, Thelma—you know that, don't you?" He said it lightly; when she didn't reply he took her chin in his hand, gently turning her face to meet his.

He hadn't said it before. She almost laughed at the absurdity of it, David professing love while admitting he planned to sleep with other women. But didn't she know, full well, the man he was when she'd first met him? Wasn't the fact that he hadn't, yet, strayed, more than she'd asked for from the start?

He smiled, stroking her cheek. "I mean it, you know. What you and I have—it's love. You must know that."

He didn't wait for her to respond but pressed against her, and she didn't care that the house was full of people packing David's trunks, preparing the speeches he would give to the applause of thousands; she kissed him with an intensity she hoped he would remember when he was surrounded by beautiful women, tall and glittering, their eyes full of the promise of what they would do, given an evening alone with the Prince of Wales.

The smell of burning fabric, so thin at first that Thelma thought David's cologne had gone off, distracted them, growing stronger by the second. David grunted and pulled away.

It was his needlepoint: his cigarette had rolled off the ashtray onto the folded fabric of his half-finished rose. With a cry,

David leaped up and grabbed the smoldering fabric. He threw it onto the fireplace surround, crushing the embroidery hoop as he stamped it out the flame with the heel of his shoe.

Gingerly, he picked it up. It was utterly destroyed: the embroidery hoop clung in listless pieces to the fabric, an unsightly hole marring the edge of the flower David had so painstakingly sewn. As though declaring defeat, the pieces of hoop fell with a clatter, leaving the prince holding little more than a crumpled napkin.

Thelma stifled a giggle; David looked at her and, unable to control herself, she burst into laughter. David smiled, tucking a hand in his pocket.

"Well," he said, tossing the remains of the needlepoint onto the fire. "Seems I'll have to find a new project for the trip over."

THIRTY-FIVE

THELMA FELT ODDLY BEREFT AFTER DAVID'S DE-
parture. She hadn't realized the extent to which she had come
to depend on his company—she had hours now, days to spend
on tasks she'd neglected. In February, she traveled to Paris to
purchase a new wardrobe and visit Gloria, who was locked in
another feud with the Surrogates.

"They keep telling me to move back to Manhattan," said
Gloria as Thelma, standing on a pedestal in Maison Vionnet,
was pinned into a new dress. "and I keep putting them off, but
I don't think I can hold out much longer. Now that Little Gloria is seven they'll want her in school. But I hate the thought
of leaving."

Thelma felt for Gloria, but she left Paris somewhat downcast.
They had spent the entire trip talking about Little Gloria and
Mamma. On the Channel crossing back home, Thelma real-
ized Gloria hadn't even asked about David.

Without David demanding her weekends at the Fort, Thelma
reestablished herself with her London friends: she lunched with

Lady Sarah and Betty Lawson-Johnson, met with Consuelo and Benny for tea. In March, she brought Tony down from Burrough Court, marveling at his growth into a sturdy, sure-legged two-year old.

He had begun to speak, Thelma realized, on a muddy afternoon excursion to St. James's Park: nonsense and snatches of nursery rhymes, but words nonetheless. She smiled at the sight of him squatting beside the pond in his sailor's suit, his coattail trailing in the mud as he splashed his hands in the brown water.

Thelma recoiled, exchanging a glance with Tony's nursemaid. It was a wet day, fresh wind lifting the air with the promise of spring; she handed her gloves to the nurse and crouched down beside Tony, wrapping her arm around his solid middle and pulling him back from the pond's edge.

"'*Mary had a little lamb, little lamb, little lamb*,'" she sang, throwing a chunk of stale bread into the pond. Several ducks flapped over, throwing up tiny wakes in the water. Tony shrieked with laughter, crumbling bread between his fingers.

"'*Whose fleece was white as snow*.' I've always considered myself more of a black sheep. More exciting to stand out, don't you think?"

Thelma looked up: Wallis and Ernest Simpson were standing arm in arm on the wet path, Wallis's red coat bright against the muted browns of the park.

"Wallis! What a surprise." Thelma handed Tony to the nurse, wiping crumbs from her coat. "You recall my son, Anthony. Come say hello to Mr. and Mrs. Simpson, Tony."

Tony buried his face in the nursemaid's chest, and Wallis laughed.

"I have that effect on most men, I'm afraid," she said. "How have you been? You look lovely in that fur collar."

"Thank you, Wallis. I've been well."

"A bit lonely, I'd imagine?" said Wallis, leaning closer to Ernest.

"We've heard His Royal Highness is abroad," said Ernest.

"Doing a cracking good job of it, too, so say all the newspapers. Chile, now? How proud you must be."

"Chile," said Thelma, "yes, of course. He's so good with crowds."

"We have such fond memories of that weekend we spent at your charming country house," said Wallis. Her jaw jutted out as she smiled, and Thelma thought of a bulldog, all jowl and underbite. "Will you be hosting much this season, do you think?"

"I hope so," said Thelma. "You and Ernest must join—we had such fun together."

"Aren't you sweet?" Wallis beamed, clasping her hands over her husband's folded arm. "Isn't she sweet, Ernest? You must come for dinner. You must be awfully lonely without your prince to keep you company. In fact, I'm having a few friends over on Friday. You ought to join. Nothing fancy. Just a little get-together."

"I'd be delighted," said Thelma.

"Shall we say five o'clock? I'm determined to teach these British the wonders of an American cocktail hour." Wallis waved and Ernest turned; they walked on and Thelma lifted Tony into her arms.

A snippet of nursery rhyme, not quite faint on the wind, floated down the pathway to Thelma: "*And everywhere that Mary went...*"

Thelma sang back, lifting her voice so that Wallis could hear: "*...the lamb was sure to go.*"

Tony threw a chunk of bread into the pond and the ducks raced to reach it, splashing and flapping their wings in a frenzy of movement.

The Simpsons' flat was in Marylebone, in a redbrick building that was nearly indistinguishable from the homes surrounding it. Looking up at the limestone columns that flanked the front door Thelma felt a strange sense of disappointment: she'd expected something more unique, somehow, from Wallis. But then, she thought as she stepped over the lintel, she didn't know the Simpsons all that well.

She rang their doorbell, listening for the sounds of a party, but she could hear nothing more than the usual rustlings of a lived-in building. She looked round, hoping to see other guests drifting up the stairs, but then Wallis, in a vibrant blue dress, opened the door.

"Our butler doesn't come for another forty-five minutes," she said. "People stand so much on ceremony here, but I pay my staff by the hour." She smiled. "It's lovely to see you."

"Am I the first to arrive?" asked Thelma, removing her coat. Wallis passed it to a waiting maid and led Thelma in.

"I've a little confession," she said. "I invited you here early— you don't mind, do you? I've been looking forward to an op-portunity to get to know you better. Burrough Court was all well and good but it can be tough finding the time for a chat between girls. Don't you agree?"

She walked quickly, her steps brisk as she led Thelma into a mint-green drawing room. Two sofas, upholstered in pale pink, flanked the unlit fireplace; between them, a vase of white lil-ies sat on a mahogany coffee table. The sofas were laden with pillows, plumped and ready to receive guests, but Wallis led Thelma to a pair of chairs by the window.

Wallis took a seat, crossed her legs at the ankle and leaned back, playing with her red-lacquered nails as though hoping a cigarette would appear between them.

"Tea?" she said, "or a proper drink? I told you I'm determined to bring cocktail hour to this damp city. I'm having a martini, if that helps you make up your mind." She perched an elbow on her knee and brushed the backs of her fingers under her chin. "I won't tell if you don't."

Thelma smiled, thinking irresistibly of Nada Mountbatten.

"Go on," she said, and Wallis picked up a crystal decanter. "Where's Ernest?"

"At the office," she said. "He'll be home soon, I hope. I need him to have a word with the cook before everyone arrives." She poured gin into a shaker. "You know, he's been spending so much time at the office I began to suspect he was having an affair—but then I realized he couldn't possibly afford to keep two women on his salary so I stopped worrying. Penury has its merits after all." She poured the mixture into glasses, stirring them with olive-pinned toothpicks.

"Oh—it can't be as bad as all that," said Thelma, looking around the immaculate room once more.

Wallis brushed the arm of her chair, as though inspecting for pulls in the fabric. "Oh, we were well enough off when we first arrived, but the Depression's been terrible for Ernest's business and his father has decided he's no longer supporting us...not that he can't afford it." She frowned, her features pulling into a grimace, then smiled languidly once more. "We moved here a few months ago, to economize. We've done it up well enough, I suppose, but it certainly lacks the grandeur you might find in other places. Such as your little bolt-hole, I'd imagine."

Thelma demurred, thinking of her comfortable apartment. "It's nothing special," she said, "And not nearly as put together. You've a real talent for decorating."

Wallis smirked. "I'd rather have the space." She leaned forward, her collarbones rising from the neckline of her dress, the rim of her glass stained with a half-moon of red lipstick. "But enough about me. How are you? Keeping busy, I hope."

"I suppose," said Thelma. "It's been nice, really, having a few weeks to myself, but I'm looking forward to David's return."

"I bet. How much longer? Two months?" Wallis shook her head. "All that time in a cold bed, I don't think I could stand it...but then, your husband's only a phone call away."

"I doubt David would be too impressed if he heard that,"

Thelma replied, trying to match Wallis's casual tone. "He asked me to go on safari with him, you know—Duke. While David's away. He wants to leave next week. I didn't know what to say... it feels dishonest. Isn't that odd? David would be furious..."

"For what? Going abroad with your husband?" said Wallis. "Surely he would see—well, if not reason, then certainly obligation?"

Thelma nodded slowly. "Obligation—that's it, exactly," she said. "I keep thinking about the end of it all. When David loses interest. Perhaps I ought to go to Kenya, keep Duke on good terms."

Wallis raised her eyebrows. "You make it sound like a chore. Africa's not exactly a second-rate holiday."

Thelma sighed, tapping the stem of her cocktail glass. "We're going for drinks on Sunday—he'll want an answer, but I don't know what to tell him. Listen to me, I sound so callous..."

"You aren't callous at all," said Wallis. "You ought to think ahead. You need to keep an eye on your future. But—speaking from a purely objective standpoint—is Duke really your only option?"

"What else could there be?"

"Marriage," said Wallis, fishing an olive out of her cocktail glass.

"To *David*?" Thelma sat back. "It's impossible."

"Why?" said Wallis. "He's crazy about you."

"He's also the Prince of Wales," Thelma replied. "He isn't—"

"What? Like other men?" Wallis tipped her head to one side, smirking. "A crown doesn't make him special. He thinks with the same part of his anatomy as they all do."

"He's got different priorities," said Thelma. "He's not free—not really. He's going to marry some foreign princess. And sooner rather than later, if his parents have anything to do with it."

"Why should they have any say in the matter?"

"Because he's the Prince of Wales!" said Thelma. She felt as though she were arguing against a brick wall: she would have a better chance of being elected Lord Mayor of London than marrying David.

"And you don't think the Prince of Wales can break with protocol, if he wants? He's going to be the most powerful man in the world one day. You really don't think he has that power?"

"I've never considered it," said Thelma. Her mind crept back to that first weekend at Fort Belvedere: David's casual proposal; her hasty rejection.

"You ought to," said Wallis. "In any case, this doesn't have to end with you returning to Furness. He would be generous, surely, in a divorce?"

"He would—but divorcing Duke doesn't mean I'd marry David," said Thelma. "More likely, I would end up alone."

"Is that so terrible? You're young, you're beautiful—you could find someone else." Wallis finished the dregs of her martini. "If you were to leave him, at least you'd be giving the prince an option that wasn't on the table before. You'd be opening the door to greater possibilities. Who knows? He might surprise you."

Thelma set her empty glass on the table. "Duke, or David?"

Wallis smiled and began to make a new set of drinks.

Thelma lingered over her conversation with Wallis for days. She wasn't so naive as to think that David might truly, one day, be free to marry where his heart lay—despite his constant grumbling, Thelma knew he wouldn't stand against the government, nor against the king and queen's inevitable opposition.

Wallis, with her American boldness, would think nothing of a prince marrying a commoner. But Thelma had lived in London long enough to know what was acceptable, and what wasn't. Marriage to David was out of the question.

But marriage to someone else? She thought back to her first divorce: living on Reggie and Gloria's charity, listening to Mamma's ceaseless criticisms. The sleepless nights and sneering publicity; the constant worry of being cast out of polite society without enough money to support herself. She would have money, this time. By divorcing Duke, Thelma would, perhaps, find further happiness— but she had no guarantee. Duke had come into her life by accident; David even more so. Could she rely on a third stroke of luck so easily, now that she was nearly thirty?

After her divorce from their father, Mamma had plunged into Gloria's life, seeking fulfillment from her grandchild and smothering her own daughter in the process. Thelma pictured herself presiding over Tony with the matriarchal authority of a despot. She couldn't—wouldn't—countenance that, for herself or for her son.

But stability—Duke offered that. He also offered his love; he'd never stopped offering it, little though Thelma deserved it. Perhaps Thelma could, in time, find contentment: not like the love she had for David, but happiness of a different sort, mellowed through years of trial and understanding. Once David, by choice or compulsion, left her, did Thelma not owe Duke her constancy? Would that not be fitting? Was that not, in itself, love?

On the night that Thelma was to meet Duke, she arrived at the Embassy Club alone, in a backless evening dress that clung to her figure. She paused at the top of the stairs, scanning the room for the telltale glint of Duke's red hair.

She walked down, noting Freda Dudley Ward, seated at a corner table, and Sibyl Colefax, who'd helped David decorate the Fort. She waved before turning back to her dining partner, a lithe young man with an easy smile. On the dance floor, the Duff Coopers waltzed slowly. Thelma had dined with them in Capri once: apparently, Lord Duff was a noted philanderer, but his wife accepted him back after every dalliance. They looked happy enough tonight, dancing cheek to cheek.

She smiled at Duke, who was waiting at the bottom of the staircase. "Thelma," he said. "How beautiful you look."

Even the flattering half-light of the Embassy Club couldn't hide the fact that Duke, for the first time in their acquaintance, looked old. He'd lost any spare roundness in his face, thin lines pulling at the corners of his mouth. Compared to David's perpetually youthful appearance, Duke looked like a grandfather: at his temples, his reddish hair had faded so far to blond that, were she feeling ungenerous, Thelma would have called it white.

She smiled, hoping to hide her shock: When had her husband stopped fighting against his years? He kissed her on the cheek, and her heart lurched at the fondness in his eyes. Those, at least, hadn't changed.

"I ordered you a sherry," he said, as he led her to their table. "But I wasn't sure whether you'd eaten already. We can order something if you're hungry."

"Sherry's lovely. I've already eaten but if you want something, by all means—"

"No," he said. "No, I'm fine."

They lapsed into silence. Thelma watched the band and Duke waved away the maître d'.

"You've been well?" asked Thelma.

"Well enough. Business has taken a bit of a knock, but we missed the worst of it." He sipped his drink. "Averill and Dickie are in good health. I know you keep up on each other, you and the children. Dickie's well—he's met someone, so Averill tells me. She's the only one who would, Dickie plays it all rather close to his chest, but so long as he's happy."

"That's good," said Thelma.

"...and Averill's told me, under no uncertain terms, that I'm not to host any parties for her in the coming season. Obstinate, that one—won't see reason half the time, and the other half she's made up her mind already."

"She sounds exactly like her father," said Thelma.

"I shouldn't be so hard on her."

"It's not a bad thing, a headstrong daughter."

Duke nodded. "She wants to come to Nairobi with me," he said.

Thelma pretended she hadn't heard him. "Always on the hunt, that girl. Have you been to Scotland recently?"

After their second cocktail Duke asked her to dance, placing his hand on the small of her back as though it belonged there. The years fell from his face and Thelma looked past the white in his hair, the new furrows in his cheeks, and she realized how easy it would be to return to him at the end of it all. He straightened, looking once more like the man she had married: not young, but younger. A man in his prime.

The song ended and Thelma stepped back. She looked up at Duke—so much taller than David—and he smiled.

"You've gotten better," she said, and he lifted her hand to his lips. He pulled away, holding her gaze longer than necessary as she tightened her grip on his fingers.

Then he glanced over her shoulder and stiffened. He released her with a hasty cough, smoothing his jacket lapels.

It felt as though the dance floor had emptied. Thelma and Duke, clearly, hadn't gone unnoticed. Freddie had the decency to look away as Thelma caught her eye; Lady Duff Cooper leaned into her husband and murmured something, her marble face impassive—but Sibyl Colefax, hand draped around her partner's neck, looked at Thelma with her eyebrows raised.

"I think I'm done dancing," said Thelma. She walked back to the table, her face reddening. Duke sat, scraping his chair away from Thelma's, taking longer than usual to trim and light his cigar as Thelma waited for a fresh drink. Once again, Duke looked old—but he looked weary, now, too.

Others had taken over the scrap of floor that Thelma and Duke had left, but people continued to glance in their direction. Lady Londonderry's daughter Margaret, seated at a crowded table, played with a folded fan, her lips set in a thin line as her eyes slid from Thelma back to one of her companions.

There would always be whispers about the woman who'd had an affair with the Prince of Wales—and about the man who'd accepted her back. They would say he did it for advantage: to curry favor with the future king, or perhaps because he enjoyed a prince's cast-offs. He would always see David when he looked at Thelma—he was seeing David now, Thelma knew, an unnamed presence conjured by the faces of those around them.

He'd had his dalliances, too, but while Duke's mistresses would sink into obscurity with each passing year, every mention of the Prince of Wales—Duke's sovereign—would be a lasting reminder of Thelma's infidelity.

Regardless of what happened with David, too much had passed between Thelma and Duke—too much pain, too much resentment, on both sides now—for them to ever find true happiness again. Thelma's selfish preoccupations—her comfort, her security—would always be the draw that pulled her back.

He deserves more, thought Thelma. He deserved to find someone for whom he wouldn't be second best; someone who viewed him as more than a safe harbor.

Thelma had been that girl once. Perhaps.

She stood first, sliding her engagement ring from her finger. It wouldn't do, for them to leave together. Duke closed his eyes, his jaw clenched, as Thelma placed the ring on the table.

"Thank you," she said leaning down to kiss the crown of his head.

THIRTY-SIX

October 14, 1934
New York, USA

EVEN DURING HER YEARS LIVING IN NEW YORK, Thelma had never thought much of the city's architecture. Where London's buildings held the story of a city built over generations, with its Georgian mansions and modern apartment blocks standing cheek by jowl, New York, by contrast, looked as though it had been built in a day. In a sense, perhaps it had: the city's downtown skyscrapers were all of a piece, the same gray stones stacked in the same stern lines, commissioned by Astors and Rockefellers over the same fifty-year period. Each building had its own undeniable magnificence, of course, and strove to say something about American exceptionalism—yet it seemed a special irony that, taken all together, the buildings that made up a city that professed to be unique looked so very monolithic.

The New York Supreme Court building, however, managed to stand out: a distinguished Roman-style block with ornate pillars that looked almost quaint next to its gleaming deco neighbors.

Seated in the back of Gloria's Rolls Royce, Thelma was

amazed at the number of people who'd come to watch Gloria's arrival: hundreds stood on the courthouse's shallow front steps, not just newspapermen but women and children, men in shiny suits seated with their elbows on their knees, shouting insults and encouragement in equal measure.

The car pulled to a stop and a woman holding a small child in a threadbare overcoat elbowed her way to the fore of the crowd. The child peered in the window, his eyes dull.

"Don't they have anything better to do?" said Thelma.

"No," said Gloria listlessly. "They're all out of work." She looked out the window without seeing, impervious to the flash-bulbs and the noise.

Thelma recoiled as a man, shoved forward by the tidal surge of people, fell against the car's rear end. "Vultures," she muttered.

Burkan, squeezed between them, shook his head. "Allies," he replied, rifling through his briefcase. "If we can get them to see reason." Gloria's team had traveled to the courthouse in three cars: Gloria, Thelma and Burkan in the second; Harry, Consuelo and Edith in the third. The first had carried a team of private detectives, hired on Burkan's recommendation, to investigate the threats against Gloria that leaked through the mailbox with alarming regularity.

The private detectives were earning their keep, thought Thelma as she watched them push the crowd back from the motorcar. They formed a cordon and cleared a pathway up the courthouse steps before opening Thelma's door.

She stepped out.

"You ought to be ashamed of yourself!"

A red-faced woman pushed to the front of the crowd, throw-ing herself into the arms of a detective who held her back, though not nearly far enough for Thelma's comfort. Spittle flew from her mouth.

"Slut! Lesbian whore!"

Thelma put a restraining arm against the car door, to warn

Gloria not to get out. It didn't matter to the woman whether she was shouting at Thelma or Gloria: to her, they were one and the same. She hurled something at Thelma and it landed at her feet with a clatter: a crucifix on a length of twine.

"That's for your daughter!" she hissed. "May God protect her from your sins!"

Burkan stepped out of the car and put an arm around Thelma. "That's enough," he said, and the detective shoved the woman aside.

Thelma blinked back tears, her heart pounding a frantic tattoo. Knowing that reporters had watched the whole interaction, she exhaled. Her eyes slid up the pillars that lined the courthouse's portico, to the words that ran across the top of the building: The True Administration of Justice is the Firmest Pillar of Good Government.

"Are you all right?" asked Burkan, helping Gloria out of the car. Thelma nodded and took Gloria's hand. "Are you ready?"

Gloria looked up at the courthouse. Without a word—without a glance to either side—she began to climb the stairs.

The sound dampened immediately after they stepped into the courthouse, the quiet of the entrance hall a sanctuary after the harsh welcome outside. Gloria led Thelma and Burkan toward central rotunda—an austere, circular atrium with a green-and-white marble sunburst on the floor and five hallways that radiated out like the spokes of a wheel. The mural on the domed ceiling was only half-finished, figures sketched out with partially painted finery, the artist's ladder leaning against a limestone pillar.

The rotunda was busy, and people walked past Thelma and Gloria without a second glance. A solemn-looking couple stood nearby, deep in a whispered conversation, and it was something of a comfort to Thelma that, contrary to what those waiting outside might think, the world was not revolving around Gloria's trial.

Gloria's case was being heard on the sixth floor, in a courtroom down a narrow hallway jammed with reporters. After the maid's testimony had nearly caused a riot, the judge presiding over Gloria's case had barred reporters from entering the courtroom but that hadn't stopped them from milling in the hall, ears pricked for raised voices or indiscreet disclosures. In his bid to keep the case private, Justice Carew had papered over the small window in the courthouse door but the press kept finding ways in: only yesterday, a reporter had rappelled down the side of the courthouse on a rope, camera in hand, to take photographs through the window.

Once again, the detectives cleared a path. The reporters backed up against the wall but clamored for Gloria's attention all the same, shouting questions and raising their hands in hopes of being noticed.

Gloria lifted her hand from Thelma's arm. She set her shoulders, replacing her weary expression with a bright smile, and waved, careful to greet them all without answering their questions. She was ingratiating herself, Thelma realized: playing nice with the reporters who would be publishing articles in tonight's newspaper. Now, they would include a sentence or two about Gloria's confidence, her grace under pressure as she glided through the courtroom's double doors.

Thelma, too, steeled herself.

"Your mum's testifying today! You nervous, Lady Furness?"

A photographer pushed forward and took a picture. The flashbulb exploded in Thelma's face, sprinkling her overcoat with glittering glass dust.

Thelma laughed at the sudden snowstorm. "Now, now—play nice," she said. Burkan held the courtroom door open, its small window obscured by green blotting paper.

Thelma walked through, brushing flashbulb fragments from her arm. "I don't know how you stand it," she murmured.

Out of sight of the reporters, Gloria wilted once more. "Nor do I," she said.

THIRTY-SEVEN

June 1931
London

WALLIS EMERGED FROM THELMA'S DRESSING room, letting her arms drop to her sides as she faced Thelma, Gloria and Nada.

"It's too short, isn't it?" she said, looking anxious. "I thought so. I've got two inches on Connie, at least."

Thelma bit her lip. The dress was, in fact, ill-fitting overall, but Wallis had only hours before she was due to be presented at Buckingham Palace—an honor that would formally launch her into London's high society.

Upon receiving her invitation, Wallis had telephoned Thelma in a panic. Thelma agreed to lend Wallis her train and ostrich feathers, her simple tiara—mandatory accessories she'd worn for her own presentation years earlier—but she'd asked Consuelo, who was closer to Wallis's size, for a dress.

Looking at Wallis now, Thelma felt she might have been better seeking help from other quarters. Whereas Consuelo had filled out the satin dress like a bride, Wallis—entirely devoid of curves—was engulfed by it, fabric gathering around her hips and bust.

"Come now, it's nothing we can't fix." Gloria rummaged through the vanity, pulling out a small box filled with safety pins as Thelma positioned Wallis in front of a full-length mirror.

Thelma pinched the excess fabric together along the pearl buttons that snaked up the back of the dress and folded it flat. Gloria handed her pins, and Wallis's face smoothed as she watched the dress pull tight across her front.

In the long months of David's South American tour, Thelma had become quite friendly with Wallis, and while she was happy to have gained a new friend, she hadn't realized just how much Wallis had come to rely on her company until today. She'd half expected Wallis to refuse her offer to help her dress for the ceremony, but Wallis had arrived at Thelma's house shortly after breakfast, her hair sculpted into glossy waves, her face impenetrably smooth and white. Despite her composure, though, Thelma could see she was nervous—and less than pleased at Nada's unexpected intrusion into the morning's activities.

"I hope you don't mind," Gloria had whispered to Thelma when she arrived with Nada in tow. Taking her time over the move to New York, Gloria had come from Paris to help Thelma host a party for the debutantes after the presentation ceremony. "She was so eager to meet Mrs. Simpson. So was I—you've told me so many stories."

There did always seem to be a story worth telling about Wallis. Although David had returned from his trip, Thelma continued to see Wallis several times a week. What she lacked in looks, Wallis made up for with outrageous wit and self-assurance. Beneath a cool exterior, she was warm and candid—at least with those she liked.

Moreover, Wallis was interested—genuinely interested—in Thelma's life. Other than Gloria, Thelma didn't have many friends with whom she could speak so openly. And Wallis spoke openly in return: she sought Thelma's advice on disputes with her domestics and disagreements with Ernest; how to make friends in London and how to make a pound stretch far enough to entertain properly.

"You're a wizard," said Wallis, watching Thelma work. "I used to do a lot of sewing myself when I was young, but it's a lot more difficult when you're the mannequin."

"Not me," said Nada, lying on a daybed in the corner of Thelma's bedroom. "My father always had people for that sort of thing."

"Well, bully for your dad," Wallis muttered.

Gloria, handing Thelma another safety pin, grinned. "We made our own clothes when we lived in New York, remember, Thelma? That green dress you made for Millicent Hearst's ball?"

"Goodness, that seems so long ago. I don't know I'd be much use with a sewing machine today, I'm so out of practice."

"So long as you remember how to close a safety pin," said Wallis. "You truly are a wonder. I don't know what I would have done without you."

"You would have spent a fortune on a new dress," said Nada, as she lit a cigarette.

Wallis twisted, upsetting Thelma's pinning job. "Would you put that out?"

"I remember my own presentation," said Gloria, as Nada stubbed out the cigarette. "I was so nervous. Nada lent me the most beautiful tiara, with diamonds and pearls... And then there she was, behind the king and queen when it came time to curtsy..."

"Why's that?" said Wallis.

"Part of the family," said Nada.

"And then you *winked*..."

"Well, you looked so nervous," said Nada, "and then you nearly laughed—"

"Because of you!" Gloria handed her pins to Thelma and collapsed on the daybed, wiping tears of laughter from her cheeks.

"Well, so long as there's no winking when I'm being presented," said Wallis, exchanging a glance with Thelma in the
mirror. "I'd like to conduct myself with something resembling
dignity."

Nada took a breath, her laughter subsiding. "I wouldn't
worry," she said. "None of them know you well enough to
bother making a joke."

It wasn't surprising to Thelma that Nada and Wallis weren't
getting along. Big personalities, the pair of them—but Wallis
let the comment pass as she studied her reflection in the mirror.

"Could you imagine, if I'd started laughing in front of His
Majesty?" said Gloria, resting her head against Nada's shoulder.

"He wouldn't have liked it," said Nada. "He's a cold fish. He
collects *stamps*."

"He's so hard on David," said Thelma. She set down the last
of the pins and picked up the heavy satin train. "You ought to
hear the stories David tells."

"Will he be there? The prince?" asked Wallis, as Gloria got
up to help once more.

Thelma handed Gloria one side of the train. "Of course," she
said, pinning the train into place on Wallis's shoulders and hiding evidence of the alterations. "He has to be there, although
he hates it."

"All those women? I would have thought he'd like it best,"
said Nada.

"It's the standing. He's by the king's side for hours. He says
his knees are stiff by the end. That's one good thing about becoming king: he'll have a chair for these sorts of things."

She and Gloria stood back and scrutinized their handiwork.

Their efforts had paid off: though the dress still didn't quite
fit, its beautiful simplicity suited Wallis's sharp features. In keeping with the custom for a court presentation, the dress was low

cut, made of ivory satin that gathered at Wallis's waist and now, thanks to Thelma's pins, sat smoothly across her bust.

"No one will notice the hem. Half the women will be in borrowed clothing," said Gloria.

"Sweep the train around the front for the photograph," advised Nada, and Wallis pulled the train forward. Unlike the dress, the train was elaborate, shot through with gold and silver thread snaking up in whorls toward Wallis's shoulders.

Wallis went to her valise and pulled out a brilliant aquamarine cross on a long chain.

"I need to wear at least one thing that's mine," she said, pulling the chain over her head. Personally, the cross wasn't to Thelma's taste: it was too heavy against the elegant satin dress, too blue for the subtle colors of the train.

Wallis turned to face Thelma. "Perfect," she said. "You know, it's nicer than my wedding dress. Truly. Men have it so easy— slap on a tuxedo and there you have it—but we need a different dress for every day of the week." She tucked in a stray pin. "It's good to have friends that are nearly the same size, it trebles your wardrobe."

"It's nothing," said Thelma. She had been presented at court two years before, and it had cost Duke a fortune. Without her help, Thelma knew, Wallis wouldn't have been able to participate in the rite of passage at all.

"I mean it, though," said Wallis. "It's not everyone that would help a girl prepare for something like this. It means a lot to me, to have girlfriends like you. I left all mine in Baltimore."

Thelma closed the pin box, suspecting that Wallis had a smaller group of friends in Baltimore than she let on.

"Well," said Thelma, "you've got us now."

Along with the train, Elise had brought Thelma's tiara and ostrich feathers out of storage; they were sitting in two boxes, one on the bed, one on the vanity. Nada opened the smaller of the two and lifted out Thelma's tiara.

"It's lovely," she said.

Thelma smiled. "A gift from Duke." It was modest, befitting Duke's status as a minor aristocrat: a circlet of round diamonds, small but brilliant, glittering as they caught the light.

"Lovely," Nada repeated. She stepped forward as though to place it on Wallis's head, but Wallis moved back.

"It took me far too long to set my hair properly. At least if I make a mess of it, I'll have no one to blame but myself," she said. Nada shrugged.

Wallis took the tiara in both hands and faced the mirror. Slowly, she placed it on the crown of her head; they all seemed to exhale as one as she took her hands away and the tiara rested atop her shellacked curls.

Wallis studied her reflection. For the first time that day she looked serene.

"Wallis in Wonderland," she said softly. She looked at Thelma, breaking the spell. "I won't say this isn't special. My mother was a landlady."

Gloria took the ostrich feathers out of their box. Together, she and Thelma pinned three feathers to Wallis's hair so that they curled, like smoke, above her head, and handed her a fourth to carry during the ceremony like a bouquet. Nada found Thelma's long white gloves and Wallis put them on.

"You really do look lovely," said Gloria, sounding almost apologetic. "I don't think we could have done much better, even with a different dress."

Thelma's party started later that evening, and while many guests had changed into evening-wear, several had come directly from Buckingham Palace in their court attire—hoping, no doubt, to prolong the magic of the evening. Even with the addition of a few modern touches like Wallis's aquamarine, presentation outfits hadn't changed much since Queen Victoria's time, and Thelma enjoyed the pageantry of the ancient clothing coupled with modern music issuing from the gramophone. She watched one young woman—she might have been a Mitford, Thelma wasn't sure—lift her hand to ensure her feathers were still firmly attached.

Thelma recalled the wide-eyed wonder she'd felt at her own presentation—and at those first few society parties she'd attended with Duke, gripping his sleeve so as not to lose him in the glittering fray. Was there anyone here who was as new to it all as she had once been? Thelma didn't think so. The women here tonight were born into wealth; their parents entertained royalty on a weekly basis. Still, she hoped to make an impression on some young person who wasn't yet so jaded by privilege.

She edged her way toward the far end of the room, waving at Betty Lawson-Johnston by the window, and sidestepping Emerald Cunard, seated next to the fireplace with a group of hangers-on. By the buffet in the dining room, George Mountbatten's brother, Louis, had just told a joke, and Fruity Metcalfe laughed so hard he nearly spilled his drink. Thelma saw Wallis at the far end of the room—she had usurped the bartender at the cocktail table and was mixing drinks while Ernest sliced lemons. As though she'd felt Thelma's eyes on her, Wallis looked up and smiled, brandishing the cocktail shaker.

What was the phrase Wallis had used? *Wonderland.* This was a world most people dreamed of, and tonight it belonged to Thelma.

She looked in the study and saw Piers Legh and G Trotter seated at a low table, playing poker with a man Thelma hadn't seen before.

"Who's winning?" she asked.

"G. He's a terrible cheat," said Legh, throwing down his cards. "Where's David?"

"Arriving shortly, I expect."

Piers reached for a bottle on the bookshelf. "Another, Khan? I don't know if you two have met. Thelma, His Highness, Prince Aly Khan."

Aly Khan stood. Thelma knew of him—apart from David, Aly Khan was the most eligible bachelor in London. His father was the spiritual leader of all the Shia Muslims in the world, but Aly himself was famous in his own right. He was enormously wealthy, known for his string of prizewinning racehorses—and for being a notorious philanderer. According to David, Aly Khan had seduced more women than any man alive.

"I hope you don't mind my coming along tonight," said Aly, raising Thelma's hand to his lips. "I've heard about you from so many people, I wanted to make your acquaintance myself."

"And yet," she said, "I had to find you. I don't know whether that's poor manners on your part, sir, or mine."

Khan smiled. He hadn't released her hand; he held it lightly, a grip she could easily break if she wanted to.

"Not that one, Khan," said Piers, lifting his glass. "She's spoken for."

"So I hear." Khan had a calm, measured voice. Though it wasn't deep, it was soothing—steady, no doubt, after years of working with horses.

"Are we dealing you in?" said Piers.

Khan released Thelma's hand. "Yes," he said. "I've a few pounds to win back. If you'll excuse me, Lady Furness."

Though Aly Khan was an interesting addition to the party, David, when he finally arrived, was truly the guest of honor. He made a slow progression through the room, stopping every few feet to greet a familiar face. Piers trailed behind him, finishing up the tails of conversations he left in his wake.

David caught Thelma's eye and smiled apologetically as he made his way over. He had changed out of the scarlet military uniform he wore for the ceremony, and was dressed in white tie and a blue sash.

She glanced at the Order of the Garter, pinned low on his chest. "A formal occasion, I see," said Thelma.

David patted the medal. "Well—one must keep some decorum at these sorts of things," he said. "Any chance of a drink? I've earned one…who are all these people?"

"Friends of yours," said Thelma, handing him a glass of champagne. "At least, the older ones are. I haven't a clue about the young ones, I assume they're connected to you somehow."

David looked around, finishing the champagne in two quick swallows. "I suppose they are. Could have used a quiet night, but I'm to go on to Lord and Lady Londonderry's."

"You're only stopping in?"

"I hate to say so, but I must. I'll come back afterward, if you're not already in bed." He looked past Thelma's shoulder, pasting a smile on his face that he generally reserved for people he didn't know.

She turned. Piers stood behind her, accompanied by a pretty young woman in a white dress and a walrus-like man with his hands clasped behind his back.

"Your Royal Highness, pardon the intrusion. Might I present Mr. Cecil Palmer and his daughter? Mr. Palmer is with the Canadian High Commission," said Fruity.

"Canada? What a lovely place. I've a ranch in Alberta," said David.

"Do you? Tell me, sir, do you get out riding while you're there? My daughter has a talent for it." Mr. Palmer rested a hand on the small of his daughter's back, coaxing her toward the prince.

Blushing, the girl stepped closer to David—too close for Thelma's liking. She really was pretty, with dark hair and fair cheeks. She looked at the prince as though she'd never seen someone so handsome.

"Charming," said the prince moments later, as Mr. Palmer and his daughter retreated.

"You think so?" murmured Thelma, handing him a second glass of champagne.

"You didn't?"

Thelma raised her eyebrow. "They were a little forward."

David smirked, casting his eyes around the room. "Now, don't be jealous... Say, haven't I met that woman before?"

Thelma followed his gaze. "Yes, darling, that's Mr. and Mrs. Simpson. They joined us at Burrough Court the weekend George had his hunting accident."

His features cleared. "Quite right. Husband's in the Grenadier Guards, isn't he?" Wallis met Thelma's eye; she took Ernest's arm and they made their way over.

"Ernest, yes," said Thelma. She raised her voice as Wallis and Ernest came within earshot. "David, you recall Mr. and Mrs. Simpson? Wallis has been such a gem in your absence, keeping me out of trouble while you were gone."

"Not too daunting a task, I hope?" said David, touching the knot of his tie as Wallis curtsied.

"Well, now, life wouldn't be fun without a little bit of trouble, sir, don't you think?" said Wallis.

"Quite," said David. "Mrs. Simpson, I must compliment you on your gown. You look lovely."

It was rote flattery. He'd said it to every woman at the party: a gallant, formulaic bit of charm.

Wallis raised her eyebrows. "Really, sir? I was under the impression that you thought we all looked ghastly."

Thelma looked up sharply; Ernest coughed into his drink.

David frowned. "I beg your pardon?" he said. Thelma could hear the censure in his voice. Could Wallis?

She smiled. "Your comment to the Duke of—Connaught, I believe? About the lighting at the ceremony." She turned to Thelma, inviting confidence. "Apparently, it made us women look like death warmed over. And after all the effort we put in."

It wasn't often that Thelma found David at a loss for words.

Wallis had no clue about how prickly David could be, particularly at the end of a long day. She opened her mouth, searching for a way to gloss over Wallis's rudeness—but then David laughed.

"That's me told. I had no idea my voice carried so far," he replied. "I hope you were the only woman with ears sharp enough to hear me."

She leaned close. "Your secret's safe," she said confidentially, "though you might want to consider a system of note-passing for future editorials."

"I just might." David smiled broadly. "Mr. and Mrs. Simpson, it's truly lovely to have met you again. We must see each other soon."

Recognizing the dismissal, Wallis dipped her head and Ernest bowed. They moved on and Piers, once again, came forward.

"Sir, might I present Mr. Jonathan Seare and his wife, Patricia?"

Mr. Seare was short and tanned, with graying hair at his temples; Mrs. Seare was round and beautiful, with a figure so curvy it made her white gown look almost indecent.

She curtsied; David started.

"Your Royal Highness might recall making the Seares' acquaintance in—"

"Valparaiso," said David.

"Your Highness is kind to remember," said Mrs. Seare. "I'm sure you meet so many on your travels that all the faces run together."

"Not yours," said David, with a note in his voice that made Thelma uneasy. She lifted her chin and smiled at Mr. Seare with dazzling insincerity. "Ah, may I present Lady Furness? Lady Furness, I met Mr. Seare and his wife in—"

"Chile," said Thelma. "So I understand."

Mr. Seare beamed, with such obvious pride that Thelma pitied him. "His Royal Highness was so very attentive toward us. He danced with my Patricia three times at the Governor's Ball."

"Did he really?" said Thelma. Jealousy, thick and bilious, rose in her throat. "And what brings you to London, Mr. Seare?"

"Jonathan had some business concerns to see to, and it just so happened to coincide with a court presentation," said Mrs. Seare, addressing Thelma but still looking at David. "I wonder, Your Highness, whether I might be so bold as to request another dance tonight."

David flushed. "I would be delighted."

Mrs. Seare rested her hand in his, and looked at Thelma beneath lowered eyes. "Thank you, Lady Furness, for such a lovely party."

Thelma stepped out onto the sidewalk, breathing in the night air. Laughter and music and light spilled out from the open windows onto the tops of the trees in Grosvenor Square.

She'd felt such pride, seeing her drawing room so full of people—many she knew and liked, and if there were a few unfamiliar faces, what did it matter? But as the evening went on, the friendly faces had melted away. Thelma's apartment, now, was brimming with strangers eager to bend the Prince of Wales's ear and throw their unmarried daughters into his arms.

She ought to have expected it. She looked up at the busy windows, knowing that the party could easily continue all evening without her. Wonderland, indeed: she doubted half her guests knew who she was.

The other half dismissed her as nothing more than a mistress.

Thelma hugged her elbows closer as goose pimples rose on her arms. She'd forgotten a shawl, but she wasn't prepared to go inside to see David dancing with some young girl in a white dress. Thelma knew how they saw her: the bed warmer, to be pushed aside when someone legitimate came along. So many women hoped to be the one to catch his eye. What did they care about Thelma? What did they care that she and David shared long years of love and affection?

But not devotion—not on David's part. She knew about his infidelities in South America: she'd read the reports in the society pages about the women he'd chosen to dance with, night after night. Young women. Beautiful. Married and discreet.

"Aren't you cold?"

Thelma looked up. Aly Khan was at the door.

"No," said Thelma, dropping her arms to her sides. Khan raised his eyebrows and removed his jacket. Before she could protest he'd draped it over her shoulders.

Thelma pulled it close. "Thank you. Did you win your game?"

"If you look in the pocket, you'll find cigarettes," he said. "I didn't win. It was well fought, though."

"I'm sorry," said Thelma, pulling out a cigarette. "What was the damage?"

Khan flicked open his lighter. "A horse."

"You bet a horse?" Thelma leaned in and allowed Khan to light her cigarette. The smell of his aftershave rose from the jacket. "A bit grand, don't you think?"

Khan shrugged. "I'm not pleased, but it will teach me to be more prudent." He sat on the front steps, squinting into the dimness of Grosvenor Square.

"Seems like a good way to lose a horse," said Thelma, sitting next to him.

Khan smiled. "It isn't fun if the stakes aren't high. There's no thrill in winning trinkets."

"What constitutes high stakes?" She nudged his shoulder with hers. "Life and death?"

He chuckled, his black eyes crinkling; his arm rested against Thelma's, as though by chance. "Nothing quite so dire," he said. "Love and money."

Thelma smiled. He did have a certain charm, she supposed—

but it was so very contrived. She doubted very much that Aly Khan had ever loved anyone in his life.

"Is love really such a poor commodity, that you'd risk losing it over a game?"

"On the contrary." He looked at her out of the corner of his eye, his face half-hidden by the shadows cast from the lamppost. "As I said, I only gamble when the stakes are highest." He finished his cigarette and flicked the butt into the street.

"Are you always so serious?"

Khan grinned. "That depends on the company. Why are you down here on your own?"

Thelma stubbed out her cigarette and Khan handed her another. "I'm not on my own."

"No," he said. "You aren't."

They sat together a few minutes more, enjoying the secondhand noise of the party and the trundle of motorcars.

The door opened again and Thelma started, shifting away as though she and Khan had been caught in the middle of something indiscreet. Khan, though, remained where he was, leaning back on the step with a cigarette between his lips.

"David." Thelma got to her feet, aware that she was still wearing Khan's jacket. "You know Prince Aly Khan, don't you, darling?" She spoke too quickly. "He came with Piers. He was telling me about a game of poker—"

"I know Khan," said David.

Khan stood, so slowly it felt like an insult. He inclined his neck, his lips curved in a half smile.

Thelma looked from David to Khan: David's light eyes boring into Khan's dark ones. David looked furious, and perhaps with good reason—but there was a small part of her that enjoyed his jealousy.

"It's late," said Thelma. "Lord and Lady Londonderry will be wondering where you are."

"I was looking for you," he said. Khan leaned against the

lamppost, finishing his cigarette. "Legh said he saw you go outside, I couldn't get away before now. Why are you wearing his jacket?"

"It was cold," said Thelma. She took it off, folding it over her arm. "Are you leaving?"

David glanced at Khan. "No," he said. "Lady Londonderry can do without me tonight."

"She'll be so disappointed." Khan threw the second butt to the ground; with one hand on his chest he bowed, first to Thelma, then to David. "I ought to return upstairs. Lady Furness, it was a pleasure keeping you company."

Thelma handed Khan his jacket and they followed him up the stairs. To Thelma's satisfaction, David didn't leave her side for the rest of the night.

THIRTY-EIGHT

ONE WEEK LATER, AVERILL CALLED ON THELMA in London.

It wasn't uncommon for Averill to visit. Since her separation from Duke, Thelma had made a point of maintaining friendships with Averill and Dickie both, exchanging letters with Dickie at university, visiting Averill at Burrough Court. That said, she hadn't seen Averill in over two months: Averill had taken Thelma's place on safari with Duke, and had only just returned to England. Thelma had sent the divorce papers to Duke shortly after their dance at the Embassy Club, and though she still felt twinges of guilt at their last encounter she thought it was fitting that Duke had taken Averill instead of her.

Averill's time abroad seemed to have done her well: she looked healthy and freckled from her time in the African sun. Thelma was used to seeing Averill at Burrough Court where, despite her efforts, she often came into dinner with grime under her fingernails from working with the horses. Today, she looked ladylike in a moss green dress, her cropped auburn hair hidden under the upturned brim of a cloche hat.

Averill pulled Thelma into a hug, enveloping her in a cloud of perfume.

"Goodness," said Thelma. "Did you really miss me that much?"

Averill smiled. "I hope you don't mind the intrusion."

"Not at all," said Thelma. "Have you eaten, or should I ring for tea?"

"No, thank you," said Averill. She sat, knitting her hands together. "I've something to tell you, and it won't take a minute."

Thelma waited, wondering at Averill's reticence. Normally, Averill was restless, only ever happy under open skies. It was one of the reasons she rebelled against the city: it was an unnecessary retreat into civility, time that could be better spent in the gardens or the stables.

"I wanted to talk to you about something that happened on the safari," she said.

"What happened? Your father?"

Averill's formal demeanor softened. "He's all right."

"It really is for the best..." said Thelma.

"I know it is—truly, I do," she said. "Father will be fine. The finality of it, I think, will take some time getting used to." She paused, and Thelma could see that, for all that Averill resembled Duke in character, she had the look of her mother.

"I've fallen in love," she said finally. It was the same tone of voice she used when purchasing a new horse: dispassionate, yet entirely self-assured.

Thelma's heart lifted. She'd expected something grave—that Duke had fallen ill, or Dickie had dropped out of school. "That's wonderful! Is it anyone we know? A friend of Dickie's?"

Averill took a breath. "Andrew Rattray," she said.

Thelma's smile faltered. She recalled Rattray indulging Duke's and Averill's passing fancy in zebras, telling stories about Kenya in his quiet Scottish brogue.

"Does Duke know?"

Averill lit a cigarette. "Of course not," she said.

Thelma could imagine Duke's reaction: Rattray was entirely unsuitable from a social—a geographical! a financial!—standpoint. "How long?"

"Since he came to Burrough Court," said Averill. "I know it's a surprise—it came as a shock to me as well. When we saw each other again on safari we realized our feelings hadn't changed. I've never felt this way about anyone. To tell you the truth, I was starting to think I never would."

Thelma closed her eyes. Averill wasn't the sort for hearts and flowers, grand gestures—she was stubborn and thoughtful, and if she'd decided that she loved Andrew Rattray, Thelma knew better than to doubt her feelings.

"I see," she said. "What do you plan to do about it?"

Averill smiled—clearly, she took Thelma's acknowledgment as acceptance. "We're going on another safari at the end of the year. Once we get to Africa, I'm going to marry him."

"I see. And Rattray agrees with this plan, does he? To elope?"

Her expression chilled. "We discussed it," she said. "He thought it was madness, too, at first, but now he agrees that it's the only way forward."

Thelma leaned forward and took Averill's hands in hers. "Please, don't do this," she said. "You don't know anything about him. He's part of your father's staff—"

"And that makes him worthless?"

"That makes him *different*. What do you know about him, really? You don't have a thing in common."

Averill pulled her hand away. "I thought of anyone, surely you would understand. You didn't come from money. Should Father have ignored you?"

"It's an entirely different situation," said Thelma. "Rattray lives in a hut, Averill—a literal *hut*—"

"How, exactly, is it different? Because you're a woman and Andy's a man? I don't care how he lives—I've got enough money, if that's what you're concerned about, but I can't imagine we'll need it. We're going to live in Kenya."

Thelma stared, shocked. For all that Averill prided herself on her hunting, her riding, she was still a peer's daughter—and an incredibly privileged girl. She'd never wanted for anything: she'd never had to budget for clothing or cook dinner. Did she truly think that she could drop everything to live in the Kenyan wilderness with a man twice her age?

"I don't doubt your feelings, but I do worry about the destruction they might cause," said Thelma gently. "You would break Duke's heart. Is it really worth risking your relationship with him?"

Averill exhaled. "And you think I would be risking it?" she said, although now she sounded as though she was seeking guidance. "Father might come round, once it's all said and done… He'll put up a fight, of course, but he'll forgive me in the end. He can't stay mad forever."

"He could," said Thelma. Averill's temper was no match for Duke's—nor her stubbornness. Thelma didn't see any future in which Duke would forgive his daughter this gravest of betrayals. "Please think about it," she continued. "You've got time. Think very hard about what you're proposing to do, and what you're planning to give up. Is everything—*everything*, Averill— worth this?"

Averill blinked hard and wiped her cheek. Did she still have dirt under her fingernails, Thelma wondered sadly—dust from the African desert, mud from Burrough Court?

She stood. "Don't breathe a word of this to Father."

"I can't promise that," Thelma replied. "Not unless I have

your word that you'll not do anything rash. Speak to me first. Please, Averill."

Averill's eyes turned to flint once more. "You won't tell Father?"

"Not unless I have your word."

She stood. "Very well," she said, and left the room.

THIRTY-NINE

October 18, 1934
New York, USA

THELMA ENTERED THE COURTROOM, SCANNING
the backs of heads in the viewing gallery for Mamma or Nurse
Kieslich, but they hadn't yet arrived: Gertrude's side of the
courtroom was almost empty, but for two men conversing with
Smyth, Gertrude's lawyer, at the front bench.

The trial had been ongoing for weeks now, and still the judge
hadn't yet called the defense. Gertrude's lawyers ran out the days
calling witnesses—doctors and lawyers and nannies—in an unrelenting line, all willing to testify to Gloria's incapacity to care
for a child. The delay infuriated Thelma. With each passing witness, it seemed, the screws were tightening around her sister,
with little in the way of defense. Burkan was earning his keep
in the cross-examination: a rebuttal here, a well-argued point
there, but for the moment, his activities lay outside the courtroom, in interviews and pictures for the press. While Gloria was
buoyed up by his activities, Thelma was uneasy with the delay.
How could Gloria withstand the mounting barrage of evidence?

On the other side of the viewing gallery, a tall man turned and greeted Thelma with a wave: Prince Gottfried zu Hohenlohe, his dark-haired wife tucking gloves into her handbag beside him.

"Good morning," he said as Thelma slid next to him. Friedel was stern and distinguished, with black hair slicked back on a high forehead. He had arrived two days after Thelma. Along with his wife, Margarita, Friedel staunchly supported Gloria, speaking to her good character and spotless reputation. Already, he and Margarita had held a press conference on Gloria's behalf, explaining European customs with an easy confidence that implied the whole to-do was simply a misunderstanding.

"Good morning," Thelma replied, giving Margarita a smile she didn't return. Margarita bore a slight resemblance to Gloria in her coloring, but where Gloria was slight Margarita was sturdy. Thelma couldn't blame her for her brusqueness: Friedel's determination to clear Gloria's name seemed to go beyond friendly devotion.

Thelma was grateful to Friedel, but she wasn't blind to the fact that he was as much on trial as Gloria. If Gloria's conduct was considered improper, Friedel's actions could be seen as nothing short of nefarious: preying on a vulnerable young widow, seeking to lay his hands on an American fortune. Mamma had done her best to paint a sordid picture, and if Thelma had learned anything from Burkan, it wasn't intent that mattered: it was what people saw in the newspapers, and in the flesh. Friedel had to be here—as much for his own reputation as for Gloria's.

The courtroom doors swung open and Gertrude Payne Whitney, accompanied by Mamma and Nurse Kieslich, strode into the room.

Gertrude walked past the viewing gallery and sat, passing her overcoat to Kieslich without sparing Gloria and Burkan a glance. Throughout the trial, Thelma had been taken aback by the woman's unfeeling actions: Couldn't she see the effect she was having on Gloria and Little Gloria both? She recalled Gertrude's words, spoken in Newport so many years ago: Reggie's choices had brought them here. Thelma hadn't heard the steel in her voice at the time, but now she could see it was that same unflinching conviction that propelled her forward now. It was Gertrude's choices, today, that kept them in the courtroom. She had little choice but to continue, now that the trial had taken on a life of its own.

Thelma turned her attention to Mamma. She sat in the viewing gallery, as close to Gertrude and the lawyers as she could without being at the bench herself, and leaned forward to listen to Gertrude's whispered conversation with Smyth. She shook her head vehemently at something Smyth said; he twisted in his seat to respond, and Thelma smiled at the identical expressions of irritation on all of their faces. Mamma, no doubt, had been elbowing her way into closed-door discussions for weeks, offering unsolicited opinions on how to run the court case.

A bailiff walked into the room. "All rise for Justice John F. Carew," he said, and Thelma stood with everyone else as the judge entered from a door behind the witness's box.

Justice Carew was a tall, broad man who looked more suited to working a farm than presiding over a courtroom. He strode to the judge's box, his robe sweeping behind him, a leather portfolio tucked beneath his arm. He looked to be in his sixties or thereabouts, with iron-gray hair, a trim goatee and steel-rimmed pince-nez.

"Take that—that covering off the window," he said as he sat down. "But be sure to tell the reporters," he continued, raising his voice as a court attendant removed the blotting paper from the courtroom door, "that I won't have anyone taking photographs or disrupting my courtroom, do you hear me? This is a court of law, not Carnegie Hall."

He waited until the attendant was finished, then looked at the assembly over the top of his pince-nez. Thelma wondered what the judge thought of the room: Mamma and Kieslich, lonely matrons on Gertrude's side of the room; Thelma, Harry, Consuelo and Edith—family, siblings, rationality—on the other.

Carew leaned back. "I believe we are still calling witnesses for the prosecution. Mr. Smyth, please proceed."

Smyth got to his feet, adjusting his glasses. "I'd like to call Mrs. Laura Kilpatrick Morgan to the stand."

Mamma approached the witness's box. Like Gertrude, she was dressed entirely in black, but for an immense silver crucifix on a chain around her neck. Was it for the judge's benefit, that blatant expression of false piety, or had she worn it as armor against the judgmental stares of her children?

Smyth smiled. "Mrs. Morgan, you testified that your granddaughter was subjected to continued neglect from her mother, yet Gloria Vanderbilt hired a professional nursemaid to care for her. Is that the action of a neglectful parent?"

Mamma raised her chin. "I selected Nurse Kieslich," she said. "My daughter did not show any desire or interest in choosing the nurse."

From his perch above the witness's box, Carew spoke without looking up from his desk. "And the mother? What contribution did she make toward the care of the child?"

Mamma clutched the crucifix. "It's not my daughter's fault," she said. "She wasn't born with a maternal instinct…"

"Objection," called Burkan.

"Denied," said Carew, almost lazily.

Smyth tucked a hand in the pocket of his waistcoat; from within the folds of his jacket, Thelma could see the yellow flash of a watch-chain. "You lived with Gloria Vanderbilt and her daughter at 14 Rue Alfred Roll in Paris, is that correct?"

"No," said Mamma. "My daughter chose that house because it didn't have room for me. It was entirely uninhabitable for a child."

"How so, Mrs. Morgan?"

"Gloria would remove her daughter to the attic when she

had friends over, to the attic where the servants—men and women!—slept, so she could make room for her friends."

"And you were excluded from this household?"

"Because of my objection to Gloria's choices," said Mamma. "I had to resort to meeting my granddaughter in secret, in the night, after Gloria and her friend—after my daughter had gone out. I used to come to the house. She was utterly alone in that house, and I was afraid for her."

Thelma straightened. Mamma had pulled back, on the brink of mentioning one of Gloria's relationships. Did she mean Nada, when she referred to Gloria's friend? Or Friedel?

Smyth stilled. "Afraid of what, Mrs. Morgan?" he asked softly, but Burkan leaped to his feet.

"Objection!" he shouted, and Mamma looked up in surprise.

Carew looked from Smyth to Burkan. "I'm afraid I'll have to sustain the objection," he said. "Have you any further questions for the witness?"

Smyth looked imminently satisfied. "No, Your Honor."

Carew cleared his throat. "Before we move on to cross-examination, I've got a question for the witness," he said. "Mr. Smyth, please read aloud Nurse Kieslich's testimony about Mrs. Vanderbilt and Prince Hohenlohe. According to the nurse, the two were seen in bed together. I'd like to hear Mrs. Morgan's testimony on that, please."

Smyth stood. Beside him, Gertrude looked up: Thelma could see her face in profile, her expression inscrutable beneath the brim of her hat.

"Mrs. Morgan, will you please tell us about when you first said anything to your daughter about the life she was living? Did you ever complain to your daughter about her friendships?"

Rather than answering Smyth, Mamma turned to the judge directly. This question, more than any other, seemed to discomfit her. She spoke quickly, color rising in her cheeks. "During the last six years, I've been telling her she ought to settle down

and love her own country—to live here, in America, and drop
her European entanglements, and European titles and desires
for a life of pleasure—"

"Your daughter's relationship with Prince Hohenlohe, Mrs.
Morgan," Carew interrupted. "That is the subject at hand. Do
you wish to tell me anything about that incident or not?"

Mamma looked out at the viewing gallery, then back at the
judge. "Your Honor," she said in an undertone, "Since she is
my daughter, may I tell you in private chambers—?"

"Objection!" roared Burkan. Thelma could picture the jour-
nalists in the hallway, their ears pressed to the door. "You look
your daughter squarely in the eye when you tell the judge what
you saw!"

"We'll hear your testimony here and now, please, Mrs. Morgan," said Carew.

Mamma closed her eyes. "Very well," she said. "It was between two and three in the morning when I heard the prince's
voice, raised very high, and my daughter sobbing." She shook her
head. "I didn't know what to do so I woke Nurse Kieslich—we
went to the door and it was open just a crack so we—we looked
in…" She trailed off, as though the recollection was too much
to bear. "We saw them in bed," she whispered, and her voice
began to catch. "This is dreadful," she said. "I love my daughter, and it's for the baby's sake that I tell you this, Your Honor.
This is the sacrifice of my life."

Carew reached into the pocket of his robe and pulled out a
handkerchief. "All right," he said. "What happened next, Mrs.
Morgan?"

"Gloria was sobbing. They were lying down in bed and he
was talking—vociferating—with my daughter. He was trying
to—trying to persuade her to marry him!"

"Let me understand you," said Burkan, walking toward the
witness's box. "You were standing outside the door and your

daughter was crying. Did you walk into the room and say, 'Are you sick, my child? What is the matter?'"

Mamma shook her head; Burkan pressed on.

"Why did you spy on your daughter, Mrs. Morgan? Why wouldn't you have gone in the room?"

Mamma put down the handkerchief. Her face was red, but Thelma knew it was a sign of anger, now, rather than distress. "My daughter loved this man," she said, "but I knew perfectly well that he was a danger to my granddaughter's future, and he didn't have a penny—a *penny!*—to support her. They would have lived off Little Gloria's money—money that's meant for *her*, not for German castles! But if I had said anything to her, she would have shown me the door right there and then. I was there to protect the baby, Mr. Burkan. Did you think I was listening at that door for pleasure? A woman my age? I'm an old woman, Mr. Burkan..."

"Protect her from what, Mrs. Morgan?"

"He wanted to adopt Little Gloria, to carry her off to Germany! Gloria was completely infatuated, she would have let him do anything he liked to Little Gloria—"

"Meaning what, exactly?"

"Have her whipped, if he wanted, handle her money—he called her the daughter of a plebeian!"

"And this is why you prevented the marriage between Gloria and Prince Hohenlohe?"

"Wouldn't you have done it, if he was trying to get all your granddaughter's money? What German has money these days? You don't think I saw what he was after?"

"Objection," called Smyth.

"Sustained," said Carew.

Thelma listened. Mamma spoke as if a dam had burst, words spilling out over months and years of resentment.

"If it weren't for me, my granddaughter would be German— or she would be dead! Gloria was so in love she would have done anything for him, spent my granddaughter's inheritance like water, keeping Little Gloria from the people who loved her most—"

"Calm yourself, please, Mrs. Morgan," said Smyth.

Mamma took a breath, twisting the handkerchief in her hands. "My daughter and I were very happy together up until the time she fell in love with the German. If she had committed *murder* I would have taken it upon my shoulders—except for the baby!" She put her head in her hands, elbows heavy on the witness's box. "Except for the baby," she repeated softly. "How has it come to this?"

Carew leaned back in his chair. Whether he believed Mamma or not, Thelma wasn't sure.

"Thank you, Mrs. Morgan," he said.

FORTY

February 1932
London

THELMA GRIPPED THE TELEPHONE, STRIVING TO quell her unease before a shuffling noise indicated that someone had resumed the call.

"Lady Averill? I'm afraid she's gone out." Webb's voice sounded thin and apologetic; Thelma could picture him threading his fingers through the telephone's wires, kneading them into collusion. "Something to do with the horses, I believe, before she departs with His Lordship to Africa…"

"Thank you, Webb," she said. "Would you let her know I've been trying to reach her?"

"Of course."

She rang off, smoothing the four half-moons her fingernails had bitten into the flesh of her palm. It was snowing outside, drifts falling from the eaves in gleeful eddies, whirling toward the white shroud blanketing Grosvenor Square.

Averill was avoiding her: that much was clear, in Webb's tactful dismissal and in Thelma's unanswered letters, her declined invitations to meet for lunch. It was a silence, which, four days before Averill and Duke were to leave on safari, made Thelma deeply uneasy, but she had kept her promise not to tell Duke about Averill's ill-conceived plan to elope with Andrew Rattray.

Snow buffeted noiselessly against the window. This silence was hardly the conduct of someone who was truly committed to her actions. Since Averill had first told Thelma about Rattray, Thelma's misgivings had only grown. Rattray was old, and unlike Duke he had little to offer his prospective bride in the way of comfort or security. While Averill considered herself a hunter in the manicured hedges of the countryside surrounding Burrough Court and the uncomplicated wilderness of Scotland, she couldn't—simply couldn't—live in Africa. There, Averill's inexperience would be a liability, regardless of how much she thought she loved Rattray. Averill had fallen for an idea, more than a man: an idea very much tied to a place where her money, her family, meant nothing.

Thelma stood, willing Averill to appear at the door. Perhaps she'd reconsidered. Thelma pictured Averill slipping a note to Rattray on her arrival in Nairobi, avoiding his hurt expression as she retreated across the gulf separating peer's daughter from servant. Her silence might be down to embarrassment: simple and clean, a cauterized wound.

But Thelma couldn't take that chance.

She arrived at Burrough Court two hours later, the drive lengthened by the snow collecting in mounds on the side of the road. She glanced at her watch—half past noon. If things with Averill went well, she would be traveling back to London by teatime.

The motorcar pulled up the drive and Thelma stared up at the familiar facade. Thick tendrils of ivy vines gripped, finger-like, to the brick. Would Averill refuse her entry? She pictured Webb barring her way and smiled as the ancient butler, heavily favoring the bannister, came down to greet her.

"I thought I'd come to wish Averill well on her trip in person," said Thelma, her voice ringing with false cheer. "Is she back from her trip to town? Or was it the stables?"

"She's—the stables, my lady," said Webb, ducking his head in a brief bow. What reason had Averill given him for avoiding her?

The stables were a short walk past the main house, a white collection of slate-roofed buildings set on three sides of a pea-gravel courtyard. Thelma slipped through a side door, blinking in the whitewashed darkness.

The stalls were along one wall, the paint chipped and worn but clean, the horses whickering softly as Thelma passed. She paused to greet the gentle roan that Tony liked to ride and passed the stalls that had once held Duke's zebras. It had all been in good fun when they'd finally harnessed them to the coach, but Duke had sold them to a zoo after they sickened in their second English winter. Such was the risk, thought Thelma, brushing aside a mess of hay with her boot, when one took a creature out of its natural habitat.

Averill was in one of the farther stalls, with the dappled mare that she'd shown at Leicester Fair. Dressed in worn trousers and a white blouse, her jacket folded over the stall door, Averill was bent over the mare's front leg, cleaning out its hoof with an iron pick. Her fringe, pinned back with a tortoiseshell clip, fell loose. She pushed it back as she continued to work the hoof with single-minded focus.

"You've been avoiding me," said Thelma. Averill looked up, resting the mare's hoof on her knee. She examined the hoof a moment more, scraping the frog with a half-hearted motion before tossing the pick in the corner of the stall.

"Gordon never takes the time to clean their hooves properly," she said, rubbing her hands clean on her breeches. "Thought I'd come and take the time before..."

"Before you leave," said Thelma. Averill dropped the towel and picked up a brush; she turned back to the mare, brushing her gray flank with a smooth, rhythmic motion. "On safari? Or for good?"

Averill didn't reply. Thelma opened the stall door and stepped inside, approaching the horse with her hand outstretched. She touched the bridge of its nose with her palm, and it nuzzled hopefully—Thelma wished she'd thought to bring an apple. "Have you given any thought to our conversation?" she said.

Averill ran her brush down the horse's haunch. "I have," she said. "Andy and I—we've been writing to each other. My feelings haven't changed."

Thelma met the mare's soft, sad eyes. "I didn't ask you about your feelings."

Averill set the brush down. "He loves me," she said flatly, and Thelma wondered how many times Averill had rehearsed this conversation in her head, during quiet moments with the horses, or brooding over cups of tea. "Would you give that up? In all honesty, would you?"

Thelma ran her hands along the mare's nose, breathing in the earthy aroma of horses that made her think of Reggie and Gloria back when they were whole.

"You know, Averill, that I was married before I met your father," she said. "I don't think I ever told you about it—not properly. It didn't seem pertinent, but now…" Thelma exhaled, dust particles dancing around her feet.

"I married too young," she said. "Far too young. He was handsome, charming… When he asked me to marry him, I didn't stop to think. We loved each other—what more did we need?"

Thelma glanced at Averill, her brush moving with slow concentration.

"We eloped. I was too young to marry without my parents' permission, and we both knew they wouldn't grant it. That ought to have been my first warning—Gloria's reaction ought to have been the second. She didn't like him, not in the slightest, but she came to the wedding just the same. I'd only known Junior two months."

She'd worn a periwinkle dress she'd borrowed from a friend—it didn't suit her but she couldn't afford a dress of her own. Not that it had mattered: Thelma had found it all wonderfully bohemian, running away in a borrowed gown. She recalled the church and the round-cheeked priest; the unseasonable cold of that May morning, which left a thin scur of frost on the daffodils in the churchyard.

"We didn't even make it through the honeymoon," she said. She closed her eyes, recalling the fragment of glass lodged in the wall behind the dining table in their apartment, the mark in the wallpaper after she'd pulled it out with shaking hands. "He hid it well, at first, but his composure began to slip. Before long, it was all just—routine.

"I stayed with him. What choice did I have? My parents had disowned me. Mamma was furious that I hadn't waited to find someone who could take care of me, but I hadn't bothered to stop and think. I was in *love*..."

She looked up, catching Averill's eye as Averill threw a heavy blanket over the mare's back.

"Gloria, thank God, stood by me. After I miscarried, she gave me the courage I needed to leave him. If she hadn't been there, I might still be in that apartment. Or worse."

Averill finished fastening the horse blanket. She walked toward the stall door, running her hand companionably along the mare's mane, passing so close to Thelma that the hem of her jacket lifted with the movement.

"You love him," Thelma continued, following Averill into an adjoining stall where a smaller horse lifted its head in welcome. "I loved Junior. Or I thought I did—I don't know which is worse, really. But I learned a lesson: no one should come so completely between you and your family. Even if you love him. If you were to end up in trouble and you've cut all ties... If he's all you've got in the world and he turns against you, the world becomes a very dark place. Believe me, Averill."

Averill lifted a limp bridle from a hook on the wall and fitted it over the horse's head. She pulled the buckles tight, testing the pressure by tugging on the rein. The horse moved with the tether, a smooth sweep of its head.

"I'm sorry about what happened to you," she said finally. "But Andy isn't Junior."

She spoke like her father: firmly, matter-of-fact; her mind already set. She opened the stall door and Thelma stepped aside as Averill led the horse out.

"I love Andy. I trust him," she said. "If I'm making a mistake—and I don't think I am—then with all due respect, Thelma, it's mine to make." She leaned forward, and kissed Thelma, her lips warm against Thelma's chilled cheek. "You know how much you mean to me. I hope you'll still be my friend, once all this is over."

It was a clear, gentle dismissal, and Thelma stepped aside. Her journey to Burrough Court had been wasted. Thelma could see that now. She ought to have known that Averill was wiser than Thelma had been back then; that her decision wasn't one of impulse but of deep, considered feeling.

Averill tugged on the horse's rein and she led him down the length of the stable toward the paddock, horse and rider walking side by side.

The motorcar idled in front of Duke's town house, the building's austere gray looming against the iron clouds. After delivering her superfluous message to Averill, Thelma had returned to London in silence, the twin relationships that tied her to Averill—stepmother and friend—plaguing her. Did her position as one give her the right to violate the confidence of the other?

She walked up the front steps and lifted the heavy doorknocker before she had the chance to lose her nerve.

"My lady," said Williams, with some surprise. Thelma hadn't

come to Arlington Place since the divorce: it was still too raw, too presumptuous, to move in and out of Duke's life with any sort of ease.

"Is Duke in?" she asked.

"His Lordship is in the study. I shall let him know you've arrived."

"Please don't trouble yourself," she said, and pushed past before he could protest.

She knocked on the door to Duke's study and he called out a muffled invitation. Thelma opened the door and Duke, sitting at his desk with a set of spectacles in his hand, looked up.

"Thelma." He frowned, stowing the spectacles in his desk drawer. "To what do I owe...?"

Thelma inched into the room as the door clicked shut behind her. "I'm sorry to come unannounced. I hope I'm not intruding—"

"Not at all," said Duke, inviting Thelma to sit down. "A few final things to sort before we sail." He sat, too, pulling the crease of his trouser-leg straight.

Thelma hesitated. Not for the first time, her ire rose. Averill ought to be telling Duke this herself, not foisting the duty off onto a messenger.

"I've come to talk about Averill," she said. "I understand you're taking her with you to Kenya."

"I am," said Duke. "She's quite looking forward to it. Dickie's going to join us when his term is up—wants to try his hand at a hippopotamus. My money's on Averill, personally... Have you eaten? Could ring for tea."

"No, thank you," said Thelma, her heart sinking at Duke's attempt at casual conversation. He had no clue. She couldn't stand to look him in the eye now that it came to it. Ending their marriage, somehow, had been easier. "It's none of my business, really," she said. "Averill's made me promise not to tell you, but I feel you ought to know. I couldn't forgive myself if you went off without the facts..."

"I'd know a damn sight quicker if you'd just come out with it," said Duke lightly. "What's this about?"

Thelma closed her eyes. "It's Averill," she said. "Once she arrives in Africa she intends to marry Andrew Rattray. I told her the idea was madness, but she seems quite set..."

She faltered into silence, her pulse beating a frantic, instinctive tattoo against her throat.

"How dare you come into my home with this disgusting falsehood?"

The room closed in; she twitched her fingers against her handbag.

"I'm trying—please, Duke, I'm trying to help. I just came from Burrough Court, and she's—"

"Let me remind you, Thelma, that you forfeited all rights to my children when you left me," said Duke, his voice low. "But now you want to play stepmother? I don't know if it's cruelty, ignorance or pure selfishness that's brought you here today, but I won't hear another word of it."

"I came because I love her," she said, "If you can't see that I'm trying to help—she's going to ruin her life!"

"Let's not pretend you've ever given a thought to Averill," Duke shot back. "You were her stepmother for years, and you've never once acted like it. Now you want to play the parent? A bit late for all that now."

Thelma was taken aback by his bitterness. "That's not fair," she said. "When you were away with your girlfriends, who did she call for advice, for companionship? *Me*, Duke—I've always been there for her, in what way I could—"

Duke snapped. He slammed his fist against the desk, the noise alone making Thelma flinch. "You don't think I know my own daughter?" he roared. "I raised that girl, on my own—despite you coming in and out of her life like you were going around a revolving door—and you're telling me I don't know her? How *dare* you insinuate—I don't believe it!"

Thelma could feel the fight leave her. If he could only set aside his anger—

"If you would just listen—" she said.

Duke stepped forward, his face red. "How *dare* you try to put a rift between me and my children? Get out! Get out or I'll throw you out!"

Thelma turned, tears falling as she fled the study.

FORTY-ONE

October 20, 1934
Long Island, USA

CLOSE AS IT WAS TO NEW YORK CITY, THELMA found the endless swath of forest on Long Island incongruous, where the tangle of trees and shrubs lining the parkway stood in thick opposition to the concrete order of Manhattan's skyscrapers. She'd come this way before as a young woman, on trips to large, effortless mansions owned by friends with far wealthier parents. She recalled driving past brown-brick monstrosities and Stanford Whites, the buildings mere dots at the end of long, wide lanes, gripping her seat in the hope that, one day, she too might be entitled to this new-world splendor.

This wasn't a social visit, although Thelma, Gloria and Consuelo, sitting side by side in the back of Gloria's Rolls Royce, were dressed as though they were out for an autumn picnic. Thelma looked at the court order in Gloria's hand, creased under the pressure of her brittle fingers. On Monday, Burkan had asked Justice Carew for a cease-fire, requesting permission for Gloria to visit her daughter, sequestered away in Gertrude Whitney's

Old Westbury mansion. Carew, to Burkan's relief and Gloria's trepidation, had granted it.

"What if she doesn't want to see me?" Gloria had said before they set out that morning, waving off the butler's attempts to help her with her jacket.

Burkan took Gloria's jacket from the butler and shook it open. "It's not about what she wants—it's about what's necessary. Gertrude's had Little Gloria all to herself since the trial began. Who knows what she's been telling her? Children can be so impressionable." He settled the tweed over Gloria's shoulders, and Thelma could see that the jacket fell looser than it ought. "Little Gloria will be testifying soon, and we don't want her to start spouting some song and dance from Kieslich. You're to remind her how much you love her. Make her realize she wants to come home."

Gloria turned. "You don't really expect he'll ask her to testify?" she said.

"I think he will," said Burkan gently. "And if so, I don't want Gertrude Whitney's voice, or your mother's, or that damned nurse's in her head. I want her to think about you."

"But why there? Why at Gertrude's house?"

Thelma and Burkan exchanged glances. Gloria knew the reason as well as anybody else—along with letters of support or condemnation, Gloria had been receiving ransom notes, arriving like daggers in the mailbox, for the past four days. Horrible, typewritten letters threatening to shoot Little Gloria, to kidnap her in broad daylight and extract what they could of the Vanderbilt fortune.

"Likely the work of a crank," they'd been told by the detective who'd been assigned to handle the threats. But Little Gloria had been under constant police surveillance since then: a state of affairs that had done nothing to calm Gloria's frayed nerves. Under Justice Carew's guidance, Little Gloria had been taken to

Gertrude's home in Old Westbury and, with Gloria's blessing, Gertrude had hired a complement of private detectives.

Moving Little Gloria out of the city had been the right thing to do—even without the threatening letters, the trial was attracting too much for any child—but now, traveling to Gertrude's mansion in the suburbs, Thelma felt as though they were crossing into enemy territory.

Gertrude's house was located on top of a hill, and the Rolls Royce purred as it climbed the subtle elevation of the drive. Columns of policemen flanked the final mile of the drive: they turned silently to watch the motorcar's progress, guns visible in holsters, faces hidden beneath the brims of their caps.

Gloria gripped Thelma's hand.

Thelma was furious. She'd expected some show of security, but this police cordon was too much. Did Gertrude expect Gloria to snatch her daughter back in broad daylight?

Gertrude's home was immense: a self-indulgent dream of a farmstead, white clapboard walls and red shingles, larger than any rural home Thelma had ever seen. What would they say, those farmwives following Gertrude and Gloria's trial, if they knew that Gertrude lived in a mockery of their modest lives?

The front door opened and a young man in a gray suit came down the redbrick steps. He didn't smile as he held out his hand to Gloria.

"Mrs. Vanderbilt, I'm Barklie Henry, Mrs. Whitney's son-in-law," he said. He was tall, with a broad, almost Grecian face. Had he been smiling, Thelma would have thought him handsome. "Mrs. Whitney sends her regrets that she's not here to greet you in person."

Gloria's hand tightened on Thelma's arm. The more time Thelma spent at court, the more she resented Gertrude Whitney's attitude: her callous entitlement, her haughty outrage masked as courtesy. Barklie Henry could apologize all he wanted, but he knew as well as they did that Gertrude's absence was mandated as part of the court order that allowed Gloria to visit her daughter—as was Justice Carew's stipulation that no lawyers were to be present.

"Thank you, Mr. Henry," said Gloria. She looked at Henry's outstretched hand. Realizing she wouldn't take it, Henry let it fall back to his side, his arm swinging with awkward bravado. "How is my daughter?"

"I don't know whether it's best for you to see her just yet," said Henry. "I told her you were coming to visit and, well, she lost her temper. Locked herself in her room." Henry leaned close, with a sigh that fell short of camaraderie. "You know how difficult children can be, Mrs. Vanderbilt. Perhaps you'd be best to return another day, when she's had time to consider..."

As Henry made his excuses, Gloria shrank farther into her overlarge jacket, her shoulders collapsing under the effort she'd made to come so far in the first place.

"Mr. Henry, this meeting was arranged a week ago," said Thelma. "If you've not given Little Gloria enough notice, that's no fault of ours." She snatched Gloria's handbag from her unresisting grasp and rifled through it, pulling out the creased envelope Gloria had been clutching in the car. "We have a court order."

They walked into a wood-lined entrance hallway where a butler should have been standing at the ready. *Good,* thought Thelma, wondering if Gertrude had sent the staff away for the day. *Fewer complications.*

Henry caught up with them as they reached the staircase, his face flushed more with embarrassment than effort.

"I understand, Mrs. Vanderbilt, that this must be a disappointment," he said, "but if you'd only listen, she's very distressed—"

"And whose fault is that?" Consuelo replied. "Policemen crawling about the place like ants—what child wouldn't be frightened? I bet you told her we were coming to roast her on a spit."

Henry flushed redder still, his outrage spilling out in sputtered bursts.

Thelma continued up the stairs. At the top, Gloria paused,
planting her hand on the newel post to catch her breath.

"I'm fine," she said in a low voice, as Consuelo and Henry
bickered below. She nodded down the long hallway. "It's at the
far end—Gloria's room," she said, and put her hand on Thelma's
arm once more for support.

They walked down the hallway and Thelma wondered again
at the deserted house. Was it for her benefit or theirs, that Gertrude had emptied the house of any staff that might leak details
of the meeting to the press? If it went well, it wasn't in Gertrude's
interest for the papers to know about it—but if the meeting went
poorly? If Little Gloria was as distraught as Henry claimed?

In that case, Gertrude's discretion would have done Gloria a
very large favor.

Gloria stopped in front of a door with a brass knob, indistinguishable from the others along the hallway. She stared at it, her
eyes wide, but didn't knock. Thelma could see her chest rising
and falling, too quickly, too lightly.

Henry and Consuelo had reached the top of the stairs. Fearing that Henry might try to stop them, Thelma knocked.

The sound spurred Gloria to movement. She cleared her
throat, resting her fingers gently on the handle.

"Gloria? Darling? It's me. It's Mummy."

The response was immediate: a piercing, panicked scream.
Gloria backed away from the door as though burnt.

"No! I don't want to see you, I don't—don't—don't kill me,
don't kill me! Don't open the door—don't open it! She'll kill me!"

Thelma stared, frozen by the sheer terror in Little Gloria's
voice. This wasn't the sound of a child's tantrum: Little Gloria
screamed as though she expected her mother to break down the
door with a knife in hand.

The scream subsided, and Gloria faltered. She dropped her

purse, her legs buckling as Barklie Henry rushed forward to catch her.

Gloria looked at Thelma, her face ashen. "Kill her?" she whispered.

"Who told her to say that?" said Consuelo, looking at Henry with incandescent rage. "Where did she hear that?"

Supporting Gloria in his arms, Henry shook his head. "I *told* you, she's not in the right mood—"

Thelma tried the handle, her shock transforming into outrage. The door was locked from the inside, and she thought once more of Gertrude emptying the house, panic rising in her chest. They had to see Little Gloria. If she truly believed such monstrous things, their case was doomed; but they could set it to rights—if only Little Gloria would see reason—

"Who else is in there?" said Consuelo.

"A nurse," said Henry. "Not Miss Kieslich—someone new. Gertrude hired her a few days ago."

Another decision made without Gloria's permission; another excuse for Gertrude to exert her influence over Little Gloria's well-being. Thelma pounded on the door.

"Nurse, this is a court order," she shouted, attempting to make herself heard over Little Gloria's screams. "I demand you open this door at once!"

Another scream "—*No!*—" and then Little Gloria was silent.

The doorknob rattled. "I can't!" came a small, harried voice— the nurse. "She took the key and threw it into the fire!" The knob shook once more, as though in illustration.

"Outrageous," spat Consuelo, her brittle voice a reminder for Thelma to maintain her composure. She turned to Henry. "You must have a locksmith, a spare key?"

Henry looked profoundly disturbed. "There's the caretaker. He might—"

"We must see Little Gloria," said Consuelo. "It's a court order—"

"I know," snapped Henry. He looked at Gloria, still in his arms. "Can you stand?"

Gloria nodded and he set her back on her feet, gingerly, and set off down the hall, Consuelo close on his heels.

Gloria stood for a moment then swayed, blood draining from her cheeks. Thelma caught her before she fainted dead away.

Thelma found a vacant room opposite Little Gloria's. She pulled Gloria onto the bed, and eased off her sister's hat. Gloria's eyelids fluttered, beads of sweat forming on her forehead as she came to.

"What happened?" she mumbled, and Thelma squeezed her hand as she returned to consciousness.

"You fainted. Nothing to worry—we're in Old Westbury—"

"She hates me," said Gloria, closing her eyes once more. "Oh, God. Why would she think—"

Thelma smoothed the hair from Gloria's forehead—another nervous attack and they would be returning to New York in the back of an ambulance. "She doesn't hate you," said Thelma. "She's confused."

Gloria didn't have the energy to argue; she lay back against the pillow, her hair coming loose from its chignon. Across the hall, they could hear the small tempest of Little Gloria's cries reach a crescendo, her pleading audible through the door.

"Don't let her kill me! Please! She's going to *kill me*..."

Thelma went back into the hallway. They couldn't stay at Gertrude's house all afternoon, but returning to New York City without seeing Little Gloria was entirely out of the question. Burkan would have to demand another court-mandated visit; the newspapers would run breathless headlines. Carew, certainly, would see it as strong evidence against Gloria's suit, and Gloria herself would lose what little confidence she still had in getting her daughter back.

Thelma knocked again, softly.

"Gloria," she said, "It's your aunt Thelma. Will you let me in?"

She pressed her ear against the door.

"It's just me out here, Gloria. Your mother isn't feeling well. Will you let me in?"

There was no response. She stepped back, defeated, as Consuelo and Barklie Henry returned with a scruffy caretaker in tow, a ring of keys hanging from his belt. Henry knocked on the door as the caretaker began to sift through the keys.

"Gloria? It's your uncle Barklie. You're being very childish," he said, as the caretaker tried the first key into the lock. "Your mother's come all this way. You must let her in, otherwise you'll be in trouble. Aunt Gertrude will be very, very cross."

The caretaker fit a second key into the lock. It turned, and Henry fell silent. The caretaker opened the door and Thelma stepped into the silent room.

It was a child's bedroom, comfortable and airy. The walls were painted white; there was a single bed in one corner, its iron head- and footboards tracing curlicues against the walls. A dollhouse sat on the floor, its back open to reveal the rooms within, and beside it stood an armchair, its seat cushion comfortably squashed with age. Was that where Kieslich told Little Gloria nightmare-stories about her mother, sowing panic in a child's impressionable mind?

A fire, close to dying, burned in the grate. A young woman, her straw-colored hair bound up beneath a nurse's bonnet, stood before it, her eyes wide.

Thelma couldn't see Little Gloria. Again, panic rose in her throat. Had the child locked herself in the closet?

Wordlessly, the nurse gathered the folds of her long skirt and stepped to one side, revealing Little Gloria crouched behind her, gripping the nurse's hem.

Thelma looked at her niece, her anger turning to shame. Little Gloria looked much younger than her ten years: she was as skinny as her mother, her face almost as white beneath listless dark hair. Thelma was thankful, now, that Gloria was across the hall. The sight of Little Gloria clinging to the nurse was enough to break her heart.

"I'm sorry, Gloria, for sounding so upset," said Thelma. "What's all this about? You're not frightened of me, are you?"

Little Gloria looked up. "No," she whispered.

Thelma knelt. "Of course, you're not. I've not done anything to hurt you, have I? Are you afraid of Mummy?"

Little Gloria glanced up at Consuelo and Barklie Henry, standing in the doorframe. She shook her head.

"There's nothing to be frightened of," said Thelma. "We're here because we love you, Gloria—your mummy, your aunt Consuelo and me. Will you come and give me a kiss?"

The nurse prized Little Gloria's fingers from her dress, and Thelma hardly dared to breathe as Little Gloria came forward with stiff, reluctant steps. She'd always been an odd child, influenced by her odd nurse, her odd grandmother—but here, locked away in the woods, surrounded by policemen and lawyers, Little Gloria had become something else entirely.

She kissed Thelma's cheek, her lips a cold, brief pressure before she pulled back.

Thelma smiled. "That wasn't so hard, was it?"

"You know, you've made your mummy very upset," said Consuelo. "Will you say hello to her?"

Little Gloria paled; Thelma, fearing another outburst, clapped her hands together. "Gloria, I see you've got a ribbon on your dresser. What did you win that for?"

Consuelo quietened with a look of consternation but Thelma pointed at the rosette, a little blue bundle of satin sitting next to a lamp. Little Gloria smiled faintly.

"Riding." She picked up the rosette, stroking it before holding it out to Thelma. "I got first place."

Thelma raised her eyebrows. "First place?" she said, accepting the worn ribbon. "You must be a very good rider."

Little Gloria nodded. "I won a cup, too, but it's in Newport."

"A cup *and* a ribbon? You must be the best rider in Old Westbury. Do you remember riding horses with Tony in Leicestershire?"

Little Gloria nodded.

"And what sort of horse do you have here?"

"I have two. One's named Black Beauty."

"*Two?* Oh, my..."

Thelma let Little Gloria talk about riding for a few minutes' more, struck by how young she seemed. Thelma didn't have much experience with children, but it felt as if she was speaking to Tony. She shouldn't have been surprised: Mamma and Kieslich had infantilized Little Gloria from the outset, and the trial clearly hadn't helped. A return to Gloria's household—a return to a normal life, filled with friends rather than nursemaids, would surely help the child thrive.

When Little Gloria went back to her dresser to retrieve more treasures, Thelma glanced back at Consuelo, who stood, arms crossed, in the doorway.

Little Gloria returned with more trinkets: a photograph of Reggie Vanderbilt in a gilt frame; a blue stone and a piece of lace that Thelma thought might have been off one of Gloria's dresses.

"This is Daddy," she said, holding the frame out so that Thelma could see. "I talk to his picture every night before bed."

Thelma looked at the portrait: he looked young and calm, serene even. She recalled Reggie's last few days: his bloated neck, spilling over the stiff collar of his dress shirt; his relentless, weary smile.

Look after them.

Thelma laid her hand across the frame. "This is very nice, Gloria," she said, "but what about your mummy? You know your father loved her very much."

Little Gloria stiffened, but Thelma pressed the advantage.

"Your mummy loves you, too, Gloria. She's come all this

way to see you, but she's feeling unwell right now. Would you go and give her a kiss?"

Little Gloria looked solemnly at the photograph. "He loved her?" she said, her voice quiet but no longer shaking.

"He did, my dear. Very much."

Little Gloria set the frame down, smoothing the glass as though it might wrinkle. "All right," she whispered.

Thelma held out her hand and Little Gloria took it. Consuelo and Barklie Henry stepped aside as Thelma led Little Gloria into the hallway.

Gloria was sitting up in the bed. She'd attempted to pin her hair back into place, and had wiped the trails of mascara from under her eyes. How could Little Gloria think she posed a threat?

"My baby," she said, holding out her arms.

Little Gloria cowered but Thelma patted her on the shoulder; she took one step forward, then another—but before she got close enough for Gloria to embrace her, she stopped.

"What's the matter?" said Thelma. "It's your mother—she wants to give you a kiss."

Little Gloria began to shake; she looked up at Thelma, her face twisting. She wrenched her hand from Thelma's and fled back into her room, slamming the door behind her.

When they returned to Gloria's town house, Burkan, Harry and Edith were waiting.

"Well?" said Burkan, coming into the front hall with a half-smoked cigar in his hand. He looked at Gloria and his face fell. "It didn't go well, did it?"

Consuelo pulled off her fur collar. "I've never seen anything so outrageous in my whole life," she said, crossing into the sitting room. Thelma and Gloria followed, and Harry made room for them on the couch. Someone had drawn the heavy curtains across the front window: it gave the room a funereal air, the chandelier casting an artificial glow.

Consuelo poured a drink. "The child is completely delu-sional," she said, as Gloria slumped into a chair, her head in her hands.

"She hates me," said Gloria. "She thinks I'm going to kill her."

Burkan lowered himself onto the couch. "Was it some sort of joke?" he asked as Consuelo poured glasses for Thelma and Gloria.

"I don't believe so," said Thelma.

"She couldn't stand to be near me," said Gloria. "What sort of child thinks her mother's a—a murderer...?"

"Was she delusional in any other way?" asked Burkan, star-ing at Gloria as though hoping she might be pulling a prank. "If it's a symptom of some greater illness..."

"I'm afraid not," said Thelma. "She was very much herself until she saw Gloria."

"Outrageous," Consuelo muttered. "I don't know what they've been telling that girl, but she was hysterical."

"You think they coerced her?" said Harry.

"They told her something. No child behaves like that with-out reason. Someone's been saying that Gloria means to hurt her," said Consuelo.

"Who would do such a thing?" said Edith. "Not Gertrude, surely. I can't imagine she'd stoop so low."

"Not Gertrude, perhaps—but Mamma? Kieslich?" said Thelma.

Burkan shook his head. "It doesn't matter if Gertrude Whit-ney isn't saying these things herself—clearly, she's not stopping it. I'll bet her lawyers have advised her to do nothing. It's their best chance of winning. What judge would force a child to live in terror?"

"It's a cowardly trick," said Consuelo.

"It is," said Burkan, He removed his glasses and pulled out a handkerchief to clean the lenses. "The nurse spends more time with Little Gloria than anyone else—except perhaps her grandmother. She's someone Little Gloria trusts—if she's telling her that Gloria means her harm, Little Gloria has no reason to doubt it." He put the glasses back on, wrapping the arms around the backs of his ears. "But to encourage the child's delusions—to sit back and allow Kieslich to spread her poison—it all feeds into their strategy. A dirty, cheap thing to do."

The room fell silent. Thelma stared at the floor.

Mamma was part of this fantasy. It sickened her to think of Mamma and Kieslich, chipping away at the foundations of Little Gloria's life: her trust in those who claimed to love her. What would be left of the child once the trial was over?

"You know the worst of it?" said Gloria. "I'm an unfit mother because I've done exactly the same thing Gertrude Whitney does in her studio."

No one responded. Thelma thought of Nada: impossibly beautiful, changeable.

"And it's all a big, terrible secret. Gertrude has her fun, same as me... And *I'm* the unfit mother."

Burkan sighed. "We agreed to civility in the proceedings because we thought it would be better for the child." He stood, stubbing the end of his cigar in an ashtray. "If they're turning Little Gloria against you, I think it's safe to assume that civility is off the table."

"What do you mean?" said Gloria.

"First thing tomorrow, I'm telephoning all of Mrs. Whitney's so-called 'art acquaintances,'" he said. "Let's see what Carew has to say about unfit parenting then."

FORTY-TWO

March 1932
Fort Belvedere, Great Windsor Park

THELMA'S MOTORCAR SLOWED AS IT REACHED the gates of the Fort. She glanced at her watch, then pulled down the divider that separated her from the driver.

"Once around the Park, please," she said. Her driver nodded and Thelma leaned back in her seat, watching the leafless forest blur past.

She had arrived at the Fort earlier than she'd anticipated, and while David always encouraged her to use the Fort as her own, it felt wrong to walk the marble floors of his beloved home unsupervised, a cuckoo roosting in a gilded nest. Most weeks, she arrived at the Fort late—David arranged his weekly schedule of ribbon-cuttings and speeches so he could leave London as early as possible on a Friday morning—but last night he'd received an early summons to Buckingham Palace.

"Do you know why?" Thelma had asked the night before, as David accepted the summons from his butler.

He read it, his face closing into a frown.

"It's Father's doing," he said. He dropped the card onto the table and returned to his meal, segmenting a piece of roast beef on his fork. "He'll want to upbraid me for something or other." He lifted the fork, examining the piece of meat before lowering it to his plate untouched. "D'you know, I've completely lost my appetite."

Thelma watched the manicured brown of Windsor Great Park pass by her window. She hoped David had behaved himself—and that His Majesty hadn't provoked him.

She ran over the guest list for the weekend in her head. It would be quiet, just friends and family—what family remained in London, with Duke and Averill gone on safari and Gloria embroiled in an argument with the Surrogates. Thelma hadn't yet received word from Nairobi: she wasn't sure whether silence was cause for relief or concern.

Family, then: Consuelo and Benny, along with Piers Legh. The Duke and Duchess of York, newly installed with their daughters in their own country home across the park, would pop in for dinner and drinks; the Simpsons, however, would be staying overnight.

They slowed at the gates of the Fort once more and turned down the drive as a weak sun struggled to break through the low clouds. Osborne was waiting at the front door, with two footmen who jogged forward to unstrap Thelma's luggage from the boot.

"Good afternoon, my lady," he said. "His Royal Highness is in the garden. Shall I let him know you've arrived?"

"No, thank you," she replied, stepping out of the motorcar. "Point me in the right direction and I'll find him myself."

Osborne led Thelma through to the back lawn. The forest surrounding the Fort was a mess of branches; rooks, stark against the gray sky, circled the tops of trees.

"I should warn you," said Osborne, "that His Royal Highness is in something of a temper."

Thelma straightened the sleeve of her coat to better block the chill. "The summons?"

Osborne nodded. "I understand the meeting didn't go quite to plan."

"Well, that's no surprise." Thelma looked down the long garden but couldn't see David; she could hear, however, a rhythmic hacking in the laurels to the east of the lawn.

"Are you sure I can't persuade you to wait here?"

"Thank you, but no," said Thelma, "I'd like to stretch my legs." She set off down the sloping ground, her heels sinking into the rain-softened lawn.

The forest was gloomy and overgrown, bare branches reaching toward the late winter sunlight. The trees were nearly silent, lacking the birdsong that Thelma had expected to hear—too early in the year?—but she followed the sound of work. Her shoes would be ruined, but she pressed on through the undergrowth, breathing in the rich, sweet smell of decayed leaves uncovered by frost. David had done well: the path was narrow but clear, flanked by piles of debris.

She picked across a hollow and came to the rise of a small valley, following the *swish-whoosh* of human endeavor. Through the gloom she saw him, dressed in plus fours and muddy white socks, shirtsleeves rolled up, his jacket and overcoat discarded on a nearby log. He was bent nearly double, hacking at the roots of a small thornbush with a machete. After a final thwack, he tossed the machete aside and tugged the bush free, throwing it aside with a crash.

"David," said Thelma. She walked closer, glad to see he was wearing heavy gloves, but his forearms were scored with bright scratches.

She raised her voice. "Darling!"

He looked up, chest heaving with exertion. He waved limply at Thelma and pushed his hair, fallen out of its usual pomade stiffness, out of his eyes. "Hello, darling," he said. He chopped at another bit of brush, the machete passing through the thinner branches like water. "You didn't have to come down. Osborne would have come."

"I wanted to," said Thelma. "You've made quite a dent. It looks wonderful."

David nodded, still short of breath, and indicated his intended path with the machete handle. "I'll be taking it through. There's a Roman ruin to the north of here, I suppose it will end up there sooner or later." He gripped the trunk of a slender beech sapling in one hand and swung the blade; it cut through and David lifted the beech easily, throwing it like a javelin atop the discarded thornbush.

"Will you come to the house?"

David shook his head, twigs snapping beneath his boots. "I'm not done yet." He knelt to attack another thornbush, his face pale.

Just off the path was a fallen tree trunk, mossy with age and large enough for Thelma to sit on. She navigated her way over and sat, smoothing the hem of her coat beneath her.

"How was your meeting with His Majesty?" she said.

He didn't answer straightaway, but continued to cut at the thornbush, planting his free hand on the ground to reach the root with his blade.

"Osborne tell you?" He swung the machete a final time and the bush shuddered; he straightened, resting his hands on his knees.

"I can't do anything right. He's so stubborn. Can't ever accept that there are other ways of going about one's business, better ways…"

"Oh dear," said Thelma. "What was it this time?"

David half-glanced at her. "Flying," he said. "That was the start—it rather unraveled from there. Said a sovereign has no business meddling in new technologies. Tells me I risk the monarchy every time I go up in an airplane." He wiped his face with a muddy glove, leaving a streak of grit across his cheek. "He doesn't see how much time I would save, getting from one place to another."

A loud crashing sound came from the direction of the Fort; Thelma turned as Cora, one of David's terriers, sprinted toward them. Thelma held out her arms and Cora leaped into them, welcoming her to the Fort with wiggling glee.

"What else did he say?"

David watched the dog with sullen interest. "Said the technology is untested—that the train was good enough for him and it bloody well ought to be good enough for me. He's forbidden me from continuing my training as a pilot."

"That's not fair," said Thelma. David had been solicitous in training with the RAF for months; more than once, Thelma had woken in the middle of the night to find him sitting up in bed, poring over a flight manual. "It's hardly untested. The RAF have been flying for nearly fifteen years."

David stood. "Tell *him* that," he said, striding partway up the path. He stopped and spun back toward Thelma on his heel, leaving a deep furrow in the mud. "He'd throw the entire country back to the dark ages if he thought he could, but what good is a sovereign who doesn't keep up with the world? He's so—so self-righteous. If he gets it in mind that there's one way to do things, one hardly stands a chance to get a word in edgewise."

He'd built up enough of a head of steam that Thelma knew it was best to let him continue. She rubbed the terrier behind its ears and it pushed its head up into her fingers, imploring her to keep scratching.

"He's stubborn," she said fondly. "It's a trait you happen to share."

David laughed. He picked up the machete once more and swung it at a mature beech. The blade bit into the tree with a heavy thud, lodging deep within the trunk, and David left it there, quivering.

"I try so hard," he said, removing his gloves as he came to sit next to Thelma, "to make an effort. I do think about it all, you know. What sort of—of *king* I'll be when the old man goes. But it's always a fight. He doesn't see that the people love me *because* I'm not him. They know that I want to be a modern king, for a modern nation." He rested his elbows on his knees, the color returning to his face. "Haven't got a cigarette, have you?"

Thelma pulled cigarettes and a lighter from her handbag. David sat up, taking the case with a nod of thanks. Thelma lifted the small chrome cap of the lighter and turned the striking mechanism; the flame burst into life as David set a cigarette between his lips.

She leaned against his shoulder. "Surely—not to sound indelicate, but surely it's a temporary problem?" she said. "Once your father goes, it won't matter what he thinks of you. You can be exactly the sort of ruler you'd like."

"Ah, but when will that be?" muttered David. "There's plenty for him to criticize before he goes. My flying isn't the only thing that's risking the monarchy. He worries the people may not tolerate my *manner of living* much longer."

Thelma took the cigarette from David. "And what manner is that?"

"Modern. Enlightened," said David. "He thinks I ought to be more traditional. Church every Sunday, marry some European princess. In bed by ten o'clock, stamp collecting in the morning."

A marriage. That was the crux of it. Thelma passed the cigarette back, smoke dispersing in the winter air. A squirrel darted through the undergrowth and the terrier on Thelma's lap began to squirm; she released it and it exploded after the squirrel, crashing through the trees.

"He wants you to give me up?" Thelma asked.

David sighed. "That's the gist of it." Without looking down, he reached for her hand. "He found out you were hosting tonight and rather flew off the handle. He's worried about a scandal—says the newspapers keep quiet on his account, but the people won't put up with my carrying on much longer. The church won't abide it...which always seemed so silly to me, their preoccupation with divorced women." He spoke lightly, but the pressure of his fingers against hers strengthened, and she squeezed back. "Says I'm not getting any younger. I ought to go about the business of settling down. But that isn't me, darling, you know that."

But it would happen, sooner or later. Despite David's impulsive proposals, Wallis's breezy assumptions—despite Thelma's divorce, the papers sitting in the topmost drawer of her desk—David would, one day, have to marry someone that wasn't likely to be her.

He finished the cigarette and flicked it into a pile of damp leaves, where the ember faded amber to gray.

"I know he thinks it would be easier if Bertie had been born first," said David, his voice hardening. "Wife and children already. No concerns about p-poor little B-B-Bertie."

"It isn't Bertie's fault," she said. "You're different people, that's all." She kissed him, hoping to ease his sudden bitterness. "Your father thinks he's right because he's only ever known his own way forward. He's been doing the job for so long…but you're going to forge a different path. You know it and so does he. I'm sure he knows you'll make a fine king."

David sighed, staring into the gray forest without any real conviction. "No, he doesn't," he said dully. "And he's right." He stood and glanced back up the path.

Thelma stood, too. She stepped closer: without the gardenwork to keep him warm, David was shivering. "All due respect to His Majesty, my love, but it's not his opinion that matters," she said. "It's yours and mine. And the people's." She pressed her lips against his, and could feel him begin to smile.

He pulled away, and she rubbed at the smudge of dirt on the bridge of his nose. "Our guests will be arriving soon. Shall we go and get ready?"

"I suppose," said David. He went back to the tree and gripped the machete in both his hands. "Couldn't find my jacket, could you? I think I dropped it somewhere back there." He set one foot against the tree trunk for leverage and pulled; with a groan, the machete came free.

Thelma handed him his jacket—crumpled though it was, he put it on and smoothed the lapels. He took Thelma's hand, his palm gritty against hers, and together, they walked back up the winding path.

Someone had turned the lights on in the Fort. The electric glow drew attention to the failing day in the gray wood, and Thelma drew closer to David. The Fort really was so much prettier from the back, she thought as they stepped onto the lawn, with all the windows lit...

Piers Legh walked across the drawing room, a glass of champagne in his hand. He held it out and Thelma took it with a nod of thanks; beside her, Consuelo and Wallis Simpson laughed at something Elizabeth had said and Thelma picked up their laughter, although she'd missed the joke.

Bertie and Elizabeth had come over shortly after dinner, providing much-needed levity to the evening. David, still preoccupied by his meeting with the king, had barely said a word over dinner, leaving Thelma and Piers to carry the conversation. Now, with the women clustered by the fireplace and the men seated round a poker table, David had retreated from his guests entirely, standing with a martini in hand by the window as he stared at the black grounds.

Thelma, too, was preoccupied. The fact that she was considered a liability by David's parents wasn't news, exactly, but she wondered at the extent of the king's opposition. Did he know that Thelma had gone through with her divorce—had David told him? If so, had it changed anything?

Not likely, she thought, as Bertie excused himself from the poker table to put on a new record.

King David. King *Edward*, she corrected herself: it was a future that she couldn't quite picture. Would there still be weekends like this, laughing by the fireplace, cutting laurels in the forest? She pictured David's beloved Fort, abandoned not by choice but by duty, his spare hours taken up by tours, diplomacy—all his hard work, crumbling into obsolescence; the Fort an escape to be made only once, twice a year when custom allowed it. The Fort, transformed into a memory of happier times.

Thelma turned back to Elizabeth, who was discussing the renovations she and Bertie had made to their own Windsor Park estate.

"It's more conventional than this, of course, all square rooms and plasterwork, but we're making it our own," said Elizabeth, her chest slumping, ever so slightly, over the round of her stomach. Compared to Wallis and Consuelo, Elizabeth looked a bit dowdy: she still hadn't lost the weight after giving birth to Margaret in August. As if to distract from her figure, she had wreathed her neck in pearls and the excess reminded Thelma of Reggie's mother, Alice Vanderbilt. "Bertie, of course, has no eye for it—he wanted to paint the drawing room mauve, bless him." She looked at her husband, the corners of her eyes crinkling fondly. "But we hired someone, and it's all turning out rather beautifully."

"It must be quite different from here," said Consuelo, looking at the drawing room's clean lines and strong colors, its wood panels and warmth. "This really is more of a bachelor's space."

"Well, with the girls we wanted a homey feel," said Elizabeth. "It's a cozy spot, really. We spent a few days there over Christmas and it looked delightful, all decorated with pine boughs and tinsel."

Cozy, to Thelma, seemed a massive understatement, having called at Royal Lodge for tea with David two Saturdays ago. The drawing room, with its sea-foam walls and family crests, its identical chandeliers dancing down the ceiling, was immense: were it not for the Axminster and upholstered furniture to dampen the sound the room would have echoed with their conversation. For all that, though, Thelma had been utterly charmed by Bertie and Elizabeth's daughters. Margaret, only an infant, had been brought down by the nursemaid and sat in her mother's arms, while Lilibet, at five years old, was engaging and energetic, running across the room as David chased her with exaggerated slowness.

"Well, I can't vouch for the Lodge, but His Royal Highness has done a lovely job here," said Wallis. She raised her voice, looking round at David's turned back. "Am I right in thinking that's a Canaletto above the fireplace, sir?"

David looked round, his eyebrows slightly raised as if he'd forgotten the room was full of people. "Hmm? Yes, part of the Royal Collection. Freddie chose it. Useful, really, to have masterworks at one's disposal."

Bertie nodded. "Q-quite so," he said, as "Tea for Two" piped through the bell of the gramophone. "We've p-plundered several pieces for the L-Lodge, haven't we, darling?"

"One of the perks of being part of the family, I suppose," said Wallis. She leaned back in her chair. "Imagine, Thelma, having a warehouse of family heirlooms…when my mother died she left me an incomplete set of silverware, a bible and a pair of glass earrings." She bit into the olive, sliding it off the toothpick. "I can't find replacements for the silverware set and the bible isn't much use, but those earrings go with just about everything I own."

"Well, dear," said Elizabeth, her blue eyes turning to ice, "we can't any of us choose our breeding, can we? We can only choose whether or not to appear well-bred."

Wallis smirked—a quick tug of her lips—and set down her glass. She inclined her head in the duchess's direction, and Thelma couldn't help comparing the two again: one, the blade beneath softness; the other, manicured bravado.

Wallis slid to Ernest's side, resting a red-nailed hand on his shoulder as she studied his cards.

"I'd like to have a go—are you boys nearly done?" she said. "Or perhaps—" she looked up. "Can I tempt you to a game, sir?"

David looked over, with an expression that made Thelma think perhaps he had heard the exchange between Elizabeth and Wallis. "Why not? Are you familiar with Red Dog?"

Wallis picked up a spare deck and walked to a separate table. "I'm not, but you could teach me."

"It would be my pleasure, Mrs. Simpson."

Thelma caught David's eye and he winked. Wallis tapped the cards out of their box and split the deck, shuffling the halves together in a brisk snap as David explained the rules of the game. She spared one final glance at Elizabeth before turning her full attention to the prince.

Situated on the east side of the house, the breakfast room at Fort Belvedere was designed to catch the morning sunlight— although, taking advantage of David's insistence on informality, most guests missed out on the room's merits by sleeping through breakfast altogether. When Thelma came down, she was unsurprised to find half the company missing: only Wallis, Ernest and Piers were at the table, with a thick pile of newspapers scattered between the place settings.

"Good morning," said Thelma. She took a piece of toast and a grapefruit half from the buffet. "Have you been up long?"

"We came down five minutes before you," said Wallis. She folded her newspaper and tossed it back on the pile. "Coffee?"

"Please," said Thelma. "How did you sleep?"

"Like logs," said Wallis. "I don't think Ernest moved in the night at all, did you, darling?"

"Mmm—very comfortable," said Ernest, setting down one paper and picking up another. "I'm done with *The Manchester Guardian*, Wallis." He handed her the paper and she put it next to her plate without looking.

"Have you seen His Royal Highness this morning?" said Thelma.

Piers chuckled. "He's in the garden. Hoping to finish his path, I think."

"Goodness, that's a tall order," said Thelma. "I hope you've brought your Wellingtons, Ernest."

Ernest frowned as he leafed through the front section of *The Telegraph*. "Doesn't he have staff for that sort of thing?"

"From Monday to Friday, yes, but he likes to work the grounds when he has the chance," said Piers. He peered at Ernest over his newspaper. "You'll notice that those who offer to help get invited back."

"I see," said Ernest, looking less than enthused at the prospect of manual labor.

"It's not a command, exactly," added Thelma, "though I've never known anybody to refuse."

"Oh, don't be such a pill, dear," said Wallis. "After all that London smog, fresh air would do you good."

Ernest's retort was interrupted by a dull knock on the windowpane. David was standing outside, a heavy set of garden shears slung over his shoulders. He waved; Thelma waved back, and David dropped the shears before jogging out of sight—to the side door, Thelma supposed.

He was preceded into the room by his dogs, who skittered under the table in search of scraps. David, in muddy trousers, smiled.

"Good morning!" he said heartily. He took an apple from the buffet and bit into it, juice erupting in a small sunburst. "It's a glorious day out there, Thelma. We ought to ask Osborne to arrange a picnic." He thumped across the carpet and kissed Thelma's cheek. "Good morning, darling."

"Hello, you. Have you made much progress?" she asked.

David squinted out the window, his hands on his hips. "Plugging along." Beneath the table, one of the terriers nudged Thelma's shin and she slipped him a crust of toast from her plate.

"Good morning, sir," said Wallis. "Thelma's told us about your gardening—we're trying to convince Ernest to join you."

"Another victim? Don't worry, old boy—I want a pound of flesh and nothing more," said David. Wallis smirked at Ernest before returning to her newspaper.

She turned to a new page and gasped.

"Dear?" said Ernest, frowning. "Is something wrong?"

"Oh, my. This is all rather..." Wallis exhaled and passed Thelma the newspaper, her usual gloss shattered in a moment of sheer discomposure. "I'm so sorry, darling."

Thelma's heart sank. She could guess what the paper contained: she'd been expecting it all weekend, a letter, a telephone call, a telegram, all but delivered on a card with a black border.

She lowered her gaze to the newspaper.

WEDDING OF PEER'S DAUGHTER—
A STRANGE SITUATION

Events of an unusual character have followed the wedding in Kenya by special license of the Hon. Averill Furness, the daughter of Viscount Furness, and Mr. Andrew Rattray, the white hunter to Viscount Furness's hunting expedition.

According to the Central News the wedding took place while Lord Furness was away shooting, and arrangements were made to acquaint him by air messenger of what had happened.

News was received yesterday that Lord Furness will return to Nairobi on Friday. Yesterday's issue of the East African Standard contains the following notice over his signature:

To all whom it may concern,

Take notice that from and after the 24th day of January 1932, Mr. A. Rattray ceased to be the white hunter to my safari, and from that date he has no authority to order anything on my account.

Thelma closed her eyes.

A scandal, then.

Wallis rested her hand on Thelma's forearm.

"I'm so sorry," she said. "If there's anything—"

Thelma looked up: David, Ernest and Piers were silent, waiting for an explanation.

She folded the newspaper so that the article was concealed from view. Wallis could tell them.

"Thank you, Wallis," she said, "but it looks as though the matter is settled, doesn't it? Would you excuse me?"

She tucked the newspaper under her arm and left as though she was removing a contaminant. Not that it mattered, really; if it was in *The Guardian*, it would be in the *Mail* and *The Telegraph* and *The Times*.

She went into the drawing room. At this hour, it was blissfully empty: blinding sunlight streamed through the windows, bleaching the wood-paneled walls. She sat down, trembling, on the piano bench and read the story through a second time.

The wedding took place while Lord Furness was away shooting... So Averill hadn't even tried to talk him round.

"Stupid girl," she said. She was too numb to be angry.

Thelma looked up as the door creaked open. David came in, barring the dogs from entering with his foot.

"Wallis told me," he said as he shut the dogs out. "I'm so sorry. Are you all right?"

Thelma began to cry and David pulled her into his arms.

"She could have warned me," she said. "What am I to tell people?"

David kissed the top of her head, his breath ruffling her hair in a sigh. "Well...you could tell them that it's not really to do with you anymore, is it?"

Thelma pulled away. "How so?"

"You've divorced him, haven't you? You're not part of their family anymore, darling."

Thelma frowned, hearing echoes of her furious last conversation with Duke.

"Of course they're family," she said, "I've a son with Duke, don't I? And Averill and Dickie...they mean the world to me."

"Still? You decided to leave Furness. You've still got your son by him, of course, but you've no claims over Averill anymore. No more than Duke has a claim over you."

"You think it's that easy, do you, signing a piece of paper and wiping my hands of them all? I can't—turn off my feelings, not when she's made such a bloody mess—"

David ran his hand down her arm. "I'm trying to help you see it from their perspective. Perhaps they thought it kinder not to pull you in." He kissed her forehead. "And it *is* kinder, isn't it? You don't need the attention. It's Furness's place to handle it, not yours."

Thelma sank back down onto the piano bench.

"I tried to tell him, but he wouldn't listen." She reread the terse statement Duke had made: not a word of congratulation or conciliation—not even an attempt to make good to the reporters. She could feel Duke's anger on the newsprint, breaking like a storm over water.

Perhaps Duke and Averill might come to common ground, if the wounds they made in these first few days of scandal didn't cut too deep.

"I need to speak with him before he does something he'll regret," said Thelma, wiping her eyes. "May I use the telephone?"

David handed her a handkerchief. "I really would prefer if you didn't," he said. "There's nothing you can do while they're in Africa, and even if you did get hold of Furness, what would you possibly say?"

Thelma nodded, folding the handkerchief over to find a dry spot. He was right, of course: short of making the journey to Africa herself, there was nothing she could do. And Duke needed time, too, to think his way past anger.

David sat with Thelma a moment longer.

"You know, we're being terrible hosts, holed up alone like this," he said. It was a half-hearted attempt at a joke, and Thelma laughed, more for his benefit than hers. "I know it's rotten luck, but there's really nothing to be done. Take a moment to compose yourself, darling, then come back and join us."

He walked to the door; Thelma could hear the terriers on the other side.

"Do you really think I don't count as family anymore?" she said. Despite the divorce, the notion seemed unbearable.

David paused. "What an odd thing to say," he said. "If I'm being entirely honest, no. I would say your duties to the family are over, and I would expect Furness feels the same. You've no longer any obligation toward them beyond civility. Make it a clean break, for your sake and theirs."

Thelma pursed her lips, weighing the implications of David's words.

The clock on the mantel chimed, a genteel nudge, and David glanced at the door. "I really ought to return to our guests. You'll be all right, won't you? I'll talk to Osborne about arranging the picnic myself."

"Of course. I'll be right in."

David smiled. "Good," he said, and left the room.

Thelma folded the handkerchief neatly on the piano bench.

A clean break. It was a simple way—too simple—to sum up six years of marriage. Easier said than done, but David had never been married, nor had he ever truly broken from his own past. Freda Dudley Ward was still a constant friend—could he cast her aside so lightly?

There was a small desk in the corner of the drawing room; Thelma opened the topmost drawer and pulled out two sheets of stationery. She wrote a short letter of congratulations on one sheet and a statement on another, then sealed them into separate envelopes. Before she returned to the drawing room, she handed two envelopes to Osborne for the morning post: one addressed to Mrs. Averill Rattray, the other to *The Manchester Guardian* relaying her wholehearted support for the happy couple.

FORTY-THREE

October 21, 1934
New York, USA

SHE HAD BEEN DREAMING OF CAMERAS. THE click, click of the shutter—a noise you heard when you were close enough to make it out over the blank explosion of the flashbulb, smoke rising into ether. It was a noise she'd loved, once: posing for an artist in Los Angeles, the feel of silk on skin, in the reckless days after her separation from Junior. Following the shine of the lens, laughing, as David lifted his sleek little Leica to take a photograph of her next to the swimming pool at the Fort. The shutter had been kind, then, the curiosity of the lens flattering—but here, the cameras flocked like wasps, their blank gaze cold, the metallic click multiplied like whispers into a roar as regular as a heartbeat.

Thelma stared up at the silk canopy of her four-poster bed. It was eight in the morning on Sunday, a blessed break from the trial, but Thelma knew that, even at this early hour, if she were to twitch open the curtains she would see reporters, clustered in twos and threes on the sidewalk. They'd been summoned by

Burkan who, following Gloria's disastrous visit to Old Westbury, planned to make an announcement.

She pressed a call button for Elise, listening for sounds of life from the other bedrooms. The house was quiet now, but it wouldn't remain so for long: the walls were too thin to accommodate the individual privacies of eight people living under the same roof.

Harry and Edith, Friedel and Margarita, Consuelo and Benny, and Thelma and Gloria were all staying in the little town house, and the strain of presenting a united front, moving from the house to the courthouse and back as though on a fixed track, was beginning to show.

Last night Thelma had heard, seeping through the shared wall like a bleed, Harry and Edith talking about Gloria's trip to Old Westbury. They were beginning to lose hope—so was Thelma, though she'd never admit it. No, Thelma would go downstairs this morning and help steady Gloria for the cameras.

She was pulled from her thoughts by a gentle tap at the door. Elise, carrying a silver breakfast tray, walked in.

"Good morning, my lady."

Thelma shifted up onto the pillows as Elise set the breakfast tray down on Thelma's lap: toast with jam, coffee in a pewter pot and a soft-boiled egg.

"Thank you. Any mail?" asked Thelma, tapping the top of her egg with a spoon.

Elise pulled a small envelope from her apron pocket. It was addressed but not postmarked: hand-delivered, then, likely an invitation to dinner. She'd received a few since her arrival, sent by acquaintances from her school days, sniffing out news of the trial. She'd rejected them all.

Thelma read the note. "Please send my regrets," she said, tucking the note back into the envelope and sliding it under her plate. She poured a cup of coffee. "Anything from London?"

Elise's professional smile softened. "I'm afraid not," she said.

Thelma poured a measure of cream into the cup. It wasn't lost on Elise, Thelma knew, that David hadn't written in over a week.

She glanced at her bedside table, where two small teddy bears, their cheap green fabric worn from frequent travel, sat propped against the base of a lamp. They slumped together, shoulders touching, glass eyes glinting in the morning sun.

Thelma lifted the breakfast tray from her lap, depositing it on the pillow beside her.

"Elise, would you bring me my dressing gown?" she said.

Minutes later, Thelma was on the telephone in Gloria's study. The small room had the air of being abandoned, with old stacks of papers piled in a corner, untouched since the trial began. Harry, it seemed, was using the room as a refuge: a heavy-bottomed ashtray stood on the writing desk, a half-smoked stogie stubbed out in the dust.

Thelma had instructed a nasal-voiced operator to put her through to London and the line had gone dead as the operator tried the connection. She sank into an armchair, arranging the folds of her dressing gown.

The line clicked back to life.

"Go ahead, please."

"Thelma?"

"Wallis. I hope I'm not interrupting?"

The sound of Wallis's voice was clear and comforting across the wire. "Not at all, Ernest and I were just sitting down to tea. How's Gloria?"

"She's coping. You've been following the papers?"

"Religiously. It will all turn out in the end, I know it."

"How are things in London?" she said. "How's David?"

Wallis waited a beat too long before answering. "He's perfectly fine. Ernest and I were out to dinner with him just the other night. Quaglino's. They've the most divine roast, even David managed a full plate and you know how picky he can be."

Thelma's heart sank at the forced levity in her voice. "Has he—taken up with anyone else?"

Once again, Wallis hesitated. "No," she said. "I won't lie to you, he's become rather—*restless*—but it's only for missing you. He talks about you constantly, of course."

Restless. According to Wallis, David hadn't strayed—but "yet" was implicit in her words.

The longer Thelma was gone, the more likely he was to find someone to pique his interest. Some dull debutante, no doubt, pushed in his direction by a grasping father...

"Darling, listen to me," said Wallis. "I know you're nervous but really, there's no reason to be. You asked me to look after him for you and I am. His heart is entirely yours. If you don't believe me, telephone him yourself."

The thought of checking up on David made Thelma cringe.

Over the line, Wallis's exhale sounded more like a sigh than anything else. "Darling, I've got to go but please stop worrying. You've enough on your plate without creating fresh intrigues." She paused. "He's likely going to drop in for a cocktail with Ernest later this evening. Is there anything you'd like me to tell him?"

Thelma cleared her throat. "Tell him—the bears send their love," she said.

"The bears send their love," Wallis repeated, and the sentiment sounded empty repeated back over the wire. "I'll tell him, Thelma. Perhaps I'll remind him how good you look in that gray Schiaparelli, he'll like that."

Wallis rang off and Thelma replaced the receiver in its cradle. The conversation hadn't been reassuring. Thelma had been able to overlook his dalliances so long as they took place in other cities or towns, but London had always been hers: London and Fort Belvedere. The quiet Berkshire hills where they could play at being husband and wife, and the restless city where they didn't have to pretend at all.

She tiptoed down the empty hallway, listening to the sound of whispered conversations behind bedroom doors.

The washroom was bone white, porcelain tiles on the floor and creeping up the walls, white sink and toilet and tub, pillowy towels on towel racks. A utilitarian room, utterly unlike the crowded excess of the rest of the house. She turned on the tap, which groaned before surrendering water, and splashed her face, welcoming the shock of the cold.

The trial had taken an obvious toll on Gloria, visible in her gaunt cheeks, her too-thin frame—but now, looking in the medicine cabinet mirror, Thelma couldn't deny that she, too, was being affected by the strain of it all. Like Gloria, she'd lost weight: her complexion looked sallow in a ghastly way that, thankfully, she could hide under powder. Powder, however, had the unintended effect of settling into lines, conferring years to her complexion that she hadn't earned through work or illness. She wet the towel and pressed it against the delicate, dark skin under her eyes. Unlike Gloria, Thelma wasn't taking anything to calm her nerves, but if things continued as they were, she would need to find a doctor willing to give her a prescription.

She returned to her room and dressed, then went downstairs.

The noise of the reporters outside was louder in the sitting room, a low murmur that the front door couldn't quite block out. The room's heavy velvet curtains hadn't yet been drawn back and the lamps were lit, giving Thelma the uneasy impression that she was living underground.

Gloria, dressed for church, paced in front of the empty fireplace. She turned as Thelma entered, her hands clasped around a cup of coffee.

"Mr. Burkan should be here soon," she said. "I hope the reporters don't tire of waiting for him. Perhaps I should go out and say something myself."

"He'll be here," said Thelma. "The reporters want to hear what he has to say. They'll wait all morning if they have to."

Moments later, the reporters began to shout. Thelma peeked through the curtain and watched them surround Burkan's car. He stepped out, waving an impatient hand as he made his way to the front door.

"Five minutes! Five minutes with my client, then I'll come speak to you," he said, his voice rising above the din. The butler opened the door and Burkan came in on a wave of sound, wiping his forehead with a handkerchief.

"Pack of buzzards," he said to no one in particular, stuffing the handkerchief back into his breast pocket. He came into the sitting room and pulled out a set of typewritten notes from his briefcase, frowning as he leafed from page to page.

"Mrs. Vanderbilt, today we turn the tide," he said. "This will be entirely painless, I assure you. You won't need to answer any questions."

"What if I want to talk to them?" said Gloria.

"If you feel you must, tell them that your visit with Little Gloria yesterday went well. You're happier than you've ever been," Burkan said. "Beyond that, I don't want you answering any questions. We don't want this turning into a press conference. Lady Furness, I hope you might join us outside. Show of support."

"Of course." She gave Gloria's arm a reassuring squeeze. "Ready?"

Gloria nodded.

Burkan opened the door and the noise hit them: reporters shouting, photographers holding their cameras aloft in the blind hope of taking the right photo. Thelma smiled, automatically— then, realizing the circumstances might warrant something different, she arranged her features into what she hoped was an expression of defiant confidence.

Burkan raised his hand and the reporters hushed, pencils poised on notepads.

"Thank you all for coming," he said. He tucked one hand into his pocket and gripped his typewritten statement with the other. "As you all know, my client, Mrs. Vanderbilt, had the opportunity to visit her daughter, Gloria Vanderbilt, at her aunt's home in Old Westbury yesterday." He looked up, his gray eyes gimlet above the rim of his glasses. "On speaking to Mrs. Vanderbilt on her return, it has become clear that there is no possibility of a settlement with Gertrude Whitney. No possibility of a settlement," he repeated slowly, pausing to allow the scribbling reporters to catch up. "As soon as Mrs. Whitney leaves the stand, I will begin to lay out our defense by subpoenaing some of Mrs. Whitney's more *bohemian* acquaintances from her work as an artist in Greenwich Village. These include Donald Hunter, a model who spent last summer at Mrs. Whitney's camp at Sabattis."

Thelma kept her expression impassive. Donald Hunter? It wasn't a name Thelma had heard before.

"Also under subpoena," Burkan continued, adjusting his glasses, "are Frederick Soldwedel, an artist; Frederick Hazeltine, a sculptor; Louis Sloden, a professional dancer; Thomas Meighan, an actor; and George Coleman—some Cody, Wyoming cowboy." He looked up. "We will be beginning our cross-examination of Mrs. Whitney as early as tomorrow and look forward to coming to a better understanding of Mrs. Whitney's character and her involvement with the bohemian arts movement. That's all."

The reporters began to shout but Burkan turned, holding out an arm to escort Gloria back indoors.

They returned to the sitting room, where Consuelo and Harry had been watching the announcement from out the window: Consuelo had opened the curtains, and Thelma felt lighter for that alone. She watched the reporters drift off, some lingering on the sidewalk over notepads to finish their scribbling.

Gloria sank into an empty armchair. "Well done, Nathan," she said. "That will give them something to chew on."

"Too right," said Burkan. "We've started the rumor mill turning before we've even begun our defense. Whitney's lawyers may still have the stand, but the media will be looking into her connections by the end of the day."

"What happens now?" asked Thelma.

Burkan settled onto the sofa and opened his briefcase to file the statement away. "I've arranged to meet with the rest of your legal team tonight, Mrs. Vanderbilt, to discuss our next steps. Mr. Mathew—Lady Milford Haven's lawyer—has asked to join us. He's petitioned Justice Carew for a copy of the testimony to determine whether Lady Milford Haven should press libel charges. I'm hoping he might have some insights to share." He snapped the clasps of his briefcase shut. "We'll iron out the particulars of how we'll proceed, finalize our list of character witnesses. All those actors and models, coming in and out of her studio—can't all be innocent. Not from what they've told me."

He turned to leave, but Consuelo spoke up.

"Is it true?"

Burkan paused. "I beg your pardon?"

Consuelo stepped forward. "Is it true?" she repeated. "About Gertrude Whitney. This whole—character assassination. It makes us no better than they are."

"Of course, it's true," said Burkan, frowning. "No respectable woman turns a child against its mother. It's not the conduct of a reasonable person—"

"I'm not asking about reasonable," Consuelo said. "I'm asking about the truth. Did she have affairs with these—these artists—"

"Does it matter?"

Consuelo didn't answer.

Burkan sighed and set down his briefcase. "Let me tell you something about Gertrude Whitney," he said. "She's no angel. She gets drunk like the rest of us, sleeps around like the rest of us. She's human."

From her armchair, Gloria huffed.

"People like her—it's not about the truth to them. If the truth is inconvenient, they pay to push it out of the way. That's the problem—money blinds. Gertrude Whitney seems to think that because she has a pot of it she's more qualified to raise a child than its own mother, that she's more honorable because she has a big bank account." Burkan looked at Gloria. "There's nothing honorable about what she's doing to that little girl. Or to you. There's nothing fancy about hypocrisy."

FORTY-FOUR

FRIEDEL HOHENLOHE STOOD IN THE FRONT HALL, inconspicuously elegant in a black suit. He shifted his weight from foot to foot, inspecting the silver glint of his wristwatch; as Thelma came down the stairs he looked up, his expression changing from hope to polite welcome as she descended.

"You look lovely," he said.

Thelma looked into the sitting room but no one else had come down for cocktails. She lingered on the bottommost step, more to keep Friedel company than out of any real sense of companionship.

"The princess must be looking forward to an evening out," she said. "The Plaza, is it?"

"Yes," said Friedel. He smiled, a hint of apology on his long face. "I can't pretend I'm not looking forward to a little time alone."

"I don't blame you," said Thelma. She wondered, briefly, if Friedel and Margarita would return—or whether they would cut and run, the pair of them, acting on the same impulse of self-preservation that had led them to New York in the first place.

"Margarita likes to take her time dressing," said Friedel. "She was nearly late for our wedding."

"Gloria's the same—well, you'd know," said Thelma. She crossed her arms, and before she could help herself she spoke once more. "Is it difficult for her?"

Friedel considered. "It's not been pleasant," he said, with a candor that Thelma hadn't really expected to receive. "Margarita knows I've got a past. But I don't think she ever expected it would confront her quite so directly."

Thelma leaned against the newel post, glancing upward once more for signs of life. She and Friedel had never been close, not even when he was engaged to Gloria. She'd visited his family home once, Schloss Langenburg, and marveled at the crumbling luxury—the castle in need of repairs that, perhaps, Little Gloria's money would have provided. "She's not like Gloria at all," said Thelma, returning Friedel's honesty with her own. "She's stronger. I shouldn't say that, it's not fair to Gloria—"

"No, it isn't," Friedel replied, without heat. "Gloria's had a remarkably difficult go of things these past few years, and she wasn't prepared for any of it. Not by her parents, nor by her late husband." He adjusted one of his cuff links. "My wife has had her own challenges, but she was raised in entirely different circumstances. As a royal, one expects some measure of adversity," he continued, smiling. "I find it difficult to pass judgment on Gloria for the choices she had never dreamed she would have to make. That Gloria's the person she is, is a testament to her determination. I wonder if you would have reacted any differently."

Thelma stepped aside as Margarita reached the bottom step and Friedel pulled her into a gentle embrace. As one, they turned, and together they walked out into the blue night.

With Friedel and Margarita gone there was space enough for all of them in the sitting room for drinks after dinner. Even with fewer bodies, the room was still unbearably warm, the fire having been overburdened earlier in the evening with letters Gloria had received from anonymous, angry people, condemning her in acid black. The flames roared with brief triumph, paper curling to ash beneath the wood.

Thelma was quiet as Harry poured drinks, letting Consuelo and Edith pick up the threads of conversation as she reflected on her conversation with Friedel. She'd been wrong, to allow Mamma's suspicions to color her opinion of him. He'd acted honorably in his defense of Gloria and devotion to his wife. If self-preservation was a by-product of those actions, was he not entitled to it?

Friedel was right, too, about Gloria: it was a mark of her strength that she'd inspired such loyalty. It was a mark of her good heart, too, that her former fiancé would, even now, not hear a word against her. Would Duke do the same? Would David? She reflected once more on his silence. Would he have come, if it had been Thelma on trial?

The doorbell rang. They heard the butler open the door and the low rumble of Burkan's voice.

"So soon?" said Gloria. She finished the last of her cigarette as Burkan entered the room, the ashtray sliding across the coffee table as she stubbed it out.

"Well?" she said.

Burkan sank onto a footstool, dropping his briefcase at his side. He leaned forward, planting his elbows on his knees.

"When you first asked me to represent you, Mrs. Vanderbilt," he said, "I asked you for honesty. I thought you'd given it to me, when you told me you'd never taken any lovers aside from Hohenlohe. Made for a rather unpleasant surprise when your *association* with Lady Milford Haven came out. Frankly, it was embarrassing to be caught so off guard." He straightened and accepted a glass of sherry from Edith with a curt nod. "After that day, I asked you for honesty once more, and you told me your affair with Lady Milford Haven was short-lived. Just the one affair. Just the one time."

Thelma looked at Gloria, who was staring, stone-faced, into the fire.

"I could have worked with once. I could have won the case with *once*," said Burkan, and Thelma's heart slipped into her stomach. "You've been untruthful, Mrs. Vanderbilt. And I don't see how you expect me to do my job when you withhold relevant facts."

Gloria paled. Thelma let out a breath, but Harry spoke first. "What happened?"

Burkan sighed. "Theobald Mathew." He reached into his breast pocket and pulled out an envelope. He handed it to Gloria. "It seems you have a few more skeletons in your closet than you let on, Mrs. Vanderbilt."

Gloria opened the envelope, her lips moving soundlessly as her eyes slid down the page.

"It wouldn't serve Mathew's purposes to divulge the extent of your relationship with Lady Milford Haven," Burkan said, "but he did provide pertinent information about a few of your other conquests, Mrs. Vanderbilt."

Gloria turned the paper over and continued to read. Thelma could feel her sister's panic rising in her own throat, the frenzied grappling for reason—she wanted to snatch the paper from Gloria's hands and throw it into the fire along with all the other meaningless vitriol.

"Mr. Mathew was quite clear," Burkan continued. "He wants the trial wrapped up, civilly, as quickly as possible." He nodded at the sheet of paper. "He's happy to provide that list of names to Whitney's lawyers, if it's the quickest way to settle it. Smyth's already seen it."

"Why?" Consuelo whispered. "What purpose could this possibly—"

"I've been offered a deal," said Burkan. "Through Mathew,

from Smyth. We say nothing about Mrs. Whitney's *friends*, and they'll call no further witnesses against Mrs. Vanderbilt. They'll cross-examine, of course, but the case will proceed based on what's already been said." He sighed. "Of course, should we accept—"

"Gloria loses," said Thelma. She recalled her conversation with Mathew on board the *Empress*, her panic turning into dread.

"We should reject it," said Consuelo. "Gloria's reputation is already ruined. Our only chance for success is retribution, discrediting Gertrude—"

"Don't be stupid," snapped Burkan. "You think Gloria would stand any chance at recovering her daughter if we gave Smyth further ammunition?"

"They hold all the cards," said Edith. "If we subject Gertrude to scandal, we both lose—if we don't, she's spared scrutiny and we lose regardless."

Burkan finished his drink and rose to pour another. "Only one lamb to the slaughter."

"And how does this slaughter serve us?" said Consuelo. "The only ones who stand to gain from this arrangement are Gertrude and Nada Mountbatten."

Burkan poured the last of the bottle of sherry into his glass without turning around. "Who do you think gave Mathew that list of names?"

Gloria closed her eyes, her trembling hands coming to a rest in her lap.

"She needs this ended as quietly as possible," said Burkan. "Not for her sake—she could sleep with the entire Russian army and still come out smelling like an English rose. Mathew didn't come for Nada. Think about who else could be implicated if this trial drags on further."

Thelma's voice sounded too loud, too final, in the dismal silence.

"It's because of me," she said. "Because of David."

Burkan nodded heavily. "If we call a halt to this mud-slinging, Smyth's agreed to not bring the Prince of Wales into it all. It's his most effective weapon—one he'd hoped not to use, I think, but now that Mathew's agreed to play by his terms…" Burkan trailed off. "Mathew's only motive is to keep the Prince of Wales out of this, and it's come too close as it is. His relation to Lady Milford Haven, his friendship with you, Lady Furness…if Smyth makes these ties known, it would be a disaster for the Royal Family. American newspapers don't have the same sort of deference as British ones."

He rubbed a hand across his jaw, gray with a shadow that would be stubble by morning.

"We're fighting on two fronts now, Mrs. Vanderbilt," he said. "We can't win against the Vanderbilts and the Royal Family combined."

Gloria closed her eyes, shielding her face with a shaking hand.

No one stopped Thelma as she walked out of the room. She opened the front door, following Friedel and Margarita's path into the night.

FORTY-FIVE

SHE STEPPED ONTO THE PAVEMENT. THERE WAS
the promise of winter beneath the red-sweet smell of autumn—
had she really been here long enough for the seasons to turn, in
futile defense of her sister's reputation? She looked back at the
house, lamp-lit in the twilight. Thankfully, there weren't any reporters lingering outside. Burkan's morning announcement had
given them enough to write about: they would be home now, in
their grimy apartment blocks with wives and colicky children,
blowing the ink dry on their stories for the morning edition.

She could only imagine the frenzy if they'd been privy to the
revelations in the sitting room.

It was cowardly to run, but there was nothing else she could
do—Mathew's intervention had seen to that. She'd never been
blind to the fact that Mathew was working for Nada, nor that
he would work against Gloria if it was in Nada's best interests.
Hadn't he said so? But Thelma had deceived herself into thinking that Gloria's and Nada's interests were one and the same.
It was Nada's scandals—Nada's alone—that Mathew sought to

bury. If Gloria's reputation was the price of silence, Mathew would pay it. He'd paid it already, with a list of names written in Nada's elegant script.

The night had gotten colder, but Thelma wasn't ready to go back. Half a block away, the gilded marquee of the Carlyle Hotel shone in the dark. She quickened her pace and slipped inside.

The lobby was monolithically elegant in black and white, shocks of mint and peach on velvet couches and silk chairs. Aside from hotel staff, it was nearly empty and Thelma thought, once more, of Friedel and Margarita at the Plaza. The Persian Room would be humming. Any other evening, Thelma would have preferred to be part of that scene, but tonight she welcomed solitude.

Her feet whispered over pools of glossy black marble, so polished it looked like water moments away from being upset by a breath. She followed neatly lettered signs through to the hotel bar—quiet, too, tonight, but for the pianist playing lingering notes of a song Thelma would have known, if she could recall the words. Three men sat at the curved bar, their backs to Thelma, and a closely entwined couple was in the far corner, their caned-back chairs touching. Thelma ordered a martini and went to an empty booth, with enough space to spread her scattered thoughts across the table.

She could blame Nada for the whole mess, were she so inclined: point fingers at the woman who'd pulled Gloria out of the wreckage of her engagement to Friedel and into a new, dangerous sphere, but to do so would be a convenient way to assuage her own guilt. She, Thelma, was the link between David and Gloria—more so than Nada, who could hide behind her title and brazen out scandal. Thelma, twin sister to the Vanderbilt widow, mistress of the Prince of Wales, had no such refuge. Like Gloria, she was now a liability. How long before Mathew sought to cut her from David's side? Had it already started?

She traced her finger down the side of her glass, leaving a trail through the condensation. Her relationship with David was an open secret—all of David's relationships had been, the king and queen turning a blind eye to their eldest son's affairs. The Royal Family—David's generation, at least—even accepted Thelma as part of David's life.

The public was a different matter. David relied on the discretion of the British press to keep his dalliances secret, and his position kept him safe from scandal: the newspapers had no desire to embarrass their future sovereign. But Burkan had been right when he said that American papers didn't have the same deference as their British counterparts. Many would relish the opportunity to cut the Prince of Wales down to size. Reporters might overlook David's affair—but his twice-over connection to the Vanderbilt widow? It was a story too sensational to ignore.

The pianist finished his song with a flourish and stood, setting a small sign on his bench—*Intermission*—and went to the bar.

"If you wait any longer that drink will be spoiled."

Thelma looked up; Aly Khan stood before her, his hand curled around the back of an empty chair. "A martini's no good unless it's cold."

"Aly," said Thelma. He sat without asking, signaling to the bartender for a new round of drinks. "I've not seen you since—"

"Lending you a jacket outside your apartment. I remember." Aly hadn't lost the habit of staring: he watched her intently, half-smiling, as though recalling a private joke. "I hope you don't mind the intrusion. You looked so serious, I thought I might try to lift your spirits."

Thelma wasn't up to the task of flirting. "In that case, a fresh drink might be a good place to start. What brings you here?"

Aly leaned back in his chair as the waiter set down two martinis. "Business. Pleasure. I'm stopping in New York on my way back to London. I spent the past month in Florida, purchasing horses for my father's stables."

"Of course. Are you staying long?"

"Tell me when you're leaving and I'll book my ticket on the same ship. The berth next to yours. Whatever it takes to have ten uninterrupted days in your company."

Thelma smiled wryly. "I'm afraid you might be waiting some time, if you plan to leave when I do," she said. "I assume you've been following it all?"

Aly pulled a cigarette case from his pocket and slid it across the table. "I have. Your sister has my sympathies. It can't be easy for her. Or you."

Thelma let out a long-held breath. "It isn't." She passed the case back to Aly, drumming the base of an unlit cigarette on the tabletop. The pianist resumed playing and Thelma lowered her voice, grateful for the music that shielded their conversation from the rest of the room. "I don't think I realized just how difficult it's all been for her. Not just the trial. Losing Reggie. Losing Friedel. Raising a baby while Mamma constantly undermines her..." She sipped her drink, not caring whether Aly followed her train of thought. He knew about Gloria and Nada, of course, but she doubted he knew about the rest, beyond what had been reported in the newspapers. "I was too busy with my own life to ask—really *ask*—how she was doing. No wonder she's in trouble."

Aly held out his lighter, flame dancing on gold. She leaned forward, cigarette poised, sensing, rather than seeing, Aly's steady gaze as she inhaled. "You can't take her troubles all on yourself. Gloria made her own choices." He shifted the flame and lit his own cigarette. "Don't flatter yourself by thinking you could have prevented her from making mistakes."

"No? I could have stopped her from turning to the least suitable person—"

"I know Nada. She's a force of nature. Do you really think desperation was the only reason Gloria chose her?"

Thelma played with the stem of her martini glass.

"Maybe I hoped it was desperation," she said. "If she'd chosen someone suitable—but then, she'd tried to, hadn't she, with Friedel? It's caused so much trouble, her and Nada…if it had been a mistake from the start, perhaps I could understand it more."

"Perhaps Gloria didn't see it as a mistake. Perhaps the risk was worth it."

"Perhaps," said Thelma. She wasn't sure why she was confiding in Aly. Maybe it was because he was the first sympathetic person she'd found since she'd come over for the trial—the only one without a vested interest in the trial's outcome. She set down her empty glass. "I can't imagine she thinks it was worth it all, now," she said. "She's losing everything, and for what? Nada hasn't sent a letter, a telegram—nothing. Just a lawyer. Not even a note in his briefcase."

Aly gestured to the bartender for another round.

"I might not have stopped her from taking up with Nada," Thelma said, "but I could have paid more attention. I should have—" She broke off as the bartender set fresh drinks on the table. Thelma took hers with a belated, automatic smile. "I should have been there," she said. "I was so happy with David that I didn't bother paying attention to Gloria. I didn't want the responsibility."

"Why is Gloria your responsibility?" said Aly, sounding brusque. "I can't imagine feeling such a sense of obligation. Do you think I feel responsible for my father's actions? Does David feel responsible for yours?"

Thelma bristled. "She's my sister."

"Did Gloria ever try to stop you from pursuing your affair with the prince?" asked Aly, tapping ash into an empty glass. "Will she tear out her hair when he breaks your heart?"

Thelma didn't respond. He sounded like Friedel. Gloria was her own person. She'd made her own choices.

She smiled, feeling the hot pressure of unshed tears. "She's going to lose the case." She finished her cigarette in a long,

shaky inhale that earned her a few more moments of composure. "Nada saw to that. Her lawyer made a deal."

Aly raised his eyebrows but said nothing; unbidden, Thelma
recounted everything that had happened with Burkan, feeling
a detached, bitter pleasure at his expression of genuine surprise.

"They closed ranks," he said simply. "I understand his position in all this, truly I do. When you've got a title to protect, you
must do what you can to protect it. That doesn't make it easier,
but it's the truth." He gestured to Thelma's drink. "Another?"

"Could we get some air?"

Aly stood and held out his arm. Together, they walked down
the hall.

"Surely, though, you see why I feel responsible for it all?"
said Thelma. "David's at the root of it—*I'm* at the root of it. He
probably doesn't even know Mathew's here."

Aly looked at Thelma with sudden disdain. "Oh, don't go
making excuses for him," he said. "Listen to yourself! Gloria's
not responsible for her actions, David isn't responsible for his.
Are you always such a martyr to fate?"

Thelma pulled away from Aly but he wheeled around to face
her head-on. "He knows," he continued, with flat conviction.
"I hate to tell you the obvious, but he knows about all of it. If
he loves you, nothing could keep him from your side. Nothing
would, if it was the woman I love." He met Thelma's eyes, fleet-
ingly vulnerable, and Thelma wondered what twist of chance,
exactly, had led him to the Carlyle bar.

Aly offered her his arm again, and they continued toward
the lobby.

"If he knows," said Aly, "and he's cutting you out deliberately, he's a weaker man than I thought. If he's truly ignorant,
he's weaker still."

Thelma had expected Aly's words to cut more, but the martinis had dulled their sharpness. David always had been weak;
always prepared to crumble at the first sign of hardship.

She'd sacrificed so much to her relationship with him: her time, her strength, her attention. Her marriage. And what, now, had her loyalty bought?

She slid her hand down Aly's forearm, turning his palm with gentle pressure so that her fingers rested in his.

"He's cheating," she said. "Or he's about to. Amounts to the same thing, really."

With unspoken understanding, they walked past the front doors in silence. Aly's fingers tightened around Thelma's, and she allowed him to lead her through the lobby, through another hallway punctuated with double doors.

Thelma didn't think as she pulled him into an alcove. She kissed him, and he responded in kind, pressing her against the door. The molded plaster was hard against her back but his lips were soft, and she wrapped her arms around his neck to pull him closer. It was a betrayal, and Thelma knew it wouldn't solve a thing—but she pushed her thoughts aside and sank deeper into something that was more real, more urgent than her good-bye from David, truer than anything she'd felt since coming to New York.

Aly pulled away, frowning.

"Are you sure?" he asked.

Reeling in the sudden glow of courage, Thelma felt invincible, reckless. "You aren't?"

Aly smiled, and ran a hand down her back. "Of course I am," he replied. "But I don't want to win by default."

"Is it a competition?"

"It's always a competition."

Thelma leaned in, letting her lips brush against his.

He pulled back once more and looked at her intently—Thelma knew he was searching for her conviction. Finding it, Aly took her hand and Thelma followed him into the lift.

FORTY-SIX

July 1933
London

OF ALL THE HOTELS IN LONDON, THE RITZ WAS Thelma's favorite.

It reminded her of Paris, in its old-world brilliance, yet to Thelma's mind the Ritz London surpassed its French cousin in glamour. She loved it all: walking beneath the arcade entrance on Piccadilly, with its marquee-bright letters. Passing an afternoon in the butter-gold tearoom, overhearing conversations from other tables, new loves and old feuds forming and dissolving around her; watching couples pass arm in arm through the flower-laden lobby.

Most of all, Thelma loved descending the marble staircase to the Ritz's subterranean ballroom. It was an entrance into another world, heralded by echoes of music that grew louder with each downward step, sound exploding into Technicolor brilliance as the double doors opened. To Thelma, her mind floating on champagne bubbles as she returned from a trip to the powder room, the ballroom's mirrored walls expanded the space into a never-ending cavern of gilt and wood and music,

a thousand-thousand dancers stretching far beneath the streets
of London. On a raised platform, a twelve-piece band played a
waltz, their stage framed by a series of painted panels depicting
a serene afternoon of Edwardian elegance. What would they
say, those staid Edwardians, if they could see the ballroom now,
filled with the crowd that David had assembled for Freda Dudley Ward's thirty-ninth birthday party? Women, bare-backed
in whispering silk and satin; men in black tuxedoes drinking
cocktails out of thin-stemmed glasses, swaying in time beneath
chandeliers and cigarette smoke.

Thelma paused at the edge of the dance floor, watching a
man in an ill-fitting suit stumble to a nearby table to speak to
a young woman in a sparkling dress. Ten years ago he would
have been handsome, with his boyish features and crumpled
carelessness, but years of overindulgence seemed to have taken
their toll, an alcoholic bloat pushing out those of his features
that ought to have been small: pouched lips, blue shadows under
overripe cheeks. He straightened his tie, watching the girl with
a devil-may-care smile that, no doubt, had carried him through
his youth. The girl rose and took his hand; together they passed,
leaving a beery scent in their wake as they went to dance.

Thelma accepted a glass of champagne from a motionless
waiter, suppressing a smile. But for the dresses and the music,
she figured the Edwardians likely wouldn't have seen anything
too far removed from their own gatherings.

It had been David's idea to have Freda Dudley Ward's birthday
party at the Ritz. He'd been planning the evening for months,
personally overseeing the menus and the guest list. As Thelma
walked through the crowd, she could see dozens of people that
David had invited, as well as a few that he hadn't but who'd decided to turn up anyway: there, by the band, was Diana Guinness
with Oswald Mosley, her body turned toward his as they spoke
in an undertone. Fruity Metcalfe, a cigar jammed between his
teeth, balanced three drinks in his hands as he walked toward a

table where Louis Mountbatten, who shared his brother George's long face, sat with Piers Legh and G Trotter. Surrounded by men at the bar, Nada, dressed in a chartreuse gown, stood out like punctuation.

Thelma returned to her table, hoping to steal a few more minutes' rest before David or anyone else pulled her back onto the dance floor and sent her head spinning again. For the moment, though, David was dancing with Freddie. Had they been anyone else their figures would have been lost in the crowd, but Freddie and David moved like oil through water, separating the tide as they turned in unison. David pulled back to say something to Freddie, smiling tenderly; she looked back with an expression closer to fondness than desire.

Wallis Simpson, seated farther down the table, shifted into the free chair next to Thelma.

"Are you jealous?" she said. Her words melted into each other with delicate precision; Wallis raised an eyebrow and Thelma could see that she'd had nearly as much to drink as Thelma herself.

Thelma rested her chin on her hand, watching as David pulled Freddie close enough for their cheeks to brush. But for her two daughters, Freda had come to the Ritz alone: since divorcing her husband two years earlier, she hadn't shown any inclination toward marrying again. Not that she would—not to David, at least. Though their affair had long since cooled to friendship, Thelma knew that David would respond to any suitors in Freddie's life with jealousy. Any man would have to be content with sharing her.

"Not in the slightest," said Thelma as the music shifted into a cheery ragtime.

"Really?" said Wallis. She looked at David and Freddie with a hard expression, as though trying to bring them into better focus. "I don't think I could stand it."

"I trust him," said Thelma as David one-stepped with Freddie, his hand low on her waist. "Or more to the point, I trust *her*."

Nada excused herself from her crowd of admirers and made her way toward Gloria and George Mountbatten, who were fox-trotting on the dance floor. She tapped her husband on the shoulder and George, conceding defeat, relinquished his lead. Nada took Gloria by the hand, and they launched into a well-practiced routine.

David swung Freddie out with an exaggerated flourish; their hands broke apart and she took the momentary distance to shake her head, laughing, before walking toward the bar. David shrugged good-naturedly and spun around, eyebrows raised as he caught sight of Thelma and Wallis.

"Too quick for her," he said once he'd weaved his way over to them, taking out a handkerchief to wipe perspiration from his forehead. "Golly, I'm hot. Another round, Thelma? Wallis?"

The song ended and the band shifted into something more sedate—an Ozzie Nelson number that had come out a few years ago, smooth and sentimentally trite, crooning stars and dreams but lovely all the same. Rather than retiring from the dance floor Gloria and Nada moved closer together and danced on. The slender train of Nada's dress drifted with their movement, brushing itself against Gloria's legs as they swayed, hands clasped, contented.

Beside her, Thelma felt Wallis shift closer.

"Your sister ought to be more discreet," she said as David relieved a waiter of a tray of drinks.

Thelma shrugged. "They're only dancing," she said. "A private room, a private party... Entirely innocent."

"A private room in a public hotel," Wallis pointed out. "And you know how people *talk*."

Thelma frowned but before she could answer, David, his elbow planted on the table to better steady his hand as he lit a cigarette, cleared his throat. "I wouldn't think too hard on it,

Mrs. Simpson," he said. He inhaled and the cigarette caught the flame; satisfied, he leaned back with an easy, heavy-lidded smile. "It's not really a concern. Not to people like us. Let the girls have their dance, they're not harming anybody."

After a few minutes, David stubbed out his cigarette with renewed vigor as the opening strains of "Blue Danube" floated through the room. He held his hand out to Thelma and she took it, head spinning, as he whirled her onto the dance floor.

"You remember this one?" he said, pulling Thelma close.

Thelma nodded, glowing in the warmth of his smile. "Lady Londonderry's ball." She closed her eyes, trusting in David's sure movements as he led her in the dance. Somewhere nearby, Thelma supposed that Nada and Gloria were still dancing together. She hoped they were.

David's words echoed in her head, making her smile at the impossibility of it all. *People like us,* he'd said. People like us, she thought, dance with the Prince of Wales. People like us buy out the ballroom at the Ritz. She opened her eyes and looked around; as she'd expected, Gloria and Nada were still dancing nearby, and it was enough to make her throw caution to the wind, lean forward and press her lips against David's.

People like us, she thought triumphantly, own the world and everything in it.

FORTY-SEVEN

October 22, 1934
Carlyle Hotel, NYC

THELMA AWOKE, STARING AT AN UNFAMILIAR ceiling in an unfamiliar room. She nestled into feather-down sheets, feeling Aly, sleep-heavy, beside her, and closed her eyes, unwilling to make the morning real. Sunlight streamed through the open window, warming her face as she listened to the muted sounds of traffic and birdsong.

Perhaps she ought to feel remorseful. Unlike her guilt over Gloria, this was a mistake entirely of Thelma's own making, though now—clear-eyed in the morning—she didn't count it a mistake at all. How long would it last, this feeling of contentedness? Until she faced Gloria? Until she reunited with David?

Aly stirred, turning onto his side to wrap his arm around Thelma's waist and pull her close. She nestled in, her back to his chest, threading her pale fingers through his dark ones.

Did he truly see the world as one endless competition, a series of battles to be won and lost, conquests of the heart and mind and body? But then, was that so very different from how others saw it—Mamma, pushing her daughters toward whichever man offered the most money or social status, encouraging them to conquer cold hearts in exchange for comfort? How naive she'd been, to think that such battles ended with marriage: that, once she'd reached the peak, she wouldn't have to fight to remain there, grasping what she could, with no guarantee that it wouldn't all end through divorce or circumstance, or the abrupt expiration of a beating heart. How little it all amounted to, when such choices were made on the promise of money or power.

Aly shifted again and Thelma turned to face him. Even in sleep, he had a casual, frowning elegance that denied him the sort of vulnerability that David, in his quiet moments, had: he looked as though he were working out some problem—another battle, even in his dreams. Thelma ran her thumb along the line of his jaw, across the thin mustache that covered the bridge of his lip, and he opened his eyes.

"Good morning," he said, his voice low with sleep.

"Good morning."

Aly closed his eyes once more; Thelma kissed him lightly and slid out of the bed.

"So early?" He raised his hand in the air, consulting his wristwatch without sitting up. "It's not even seven o'clock. Come back to bed. We'll order breakfast."

Thelma wrapped a quilt around her shoulders. "The courtroom opens at nine," she said, finding her undergarments on a nearby chair. "And I'll have enough to explain as it is. As fun as this has been, time didn't stop last night."

Aly smiled. "Didn't it, just for a moment?" He sat up, reaching for his cigarettes. "You'll return afterward?"

Thelma finished fastening her brassiere and retrieved her slip. Aly exhaled, drumming his fingers on the end of the cigarette.

"I thought not," he said.

Thelma returned to the bed, perching on the edge as he ran a hand down her back. "I can't," she replied. "You know where I've got to be."

Aly held her gaze before kissing her, once, softly, on the lips.

"You're wasted on him, you know," he said as she rose to continue dressing.

Thelma leaned forward to check her reflection in a mirror, twisting her hair back into place. "Is that so?"

She watched him nod in the mirror's reflection. "When all this is over, we should go away together. Leave the prince to his toys and marry me."

Thelma smiled. "Do you say that to all the women you sleep with?"

"Yes. But this time I mean it."

She sat on the edge of the bed. It was tempting: wipe the slate clean. Run away from David, from Gloria—from all of it.

She kissed Aly once more, lingering as long as she dared, willing herself to remember all the details: his cologne, the feel of his hands on her; her carefree joy.

They broke apart.

"Goodbye, Aly," she said.

Though Thelma hoped she might be able to slip into Gloria's house unnoticed, she had no such luck. When the butler opened the door, he nodded toward the sitting room, his youthful face solemn. Thelma, with no small amount of trepidation, looked in.

It was clear that Gloria hadn't slept: she was sitting in the same chair she'd occupied last night, legs curled beneath her, a bird's nest of cigarettes in a nearby ashtray filling the room with a tobacco stench. Someone had covered her feet with a quilt but Gloria was still wearing last night's dark dress, rumpled creases scoring the fabric from top to bottom, her hair falling from its pins. She looked at Thelma, an anesthetized stillness in her expression.

"I wasn't sure you were coming back," she said.

Thelma came closer. "Neither was I."

Gloria eased out of the chair, her hands heavy on the armrests as she pushed herself upright. "Coffee?"

Thelma nodded and Gloria left, padding toward the dining room barefoot. Thelma wondered at the silence: no noise from upstairs, no voices from the kitchen.

Gloria returned, coffee in hand. She handed the cup to Thelma and sank back into her chair, making Thelma feel as though she'd been granted an audience.

"You must know how sorry I am."

Gloria looked down, her fingers curling around her coffee mug. "Me, too," she said.

"If it weren't for me, you could have stood a chance. Mathew wouldn't have gotten involved—"

Gloria shook her head. "You know that's not true. It would have happened sooner or later. Nada's too close to David. Even if you'd never met him, Mathew would still have intervened."

"I can't help feeling like it's my fault," said Thelma.

Gloria shrugged. "We could go over it all, but what would it solve? I chose Nada. And Friedel. The blame lies with me."

They sat in silence for a few minutes; upstairs, Thelma could hear footsteps.

"Why Nada?" she said finally. She couldn't stop herself from asking: she'd been wondering it for years, from the moment she first met Nada Mountbatten, when she realized the bond between Nada and Gloria was almost as strong as the one between Gloria and Thelma. At its root, it was a question born of jealousy: the ugly, childish assumption that no one had the right to such intimacy with her sister, a question asked by a six-year-old screaming at the parental directive to share.

Gloria set down her coffee. "She made me happy," she said. "It's as simple as that. She made me feel like I was the only other person in the world who mattered. Like I was as exciting as she was." She looked down. "Isn't that silly? She made me like what I saw—what she saw in me. Perhaps that's all I was looking for—someone who made me like my own reflection."

She drifted off, pulling a lace-trimmed handkerchief from a drawer.

"It's all still there, you know," said Thelma. "Everything Nada saw in you. Everything Reggie saw in you, God rest his soul. People don't see what isn't there."

Gloria shrugged. "Maybe it is," she said. "The good and the bad. Nada wasn't perfect—she never pretended to be. Neither did I." She looked up. "I don't blame you, Thelma. My mistakes were my own—my mistakes as a mother. But my biggest mistake was in trusting the wrong person with my secrets. Not when she had secrets of her own to protect."

Thelma was helpless in the face of facts: helpless against Gloria's calm, Burkan's impotence, Mathew's firm, merciless grip. "We can fix this," she said. "I've got the money to continue fighting. An appeal. I'll support you and Little Gloria both, you'll never need to touch a penny of her inheritance. I'll act as an assurance—I'll adopt Little Gloria if necessary—"

She could picture it, the scene blooming in her mind like a morning glory. Why hadn't she thought of it before? Duke had given her enough money, if she was careful, to support Gloria and Little Gloria both: a larger flat in London, or something in the country if the Surrogates preferred it, a house with a nursery and garden large enough for Tony and Little Gloria to grow up together. Thelma could take over the finances but she would share, with Gloria, the task of motherhood—

Gloria smiled, and the picture died as quickly as it lived. "If only it were still about the money," she said. She leaned back in her chair, balancing her coffee cup on her lap, looking into space as though contemplating something as trivial as the weather. "She was always going to get Little Gloria. I wonder when she first started plotting—probably before the ink was dry on Reggie's death certificate."

"Gertrude?"

"Mamma." Gloria looked at Thelma. "She wanted a pretext,

and I gave her one. She wanted an ally, and Gertrude was willing. She's not thought it all through, though, if she thinks Gertrude will allow her to dictate Little Gloria's life."

Had Gertrude realized how much control Mamma would expect to continue wielding over Little Gloria? Chances were, Mamma was already measuring up for drapes in the spare bedroom at Old Westbury. Gloria had put up with Mamma's toxic influence because of filial duty, but Gertrude owed Mamma no such courtesy. They might win the courtroom battle, Mamma and Gertrude, but how long would their alliance last, once the practicalities of raising a child began to grate on them both?

"Poor Gertrude," said Thelma.

"She won't be as easily handled as I was. And once Gertrude starts making her own decisions on Little Gloria's behalf…" Gloria drifted off, her features sinking into melancholy once more. "The thing I regret most is that she believes all the lies. Gertrude was so good to me when Reggie died. We were friends. Did she think of me as an unfit mother the whole time?"

Gloria looked up, and Thelma knew the question had pained her since the start of the trial—the question of reputation, of dignity. What would Little Gloria think of her, once she was living in another house, with a woman who'd fought to keep her from her mother?

"Gertrude's relying on Mamma's lies," said Thelma. "One day, she'll realize that—if she hasn't already. And when she does, she'll see you for who you really are. So will Little Gloria, when she's old enough to understand."

Taking Gloria's hands in her own, Thelma leaned forward; Gloria leaned, too, their foreheads pressing together like they used to do when they were children, each the reflection of the other, two sides of a coin.

"Until that day comes," she continued, "you've got me."

FORTY-EIGHT

THE CAR TURNED ONTO LEXINGTON AVENUE, and Thelma, Consuelo and Gloria, wedged together in the back seat, began the traffic-clogged journey to the courthouse. Gloria, seated next to the window, closed her eyes and leaned against Consuelo's shoulder.

"You might be called to testify today, Thelma," said Consuelo. Disapproval hung over her tone: according to Gloria, Consuelo and Burkan had stayed up late into the night discussing the trial. Thelma couldn't blame her older sister for thinking she was the only adult left in the room.

"You're to speak to Gloria's good character," she continued. "Her morality, her church attendance. Her devotion to Little Gloria. Nothing else, you understand?"

"Yes," said Thelma. She looked out the window, watching green slivers of Central Park appear, two blocks away, as the street names dropped from the Seventies to the Sixties. She was glad they were taking Lexington rather than Fifth, where the palatial Vanderbilt mansions, delicate as spun sugar, took up entire city blocks.

As Lexington merged into Park Avenue, they passed the Commodore Hotel, named for Reggie's great-grandfather, who'd built the family fortune in railroads. If she were to walk a few blocks from the Commodore, Thelma would find Vanderbilt Avenue, a slim little street named in honor of the family—as though not enough of the city already bore their name, in statues and buildings and boardrooms and parks.

How had she never noticed the stamp that the Vanderbilts had made on the city before? She'd seen power in that name, once, but now she saw only an obsessive insecurity in their need to paper their surroundings with reminders of their own prominence; to cement their hold on authority by crafting the city in their own gilt image.

There was little Thelma could do, now, to change fate. She'd not missed the implication behind Consuelo's instructions: Thelma was being hurried onto the stand so that she could be hurried off it again. She was a liability now, to Gloria as much as to David, to David as much as to Nada. And she was a liability to Gertrude as well, for wasn't the threat of David's connection the only reason Burkan wasn't pulling Gertrude's skeletons out of the closet, too? No, when Thelma got on the stand Smyth would play nicely. It was in everyone's best interests.

She closed her eyes for a moment as the motorcar, snagged in traffic, slowed. She hoped she would testify today. She feared that if she waited any longer, anger would spill out of her in a screaming condemnation of Gertrude and Mamma and Nada Mountbatten, of sheer hypocrisy; of the fact that Gloria's only crime was not having a pile of coins large enough to hide her sins.

Beyond the autumn leaves in Foley Square, Thelma could see the courthouse, gray and austere, morning sunlight catching on the pillars and sending the portico into ribbons of light and shadow. Consuelo nudged Gloria awake and she sat up, pinching color into her cheeks as the car stopped.

The crowd was overwhelming: hundreds, it seemed, had come to witness the arrival of the Vanderbilt Widow. Along the courthouse steps, police officers had formed a barricade. They waved the car forward as the crowd shouted words of encouragement and condemnation in equal measure. Newspapermen pushed against the police cordon as they raised cameras, lenses flashing in the sunlight like beetle shells. A few hefted heavy newsreel cameras onto their shoulders, waving their hands to attract Thelma's attention as a policeman opened her car door. Thelma searched the crowd, and met the eyes of a woman in gray. She shifted closer to her husband, unsmiling, staring at Thelma's fur coat.

Consuelo followed Thelma onto the pavement, ignoring the noise as she bent to help Gloria out of the car. Gloria lifted a gloved hand and waved to the crowd, her red lips the only color on her pallid face, and the crowd roared in response.

"You tell 'em, Mrs. V!"

"Go get your baby back!"

"Sinner! *Sinner!*"

Gloria drifted toward Thelma as Consuelo consulted her watch. "Burkan and the rest should be arriving shortly," she murmured, glancing up Lafayette Street.

Wordlessly, Gloria slipped her hand in the crook of Thelma's arm, their shoulders touching. She tilted her chin, turning her face to the sun, and smiled.

Gloria would lose the trial, yet here she was, ready for another day of scandal. Thelma tightened her grip on Gloria's hand, willing herself to hope. Carew might yet grant Gloria partial custody of her child; at the very least, he would allow visiting rights. Over the years to come, Gloria might yet salvage her relationship with her daughter.

Consuelo let in a sharp intake of breath and Thelma looked

up: a dark Rolls Royce was coming down the road. Gloria's grip on Thelma's arm tightened but she stood her ground, watching the car make its way to the break in the police cordon, coming to a stop only feet from where they stood.

Mamma Morgan was the first to get out: she stood with her dark eyes fixed on the courthouse, her jaw jutted forward like a pugilist. She didn't acknowledge her three daughters, but walked past as though they were nothing more than faces in the crowd.

Thelma couldn't help pitying her. Mamma had lost all four of her children in this fight. Of course, she would have said she was acting out of love. One day, Thelma hoped, she might realize the tragedy of it all.

Gertrude, at least, had the decency to nod to Thelma, Gloria and Consuelo as she exited the car. Like Gloria, Gertrude was dressed entirely in black—she seemed determined not to let Gloria's presence ruffle her, turning her full attention to the car and its final inhabitant.

Little Gloria slid across the car seat, her legs—white stockings and black Mary Janes—hovering, too short to reach the ground from the height of the seat. She hopped out of the car, glancing left and right as the crowd roared for her attention. Thelma wouldn't have blamed the child if she'd retreated, but Little Gloria stood firm. She looked healthy, at least, dressed in a tweed blouse and dark skirt, an autumn cape tied around her neck with a ribbon. Still a child, in most respects—but Thelma could see the weight behind her eyes.

The crowd fell silent as mother and daughter looked at each other. This was what they'd come for: live entertainment, a bloodletting in the streets.

Gloria released her hold on Thelma's arm and looked down at her daughter. "Hello, darling," she said. "Are you well?"

The child reddened, and she turned from her mother without a word. Like her grandmother, she set her jaw and began walking up the stairs, her white-gloved hand gripping the iron railing.

Gloria looked as though she'd been slapped. Even Gertrude looked stunned. She turned to Gloria and opened her mouth as if to say something, but then closed it again. She let out a breath, shook her head and followed her niece into the courthouse.

Gloria watched them go. Thelma took her hand once more and Consuelo pulled a case of cigarettes from her bag.

"To calm your nerves," she said. Thelma took one, but Gloria shook her head. She followed Gertrude up the stairs, her head held high.

Thelma lit a cigarette for herself, her hands shaking. Burkan's words came back to her, unyielding: *no possibility of a settlement.* Once the court case was decided, things would continue to be troubled. Gloria would have to keep fighting. It was all she had left—the fight to reclaim custody of Little Gloria, and then, when that failed, the fight to win back her love.

It was something Gloria could do, but not alone. Once Carew ruled against Gloria, she would lose access to the income from Little Gloria's estate. She would need support—financial and emotional—to endure the overwhelming challenges that lay ahead.

A third Rolls Royce pulled up in front of the courthouse: Burkan and Harry and Edith. Consuelo crossed to the car as Burkan exited, greeting him in a low voice as Thelma walked up the stairs.

Thelma's future was here, by her sister's side. She would return to London, of course, to wrap up loose ends: close the Grosvenor Square flat, discuss Tony's schooling with Duke. Perhaps they would find him a place in a New York school, if they were lucky; maybe a house outside the city, with land enough for horses. Tony took after his half sister in that way.

She lingered at the edge of the portico, looking back past the crowds toward Foley Square. It was a blindingly bright autumn morning, the sun peeking through the gaps between skyscrapers. Were she standing atop the turret at Fort Belvedere, Thelma would be looking over nothing but a blanket of blue sky, green fields rushing up to meet the horizon in the distance.

"Lady Furness!"

Thelma looked down. Below, a small woman had pushed her way past the reporters. She was clearly hard done by—a husband put out of work by the Depression, perhaps, but she had her pride: she wore a patched dress, ironed like it was new. She waved, as though she was greeting an old friend.

Thelma paused, lifting the half-smoked cigarette from her lips.

"You give them hell," the woman said, and though she didn't shout Thelma could hear her as clearly as if she were standing right beside her. "From one mother to another. You tell that Whitney bitch to go to hell."

Thelma held the woman's gaze for a moment. She nodded, then flicked the cigarette from her fingers. She watched it fly and land, ember fading, on the stairs.

She glanced back, but the woman had sunk once more into the crowd of onlookers. Thelma turned, squaring her shoulders as she faced the darkness of the courtroom, and walked inside.

EPILOGUE

May 1946
Buckingham Palace

TWO HUNDRED PAIRS OF EYES GAZED AT HER AS she walked down the long hallway of the Picture Gallery: a hundred different expressions, serene and judgmental and wise, dressed in Tudor finery and ermine robes, damask and silk and finery, jewels so heavy the sitters, surely, had never been able to wear them all at once in real life. The procession of people around her—who, like Thelma, had been invited to the investiture—slowed as they walked through the room, lingering over the frames as though expecting a tour guide to appear and begin explaining this painting or that, the Van Dyck or the Canaletto or the Reubens, the canvases that hung cheek by jowl in a higgledy-piggledy overload that only the British could find dignified.

Thelma knew she stood out in the threadbare crowd, with her manicured nails and glossy hair, her chic American clothing. She had been lucky, choosing to return to New York with Gloria in the latter half of the 1930s—luckier still that her settlement from Duke had safeguarded her during the worst years of the Depression. She'd watched from afar as German bombs decimated her former home, thankful to have Tony safe at her side, wishing she could have taken Dickie, too—to have instilled in her heroic stepson the wisdom of cowardly life, rather than the futile romanticism of a glorious death. She would have given anything for him to be here, rather than for Tony to be collecting medals on his behalf. Heroism was cold comfort, now that Thelma and Tony were the last surviving members of the Furness family.

She walked on, passing portraits of prior monarchs, generations of kings and queens whose stories were as well-known as their faces. Their personal triumphs and failures were woven into the fabric of Britain: the Empire rose and fell with the choices they made, followed through with the stroke of a sword or a pen. The man who now sat on the throne bore the burden of decision heavily—Thelma could see that in the pictures they printed in the newspapers. Bertie had always been duty-bound, even before fate tapped him on the shoulder.

She walked into the ballroom, where silk chairs had been set up in rows facing two empty thrones on a platform. She made her way to the front of the room and filed into the row of seats reserved for Victoria Cross families. She chose a chair off to the side, knowing that, within moments, she would be facing the monarchs she'd once known as friends.

She nearly smiled at the incongruity of it all: Thelma, representing the family she'd abandoned for David; Bertie, standing in place of the brother who'd tossed him a crown as easily as he might the reins of a horse. She could see, now, that David had always intended to reject the throne and push the burden onto his younger, infinitely nobler brother. He'd told her as much, once—she hadn't believed him, but here they were, Bertie and Elizabeth, in circumstances of David's making. Perhaps he would laugh, to know the old Fort Belvedere crowd had gathered together, jumping to his tune for one final dance. Wallis, at least, would find it amusing. Thelma found her seat, settling her handbag on her lap. Perhaps she'd send the Duchess of Windsor a clipping of the day from the court circular.

As people filed into their seats, Thelma saw a familiar-looking man with slicked-back hair emerge from a side door. He made his way toward her, head lowered, glancing around the room in a futile attempt at inconspicuousness. Thelma had heard Piers Legh had become Master of the Household—a lofty position for one who'd once been so devoted to the Prince of Wales. She was pleased he'd done so well in Bertie's employ. It would have been a shame to visit David's sins upon a loyal friend.

Legh sat next to her. "Lady Furness," he said, "What a pleasure to see you again."

"It's been too long, Piers," said Thelma. "How are you?"

He looked up at the chairs. "As well as can be expected," he replied, "though I'll admit we have a rather long to-do list before things settle down properly."

Thelma thought to her ride to the palace: the crater they'd had to navigate in the quadrangle, the tarpaulins and rubble marking the remains of the north lodge. "How times have changed."

"Indeed," said Piers. She and Piers had never been close, but he'd always been there, as much a part of her life back then as anyone else. "Lady Furness, I wanted to pass along a message from Their Majesties. They were hoping they might find time to meet with you in private, but it seems the newspapers have caught wind that you're here. Perhaps, for all involved…"

"I understand," said Thelma.

"If it were a more private venue… They were always so fond of you."

"I understand. Really, I do," she said, and patted Piers's hand. Then, before she could help herself, she spoke again. "How is he?"

Legh stiffened; he seemed to retreat into the dignity of his position, but Thelma held his gaze until he leaned in and lowered his voice further. "He writes. Frequently. Much of his correspondence goes unanswered."

The band at the back of the room fell silent, and Piers, catching the eye of one of the liveried attendants along the side wall, stood. "Lady Furness, I must dash. My deepest condolences for your loss. Your stepson was a brave man."

"Thank you. Please pass along my regards to Their Majesties," said Thelma, and Piers vanished once more through the side door.

He writes... Thelma thought of the notes they once passed, sentimental and sweet and needy. What had happened to the ones she'd sent back? Burned, most likely. According to a few of her old friends, Wallis had destroyed all of Freddie's correspondences to David. Thelma doubted that her own would have survived the purge.

The band trilled a fanfare and the room rose to its feet. Thelma half-expected David to walk through the door, smiling that old, familiar grin that had broken hearts around the world, but the king and queen that entered were old friends nonetheless, and Thelma caught Elizabeth's eye. She smiled, too quickly, and shifted her gaze up and over the crowd. Thelma, with a pang, understood: the digging up of ghosts was never a pleasant business, and Thelma's ghost—David's ghost—would always loom large for Bertie and Elizabeth.

The king and queen would never allow Wallis and David to return to England: not with their tacky tabloid tell-alls and their appalling prewar sympathies, their single-handed attempt to destroy the fabric of the British monarchy. Thelma wasn't surprised that David had painted himself as victim of the whole sorry business, unfairly maligned by a monarchy blind to the eclipsing nature of true love. She stared at the silk crest behind Bertie and Elizabeth, knowing just how cold it would have been for David to have fallen into the shadow of the world where he'd once belonged.

The band played "God Save the King", and Thelma sang along with the rest, attempting to mask the sudden, frustrating sorrow that made her cheeks grow hot. It wasn't fair, that she was the only one left to watch Tony receive Dickie's commendation—that Averill and Duke both had perished under the weight of heartache and strain. It wasn't fair that Dickie couldn't be lauded for his bravery in person, rather than buried in some far-off field in France. It wasn't fair that Bertie, up on his dais, looked so old; that Elizabeth had finally aged into the matron she'd always been, the weight of the nation resting heavily—jointly—on their shoulders. It wasn't fair, what Wallis had done all those years ago: letting David indulge his selfish impulses and run away from a responsibility he never truly wanted.

The anthem came to an end and Thelma sat back down. She didn't regret a single decision she'd made, all those years ago—not the decision to take up with David, nor the decision to leave him. She'd lived with the consequences of her choices—they'd all had to, Gertrude and Gloria and Mamma; Thelma and Wallis and David. She thought of David, exiled to France; Wallis who was anathema to the House of Windsor, and would likely remain so until the end of her days; Gertrude, whose relationship with Little Gloria had never truly grown into one of love.

Perhaps there was a little fairness in the world after all.

The court attendant read out Dickie's name, and Tony—fifteen years old, tall and handsome, his straw-blond hair pulled back from his sharp features—walked up. Thelma held her breath as her son bowed in front of the King of England. Did he remember meeting Bertie before, as a toddler at Burrough Court?

Bertie presented Tony with the Victoria Cross, its iron glint visible within its black velvet box. He leaned in as Tony accepted it, and murmured something; Tony replied, and Bertie looked up, searching past Tony's shoulder.

His smile hadn't changed in the years since Thelma had last seen him: she'd seen it a hundred times, from across the dining table at the Ritz or in the drawing room at Fort Belvedere. She inclined her head, returning affection with affection, seeing in the king's face the warmth of his brother's smile.

Bertie turned back to Tony, and with a final bow, Tony walked on. The court attendant read out the next commendation, the king picked up the next medal and the ceremony continued.

★ ★ ★ ★ ★

AUTHOR'S NOTE

Thelma Morgan Furness died of a heart attack on January 29, 1970. According to her niece, Gloria Vanderbilt, Thelma collapsed in the street in New York City on the way to a doctor's appointment. In her handbag, Thelma was carrying one of the green bears that she and David had exchanged so many years before.

Thelma's story is one of many contradictions, and while I've taken some artistic license with it, I hope that she and Gloria would recognize themselves in the characters I've created. For the purposes of the plot, I changed a few key dates in Thelma's story. In reality, Thelma took two trips to the United States in 1934: one in January, and one in October, for Gloria's trial. It was on the first trip that Thelma and David grew apart; their relationship was already over when Thelma journeyed back to New York to stand in Gloria's defense in the custody trial. That said, according to Barbara Goldsmith, author of *Little Gloria... Happy At Last*, Nadejda Milford Haven did send Theobald Mathew to represent her at the trial—and to keep the Prince of Wales's name from being raised in connection with Thelma and Gloria. Gloria's defense was indeed ruined by a list of names that Mathew provided in exchange for keeping "a certain royal party's" name out of the courtroom.

On November 21, 1934, Justice Carew issued his decision on the Matter of Vanderbilt, giving Gertrude Whitney primary custody of Little Gloria Morgan Vanderbilt. Gloria was granted weekend custody of her daughter in an arrangement that left Carew with the nickname The Socialites' Solomon. He directed the courts to seal the record of the Matter of Vanderbilt, but the trial continued to be a topic of public speculation. His ruling was roundly criticized by the press, who saw Gloria as the victim and Gertrude as the villain, and felt that his decision served only to prolong an untenable, unworkable living arrangement for the child:

> *What kind of provision for the child's welfare is all this, anyway?*
> *The judge has taken the child from its mother and awarded it to*
> *the woman whom the mother probably hates most in the world,*
> *and who probably returns the mother's hate with interest. How can*
> *either of these women refrain from trying to poison the child's mind*
> *against the other, and what will that do to the child?*
>
> –*Mirror* editorial, reprinted in Goldsmith, p. 474

The trial made Gloria Vanderbilt a notorious figure in New York society, and it made Little Gloria an object of constant, unrelenting fascination. For years, Little Gloria was hounded by reporters and hangers-on; weekend visits between mother and daughter were attended by private detectives, and in the wake of several kidnapping threats Gertrude Whitney hired a team of bodyguards to protect Little Gloria at school. In 1936, the United States Supreme Court declined to review the Matter of Vanderbilt, and with no more legal options open to her, Gloria stopped fighting. Her relationship with her daughter remained strained throughout the rest of her life.

After the trial, Thelma moved back to the United States to support her sister, financially and emotionally. In 1935, they started a dressmaking business—a company that, three years later, was so heavily in debt the business folded, and Gloria filed for bankruptcy. With no business experience or acumen, Gloria's subsequent business ventures also failed. In 1940, she was diagnosed with glaucoma; by the mid 1950s, she was almost completely blind. Thelma took on the role of Gloria's carer, and when Gloria died in February 1965, it was with her twin sister by her bedside.

Marmaduke Furness never truly forgave Averill for eloping with Andrew Rattray, though Thelma continued to fight in her stepdaughter's corner. After her marriage, Averill Furness—Averill Rattray—remained in Kenya with her husband, though their happiness was short-lived. In 1933, Andrew Rattray died of a sudden illness; and though Thelma persuaded Duke to forgive his daughter and welcome her back to England in the wake of the tragedy, Averill refused to go. She remained in the hut that had been her marital home and died a year later, at the age of twenty-seven, of heart failure. In her memoirs, Thelma maintained that her beloved stepdaughter had died, quite literally, of a broken heart.

After his divorce from Thelma was finalized Duke wed a third time, but the marriage—to Australian-born widow Enid Maud Cavendish—was not a happy one. In 1940, Duke received word that Dickie, fighting in the Battle of France, was missing in action; the strain of the news, combined with the untimely death of his daughter, caused him to turn to drugs. He died a broken man at the age of fifty-six, leaving his title and fortune—totalling £20 million—to his second son, Tony.

Dickie Furness died in Arras in May 1940, fighting as a lieutenant with the Welsh Guards, covering the withdrawal of a large transport column to Douai. As enemy fire advanced on the transport vehicles, Dickie spearheaded an attack, inflicting heavy losses on the German troops and wounding himself in the process. When all of the tanks, carriers and crew under his command were gone, Dickie kept fighting, engaging the enemy in hand-to-hand combat until he finally fell. He was awarded the Victoria Cross for his sacrifice; in his commendation, he was praised for having "displayed the highest qualities of leadership and dash" and "imbued his command with a magnificent offensive spirit."

As for Wallis and Edward—theirs is a well-known story. Upon George V's death on January 20, 1936, Edward ascended to the throne, but he didn't stay there long; less than a year later, on December 11, 1936, Edward gave the speech for which he is best remembered: "You must believe me when I tell you that I have found it impossible to carry the heavy burden of responsibility and to discharge my duties as king as I would wish to do without the help and support of the woman I love…"

The abdication crisis rocked the British establishment. As a divorcée, Wallis was ineligible to marry the Head of the Church of England; as a brash and opinionated American, she was considered a crass and unsuitable partner for the Head of State. The Royal Family was mired in a scandal they'd hoped they could avoid—a scandal that had been brewing ever since a lunchtime meeting in the Ritz Hotel, when Thelma Furness asked a fateful favor of a close friend.

ACKNOWLEDGMENTS

As a first-time novelist, I entered the writing world with complete naivete, eyes wide open and shining at the possibility of being a WRITER. It wouldn't take more than a year to finish it, I told people, shrugging off their looks of incredulity. Just a year, I said, as I began plugging away at the earliest drafts of what would become *The Woman Before Wallis*.

As everyone in this acknowledgment section can attest to, it took me far longer than a year to write this book, and I count myself so very fortunate to have had such an incredible network of people helping me bring Thelma's story to life.

First, to my Scottish writing family in the Creative Writing department at the University of St. Andrews. To John Burnside, my academic advisor, and my colleagues Devon Stark-MacLise, Tamara Mathias, Esther Nisbett, Francesca Bellei, and Queenie Au, whose advice, support and creativity made this book better than I could ever have done alone. To my favourite Scottish bookstore, Toppings and Company in St. Andrews: I promised to have a book for your shelves one day and here it is.

I'd like to offer my deepest gratitude to my agent, Kevan Lyon, for being my champion and guide through this whirlwind industry. I count myself so fortunate to have you and your incredible team at Marsal Lyon in my corner.

This book simply would not be what it is without the insight, support, and steady hand of my editor, April Osborn. Thank you for believing in me, and for seeing the potential in Thelma's story. To the entire team at Mira for putting their considerable talents behind my book—especially Elita Sidiropoulou and Kathleen Oudit, who provided me with my beautiful cover: Thank you for making this debut writer's dreams come true.

Thank you, as well, to the Lyonesses. I'm honoured to be in your company, inspired by the remarkable stories you tell about strong women, and awed by the strength of your support. I promise I will pay it forward in my career.

While a complete bibliography of the resources I consulted to write this project would constitute another book in its entirety, I'm heavily indebted to the following: Barbara Goldsmith's *Little Gloria… Happy At Last*, which gave me a glimpse into a court case where the records were otherwise sealed; Anderson Cooper and Gloria Vanderbilt's *The Rainbow Comes and Goes: A Mother and a Son on Life, Love and Loss*; Anne Sebba's *That Woman: The Life of Wallis Simpson, Duchess of Windsor*; Frances Donaldson's *Edward VIII: The Road to Abdication*; Philip Ziegler's *Edward VIII*; Gloria Vanderbilt's *Once Upon a Time: A True Story*; and Thelma and Gloria's co-written autobiography, *Double Exposure*. I'd also like to thank the New York Public Library, the Toronto Reference Library, and the University of St. Andrews Library for their incredible newspaper archives. A more robust list of resources and works consulted can be found at brynturnbull.com.

I'd also be remiss if I didn't express my gratitude to Madonna, whose 2011 movie *W.E.* led me to Thelma in the first place.

This book is, at heart, a love story—but it's not a royal romance. It's about the unbreakable bond between sisters. I am immeasurably lucky to have a sister who inspires me to keep pushing forward, every day. Hayley, I dedicate this book to you.

I am so pleased to be welcoming another sister into my family this year—one who embodies Nada's joy, Thelma's sensibility, and Averill's adventurousness. Coretta King, I look forward to forging our bonds of sisterhood today and all the days to come.

To my brother Alec, whose late-night plot twists help me think through any challenges my characters might face. To Brenda Doig, Derek Plaxton, Sally Dakers, Jill and Michael, Louise Claire Johnson, Amber Crawford, my McGill crew, Kealy Simpson, and Mike Schneider, who have all been constant voices of support. To my grandparents: Don, Dorothy, and Mary: Thank you.

Finally, to my parents. Mom and Dad, this book belongs to you. Every single day, I'm thankful for whatever alignment of stars led me into your remarkable lives. When I finally screwed up the courage to tell you I was leaving my job to become a WRITER, you gave me the best response I could have ever hoped for: "What took you so long to figure that out?"

It took me a while, but I got there in the end.

THE WOMAN
BEFORE
WALLIS

BRYN TURNBULL

Reader's Guide

mira

QUESTIONS FOR DISCUSSION

1. How does Thelma's relationship with her mother fundamentally shape her attitudes towards men and money?

2. Thelma's abusive first marriage occurs in the years before the book begins. How does that experience impact her relationships, not only with David and Duke but with all of the people in her life?

3. Thelma's relationship with Gloria has room for criticism, but never disloyalty. How does her attitude towards homosexuality differ from other characters in the novel? How does class distinction play into rules of gender in the 1930s?

4. When Thelma first meets Gertrude Whitney, Gertrude blames Reggie's choices for leaving Gloria in such a dire financial state. Do you think her own choices are justified in seeking custody of Little Gloria?

5. Thelma is genuinely surprised that Duke believes their marriage fell apart because of her relationship with David. Do you think this is a fair judgment on Duke? How do Duke's own actions contribute to the end of the marriage?

6. Thelma's relationship with Averill grows and deepens over the course of the book, but Thelma struggles with the idea of being Averill's stepmother. How does that struggle shape her decision to tell Duke about Averill's plan to elope?

7. At the end of the book Thelma calls David a "weak" man. Given his actions over the course of the novel, do you feel he would have made a weak king?

8. Thelma considers Wallis a trusted friend. Do you think her feelings were reciprocated? How does Wallis's conduct change during the course of the book?

Fur coats and beaded fringes. Champagne in coupes held aloft by silk-gloved hands. Lipstick-stained laughter from across the room, drifting over the heads of black-tie dancers poised in the moment before the music begins. The sights and sounds of the interwar period are familiar—irresistible, really— to those with a taste for glamour and an airy disregard for social stratification.

Those are some of the qualities with which I imbued Thelma Morgan Furness, the heroine in The Woman Before Wallis, and which I confess to share, to no small degree. Thelma is a creature of her time, limitless in her ambition yet boxed in by circumstance. She is, by all the measures of her world, successful—yet powerless when pitched against the true titans of high society.

This is a book about power and belonging: how power is created, and ultimately wielded, both by those born to it and those who believe themselves immune to its thrall. I wrote The Woman Before Wallis while attending one of the UK's powerful, old-world universities. As a middle-class "colonial," I shared Thelma's sense of unbelonging, an outsider fascinated by the wealth around me. Champagne drinking games and beachside polo; weekly black-tie balls and scarlet academic robes. I asked the question that plagues Thelma throughout the whole of this novel: Do I truly belong here?

As a woman eclipsed by the world's most enduring love story, Thelma was fascinating to me from the outset. Given what I already knew about Edward and his overbearing neediness, I had to wonder whether Thelma's directive to Wallis (Take care of him) was truly a favor asked of a close friend—or whether she was giving Wallis implicit permission to pursue the world's most powerful man. I was genuinely surprised when I found out that final, poignant detail of Thelma's life: she died with one of Edward's keepsakes in her handbag. That was the genesis for my story and ultimately shaped Thelma's direction toward self-determination. It's noble to love a flawed individual; it's nobler still to recognize when a relationship has run its course.

This book is, at its heart, a love story—but it's not a royal romance. It's about the unbreakable love between sisters: a love that overcomes prejudice, greed and jealousy. Thelma and Gloria share a connection that leaves room for criticism, but never for disloyalty. Gloria's story line gave me space to grapple with some of the more interesting idiosyncrasies of the 1930s, including attitudes toward homosexuality and motherhood. Did upper-crust parents really limit the time they spent with their children to the short hour between teatime and dinner?

I truly enjoyed conducting research for this novel—a journey that took me to Thelma's old stomping grounds in Mayfair and St. James, Scotland and New York. I had cocktails at the Carlyle Hotel and traveled through the archives of the New York Supreme Court in pursuit of transcripts from Gloria's court case. I traveled the greens of Melton Mowbray and dived deep into ever-growing piles of newspapers and biographies in libraries on two continents. I lost sleep over communication methods of the 1920s and 1930s, and admired the impeccable tailoring on gowns by Schiaparelli, Lanvin and

Chanel. I sat in Edward's flashy biplane and took flight in a plane of similar vintage (sadly, for a scene that never made it into the final edit—all that engine oil in my hair for nothing!).

When I first encountered Thelma's story (in a movie directed by Madonna!) I thought I'd found an interesting sidebar in history—fodder for a blog post, or perhaps an hour or two of time spent down a Wikipedia rabbit hole. What I discovered was something so much more: my first novel.

Everyone knows the story of Edward and Wallis. What drew you to Thelma's story instead?

Thelma's affair with Edward is only one aspect of her story: she was on the periphery of not only the abdication crisis but also the biggest custody battle in US history to date. She was something of a Kardashian in her day—famous for being famous—but she was also strong-willed and willing to stand up for those she loved. Other people have written beautifully about Wallis and Edward, but Thelma's story deserved to be told on its own merits.

This novel contains the real-life stories of real-life people—some of whom have living descendants. How did you balance the drive to tell a good story against the historical record in terms of character development?

It's a tricky balance to strike, but at the end of the day my job is to tell a good story, taking as much historical fact into consideration as I can without sacrificing the plot. I spent a lot of time researching the people who make up my book. Luckily, Thelma and Gloria wrote a memoir, and we have plenty of letters, biographies and recordings of Edward VIII and Wallis Simpson, so by the time I started actually writing, I had a very good sense of who they were. Wallis, in particular, leaped out of the pen, and I think that's because she's left such a legacy behind. I certainly hope that they would see themselves in the characters I've created, but at the end of the day these are fictional representations.

How did you find Thelma's story?

I'd long been interested in the abdication crisis and had read biographies of Wallis Simpson before, but I'd never really picked up on Thelma's story until I watched W.E., a movie directed by Madonna about Wallis and Edward's relationship. In the film, we see Wallis and Thelma have that conversation where Thelma asks Wallis to "take care" of Edward for her while she's traveling, and I remember thinking it was such a strange request to make of a friend—even one as close as Wallis was to Thelma. After the movie ended, I found myself down a bit of a Wikipedia rabbit hole, where I discovered her connection to the Gloria Vanderbilt trial and recognized that this was a story that ought to be told.

One of the major relationships in this novel is between Gloria and Nada. Why was it important to you to show a relationship between two women in the 1930s?

Their relationship is historical fact. It would have been disingenuous to omit it from the book. I truly believe that Gloria loved Nada and that their story would have ended quite differently had they lived in a different time period. What's more interesting to me is the fact that their relationship was permitted because of social privilege—and when Gloria lost that privilege, their relationship fell apart.

How does Gloria's experience as a queer woman shape Thelma's actions?

To me, The Woman Before Wallis is a love story—but it's not a royal romance. While the abdication crisis looms large over Thelma's life, this is a book about the love between sisters:

Thelma supported her sister in a day and age when being gay was seen as unacceptable—except, as Gloria points out, in the highest echelons of society. In the history books, Thelma has often been dismissed as a lesser socialite, but when it comes down to it, she was a deeply principled woman, and her experience as an ally spoke to me.

After spending so long with his character, how do you feel about Edward VIII and his decision to abdicate?

I think Edward VIII would have found an excuse to abdicate, regardless of whether Wallis Simpson had come into his life or not. He was a fundamentally weak man and would have made a fundamentally weak king—and while in my novel I have him talk to Thelma about the sort of king he wants to be, I don't think he ever intended on taking up his crown. If it hadn't been Wallis, he would have found another excuse to abdicate.

That said, Thelma was genuinely in love with him. It was important for me to find a way into that love and to be able to portray him with some compassion.

Edward VIII and Wallis Simpson are known to have been Nazi sympathizers. Why don't you address this in your book?

I don't address it for three reasons. First, Thelma and Edward's relationship ended in 1934. Hitler only became chancellor in 1933, so while he would have been a topic of conversation around the dinner table, he wouldn't have been the main topic of conversation. Second, Thelma was not a political person. One of the biggest complaints the government levied against Wallis Simpson was her political activism—in fact, when it became clear Edward wouldn't give Wallis up, there was a movement within government to invite Thelma back to England because she wasn't seen as someone who would interfere in politics the way Wallis did. Finally, the sad fact is that many members of Britain's upper crust had extreme right-wing leanings in the 1930s, and many were generally supportive of Hitler's policies. At the time, socialism was seen as a far greater threat than fascism, particularly because the General Strike of 1926 had been so successful in disrupting industrial production. Oswald Mosley's British Union of Fascists had fifty thousand members at the height of its popularity in the 1930s.

In the end, I find it incredibly interesting that history played out in such a way that Britain had the king it needed during the war. Could you imagine what would have happened if George VI hadn't been on the throne during the Blitz?

Do you think Wallis intended to replace Thelma?

I don't think she did. Whatever else has been written about her—and there has been a lot written about her—Wallis was an extremely ambitious social climber. I believe that Wallis was genuinely trying to keep Edward's eye from straying, for Thelma's sake, but when it became clear that his affection had transferred to her, she didn't feel too much guilt in taking advantage of the situation.

She certainly didn't intend to marry Edward—that much is clear. In 2011, Anne Sebba published a biography of Wallis Simpson that contains previously unpublished letters between Wallis and Ernest Simpson. She wrote to him until the end of her life and expressed regret at having ended their marriage. I believe that Wallis had hoped to take advantage of Edward's attraction to make new friends and move in the highest social circle in Britain. She genuinely believed that Edward would tire of her before too long. When he didn't, I think she was as surprised as anyone else.

What did you enjoy most about researching this book?

I wasn't on any fixed timeline to complete this book, so I was able to spend two full years researching—just researching!—

the time period. I particularly enjoyed researching the fashion of the 1930s—the attention to detail is incredible, especially for someone who had Thelma's budget. I was able to access a lot of newspaper articles about the Vanderbilt trial at the New York Public Library, which really helped me understand the frenzy that the trial had created. A photographer actually did try to rappel down the side of the courthouse to get a picture of the proceedings! The trial reached newspapers in Pakistan! I went to London and walked Thelma's neighborhood—while Duke's Arlington town house is no longer there, I visited her home in Mayfair and had drinks at the Ritz.

My favorite research moment, though, was finding Edward's plane, and while I wish I'd had the right place to put it in the manuscript, it did help me come to an understanding of who he was as a person. One of his planes is at the Vintage Wings museum in Gatineau, Quebec, and I was able to visit it. It's a beautiful little biplane with an open cockpit and a closed cabin for passengers. The plane itself looks like a Rolls-Royce, with a beautiful chrome and indigo body and burgundy leather interior, but the best part of it is that Edward had a small generator installed on one of the wings so that he could power a wireless radio. While that sounds like a good idea, Vintage Wings was kind enough to take me up in a plane of a similar vintage, and I was struck by how unbelievably loud it was up in the air. Even with headphones on, it would have been extremely difficult to hear anything on a wireless radio.

I think this really sums up who Edward was. He was so concerned with his image—with looking and feeling like a modern royal—that he forgot to take into account the practicalities of the situation.